NEFARIUS

MAGITECH CHRONICLES BOOK 6

CHRIS FOX

CHRIS FOX WRITES LLC

For Pat. I am incredibly grateful for your quiet wisdom, and unfailing enthusiasm. Thanks, Dad.

CAST OF CHARACTERS

The Magitech Chronicles are vast, and we now have a dizzying array of gods, demigods, drifters, Shayans, planets, and other stuff. Below you'll find a mostly complete list to remind you who's what.

If you find anything missing, please shoot me an email at chris@chrisfoxwrites.com and I'll get it added!

Gods, Wyrms, & Demigods

Arkelion- Son of Drakkon. Currently works for the Krox and was recently involved in the assault on New Texas.

Drakkon- The Guardian of Marid. Dwells on the world of the same name.

The Earthmother- A Wyrm of tremendous power. Sibling to Virkonna and Inura. Killed by Krox during the godswar. Her body is now used to lure primal drakes, which Krox has been enslaving for millennia.

<u>Inura</u>- The undisputed master of *air* in the sector. Inura was the chief architect of the *Spellship*. Sibling to Virkonna and the Earthmother.

<u>Krox</u>- One of the most ancient gods in the sector. Krox was dismembered during the last godswar, but his children have been conspiring to raise him. Nebiat finally succeeded in doing so, and is in control of Krox.

<u>Malila</u>- The guardian of Xal, a demon queen who rules the Skull of Xal and who is connected to both Aran and Nara.

<u>Marid</u>- Marid is an elder god slain by Shivan in the early days of the godswar. Her body lies on the world of the same name, and is protected by her Guardian and son, Drakkon.

<u>Nefarius</u>- Nefarius is a Void Wyrm of immense power who ascended to godhood in the earliest days of the godswar. She is sometimes referred to as a he, though the reason for the change in gender is unclear. Nefarius was slain at the end of the last godswar, but her Guardian, Talifax, is conspiring to bring her back.

<u>Neith</u>- The first arachnidrake, and the eldest of the draconic siblings. Sister to Virkonna, Inura, and the Earthmother, but much, much older.

<u>Shaya</u>- A mortal raised to godhood by Inura in order to defend her people. Died doing exactly that. Now entombed under the great tree on the planet Shaya.

<u>Talifax</u>- Guardian of Nefarius. Talifax's age and race are unknown, but he is rumored to be nearly as old as Xal.

Virkonna- The Wyrm of *air*, sister of Inura, Neith, and the Earthmother. Virkonna is known as the mother of the last dragonflight, and slumbers in torpor on the planet Virkonna, watched over by her children. Virkonna helped Inura build the first *Spellship*.

Xal- One of the eldest gods in the sector, and also one of the largest repositories of *void* magic. Xal allowed himself to be killed by a pantheon including most of the other gods on the list, because he knew eventually that would allow for his return. Best known now as the Skull of Xal.

Inurans

Jolene- A powerful Inuran matriarch. Mother to Kazon and Voria.

Kazon- Brother to Voria, son of Jolene. Kazon was mind-wiped alongside Aran, but has since returned to take his place in the Inuran hierarchy. Kazon owns a huge chunk of Consortium stock, but has turned over his voting rights to his mother.

Skare- A powerful Inuran patriarch. Skare is a rarity among Inurans. He's ugly. Skare is also corrupted by Nefarius, and is working with Talifax to raise their dark goddess.

The Krox

Frit- Frit is an escaped Shayan slave, one of the Ifrit, who were molded by Shayan slavers into beautiful women made completely of flame.

Kahotep- Son of Nebiat, grandson of Teodros. Kahotep, or Kaho for short, is Nebiat's last surviving son. He is a powerful true mage and master scholar.

Nebiat- Daughter of Teodros, granddaughter of Krox, mother of Kahotep. Nebiat is a centuries-old Wyrm, and one of the most powerful true mages in the sector. Her hatred of Voria borders on irrational.

Teodros- Son of Krox, father of Nebiat. Teodros was a hatchling during the last godswar, and played no notable role. However, he's spent the intervening millennia gathering strength, and building his people into a military powerhouse. Teodros orchestrated the rise of Krox, but did not live to see his work completed.

Shayans & Drifters

Bord- Bord is a lower-class Shayan born in the dims at the feet of the great tree. He was conscripted into the Confederate Marines just before the Battle of Starn, and has been cracking bad jokes ever since. Kezia's boyfriend.

Ducius- Thalas's father. Ducius has been a Caretaker of Shaya for many years, one of the most powerful political positions, second only to the Tender. After Eros's death, Ducius took up the role of Tender, and is currently the leader of the Shayan people. However, he is Tender in name only and lacks the divine infusion that both Eros and Aurelia had.

Ducius hates Voria. Kind of a lot.

Eros- Eros was the head of the Temple of Enlightenment on

Shaya, and Voria's original master. Eros became Tender of Shaya when Aurelia died. Eros died shortly thereafter fighting Teodros in the Chamber of the First.

Kezia- Kezia is a blonde, curly-haired tech mage drifter born in the dims, not far from where Bord was raised. She was conscripted in the same wave, and went through basic training beside him. Bord's girlfriend.

Thalas- Son of Ducius. Thalas was Voria's second in command for several years. He was executed by Voria for insubordination during the Battle of Marid.

Voria- Daughter of Jolene and Dirk. Sister of Kazon. Voria served as a major in the confederate military, and commanded the *Wyrm Hunter* until she acquired the mythical *Spellship*. She now commands the Shayan defense against Krox's inevitable invasion.

Ternus

Governor Austin- Austin is a young, ambitious politician in the wrong place at the wrong time. He is woefully unprepared to lead his people during a time of war, and is desperate for allies that can help his people survive. Seriously distrusts magic.

Fleet Admiral Kerr- Commander of the Ternus fleet during the Battle for Marid, and subsequently promoted to Fleet Admiral and placed in charge of all Ternus fleets.

Nara- Former space pirate, now powerful true mage. Nara was mindwiped by Voria, and conscripted into the Confederate Marines. She's fought alongside Aran, Crewes, Bord, Kez, and Voria ever since.

Pickus- Pickus is a freckle-faced grease monkey turned tech mage who has somehow found himself as Voria's right-hand man.

Virkonans

Aran- Born on Virkon. Manipulated by Neith into being mindwiped in preparation to forge him into a tool to kill Krox and Nefarius. Aran is currently the Captain of Aran's Outriders, a mercenary unit based out of the *Talon*.

Kheross- Father of Rhea. An ancient Wyrm from an alternate timeline where Virkonna was overcome by a sea of blood. Kheross was corrupted by Nefarius, and despite being cleansed on Shaya, still bears the mark. He's currently allied with Aran's Outriders, but Aran doesn't trust him, and Kheross knows it.

Rhea- Daughter of Kheross. Rhea is an unknown quantity. She believes herself to be a human Outrider, but is in fact a Void Wyrm. She is a powerful war mage, with limited true magic. Until recently she was held on Yanthara, in the custody of the Temple of Shi.

After Crewes freed her, she joined the Outriders with the rank of lieutenant, and has become a devoted member of the company.

Yantharans

Marcelus Crewes- Brother of Sergeant Crewes. Marcelus is a prosecutor living on Shaya. He prosecuted Voria during her trial.

Sergeant Crewes- Brother of Marcelus Crewes. Sergeant Crewes was born on Yanthara. He voluntarily joined the Confederate Marines, and was quickly assigned to the *Wyrm Hunter*. He is one of the strongest tech mages in the sector, and his mastery of *fire* is unrivaled.

Sarala- Priestess of Shi, and former girlfriend of Sergeant Crewes. Sarala is the head of the Temple of Shi, and is responsible for guiding new members to the Catalyst. She dated Crewes briefly in secondary school, but that ended when Crewes enlisted in the Confederate Marines.

PREVIOUSLY ON

You guys all know the drill by now. The *Previously On* is where I get to snarkily relate the previous book, and is always my favorite part to write. That said, having recaps for every book is getting longer and longer, and we're reaching a point where it is no longer feasible.

You can check out all the recaps at magitechchronicles.com/previously-on. Odds are really good there will only be one more in the main series, as I plan book 7 to have a real ending. There will be spin-off series!

One last thing before I let you get to the recap. **We've begun play testing the Magitech Chronicles pen and paper RPG**, so if that's something you're interested in, sign up to the mailing list at magitechchronicles.com and I'll get you some details.

The first ever game was run at the 20BooksTo50k convention. I played with five science fiction authors, several of whom I'm betting you'd recognize. By this fall I'm hoping you'll be playing too.

Okay, enough about me. Let's get to the recap.

Last time, on The Magitech Chronicles...

Shit just got real, yo. At the end of *War Mage*, Nebiat seized control of Krox through the spell her father Teodros had created. Our Main Bad Guy (TM) is more powerful than ever, and we know right off the bat that she wants to blow up Shaya.

In *Krox Rises*, we get a scene with Nebiat asking Krox for the God Instruction Manual, but Krox gives some predictably cryptic replies. Nebiat decides she's going to lay the smack down on her enemies, and is more than a little butthurt at how things played out in *War Mage*.

The Krox were supposed to win. Now she has the power of an elder god. She can cheat.

Nebiat tries to open a Fissure, but it collapses on itself, because she is a star, and a Fissure can't survive in the presence of a star. Krox explains that there are denizens in the Umbral Depths that even he fears, and that this is a security measure to prevent the denizens from getting out. It's almost like the author is preparing for a spin-off series.

Krox tells Nebiat that if she wants to throw around god-sized spells she needs god-sized magic. She goes to the planet where her species were born, and finds that the Krox are born from primals attracted to the headless corpse of the Earthmother, one of the oldest Wyrms in the sector. Krox has been using her to create armies of dragons, which the sector has taken to calling 'Krox'.

He drains a bit of the Earthmother's magic, but is very careful not to take too much. Now Nebiat has enough *earth* to do some truly dastardly stuff.

We flip to Aran.

He and the rest of the company are being led onto a talk show set to meet with Governor Austin, the leader of

Ternus. Aran and company are hailed as war heroes, presented by Erica Tharn, the reporter we met in *War Mage*.

Then a second star appears over Ternus. Guess who it is? Yup, Krox is here and he's playing for all the marbles. Aran feels immense *earth* magic, and it turns out that Nebiat has increased the density of all minerals comprising the crust, mantle, and core of the planet.

This was super fun to research, and I got to learn all about what would happen to a planet if you suddenly doubled its density. Try to imagine doubling your weight. Many people wouldn't be able to walk. Even those who could would have trouble surviving for very long. Heart attacks would kill hundreds of millions in the first few days. Within a few weeks almost everything would be dead.

Most stuff wouldn't live that long though. Every satellite, ship, and defense platform in orbit would come crashing down, and be completely incapable of escaping the planet's gravity well. The raining debris would create a nuclear winter.

Nebiat is not a very nice person.

Aran and company are at the top of a giant space elevator, which begins to buckle under the increased gravity. The governor tells them that the *Talon* is here, and he will give them their ship back if they'll get him off the station.

We get a tense run back to the ship with Aran carrying Tharn. She grows pale, and has a heart attack just as they reach the airlock. I felt pretty bad about killing her, but it made sense. The human body can only withstand so much.

Our heroes pull some standard heroics, and safely get the *Talon* airborne. We see the space elevator slam into the doomed planet, and watch all the stations and ships crashing. It was a hell of a way to kick off a book.

Meanwhile, Voria is trying to muster a defense at Shaya.

Her godsight tells her that Krox is coming, and that Shaya is doomed unless she can somehow find a way to resurrect Shaya. They need a goddess to oppose a god, but that seems impossible since Teodros drank the pool of life, and now they don't even have enough magic to keep the dome going that protects the part of the planet with an atmosphere.

Voria meets with Ducius and the caretakers and they perform a ritual to stabilize the pool. It takes some of their magic, and amplifies it through Ikadra. It's enough to keep the dome going for a year, and then they can perform another ritual...assuming there's a planet left after Krox comes.

Inura and Kazon show up in her quarters and Inura tells her that she's going to have to figure this out on her own, but that she can do it, and all the tools she needs are here. Have you ever had a boss who gave you an impossible job and no resources? Voria is pretty pissed, but Inura just translocates away. We're very annoyed.

Flip back to Aran, who is still helping the Ternus government. They're running relief efforts from the *Talon* until they can get the *Wyrm Hunter* back and transfer command. Ternus has a smashing plan. They want to buy a fleet of corrupted ships from the Inurans so they can fight back against Krox.

Aran knows this is a terrible idea, but also knows they'll never listen to him. Plus, it turns out he has other problems. Kheross is all over his ass about getting his daughter Rhea back. Plus, Nara, Kaho, and Frit are in the brig, a gift from Ternus to Voria.

Aran heads down to ask Nara why she betrayed them. She explains that Talifax returned her memories, and that she can no longer be trusted. Talifax wants her to kill Voria, so she should be kept locked up to prevent that.

Aran gets some coffee, which I think I'm going to do too. BRB.

Now armed with coffee, Aran sends a missive to Voria, and they finally get a chance to compare notes. Voria thinks Aran should go with the governor to Yanthara, where they can buy this fleet they're after.

Apparently one of Eros's last acts was to hide Rhea, because he thought she'd be important. He chose to hide her on Yanthara at a *dream* catalyst. Aran is thrilled to hear this, because it means he can finally get Kheross off his ass.

Crewes is from Yanthara, and we're shocked (not shocked) when it turns out that the priestess at the temple is his ex-girlfriend. We get to see Crewes put into an uncomfortable romantic situation, and instead of Aran going into the Catalyst, like everyone expects, poor Crewes has to do it.

He finds himself in a jungle that stretches in all directions. Sarala, his ex and the priestess of Shi, tells him that if he uses his technology it will betray him, so he has to abandon his armor and weapons.

Crewes laughs and refuses. He flies up over the jungle using his spellarmor and sees a purple glow in the middle of a crater. Crewes starts flying toward it, but doesn't get very far when his armor disappears and he plummets into the canopy...buck-ass naked.

For the first time Crewes directly manifests *fire* magic the way a war mage would. He saves himself, just barely, but is pretty banged up when he hits the forest floor. He lands on top of a long, straight branch, which seems perfect for a walking stick.

Before he gets far he realizes he's being shadowed by a ghost leopard, which are ruthless killers of the deep jungle. The cat attacks him and he fends it off, but it continues to follow him for some reason.

Eventually Crewes reaches the center of the crater, and falls backwards onto a bed of leaves. He stares up at the sky and sees a battle playing out between gods. The elder god Shivan is cut in half, and those halves land on separate hemispheres. One is *fire*, and the other *dream*.

Clever readers figured out that the Temple of Shi and the Temple of Van are worshipping halves of the same elder god. That will definitely play a role in book 7. Kudos for figuring it out.

Anyway, Crewes realizes that the cat that's following him is actually his armor, and the walking stick is his rifle. He's pretty annoyed by all this symbolic representation crap, and more annoyed when it turns out that his armor can turn into a cat whenever it wants. He now has a ghost leopard named Neeko-Kan following him around.

Crewes journeys into the dream and rescues Rhea, the Outrider. We see a vision from Rhea's point of view where she and Kheross are fighting off their corrupted brethren. Crewes convinces Rhea that it's just a memory, and she returns...only to immediately reject Kheross because he is still corrupted by the blood of Nefarius.

She reveals that anyone touched by it is a conduit for Nefarius. The goddess can see through their eyes, and learn all their secrets. She urges them to kill her father. Aran refuses and won't turn on an ally. He allows Kheross to leave peacefully, and wishes him well.

Flash back to Voria as she journeys down to the Chamber of Shaya for answers. Shaya shows her that there is a cavern under the tree, and we get to see Shaya's death scene. It turns out that the tree is over her grave, and the goddess isn't really a tree.

In fact, the tree is actually the great spear Worldender, wielded by Shivan when he killed Shaya. Voria realizes that

Shaya's magic is still under the tree, and that losing the pool isn't as catastrophic as we first thought.

A bit later in the book we get another vision, and this time we see Shaya becoming a goddess. She's the commander of something called the Vagrant Fleet (uh oh... another spin-off series), and she uses worship from every person on every ship to help transform her into a goddess.

Inura provides the rest of the magic, and Voria watches him funnel the magic through Ikadra. We see a version of Ikadra that is naive, and quickly realize that the source of the poop jokes is actually Shaya. She's a terrible influence.

Now Voria understands what she needs to do (more poop jokes, obviously).

She calls a meeting with Ducius and the caretakers and explains that they need to convince their people that not only can she become a goddess, but she'll be strong enough to stop Krox. She herself doesn't believe it, but she somehow needs to convince them. Ducius agrees to put his hatred aside, and he and the caretakers start convincing the people to help her rise as a goddess.

Flash back to Aran. Skare has delivered a fleet of black ships to Ternus, and Ternus wants Aran to help power them up. Since the ships can drain magic it stands to reason that they can suck a Catalyst dry. Ternus believes that *void* is the most important aspect, so they want him to lead a raid on the Skull of Xal.

Aran's initial instinct is to say no, but Austin agrees to use those ships to fight Krox when he attacks Shaya. They're desperately short on tools that will hurt a god, and Ternus wants payback for what Krox did to their homeworld. Aran reluctantly agrees.

They arrive at the Skull and the governor wants to fly right in and take what they need. Aran explains that Catalysts have guardians, and that they have no idea what this one is capable of. They need to be cautious.

Sure enough, they are opposed by a potent demon army, led by the demon queen Malila. The black ships try to use their magic-draining tendrils, which have some success against the lesser demons. The ships vacuum up a little *void* magic, but then they try assaulting Malila directly.

It doesn't go well.

Malila reverses the flow and sucks the magic from one of the ships, which starts falling toward the Ternus troops. Aran and Nara manage to knock it out of the way, and the other Ternus ships retreat, leaving them to deal with an angry demigod. Not that angry, though, as it turns out.

Aran and Nara are invited to speak with her, and she tells them that they are, in fact, tools she created. Haven't they ever wondered why their names were so similar? She is trying to resurrect her father, and they are a part of that plan.

She agrees to allow one hundred mages to enter the light, and come away with a piece of Xal. But Aran and Nara must be two of the mages. They agree.

We get some more cool scenes of the godswar. Nara sees how Talifax first tricked Xal. Aran sees how Xal's body was devoured by a host of gods, including the 'good' ones. Xal turns Aran into something called a Hound of Xal, which effectively allows him to track and drain magic. He's designed to kill gods, though Aran doesn't yet realize it.

Flip over to Kheross, who is hovering in space as a dragon. Talifax appears near him and we basically get a 'one more job' scenario. If Kheross will do one more job for Talifax, the Talifax will drain the *void* magic from him, and purge him of Nefarius's black touch.

Kheross knows it's probably a trick, but all Talifax wants

him to do is open a door at the right time. Sounds pretty simple, so Kheross agrees.

Flip back to Voria. She's got the ritual set up and is pretty much good to go, but Drakkon arrives in human form. He brings her enough of Marid's *water* magic to turn Voria into a demigod, because he knows that Shaya's power will not be enough. Yay! We finally get a win.

The magic gives Voria a heightened sense of euphoria, basically making her drunk/high until she crashes. Voria greets her mother and Skare, and thanks them and Ternus for bringing the black ships to help them fight.

We get a reunion between Voria and the company, and everybody is feeling good! It's totally a trap. Voria goes back to her quarters to sleep it off, because she has to become a god in the morning.

Flash over to Nara who is still sitting in a cell with Frit and Kaho. Time stops, and Talifax steps out of the shadows. He taunts her, and says she'll kill Voria. She says she won't.

A few scenes later Kheross comes walking into the brig. Guess which door he has to open to get his freedom? Kheross releases Nara, Frit, and, Kaho and then disappears for the rest of the book.

Nara is terrified. She doesn't want to kill Voria, but realizes that Talifax is 100% certain that she will. Up until this point I planted several little clues about how the ritual of raising a goddess works. You don't need a body. You only need a soul. Ikadra can store a soul.

Nara goes to Voria's chamber and straight gats her. We get to see Voria's cooling corpse, and Nara crying over it. The scene was pretty brutal to write, even though I knew Voria was coming back.

Meanwhile, Nebiat/Krox are getting ready to attack. Nebiat does something that triggers Krox, not that he can do anything about it. She consumes all of the Earthmother's magic at once, removing her as a permanent resource. Basically she eats the Catalyst.

Nebiat spends the magic to awaken every drake on the planet. Effectively she rebuilds the Krox race, and replaces all the dragons that have been killed fighting against the Confederacy and in previous wars.

She takes a few hundred of those dragons, and a bunch of fire elementals, and then heads to Shaya to crush her hated rival.

When she arrives, Voria hasn't risen, and Krox is able to attack the shield directly. Aran and the *Talon* do what they can to fight her army, but it isn't going well. Aran gets ballsy, and attacks Krox directly. He guides the *Talon* inside the body of a god.

Back to Voria. Nara finds a way to modify the ritual, and they are able to raise Voria as a goddess. Voria steps up and starts to fight Krox, but it's clear that she's totally outclassed. The Shade of Shaya tells Voria that the *Spellship* is that weapon. The ship fits in Voria's palm as a goddess, and she ignites it into a double bladed light—uh—sword, which is powered by the faith of the people inside the ship.

Voria brawls with Krox, but Krox is simply too strong. She's losing. There's no hope. =O

We flash back to Aran inside Krox. Aran uses his newfound ability to track and absorb magic. First he rips out the *void* magic Krox took from Xal all those millennia ago. Then he finds the Heart of Fire, and sucks away a bunch of flame.

The *Talon* grows massively in size and power, and so does Aran (he grows in power, not size). He hasn't quite passed the threshold into true godhood, but by the rules of the roleplaying system we're building he's at the very edge of heroic mortal.

Unfortunately, Krox still rips the great tree out of the planet and shatters it. He claims Worldender, the oldest object in creation. Aran does enough damage that Krox retreats since he and Nebiat have what they want.

Voria looks at her ruined world, and replaces the tree, then gives the entire planet an atmosphere. Never again will they need a ritual or a dome. She creates a self-sustaining world, though there are few survivors to populate it. Most died in Krox's assault.

In the last chapter Nebiat returns to her world and brags to Krox about what a badass she is. She didn't kill Voria, but she removed her power base, and claimed the most powerful object in creation.

Now, she plans to sit back and grow in strength while her enemies fight each other, then strike at a critical moment when they are all weakened.

Which brings us to the book you're holding. Nefarius will rise, and Nebiat has not been idle.

AMBUSHED

Aran scanned the newly expanded bridge of the *Talon* as he strode through the vaulted doorway, and was pleased by what he saw. Rhea had command, and currently sat in the central matrix. The contoured couch was designed for pilot comfort, but her posture was stiff and her shoulders squared. A slender spell-blade was belted around her waist, the scabbard resting against the chair's golden frame and the tip of the blade nearly touching the bronze ring as it swung past. That was new.

"Captain on deck," the raven-haired Outrider barked, drawing the attention of the rest of the bridge crew.

Crewes manned the matrix on the far side of the room, his oversized legs dangling off the chair. Unlike Rhea, the sergeant lounged in his matrix, though the dark-skinned man offered Aran a crisp salute. "Love that we got a proper chain of command again. Welcome back, sir. How did it go?"

Aran offered a nod to Davidson in the last matrix. The blond officer's bearded cheeks were more gaunt than they had been, and he still wore the haunted expression that had settled in immediately after the Battle of Shaya.

Davidson returned the nod, his icy eyes focusing for a moment. "Welcome aboard, Captain."

Aran returned Crewes's salute, then willed a bit of *air* from his chest to craft an invisible chair. He adjusted Narlifex as he sat, and considered how to answer Crewes's question. As with most things these days, it was complicated.

"Good, I guess?" He focused his attention on the scry-screen, which currently showed the planet's growing umbral shadow. They'd be in Fissure range soon. He turned back to the sergeant. "Voria is going to head to Ternus once she's done fluffing Ducius's ego."

Crewes licked his lips, and adopted an uncomfortable expression. "That's not what I meant. What about Nara, sir? She coming back?"

It meant a lot to Aran that the sergeant had forgiven Nara, though he had a feeling that clemency didn't extend to either Frit or Kaho. He still wasn't sure where he came down, and was thankful he didn't have to find out. Nara he trusted, to a point. The others? Enemy of my enemy and all that.

Aran shook his head. "Nara's taken Voria's offer. Last I saw her she was surrounded by a dozen advisors in the *Spellship*'s library." Something eased in him, and he relaxed into his invisible chair. "She looked happy. I'm not sure I've ever seen that, and it looks good on her."

Crewes barked a short laugh. "Guess I really am going soft. Kid probably made the right choice, and the major— uhh, Lady Voria, I guess, could use the help so she don't get overwhelmed by snakes like Ducius."

The sergeant's laugh caused sudden motion from the

base of the matrix, and Aran gave a start when he realized that Neeko, Crewes's ghost leopard, was curled up near the sergeant's feet. The cat's fur had faded to a dull bronze, and now perfectly matched the ship's hull. Only a sudden flick from the tail had given its presence away, the motion caused when Crewes laughed. He noted that the cat's ears were tilted toward the sergeant, though her eyes were closed.

Davidson stifled a yawn. "Captain, if we hit another Catalyst do you think the *Talon* might grow again? Right now we can maybe fit a little armor, but if you get us up to a full cruiser we could field a whole tank battalion. We've got the funds to buy them."

"Theoretically," Aran allowed, "but much as I hate to say it we're short on time. We need to get to...our friend in the Umbral Depths. Voria claims that Inura says that Nefarius is about to resurrect. It's like one of those...what do you call those holoshows, Davidson?"

"Soap operas," the blond man drawled.

Aran snapped his fingers. "That's the term. It's like a soap opera. Anyway, Voria believes that the most valuable thing we can do right now is to gather intel. I can't think of a better place than where we originally found this ship."

"Why do I get the feeling that we're all dancing around a topic?" Davidson asked. He scrubbed his fingers through his beard, a straw-colored mirror of Aran's own. "It's like we're all talking about the same thing, but not saying it. I thought this ship was warded by gods or some such. Are we really afraid to say out loud what the mission is?"

"Lieutenant Davidson is right." Rhea swiveled her command chair to face Aran, the rings temporarily obstructing her angular face as they rotated around her. She spoke again when they'd passed, her raven ponytail curled over one shoulder. "If we are to accomplish our mission we must understand what it is. I am given to understand that you are an able commander. Surely you recognize the value of sharing intelligence with your most capable officers."

Crewes started to laugh, though it subsided when Rhea shifted a very intense gaze in his direction. Not a glare, exactly, but more the kind of judgmental stare that Voria had often managed.

"The sergeant is amused, because we literally cannot talk about the mission." Aran hopped down from the invisible chair and began pacing across the deck. The scry-screen showed nothing but darkness now, broken by a few glittering lights on Shaya's surface far below them. "We met a goddess, and she...altered us so that we cannot discuss her, or where we met her. It's a security precaution to ensure that no one finds her world."

Aran was relieved that he'd been able to explain the situation well enough. Some topics were more taboo than others to speak about, and he never knew what he'd be allowed to say when Neith was involved. The spider goddess had been quite thorough with her binding.

He was even more relieved that he didn't need to discuss his personal reasons for pushing for this. Voria hadn't fought him on it, though she was of the mind that they could learn anything they needed to from the Mirror of Shaya.

Aran doubted it. He needed to know more about Xal, and what the god was like. Part of that god lived within him, a large part. Aran wanted answers, and Neith seemed the most impartial of the gods. He felt that she'd deal straight with him, or as straight as an elder goddess could.

"I see." Rhea's expression relaxed, almost imperceptibly.

"What *can* you tell us?" Davidson stifled another yawn,

which was unsurprising given that he'd been on duty for a full twelve hours.

Aran considered that before answering. What would Neith allow him to divulge? "We're heading to the library of the gods. Every action taken in every possible reality is recorded, and the people running this place can help us understand both Krox and Nefarius, and maybe what they're planning."

"So it's like Ternipedia meets quantum, basically." Davidson gave a chuckle. "Well, the divine version anyway. All right, I'm on board. If we can learn about our enemies in the five minutes they give us before the next attack, I'm all for it."

"Well, I ain't okay with it," Crewes groused. "Sir, I get wanting intel, but we kicked Nebiat's ass and she went high-tailing back to her planet. Why don't we get a bunch of allies, fly into the rift, and kick her no-longer-scaly ass across the sector? We cannot give that bitch time to recover."

He was about to respond when something stirred around Aran, a potent, dark magic that was answered by the *void* in his chest. A thick purple crack spread across the blackness outside the ship, and quickly veined outward as the Fissure opened.

"Is someone entering the system?" Rhea asked. She raised a finger, but didn't quite brush the *fire* sigil on the silver ring. "Should we be ready for combat?"

"That was the *Talon*," Aran realized aloud. "I didn't ask it to do it, either. The ship opened the Fissure."

"Well, ain't that the shit. Nice work, ship." Crewes gave a wide grin, and patted the arm of his matrix's command couch. "Guess we don't need a true mage as much as I thought."

"Taking us in," Rhea said, her tone clipped and professional.

Aran couldn't avoid the tension, though he managed to stop pacing. Entering the depths would never be anything but terrifying, because they couldn't predict what might be waiting on the other side. He'd only seen a fraction of the horrors living within that endless darkness, and he prayed he'd never meet another.

The *Talon* glided slowly forward, and the Fissure grew larger on the scry-screen. They quickly passed through, and the Fissure snapped efficiently shut in their wake, trapping them in darkness.

"Prepare the ship for silent running," Davidson ordered. He stifled a third yawn, then climbed from his matrix. "Permission to get some rest, sir?"

"You are relieved, Lieutenant." Aran squeezed his friend's shoulder, then slipped into the matrix Davidson had been sitting in. He tapped *void* on all three rings, then repeated it with *fire*, fully linking with the ship.

"Sir, is there a course you'd like me to set?" Rhea's discomfort was clear, though Aran had no idea what the cause was, or how to correct it. It seemed linked to him.

"I'm leaving that up to the *Talon*," he explained, understanding instinctively that it was the right answer. "He's been to the world where we're going, and can get us back."

"He?" Crewes asked, raising a thick eyebrow.

"We weren't the only ones changed by draining Krox," Aran explained. "The *Talon*...awoke, for lack of a better term. It happened when we consumed the *void*. The ship benefited from the *fire*, too, but it was the *void* that—"

A shape swam in their direction through the darkness, perceptible only because Aran could see it through the *Talon*'s magical senses. He spotted another, and another.

There were twenty in all, each vessel fanning out to create a net around the *Talon*. All were shielded with illusion magic, the same invisibility spell Nara so often employed.

"Battle stations," Aran barked. "We're about to be under assault. Crewes, get Bord and Kezia up here. Put Davidson on standby. Rhea, get ready to cast a full suite of wards, but don't start until I give the word. They don't know we've seen them yet."

Aran drummed his fingers on the command chair's arm. Should he fight? Or flee?

"What are we dealing with, sir?" Crewes asked as he climbed from the matrix and headed for the doorway.

"My guess?" Aran surveyed the approaching ships, his stomach roiling as his suspicions were confirmed. "Black ships. The Inurans probably left them here to ambush us when we departed the system."

2

DISQUIETING

Aran's breathing slowed as he synced fully with the *Talon*. The ship was more responsive now, to the point of almost anticipating his commands. They'd received a huge dose of divine power from Krox, and were now staffed by some of the strongest mages in the sector. They might not have Nara, but theoretically Rhea could make up for it.

The old Aran would have blindly attacked, and assumed he could win by overcoming all enemies. The Aran who'd emerged from Virkon would probably have chosen discretion, and simply run. It wasn't as if these ships could catch them in the depths. Any magic they used to try to locate the *Talon* exposed them to whatever lurked there.

But Aran was neither of those men any longer.

The Aran who'd assaulted a god was starting to understand that he was capable of a great deal more than any ordinary war mage. And he was damnably tired of running. If he assaulted the black ships and things went south he'd simply flee. A risk, but a calculated one.

He guided the *Talon* along the same course, making no

move that might show that they were aware of the approaching net. Aran waited until the ships were within firing range, and then waited another few moments. Tension radiated from Rhea, but she maintained her calm exterior.

"Now, Rhea." Aran tapped the *void* sigil on the gold ring, then the silver, and finally the bronze. He funneled a large amount of *void* into the ship, and felt the *Talon* supply an equal quantity to match the spell. He repeated the sequence with *fire*, and poured an equal amount into it, fueling the disintegrate spell. It was the first time he'd attempted a spell this complex all on his own, and he was shocked by how easy it was.

In his peripheral vision he spotted Rhea tapping *life*, *water*, and *spirit* sigils on all three rings. Her fingers flew across them with incredible precision, more than Aran himself was capable of, if he was being honest.

A latticework of wards sprang up over the skin of the ship, and Rhea grunted with effort as the spell completed. He eyed her sidelong, and she glared back a challenge. "What? The ship is sixty percent larger than it was. Wards take a lot more strength now. I'm used to having co-pilots to help."

"I'm not complaining, just admiring." Aran focused on the closest vessel, which had drifted just a hair ahead of the rest of the fleet. He poured the last bits of *fire* and *void* into the ship, and smiled in satisfaction as a bolt of disintegration lanced out of the spellcannon. The crackling beam of negative energy appeared to impact with empty space, but an explosion of particles revealed the black ship for a fraction of a second before it ceased to exist. "Guess their magic resistance has limits."

"True, but even you cannot disintegrate them all. There

are nineteen more." Rhea grabbed the arms of her chair, and swiveled to face the doorway. Footsteps pounded up the hallway from the mess, but there was no sign of Bord or Kez yet. "Where are those laggards? I do not wish to second guess your choices, Captain, but—"

"Then don't," he interrupted as he guided the *Talon* into a steep dive. Black ships shimmered into existence all around them, and Aran's stomach lurched. His skin beaded with sweat, exactly as it had when he'd stepped inside one of the black ships.

Several of the closest vessels discharged tendrils of writhing energy, tinged with the faint purplish light of *void*. Aran had seen the attack back at the Skull of Xal, and had spent a long time thinking about the best response. Thankfully, the *Talon* hadn't lost much maneuverability despite the increased size, and he twisted adeptly around the grasping tendrils.

The fleet accelerated in his direction, the ships beginning to clump as they pursued. Aran accelerated enough to outpace them, but not enough for the black ships to lose them entirely.

Crewes pounded back onto the bridge, his chest heaving as he climbed back into his Matrix. "Bord and Kez are right behind me."

The couple tumbled into the room after him, and moved to flank the matrices on the opposite sides of the room. He felt immediate relief knowing everyone had back up.

"What's the play, sir?" Crewes prompted.

"I'm going to need every bit of *fire* that you can supply." Aran accelerated slightly, and the enemy ships fell into a tighter cluster as each flew in a perfectly straight line to reach them. "Rhea, same goes for you. Every bit of it."

"Yes, sir," Rhea's voice was quiet, but resolved.

Both tapped their respective sigils, and Aran did the same with his own. His command of *fire* was impressive, as was Rhea's, but they both knew that Crewes would really be the one powering this spell. The sergeant might be the only person in the sector to have been to three *fire* Catalysts, and outside of a guardian or a god he was probably the strongest user living. Or so Aran hoped anyway.

Fire rolled out of Aran into the deck, wave after wave joining the magic from his co-pilots. The amount of magic they collected was staggering, but it grew even more so when the *Talon* matched the spell's power.

Aran tapped a final series of *fire* sigils, then abruptly flipped the ship and began accelerating toward the enemy. "Sergeant Crewes, make me some dead Inurans, please."

"With pleasure, sir." The sergeant gripped the arms of his command chair, and gave a roar of effort as a river of flame pulsed from him into the ship.

The spellcannon began to glow, and a moment later a beam of pure heat, as hot as any star, surged out of the *Talon*'s spellcannon. The flame was easily a kilometer wide, and caught six ships, which had been clustered together at the center of the pack.

All six vessels burst into brilliance, and the front two ranks detonated spectacularly. The rear rank, though, contained a pair of vessels that were larger that the rest. Those vessels smoldered an angry orange, and then their hulls resumed their flat black exterior.

"Uh, sir, I think I just pissed them off." Crewes eyed Aran helplessly. "Think we should run?"

"If we do," Aran thought aloud, "they'll be here to hit the next ships that depart Shaya. If it were me I'd blockade the system, and destroy any ships trying to enter or exit. Since they can drain magic they'll only get stronger over time."

There was no more time for words as they closed with the enemy.

"I hope your wards are as good as you say," Bord ventured from behind Rhea's matrix, "'cause there sure are a lot of those things left."

As if on cue, a dozen black ships unleashed their tendrils, and the two larger ships that had survived Crewes's spell were the first to reach them. The oily magic latched onto the wards, which began to discolor around the affected areas.

Rhea gave a grunt, and renewed waves of *water* and *spirit* poured into the hull. "I'm not sure...how long...I can hold this."

Four more tendrils slammed into the wards, catching like hooks in a net. The *Talon's* forward momentum slowed as they were jerked to a near halt by the combined force of the enemy ships.

"Bord, relieve Crewes and give the wards everything you have," Aran roared. He was only vaguely aware of the curly-haired specialist replacing the dark-skinned man. He knew that would only buy them a little time, and needed an answer quickly.

They treat us as prey, Narlifex pulsed in his mind. *We are NOT prey. Slay them. Slay them all. Use the dark magics given to us by our father. It is the only way.*

Aran seized the arms of his chair and concentrated. He reached out with the senses Xal had given him, and felt the power of the tendrils, and of the vessels employing them. It was layered and complex, and he couldn't pretend to understand all of it. He didn't need to understand their magic though.

He just needed to devour it.

Aran reached for the thing or quality that made him a

Hound of Xal, and the magic answered eagerly. It reached through him, through the *Talon*, out to the tendrils gripping the wards.

Time seemed to slow, and Aran became aware of a million, million tiny little factors. He could hear Crewes's labored breathing, and Kez quietly praying under her breath, and Rhea's thundering heartbeat. Through the *Talon* he could feel the cold of the void, and the deeper chill of the tendrils draining the power from their wards.

Aran focused on the first tendril that had gripped them, the one belonging to the larger of the two ships. He sent a surge of magic up the tendril, his own strength eagerly devouring the magic he found there. The tendril began to collapse in on itself, but Aran wouldn't allow it. He flooded the tendril with more magic, and it began to expand, and then flow back to the enemy ship.

The dark energy latched onto the Inuran hull in much the same way the tendril had done to theirs. Aran reached into their vessel, and began to drink. Power, immense glorious power, flowed through the tendril, through the *Talon*, and into Aran. He sipped *spirit*, and *void*, and *fire*. A little taste of each.

In the distance he could hear Rhea and Bord struggling to keep the wards going. He needed to be quick. Aran gritted his teeth, and pulled harder. He blanked out the world, narrowing it down to a pinprick of focus. The enemy ship became his entire reality, and Aran was acutely aware of the veins of dark energy running through the walls of the vessel.

He drew that magic forth, coaxing it from every part of the titanic craft. That magic flowed back up the tendril, into the *Talon*, and into him. The process continued, pulse after glorious pulse, until the enemy ship peeled off and began to flee.

Aran continued to drain, sucking a final pulse from the enemy vessel. Another ship slammed into the tendril, and it snapped, separating them from their wounded prey.

He instantly reversed course, and began to accelerate away from the Inuran fleet. A few vessels tried to respond to the sudden shift, but most of their fleet was still in retreat.

"Get ready for silent running." Aran relaxed back into the command couch, conscious now of the sweat soaking his uniform.

"We're not gonna finish 'em off?" Crewes asked, his gaze locked intently on the scry-screen. "They ain't done much damage to us, and they seem scared."

"Look at Bord." Aran nodded in the specialist's direction, and the sergeant seemed to notice Bord's ashen complexion. "He doesn't have much left, and Rhea probably doesn't either."

Rhea avoided eye contact, but didn't contradict his words.

"We've got a mission to take care of." Aran tapped a *fire* sigil. "I'll get a missive off to Ducius so they can prepare a defense in case the ships attack, but I expect they'll stay in the depths for the time being."

"Damned straight." Crewes gave another grin. "We gave 'em something to think about. Outriders four, bad guys zip."

"You fought well, Sergeant." Rhea gave the dark-skinned man an approving nod, then shifted her attention to Bord. "As did you. I cannot condone your cavalier attitude or utter lack of discipline, but you've the talent and skill to make an excellent soldier."

Kez rose from one of the couches along the wall, and moved to stand protectively next to Bord's matrix as she bristled at Rhea. "I like him joost the way he is, thank you very much. His 'undisciplined' self has saved us more times than you, that's for sure."

"Rhea, you've got command." Aran rose from the command chair and ducked through the spinning rings.

"Where are you going, sir?" Crewes called as Aran reached the door.

He stopped and turned to face the sergeant. "I get the feeling Skare is playing a deeper game, one we're not seeing. I want to know what it is, and I'm going to see if I can puzzle it out."

"Yes, sir." Crewes snapped a salute. "Might get a nap while you're at it. You could use it."

"If I can find time." Aran never seemed to have enough of it.

3

THE CHILDREN OF NEBIAT

Nebiat looked down upon her world, and was pleased. The citizens of her empire did not know the word Krox. They did not call themselves the Krox. They called their world Nebiat, and knew themselves as the Children of Nebiat.

She could see all of them, every drake, and Wyrm, and hatchling. She'd watched over them from orbit, still cradling Worldender like a talisman.

You place too much value on that weapon. Krox rumbled in her mind. *Its sole use is combat, and combat has never been my chief strength. We are best served to gift it to a potential ally, one who might help us achieve dominance. One we can manipulate, ideally.*

And you have such a candidate in mind? Nebiat snapped. She was growing more and more weary of sharing a head with Krox, and the fact that he knew it only made it worse.

I do not. Krox admitted. *But one will present itself. There are many gods in this sector, and in other sectors if we must venture further. Translocation knows no distance, and there are many corners of the galaxy where we could find aid. We might even recover additional pieces of myself.*

And thus weaken me. Is that it? No, I think we have quite enough power for the time being. It shocked her that she could so casually turn from more strength, but she'd learned that some prices were simply too high. Her whole life had been spent in pursuit of something she hadn't fully understood. *No, I'll keep this weapon for the time being. Thank you very much. The time will come when I either wield it or bestow it to an ally.*

Krox pulsed thoughtfully, and Nebiat could see the shape of some of those thoughts. He thought her weak and shortsighted. She tried to focus on her world, but even her children brought her no pleasure right now. She longed to be able to manifest, to escape this horrendous god and be mortal, just for a day. An hour.

How am I to enact my will in the galaxy? Nebiat demanded, shifting the subject. She tightened her grip around Worldender, and focused on the sensation of holding the spear with one of her celestial limbs. It wasn't the same, not exactly. *Do I need to somehow train worshippers? That seems impractical.*

Krox's amusement rippled through his thoughts. *You have seen the pieces, but you do not grasp the whole. Why do you think that Shaya had a guardian that your father must first overcome? Why do all Catalysts have one, even those gods who've been dead for eons?*

Nebiat considered that. Every Catalyst did have a guardian. If a guardian was slain, and that Catalyst left in peace, then eventually primals would come. One would become stronger than the rest, eventually assuming the role of guardian. It was a nearly immutable law, so far as she knew.

It wasn't difficult to see where Krox was going with this. She needed a guardian if she wanted to interact directly with mortals. *Very well. Lord my ignorance over me. How do I create a guardian, and what are the pitfalls I should know of when choosing one?*

You misjudge me. Amusement still flitted across his thoughts. *You would react the same were a being you deemed a child to ask you questions it felt were very important. I mean no insult. You are a part of me now, after all. If you wish to raise a guardian I can aid you. They are more than merely protectors. They are our agents in the galaxy. We gift them with phenomenal power, and they enact our will.*

And what if they turn that power against us, as my father did?

Clever gods, Krox explained, *do not invest enough power to create such threats. In my case, I had little choice in the matter. I knew my consciousness would be shattered, and I foresaw that your father was capable of healing me. In the end, I was right. The price is a small and very temporary one, I assure you.*

Krox directed her at memories of his various guardians, and there had apparently been a dizzying array of them. Some were dragons, as her father had been, but others were strange alien races she didn't recognize. When she went far enough back those creatures became unrecognizable, and were more the embodiment of magical forces than anything she would deem a sentient race.

A guardian can war on your enemies, and if they die you lose nothing but the magic you invested in them. They can inspire your religion, acting as a hero that your other followers seek to emulate. When you select a guardian, you must choose someone your children will respect, and eventually fear. They should be competent and loyal. Some gods choose to allow their guardians free will, though I did not. There is too much danger of betrayal.

Nebiat went down her very short list of candidates, none of whom were present on her world below. She loved these new children, but not a single one had proven themselves. She needed someone who'd seen war. Someone whom she trusted, but that would also look out for the best interests of the people below.

She had just the candidate, one who fulfilled all the requirements. *It's time to bring my wayward son home, I think. Kaho will make an excellent guardian.*

Krox pulsed displeasure. *I have seen your memories. Your son is not loyal to you. He is dangerous. Giving him this power is ill advised, unless you also plan to shackle his will.*

No, Nebiat thought back, utterly furious now. *Enough of your binding and your games. We see where that took my people. I am already sick of your schemes. I will elevate someone who seeks the betterment of this world, and I will not make them a puppet. I will make them an ally.*

That, she realized, was what she desperately needed. A friend. An equal. Someone she could converse with. Someone who shared her goals.

Is it possible to project myself? How do I speak with a potential candidate?

If you must do this, Krox groused, *then I will aid you. Create a sliver of yourself, and fill it with your consciousness. This simulacrum can translocate, as you do, and it can cast spells as you do. However, its creation is expensive, and leaves you vulnerable. If you are attacked, your consciousness can be destroyed, which makes such endeavors extremely ill advised. If you must do so, then do it quickly, speak to your candidate, and then return as fast as you are able.*

Nebiat smiled, her cosmic face creasing as the expression grew. Her children would make all sorts of portents about it, no doubt. She only hoped her son would see reason.

4

LOST

Frit couldn't shake the persistent feeling that she was a traitor one step ahead of the executioner. It followed her almost everywhere in the *Spellship*, and it didn't help that passersby stared and whispered wherever she went.

She wasn't the only Ifrit on board, but she was the only one who'd betrayed Shaya. Voria had forgiven her, and Nara had as well. Both had entreated her to stay, and as Frit had no other home she'd accepted their offer. But letting her stay and considering her one of them were two totally different things.

Frit braced herself as she stepped into the library, and almost turned around and ran. Nara was there, as expected, but she was surrounded by a dozen attendants. Most had datapads and were asking questions, then jotting down their accusatory little notes.

They weren't the only people in the library, either. Almost every table had at least one person seated at it, and many were completely surrounded.

"Frit!" rumbled a familiar voice from a nearby table. She

turned to see Kaho rise to his feet, his considerable height drawing the attention from her, for once. "Have you come to study? I've not seen you in a few days, and was starting to get worried. I wanted to give you your space, but, well...I've missed you."

She found his nervousness endearing, especially given the frightening form he wore. Well, frightening to most people. Nothing about Kaho's draconic visage frightened her, quite the opposite. She found him handsome and dignified. He was one of the brightest scholars she'd ever met, the path she'd have chosen if Shaya hadn't bred her for war.

"Nara and I are supposed to have lunch." Frit moved to lean against the table, and smiled up at Kaho. His was one of the few friendly faces to be found, and she felt a little bad for not showing more of her face lately. Depression wasn't doing her any favors. She hated it. "I'm starting to wonder, though. She looks pretty busy."

"Well, if she can't break away, then I can." Kaho brightened and gave her a toothy smile. "I'd enjoy the conversation. I've been reading all sorts of fascinating things. This place is utterly ancient, and every tome dates from...well, you know all this." He gave another nervous laugh. "Listen to me. Go enjoy your lunch, mahaya."

She'd done a little reading and learned that mahaya was draconic for single star, and referenced the idea that everyone had one star in the heavens that they were connected to. She didn't need another reason to care for him, but that endearment gave it to her anyway.

Frit squared her shoulders and marched through the tables, and then through the students and aides seeking Nara's attention. She walked right up to the newly appointed high priestess. Nara's irritated gaze came up, and Frit wilted.

"Frit." Nara blinked a few times. "I'm sorry. I thought you

were another acolyte." Her face softened into a smile, and she rose from her chair and took Frit in a deep hug.

Nara possessed *fire* magic, and that meant she was one of the few people Frit could actually hug. She took full advantage, and squeezed her friend fiercely. "I missed you."

"I missed you too." Nara took a step back and her smile grew. "So what can I do for you?"

"We were supposed to..." Frit trailed off.

"Oh, my." Nara's hand shot up to cover her mouth. "I'm so sorry, Frit. I can't. We're trying to research a ritual that will restore Ternus, and Voria plans to take us there in the morning. We need to get this done. Is there any way we can push lunch to tomorrow, or the day after?"

"Of course," Frit replied cheerfully, dying inside. "Do what you need to. I have lots of studying I want to get done anyway." She gave her friend a smile, and then turned and all but bolted.

"Frit!" Nara called, but Frit plunged away from her friend, not wanting Nara to see the tears. Her sycophants would prevent her from chasing Frit in any case.

She wound deeper into the library, threading through the stacks as she sought to master her emotions. That was growing more and more difficult. She just felt so damned alone. Theoretically Kaho should make her feel less lonely, but the way he'd eagerly adopted his studies, and the way he laughed off the blatant racism leveled at him every day, made it hard to relate to him.

Frit couldn't tell him about problems when she knew that if he ran into similar problems he'd shoulder them without complaint. That made her feel petty. She knew it wasn't Kaho's fault, but it also made it difficult to confide in him, about this at least.

She finally stopped when she reached a part of the

library she recognized. Frit hurried to the history section, and circled the shelf until she found the knowledge scale she was looking for. It wasn't quite a hologram, per se, but it was almost as good. The library was full of historical accounts, some written in the first person by the actual witness, and while she didn't know where or when they'd lived she found their lives fascinating.

She brought the scale to a table, and tried to think about how much fun it would be to read, and not how devastatingly alone she felt.

5

BLESSING OF VORIA

Voria manifested in the sky over the great tree, the tree she herself had created to replace the original, and made herself known to her people. The survivors of Krox's wrath had already begun constructing homes on the upper branches, those that had been deemed the most valuable on the original tree.

That had only been the case because there were enough people to fill every branch, and spill over the roots at the base of the tree. Now? Only the top four branches had significant settlement, with a few more on lower branches set up by groups that valued privacy.

Faces turned skyward as she descended, a literal lady of light. She basked in their attention, their worship she realized. It strengthened her as a sun strengthened the plants at winter's end. They believed in her, despite all reasonable evidence to the contrary.

Voria fortified herself with their worship as she shrank to a more human-sized form. She landed on the uppermost branch in the center of an amphitheater Ducius had shaped from the tree's whorled red wood.

As expected, every seat was occupied. Ducius had appointed dozens of new caretakers, each with different areas of the world as their stewardship. That hadn't been surprising. What did surprise her was the number of drifters among the assembly. There were even a few humans.

Necessity had forced Ducius to tolerance. There simply weren't enough survivors for his Shayan superiority to flourish. Not any more.

"Welcome, great mother," Ducius intoned as he stepped forward to greet her. He bowed, but not as low as he would have for Eros. "We receive you with joy, and greet you with honor."

"And I greet you, honored child." Voria did not bow, though she inclined her head respectfully. She turned her attention to the assembly. "Caretakers, it is a pleasure to see you gathered and working together to restore this world. The best revenge we can have against Krox is ensuring our children live free and prosperously."

"The best revenge," Ducius shot back, his tone acidic, "is *actual revenge* against Krox. I still do not understand why you haven't taken your forces and pursued that thing into the Rift. What guarantee do we have that he will not wait until you are gone, and then return to destroy us all?"

Voria briefly entertained a fantasy where she disintegrated Ducius on the spot, even though she knew how impractical that was. Gods but she loathed this man. She folded her arms, and delivered what she hoped was an imperious stare. "Krox fled back to the heart of his strength, and he did it carrying an unparalleled god-slaying weapon. Worldender is enough reason to tread lightly. The fact that Krox is dramatically more powerful than I am is a second. The fact that Nefarius is about to rise is a third. The landscape is shifting, Ducius, and I need to act quickly to secure what allies we have left. Ternus needs us, whatever you might think. They were here for us when Krox came. We must do the same."

Ducius frowned darkly, and the expression was mirrored on a number of caretakers. They wore their hostility openly, which didn't say much for their faith in her.

"Voria," Ducius began, as if instructing a child, "If you believe you can make any difference on that doomed world, then you are a fool. Your magic is not limitless, nor is the faith of your people. We are weary. We are grieving. A war of vengeance we can stomach. Call for our aid, and we will ride into the Rift. But presiding over a planetary funeral in the guise of helping? I won't be a party to it. Your magic is vast, but we know what gods are now. We know that you are no more divine than when you first blasphemed in my presence all those years ago."

Voria began to laugh, and reveled in the reminder that she could still experience human emotions. She stilled her mirth and shook her head. "Oh, Ducius, please don't ever change. To you I am simply a glowy mage, yes? Like you, but a hair stronger? You have no idea what I can perceive now, Ducius. And long after you, your descendants, and their descendants are dust I will be here, unchanged, fighting to protect this sector from those who mean its citizens harm. I *am* a goddess. I can assure you of that."

"So you've come here to lecture us then?" Ducius demanded, shifting the battlefield since he knew he'd lost ground.

"I have come to offer my blessing." Voria raised both arms, and intense golden light flowed from her. "Once, Shaya did the same, and gifted key followers with the ability to heal. She gave them *life* magic, so they could protect. I make the same gift to you."

Life magic pulsed from Voria, rolling out over the assembled caretakers in a crackling wave. It washed through them, changing and enhancing as it bonded to each mage. Voria gave each a small sliver, enough to cast basic *life* spells, and was shocked by how little it tapped her reservoir to do so. Several hundred new mages blinked at her in wonder, and in that moment she was certain she'd made the right choice.

She turned back to Ducius, who'd received the same gift as the others. His expression hadn't softened. She didn't care. "I've given you the tools to protect this world, Ducius. There is only one more thing I can do."

"You've done quite enough," Ducius sneered, the hatred once again making him ugly.

"Oh, I think you'll like this last gift." She rose into the air in as dramatic a fashion as she could manage. "I'm going to leave, Ducius. Without me here, with no Catalyst, you are no longer a target. Yet you also possess the magical strength to protect yourselves. That's all I ever wanted. You will be safe, for a time, with me gone. Wish me luck, Tender, for if I fail, your reign will be nearly as short as Eros's."

She translocated before he could get the last word. Petty, but so very satisfying.

6

EXPECTED

I t took Aran almost the entirety of their three-day flight to figure out why the crew was avoiding him, especially Rhea. He walked slowly into the mess, and moved to the food thingie and thought about eggs and bacon. Davidson had hooked him on the dish, and claimed that over sixty percent of Ternus citizens broke their fast with it.

He took the plate over to the far side of the room, and sat with his back to the door. No one else was in the mess, and short of being in his quarters it was the most privacy he usually got. He'd been seeking a lot of it, because he understood why the crew was so horrified.

Aran had drained magic from the Inurans in precisely the same manner they utilized, which begged the question: How was he really different? And what might he become if he kept draining magic? Had taking a sliver of Nefarius's magic from that ship been enough for Talifax to see through his eyes in the same way he could see those who'd taken from Xal?

There were so many questions, but he had neither Nara

nor Voria to help him find answers. That was what he missed most, really. He'd become a decent enough commander, he figured, but he lacked their knowledge of history, magic, and the gods themselves. That kind of data was critical, because it allowed you to anticipate your enemy.

That meant if he were going to obtain that data he'd have to rely on himself to get it. That made this mission even more valuable, to his mind.

"Eggs, bacon, and two pancakes," came Davidson's drawl from behind him.

The newly minted lieutenant moved to sit across from Aran, and began wordlessly spooning eggs into his mouth. The self-demotion in rank had seemed to make him much happier, and Aran understood why. He didn't much enjoy command either, and it was nice knowing someone else would make the final call.

Aran slowly spooned eggs into his mouth, silently eating next to Davidson until both parties had run out of eggs. He set down his fork, and broke the silence. "You think they're right to be scared?"

"Figured it out, then. I shouldn't be surprised." Davidson sawed off a piece of pancake and popped it into his mouth. He chewed thoughtfully before speaking again. "Yeah, I think they're right to be scared. We got a saying."

"Ternus has a saying for everything. Most of them involving beef, or grit."

"True," Davidson allowed, "and I don't even know where this one originated. Terra I imagine. Sometimes to kill the devil you got to become one yourself."

Aran considered that. "Shit."

"Yeah." Davidson set down his fork, and clapped Aran on the shoulder. "Don't let it get to you, brother. If you ever go bad I'll quietly put a tank shell in the back of your skull."

"Ugh, why don't you two joost get married already?" Kez called from the doorway. She gave Aran a wink as she moved to the food thingie, then settled at a neighboring table armed with a slice of apple pie. "Lieutenant tight-pants says we should reach the coordinates in joost under ten minutes. She sent me down to get you, and I figured I had joost enough time for something to fortify me 'fore we walk into whatever this mess is."

Aran snorted a laugh at the tight-pants comment, and noticed that Davidson was hiding a smile. They all liked Rhea, but she was a stickler for protocol. "Guess I should head up there." He gave Davidson a grateful nod, then deposited his plate back in the food thingie before heading up to the bridge.

Rhea, Crewes, and Bord had all taken a matrix, with Rhea commanding from the center. Her hair had been brushed into a tight ponytail, and her midnight flight suit was immaculate, not a wrinkle to be found. She was a marked contrast to Bord's rumpled trousers and shirt, which still bore chocolate stains across the chest from his last shift. Rhea was pretty, in a severe sort of way, though knowledge of her true nature muted any attraction Aran might have felt.

Crewes wore his armor, currently a deep purple, and Aran didn't really blame him. In fact, he considered heading down to the cargo hold and equipping his own.

Not necessary, Narlifex buzzed. *I remember fire god. Fire god awakened me. There is no danger here, only allies.*

He knew intellectually the blade was right, but the feeling persisted. *I'll never be comfortable approaching a god that could accidentally kill me with a casual step.*

"Officer on deck," Rhea barked as she spun the chair in

her command matrix to face him. She snapped a tight salute, one Crewes and Bord immediately echoed.

"Morning, Rhea. You're relieved." Aran moved to stand outside her matrix as she exited. He almost took an instinctive step inside, which had become habit. The fact that he didn't need to was going to take some getting used to. "Will you head down to the cargo hold, and get the squad ready for deployment? Sergeant, Specialist, please go with her."

Crewes gave Aran a respectful nod as he exited the bridge, while all Bord offered was a weak smile as he followed. Aran's shoulders slumped. It felt like there was a distance that hadn't been there before.

Aran reached for his link to the ship in the same way he did when communicating with Narlifex. "Bring us home, boy. You can set down right where you picked us up."

Something pulsed through the ship, a quick magical shine infused the walls, then was gone. An answer? Perhaps the only one the ship was capable of giving. The view on the scry-screen didn't change, still unbroken blackness, but the position indicator in the lower corner began to scroll as they picked up speed.

A moment later they broke through the illusion cloaking Neith's world, and Aran perceived her planet through the *Talon's* senses. It was unchanged, a mostly barren rock with a bit of water, and a whole lot of mountainous caves where countless arachnidrake hatchlings lived.

The *Talon* approached the planet at an angle, its shadowed grey mass growing larger as they approached. Aran turned and left the bridge, threading his way down to the cargo hold. He'd intentionally waited, and not just because of the fear.

More and more Aran was realizing that as the commanding officer he couldn't fraternize like he once could. Much as he wanted to pretend otherwise, barriers were growing. Bord and Kez and Crewes were still the same soldiers, but he'd gone from a raw wipe to a captain, though if he was being honest his responsibilities warranted a rank more like major, or maybe even commander.

He let the distractions fall away as he entered the cargo hold, and pride swelled when he saw his people ready for battle. Rhea hovered in her Mark XI spellarmor, which had been painted a deep blue with gold highlights. It reminded him of the Confederacy, and he rather liked it.

Crewes, Bord, and Kezia all stood in a line, each in their armor, and each cradling their respective weapons. Bord and Kez had their faceplates down, so he couldn't judge their mood.

"All right, people," he began. "We're going to be landing in just under sixty seconds. Once we touch down, we're going to move through the hangar in cover formation. Rhea, I want you to advance until we reach the giant double doors at the far side. Hopefully we'll run into a caretaker, one of Neith's people, and they'll guide us. Don't cast unless cast upon."

"You said her name," Crewes said, blinking.

"I think her prohibition doesn't work here." Aran offered a shrug, then moved to his spellarmor. He sketched a *void* sigil, and slid inside. The comfortable tang of old sweat surrounded him as the foam tightened around his body, and the HUD flared to life.

A moment later there was an audible thunk as the *Talon* set down.

"Let's move, Outriders," Rhea ordered, as she snapped her faceplate down and glided toward the *Talon*'s shimmering, blue field. It winked out of existence at her approach, exposing both the golden ramp and cavernous hangar they'd landed in.

Aran had the freedom to examine his surroundings as he trailed after the squad. Not having to run the combat op was kind of nice, and he really studied the immense pillars they passed as they threaded toward the doors leading to Neith.

There was no movement, and no sound. This place could have been a tomb, and for a single instant Aran worried that some dark god had found this place and killed off Neith.

Then he sensed the ocean of *fire* in the distance. It was a vast reservoir of immense strength, and now that Aran had met several gods he could properly categorize Neith. She was much, much stronger than Voria, but considerably weaker than Krox.

Something skittered in the darkness ahead, and the light of the globe of fire hanging over Crewes's head glinted off multi-faceted eyes. Eight eyes.

"You are expected," a voice like rustling cloth came from the shadows, "The one called Aran may approach. The rest of you must return to your ship, immediately." There was a touch of urgency to the command, which seemed out of keeping. The caretakers he'd met previously were almost servile, and expressed no emotions.

"Captain?" Rhea pivoted her armor in the air to face him. "Shall I escort the company back to the *Talon*?"

"Affirmative." Aran rose up into the air near her, and willed a bit of flame to illuminate the skin of his armor. The light brightened gradually, exposing the caretaker's many-limbed body. Nara had hated these things, but for Aran they merely made him uncomfortable, though he wasn't sure why. "Keep the *Talon* ready to move. I don't know how long

I'll be, but I expect not long. Remember, people, we're guests here."

Rhea began herding the company back the way they'd come, leaving Aran in the custody of the caretaker. The creature's jaws quivered as it spoke. "If you'll come with me, Captain, Neith awaits."

7

ACTIONABLE INTEL

A ran followed the caretaker as it shuffled deeper into the hangar, though that term didn't seem entirely accurate. They housed ships here, and a number of berths were scattered seemingly at random, but the bulk of every area contained shelves lined with knowledge scales. They glowed with their own inner light, like a sea of orderly fireflies, lining his path toward the titanic double doors sealing Neith's chamber.

He snapped his faceplate down, and drifted toward the doors. As expected, the doors swung silently open. As they did so, the caretaker turned wordlessly and scuttled back the direction it had come, no doubt returning to whatever errand it had been about.

Aran flew between the golden doors, which began to close behind him. A wide stairway descended down into darkness, and he knew it ended in a room large enough to house a goddess of Neith's considerable size.

The last time he hadn't been able to see her until she'd lit a flame, and the illumination from his armor wasn't nearly enough to banish the shadows. But he knew exactly where she was standing. A mountain-sized shape lounged against one wall, her bulk blazing to Aran's supernatural senses. She contained so much *fire*, perhaps as much as Krox had.

"You have changed much, little vessel," Neith's voice broke over Aran like thunder, and it actually knocked him back a step in midair. If not for the armor his ears would have bled, like last time. "I can feel Xal's touch upon you. He has claimed you, and invested a not inconsiderable amount of his power to do so. Tell me, Outrider, do you understand what being a Hound of Xal signifies?"

She is my Mother. Narlifex pulsed. *In the same way Xal is my father*.

Aran supposed the blade was right, in a way. Maybe that made Virkonna its aunt. He drifted closer to Neith, and willed a sliver of *fire* to amplify his voice. "I'm beginning to, and I don't much like it. In fact, that's why I've come. For answers. Hounds exist to find and devour magic, don't they?"

"That is their primary function," Neith allowed. The titanic goddess scooted forward, the ground trembling as she moved. "But it does not answer the question. Being a Hound of Xal means that you are designed to hunt Xal's enemies, to slay them, and upon your death to return all the magical energies you have collected to your master, like a bee to the hive."

"How does that work if that master is dead?" Aran wondered aloud. He drifted closer, moving higher until he was roughly at eye level with the world's largest arach-nidrake. Curiously, he experienced none of the fear or rever-ence that he had the last time he'd been here. Of course, he'd seen a lot since then.

"How do you define death?" Neith mused, her jaws quivering. She gestured, and a vast illusion covered the upper portion of the room. Stars and planets spun out all around them, then the illusion zoomed in on a remote sector, one with a fading red dwarf in the last phase of the sun's existence.

A headless corpse floated in the void, and at first Aran thought it might be a Wyrm. It had wings, arms, and legs, like a hatchling. But it wasn't a hatchling. The body looked a good deal more like the demon queen Malila's had, back at the Skull of Xal. It was a demon, not a dragon. And the sheer size of the thing against the backdrop of the sun made something chillingly clear to Aran.

This body was large enough to be attached to the Skull of Xal.

"What am I looking at?" Aran asked as he gazed up at the illusion.

"It is called the Husk of Xal," she explained, and raised a scaled appendage to gesture. "You saw Xal's death. This is what remains of his body. The magic has been stripped away, and the head moved thirty light years from the body. Yet is Xal truly dead? I often wonder. Xal allowed himself to be killed. He neither resisted, nor attempted to flee. Why? Why allow himself to be consumed, unless he had some sort of plan?"

It was a good question. What had Xal seen that caused him to choose the course he had? Aran thought back to the first time he'd touched the god's mind. Xal had gone calmly to his death, and had seemed certain that it was a necessary part of whatever victory he ultimately sought.

"Do you have any theories?" Aran rose a bit higher, and turned his attention from the illusion back to the goddess.

"I do, but they are immaterial to your current need," Neith countered. She waved a clawed appendage and the illusion disappeared. "You have come seeking 'actionable intel', have you not?"

"Effectively," Aran admitted. "We need to understand our enemies, and that's proving difficult. There's no hard data about either Krox or Nefarius, and I don't know who to concentrate on or what the real threat is. Krox attacked Shaya, and now has Worldender. That makes him the primary threat in my book, and I'm sure whatever he's planning it isn't good. But we know Talifax is scheming to bring Nefarius back, and I've seen enough to realize how bad that will be. So what do I do? Where do I focus? I can only be in one place at a time, and I feel like whichever choice I make will leave us screwed in the end."

"Neither is the true question you wish to ask, which is whether or not you will become evil now that you are a hound. I do not have the answer for that, because evil isn't so easily defined. It will certainly change you, but how remains to be seen." Neith settled onto her haunches, somehow managing to look like a typical house cat. "I can, however, shed a great deal of light on your dilemma with Krox and Nefarius. Krox is the lesser threat for the time being. It is true that he possesses Worldender, but the addition of Nebiat as a factor has dramatically altered Krox's motives. She has used immense magic to breathe life into her world."

The goddess gestured again, and this time the illusion showed the Erkadi Rift, their perspective zooming inside the purple nebula, whizzing past stars and planets and dust clouds. It finally slowed, and stopped at an unfamiliar green-blue world.

Aran was somehow able to perceive the entire world at once, and saw hundreds of thousands of hatchlings scattered across a half-dozen continents. They lived in small flights, and more than one group had begun warring on their neighbors.

"None of this existed a cycle ago," Neith explained. "Nebiat has re-created her species, and in the process undone Krox's plans. She wishes to see her people rise and conquer, which is very different than devouring every living being, as Nefarius seeks. It will take Nebiat many years to develop her power, and while she will be a threat, we will always have the advantage of knowing what she values."

Aran considered that. Nebiat wanting to preserve her people made sense, and if she really did control Krox it meant that she'd force him to look out for her interests. Those almost certainly ran counter to their own, but at least he understood her motivation.

"What does Nefarius want?" Aran found himself asking. "And better yet, what does Talifax get out of it? You've implied they're the greater threat. How?"

Neith rose again, and began doing something very ungodlike. She paced back and forth across the chamber, swaying as she shuffled. "I have dedicated a dozen millennia in contemplation of that question." She closed her many-faceted eyes and spoke again. "Nefarius is a Wyrm, and one of my siblings. Our mother was known as the Wyrm Mother. Not *a* Wyrm Mother, but *the* Wyrm Mother. The progenitor of our entire race. As ancient as I am...she remembered a time before what Ternus scientists would call the Big Bang."

The illusion shifted as she spoke, and Aran focused his attention on it. The sky went fully dark, like the umbral depths. Then sudden light flared, and light, matter, and heat exploded outward from a single point.

It spun through the cosmos, flung in all directions.

Magic and mundane matter and energy in every form, all scattered across the cosmos.

"My mother," Neith continued, "was one of the original elder gods. She was created by the titans, who in turn were created by a being we call Om."

"Om?" Aran asked.

Neith waved an appendage, and the illusion shifted. Now it showed a terrestrial world, a temple carved directly into a mountainside, peopled by dozens of monks in orange robes. Those monks knelt in even lines, and as one they sucked in a breath and began to chant.

A single sound issued from every throat, forming a layered, wordless sound, "Ohhhhmmmmmmmmmmmm." On and on it went, then ceased and began again, arising and ceasing like the song of the universe.

"Do you see?" Neith asked. "They do not understand, but what they are doing is venerating the creator of us all. The sound they make is the name of god, or goddess perhaps. Such things may be irrelevant to such a deity. A deity that may no longer exist."

That was a lot to take in. Aran added the new information to his hierarchy of the universe. Lesser gods, like Voria, then elder gods, like Krox or Neith, or this Wyrm Mother, and then something above them called a titan. All created by a single being from the sound of it.

"What happened to your mother?" Aran clasped his hands behind his back, and tried to be as respectful as possible. He might not fear Neith in the same way, but if anything his veneration had grown.

"Over the eons she created many Wyrms." The vision shifted again, now showing an unfamiliar world where two massive Wyrms battled. "She created dozens of species, from lowly wyverns to unintelligent drakes, to my own unique species. The more modern Wyrm that now dominates the sector came from a relatively recent experiment. Our people have always formed dragon flights, and for countless millennia they policed much of this galaxy. Every Wyrm among them prayed to be elevated, and in her lifetime my mother granted that request precisely eight times. Each of her divine offspring, myself included, were gifted with mastery over one aspect of the Circle of Eight. I embody *fire*, as you know. Nefarius embodied *void*. She was a fierce warrior, rivaled only by our younger sister, Virkonna."

Neith hunched down, and sadness wafted off of her in divine waves. The magic overpowered Aran, and he felt her grief become his own. Tears streamed down his face as the illusion shifted and showed a dragon with black scales dismembering an eight-headed dragon with iridescent scales that shifted in color as she fell through the skies of some distant world.

The midnight dragon tore out her throats, and began feasting on her corpse.

"My mother bore many gifts," Neith explained, her grief total, "but she did not possess the same foresight I do. She was unable to predict her fate, to see the growing darkness in Nefarius. For a hundred millennia Nefarius had been a champion. A protector. I do not know what changed her, but it happened after Talifax was named guardian. Is he a symptom or the cause? We cannot know."

Aran cocked his head, and wondered if there was anything actionable he could take back. "How strong is Nefarius relative to you or Krox? What kind of force will it take to bring her down if she comes back? I mean, I'd prefer we never let her come back at all, but you seem unsure how to prevent it."

"Indeed." Neith's jaws quivered in a disturbing way that might have been anger. "Talifax has carefully cloaked my sister's return. I do not know how he will achieve it, only that he will. When she returns she will be weaker than she was, but every god in the sector is weaker. Nor will she remain weak. Nefarius will begin a campaign of conquest and destruction, and she will devour every Catalyst and god she can find until she has consumed all magic in this sector. Once it is drained she will do the same to every other sector, and presumably every galaxy if not stopped. I do not know her ultimate goal, but I do know that our extinction is merely a step on her path."

"And how do you suggest I stop her?" Aran asked. Neith's logic was inescapable, and it did appear Nefarius was the greater threat. The fact that her guardian was making Nara's life hell added a little weight to that need. He didn't like the idea that this guy could materialize inside his quarters at will.

"You gather allies," Neith suggested. "Beginning with my sister. Virkonna is powerful. Perhaps the most powerful goddess living. Wake her, and you may have a chance to stop Nefarius before her rebirth."

Aran exhaled a heavy sigh. Why did doing what he needed to do always come at a personal cost? He'd felt supremely uncomfortable on Virkon, especially around his sister Astria. Going back was pretty much the last thing he wanted to do. Olyssa had turned Rhea away when she'd needed help the most, and it didn't exactly endear her to him.

"All right." He straightened, accepting what he must do. "I'll go to Virkon, and I'll get your sister up from her nap. We'll find a way to stop Nefarius, or die trying."

"Take great care, Outrider," Neith cautioned. "You will

soon learn the full cost of being a Hound of Xal. There are worse threats than Nefarius. Be certain you do not become one of them."

Well, that was just lovely. This trip wouldn't have been complete without some sort of cryptic warning he couldn't really do anything with.

8

AN OFFER

Kahotep crawled wearily atop the floating bed he'd been provided, the irritation at his scaly feet dangling off the edge having long since faded. It wasn't as large as the bed on a Krox vessel, but it wasn't so bad, and he was fortunate his quarters weren't in an unfurnished cell somewhere.

He wrapped his wings around himself for warmth, and settled in for sleep. There was so much knowledge here, and study was the thing he'd always been most passionate about. He cared nothing for war, and if he could live in a tower somewhere, then that's exactly what he'd do.

"Kahoooo," a faint voice hissed through the room, like a breeze on a still day.

Kaho's eyes shot open, and he rolled awkwardly from the bed, landing in a heap. He scrambled to his feet, and grabbed his staff from its place against the wall. "Show yourself. Who are you?"

The voice was damnably familiar, but he hadn't heard enough of it to place it.

"You wound me, my son." A translucent figure shimmered into existence a couple meters away, in the room's shadowed corner. Nebiat's ebony skin and white hair were unmistakable. If anything, that form suited her more than her draconic one. She smiled coyly. "I didn't expect joy at seeing me, but I thought you'd recognize your mother at the very least."

Kahotep's hands began to tremble. Nebiat was here, on the *Spellship*. In his quarters. If Voria discovered this, or even Nara, they would not wait for an explanation. They would assume he was a traitor, and execute him. It's certainly what he would do in their stead.

"Why have you come?" Kaho growled, his eyes narrowing. He took a threatening step closer, though he wasn't certain what he could even do. "I want nothing to do with you, or your mad schemes. You're as bad as grandfather. Worse."

Nebiat's face fell, and Kaho could tell he'd scored with that one.

"You have no idea how right you are." Her shoulders slumped, and if he didn't know better he'd say she was on the verge of tears. That would imply that his mother had feelings, and he was fairly certain that wasn't the case. "My father had a plan to control Krox. Since you've cozied up with Voria I'm sure she's told you that I am now controlling him. There is a cost. A bitter one, I assure you."

"What of it?" Kaho snapped. He knew his temper ruled, but he didn't care. This woman had brought him nothing but grief, and had brought worse to their species. Countless Wyrms, and far more hatchlings, had died at her command. Enough that their extinction was a real possibility.

"Well, I can see that regard for my well being isn't reason enough to care." Some of the distress shifted to anger. "Very well, I'll get to my offer. Look, Kaho. See the world I have wrought."

Nebiat didn't move. There was no sketching, and nothing to counter. A wave of *spirit* rushed out of her and swirled around Kaho, seeping into his body and his mind. His senses were overwhelmed, and when he regained them he appeared to be in orbit over an unfamiliar world.

"Where are we?" he asked, twisting in the black as he struggled to locate Nebiat. There was no sign of her.

Instead, something on the world below pulled his attention. Movement. Somehow he could sense hundreds of Wyrms. Thousands. More. So many more. And these were not Virkonna's kin or some new species. These were Krox. They were his people. More than had ever existed in his lifetime.

Had this world been hidden somewhere the entire time?

The memory faded as quickly as it began, and Kaho was back in his quarters, clutching his staff protectively. His mother had well and truly become a goddess, and now she wanted something from him. What he'd just seen was no doubt part of the bait.

"Did you see it?" Her mouth curved into an excited smile. "It is wonderful, Kaho. Our people live in peace, with no fear of invasion. Free to learn and grow, and thrive. I created this paradise, my son. I used the power I have seized to create the future for our people that neither Krox nor Teodros would have given us."

Kaho folded his arms and eyed her evenly. "What do you want, mother? You know I am too canny to fall for your wordplay. Abandon the games and just tell me what you're after."

She heaved a heavy, and very nearly believable, sigh. "There are no games here, Kaho. I will speak plainly. I am trapped. My father created a prison for Krox, but the jailer is also caught. I cannot escape, and the very real possibility that Krox will devour me exists. If that happens everything I have created will be wiped away. The world I showed you will be used just as you were used, until every last Wyrm is dead."

Kaho knew she was appealing to his sense of nationalism. She knew he loved his people. But she also loved them; of that he was fairly certain. If she was telling the truth, she'd been caught in a truly awful way. A way perhaps not even she deserved. Though, perhaps it was exactly what she deserved.

"And what is it you think I can do to help you escape this trap?" He straightened, and forced the fear away. She couldn't force this on him or she already would have.

Nebiat's smile faded. She hugged herself with both arms, and looked very small. "I don't know. But I have been studying what it means to be a deity. One of our tools is the ability to invest our strength in a guardian."

"Just like a Catalyst."

"Exactly." Nebiat nodded. "Except that I can consciously direct the magic. I can reshape you to make you the most powerful mortal sorcerer in the sector."

Kaho barked a bitter laugh. "And I'm sure that carries no cost with it."

"Not as high a cost as you might think," Nebiat corrected. She shook her head sadly. "If you accept this blessing it will not shackle you to my will. You will be your own creature, even if that means opposing me. I'm hoping that after you see the world I have created you'll agree that our people are more important than either one of us. You can help me bring them to dominance in the sector, Kaho. You can shape their cultural identity, and help ensure that they are more peaceful. You could help them learn to value knowledge as you do."

"And, most importantly," Kaho supplied, suddenly realizing what she needed most, "I will find a way to free you from Krox?"

"Precisely." She smiled at him again. "You always were the brightest. I just want us to be free, Kaho, and I need your help to do that."

"I have a life here now, mother. A mahaya, if you can believe that. One who is, for whatever reason, not repulsed by me. Why would I leave Frit behind?" Kaho propped his staff against the wall, then heaved his bulk back onto the bed. He turned to face the specter in his quarters, even as he began wrapping his wings around himself, preparing for sleep. "In the morning I will go to Voria and tell her that you came to me. You have until then to withdraw. I will not help you, mother. I have no ill will toward you, but I won't help you. Simply put, you are not trustworthy, and I will not be taken in by your schemes."

"And if I am telling the truth?" Her voice was tiny.

"Then you are paying the price for all your lies. Good night, mother. Please don't visit me again." Kaho closed his eyes, and prayed she would go away and never return.

"You will regret this decision, my son." Her voice carried no malice, and in fact was tinged with sadness.

Kaho kept his eyes closed and said nothing.

9

A PLAN

Surreal utterly failed to capture Nara's new life. Three weeks ago she'd been a traitor on her way to probable execution. Her friends had hated and mistrusted her, and all the people she'd once helped save called for her death.

Today she was the savior who'd resurrected a goddess. The archmage and high priestess who'd architected the return of the lady of light, Shaya, reborn as Voria—whatever that meant. The sudden and violent change in her position was more than jarring. It had caused her to disassociate from her own life, in a way.

Nara reluctantly threw back the covers and forced herself from the floating bed, the opulence a welcome change from the austere cells she'd spent so much time in recently. She summoned a bit of *water* magic, heated it with *fire*, then swirled it around her body until she was clean. So much faster than a shower.

She reached for her stealth suit, which sat on the chair next to the bed. The strange polymer was self-cleaning, and not even Pickus had any theories as to its creation. Some sort of Ternus breakthrough they hadn't shared, and one she probably wouldn't be able to replace. All the more reason to take care of it.

She zipped up the suit, and enjoyed the way it cradled her body. It had all the best parts of armor, but none of the restricted movement. And, as she admired herself in the wall mirror, she admitted it was rather flattering to her figure.

A chime came from the door, and Nara half turned to face it as she tucked her hair into a ponytail. "Come in."

The door went translucent, and Pickus stepped inside. The once-mousey tech had grown in confidence, if not in stature. The freckles no longer looked goofy, and he stood straighter than he used to. The outfit completed the transformation, though. Pickus wore a deep-blue uniform, with five starbursts along the collar.

It was a marked difference from the baggy clothes the former tech usually wore, and it showed that Pickus actually had some muscles. He gave her a weary nod as he stepped inside. His demeanor was stiff, as it had been since her return. Not everyone had forgiven her. "Sorry to bug you, but Voria requested our presence. She's in the chamber."

"She's always in the chamber." Nara grabbed a Ternus chocolate chip cookie dough protein bar from the box next to her desk and peeled the wrapper as she followed Pickus out of her quarters. Just before exiting she paused, and retrieved Ikadra with her free hand. The staff still emanated magic, though the sapphire was cracked and dark. "Do you have any idea what it is this time?"

"No," Pickus admitted. He walked briskly up the corridor, and avoided looking in her direction. "She's still obsessed with saving Ternus as the miracle she needs to establish herself in the eyes of her followers. I think she feels guilty about what Krox did to them, though it isn't her fault."

"Her and Aran are a lot alike in that way," Nara mused as they threaded through the *Spellship*. They passed a number of techs hurrying about tasks, each of whom took a moment to snap their hand over their heart as they passed. It was unclear if that was meant for Pickus, or her, or maybe both. "She might not be wrong. The more I understand how worship seems to work, the more clear it is that divine miracles probably get you a lot of mileage with your followers. Voria giving *life* to all of Shaya is a great example. The people here love her."

Pickus nodded soberly and picked up his already brisk pace. "It's good that something came out of the tragedy of Krox's attack. People here will follow her, even if most of the caretakers have their heads firmly lodged up their asses."

Nara barked a short, unexpected laugh, and blushed when Pickus eyed her askance. "Sorry. I was just picturing Ducius."

"Guess I can't blame you." Pickus's expression softened into a smile. "He's the worst of the lot and I can't say I wouldn't pay a good bit of credits to see someone firmly wedge that smug face right up his posterior."

Nara felt a little better as they reached the Chamber of the Mirror. She knew Pickus still didn't trust her, with good reason, but he seemed to be accepting her as a coworker at least. They needed each other, for a variety of reasons, and it was good he recognized that. This would be a lot harder if he was giving her pushback.

Conversation ceased as they stopped outside the golden double doors protecting the chamber. Voria could order them sealed, and not even a god could violate the ward, as Nara understood it. It would even be safe from Talifax.

The doors opened at their approach, which shouldn't be surprising. Voria was a goddess after all, and knowing when worshippers approached was probably a trivial divine ability.

The mirror bobbed slowly up and down as it rotated in a slow circle, a deep thrum accompanying each revolution. Voria stood before the mirror with her hands clasped behind her back. If not for the divine nimbus shining from her skin, she'd have looked exactly the same as the day Nara had met her.

"Nara. Pickus." Voria nodded brusquely, and her attention never fully left the mirror. "Thank you for coming. I have a plan, I believe, but before I approach Ternus with it I want to see what holes the two of you can poke in it."

Nara nodded, but didn't say anything. She moved to stand near Voria, so that she could see the surface of the mirror. It showed a grey-green planet that sent a shiver up her spine. Many of her earliest memories came from that world, fragments that hadn't been obliterated by the Zephyr training.

Of course the world looked different now. The glittering corona of satellites, space stations, and ships was utterly absent, leaving the world naked. The space elevator, which was normally visible extending up into orbit, was...gone. Aran had described it to her, and she winced as she pictured something that titanic slamming into the world below.

"I've used life sense, a basic ability, to ascertain how many people still live." Voria stretched out a delicate hand, and very nearly caressed the mirror. A pulse of gold flowed from her palm, into the shining surface. "I estimate twelve million survivors. I don't know how, but they must be a hardy people to have survived the sudden doubling of gravity on their world."

"Ma'am," Pickus all but whispered, his eyes shining. "There were four billion people on that world. Maybe more, if you count all the tourists. You're telling me all that's left is twelve million?"

Voria nodded, the ghostly glow around her dimming slightly. "A remnant, but an important one. Saving them will do more than allow the survivors to re-colonize some other world. It will show the sector that we can resist a god."

"And it will also legitimize your religion, which still needs a name," Nara pointed out, aware of her own lack of compassion. Someone had to be the pragmatic one. "The sector needs to see you as the rally point against Krox, and theoretically, Nefarius. Save these people, and you'll have proven we have a divine counter. There's no way to give people hope without that counter. We need a god to stop their god, and people know it."

"Surviving Krox's assault was a good start," Pickus pointed out. He scratched at the back of his head as he studied the mirror. "It showed we can push back, and you wallpapering the planet with trees helped too. Are you going to do something similar with Ternus? Where are the survivors going to go?"

"That's where your knowledge comes in." Voria waved a hand and the view on the mirror zoomed out, then in on a planet further out in the system. It was smaller than Ternus, and the surface swirled with snow. "That is Ternus IV. Is it not?"

"Yeah," Pickus allowed, his confusion evident. "It's not fully terraformed, though. The atmosphere is a methane soup, and the only inhabitants are within a few research facilities. There's a terraforming station, but we're a hundred and eighty years from that world being livable. Even then it's going to suck ten months out of a fourteen-month year."

"What if the planet was moved into the same orbit as Ternus, and the atmosphere magically cleansed to perfectly match the original Ternus?" Voria gave a satisfied smile as she folded her arms, a habit Nara was used to. She was glad it had survived into godhood.

Pickus blinked a few times, and seemed to struggle with the location of any words. Eventually he scrunched his eyes and looked from the mirror to Voria. "Let me see if I understand this. You can basically move a worthless planet into the same position, and terraform it instantly so those twelve million people have a place to live?"

"Precisely." Voria's smile didn't slip. If anything, it grew. "I have the power to accomplish both of those things, provided we can get the people off that world. It will require a little research, I think, mostly on Nara's part."

"Why not simply translocate them all?" Nara wondered aloud. "You could do everyone at once, right?"

Voria shook her head, and her mouth creased into a frown. "That was my first instinct as well, but as Shaya pointed out, the amount of magic required is massive. We need a less expensive way, magically speaking."

Nara considered that. As she understood it, the amount of people being transported was the problem. "Voria, mass increases the amount of magic required, right?"

Voria nodded silently and eyed Nara with curiosity.

"What if we shrank them?" She blinked, and wondered if it was a stupid suggestion.

"That...that might actually be possible. I have access to the greater path of Nature, which allows me to create and modify life as I see fit. I believe I can shrink these people to be a fraction of their current size. We stuff them aboard the *Spellship*, which is powerful enough to break orbit even with the increased gravity. Then we build a new home, and I return your people to their original size."

Nara couldn't believe the audaciousness of it. She loved it. "I'll get to work calculating the requirements. I'm worried about side effects from changing their size so dramatically, and then changing it back."

Voria nodded impatiently. "I assume there might be cognitive issues especially, so we'll need to solve that before we can rescue them. For now, it's time we translocate to Ternus. Let them see that we're doing something. I'll begin terraforming Ternus IV, while you find a way to safely morph an entire population."

Nara nodded. "I can handle that, but while we've got you here, and since we're going to Ternus, I had something I wanted to address." She glanced at Pickus too, as his input would be needed. "If we're going to capitalize on this miracle, we need people to see it. This ship relies exclusively on magic, but we're going to a system where the people are dead and the tech has been abandoned. We can take discarded cameras, drones, and transmitters and retrofit this ship to use both tech and magic. We can start broadcasting to everyone in the sector, to make sure they see you trying to save the sector."

"I don't like it." Voria's smile slipped. "But I admit the need. Pickus, is this something you can tend to?"

"Yeah. It will be nice to have a solvable problem, and I do miss working with tech. I'll start getting crewes together. Sounds like we all got our work cut out for us."

"That we do, Administrator, that we do." Voria turned back to the mirror, a clear dismissal.

It was just as well. Nara had work to do.

10

DIVINE TERRAFORMING

Voria appeared in the sky over a doomed world, the *Spellship* and the ragged remains of her fleet cupped in her hands as the translocation resolved. She stepped back, and took a moment to survey the system she'd arrived in.

It wasn't the first time Voria had been to Ternus, but it was the first time she'd been here as a goddess. Her senses perceived so much more. Every life sign, no matter how microscopic. Every quanta, and every signal. The dizzying tapestry resolved into a simple perception of the universe around her, one she was already growing used to.

"Wow, kid, looks like you've got your work cut out for you." The Shade of Shaya materialized near Voria's cheek, and she pointed down at Ternus, the world she'd come to save, if it could be done. "Those people are screwed. If you pull this off you're going to have one heck of a fan club."

Voria frowned slightly as she surveyed the rest of the system, including Ternus IV, the white world a good ways further into the system. "In my experience it's best not to get attached to outcomes. The possibilities I've examined look promising, but if we successfully surprised Nebiat at Shaya, then there is no reason she can't do the same to us here."

"Or another god," Shaya pointed out. "Talifax is out there."

Voria was growing damnably tired of hearing that name. She drifted away from her fleet, toward the world she'd targeted to become the new Ternus homeworld. As she drew closer, she could feel the handful of life signs more closely. The world had no natural life, and all that existed was confined to a handful of installations dotting its frigid surface.

She extended a hand toward the world, though the gesture wasn't strictly necessary. It harkened back to the magic she'd grown up with, though, and the familiar comforted her. A wave of *life* and *water* twisted toward the world, and flowed over every meter of the small planet. Wherever the magic passed the methane was remade into nitrogen, or oxygen. The process happened nearly instantly, and within moments the atmosphere became breathable to humans and similar species.

"It's humbling, isn't it?" Shaya gave a little chuckle, and nodded at Ternus IV. "You can literally reshape planets, and create armies to populate them. *Life* is powerful, and so is *water*, but together? Nature is amazing. I was never able to fully exploit it, but maybe you'll get a chance to do what I never did."

"I lack words." Voria reveled in the power, drunk with it, she realized. Who wouldn't be? "Let's hope this works."

This next part was tricky, but she'd given it a lot of thought. Changing a world's orbit required immense magic of a very specific type. Using *void* to pull the planet would have been easiest, but Voria didn't possess nearly enough *void* magic to pull it off. Her solution needed to come from *life*, *water*, or Nature.

The ultimate solution was only possible because there were so few lifeforms on the planet. She swirled *life* and *water* around herself in roughly equal measure, the magic mixing and flowing until it formed one azure whole. That magic coalesced into living ice, enough to form a hand, an arm, and then a torso.

Voria reached down and plunged her fingers into the unused arctic surface. They sank deep into the planet, far enough to get a solid hold. Then Voria pulled. She dragged the world from its orbit, slowly at first, then faster as she gained momentum.

The planet's orbit became more elliptical, slowly tightening into a spiral as she dragged it closer to the orange star. She continued the process for long minutes, gradually maneuvering it into the right orbit. Voria tried not to pay attention to the sea of signals rising from Ternus, and from the small fleet arrayed around one of the few surviving stations, the one Austin had declared the seat of their governing body.

She heard her name over and over, sometimes in awe, and other times in rage or confusion. They were aware she was here and doing something, but most didn't yet know that. That was by design, of course. Voria didn't want to attempt this, fail, and then have to explain. This way they wouldn't get their hopes up, unless she succeeded.

One final tug dragged the planet into a mostly stable orbit. It wasn't perfect, but that would sort itself out in the first few revolutions. That might mean some wild seasons, at first, but they would calm, and the world would be every bit as habitable as the one Krox had doomed.

The first part of her work was now completed, but

before she could go further she needed to consult with Nara. Voria concentrated, then teleported into the library where she knew Nara would be working.

As expected, the dark-haired scholar sat behind a desk, a knowledge scale playing images over her outstretched palm.

"I apologize for interrupting," Voria offered as she approached the table. Nara sat alone, a testament to Pickus's fierce insistence that no one bother her while she solved Voria's problem. "Have you made any progress?"

"I've solved it." Nara set the scale down, and glanced up at Voria. "I've reviewed the spell countless times, and every case study of a sentient being after having their size radically altered. The data is clear. If we keep them miniaturized for no longer than four hours there will be no permanent cognitive damage. We might be able to press it to six, but I'd rather not test that."

Voria considered that timeline. She could use a simple teleport to gather all the people inside the *Spellship*, which meant collecting them would be effectively instant.

"I don't think we'll need anywhere close to four hours." Voria raised a hand and an illusion appeared. She showed the *Spellship* materializing on the surface. A wave of *void* energy pulsed out of the ship, and washed slowly over the entire planet. "We'll need your mastery of *void*, but I think with the *Spellship*'s amplification we can pull it off. You teleport them aboard, and I translocate the ship instantly to New Ternus. If you've got strength left, then you teleport them out onto the surface, and then I return them to normal size."

Nara bit her lip, a sign that the timid girl was still in there somewhere. "If my math is off by even a little, thousands of people could die. More. I need to spread them far enough apart that when they return to full size they won't crush each other, and I need to determine where to put them all."

"That's where I come in." Voria gave a confident smile. "I'll determine safe locations, and you can set people there. There's a chance we'll take some casualties, but I believe we can save nearly everyone."

Nara shook her head. "I'm not sure I really believe it. Nothing ever goes that easy for us."

Voria prayed to—well, the universe, she supposed—that Nara was wrong. She wasn't certain how much more failure and heartbreak she could endure.

11

FORGIVENESS IS BETTER THAN
PERMISSION

Pickus braced himself as the scry-screen resolved onto the bridge of Ternus's last remaining station. Admiral Nimitz's granite features filled the screen, his narrow eyes locking on like missiles. He stared at Pickus for several moments, then his eyes flicked around the room where Pickus stood.

Pickus had set up his workshop to look somewhat professional, but there were still half finished computers all over the room. In his defense he'd been trying to retrofit the ship, and there weren't enough techs to delegate this stuff to.

"Son," Nimitz rumbled like a dog making its first lazy bark after napping, "You had better have a damned good explanation as to why a goddess just manifested in our system and started mucking with one of our worlds. We don't have many people on that rock, but it's our rock, and there ain't no Confederacy any more, which means we aren't allies."

Pickus squared his shoulders, and reminded himself that he was the chosen representative of a goddess, not just a JC-educated tech totally out of his depths. "I'll make it quick, Admiral. Voria is going to try something risky—"

"Course she is," the admiral interrupted. "Sorry. Continue, please."

"She's going to terraform Ternus IV, and move it into a sympathetic orbit." That got Nimitz's attention. The grizzled officer's eyes widened, and Pickus continued. "The part that comes after is risky, and that's why she didn't want to explain ahead of time. She wants to save the survivors on Ternus, and then relocate them to the world she's prepared."

Nimitz just sat there. He sat there so long that Pickus was positive they'd lost signal, except that they were using magic and magic didn't drop calls. The admiral removed his hat, and tucked it under his arm. "Son, if you can pull it off you have no idea what it will mean to the Ternus people. Many of those that have survived, well, they've been sending footage of their struggle. Colony 3 and New Texas can both see what they're going through. Up until now we've been powerless."

"I can't make promises, Admiral." Pickus folded his arms, like Voria would have. "She could fail. And I guess that's where you come in. I need to know that you're okay with her making this attempt, and when I say that, what I mean is I need formal permission to move those people."

"You didn't ask permission to move one of our planets, but you want it to save people? I will never understand that up-jumped Shayan you follow."

"Respectfully, Admiral." Pickus leaned in closer to the screen. "That up-jumped Shayan saved New Texas. Her high priestess saved Colony 3. If not for Voria, you'd be down to Marid, and whatever is left in this system. So how about a little gratitude, sir? As you've pointed out, there is no Confederacy. We don't have to help you. We're choosing to."

"Except we just helped you fight off a god," Nimitz pointed out, with absolutely no humor. "You owe us, son. Now if you can pull this off, you'll have my apologies. But you want to know what I think? Voria's going to screw it up, and my people are going to pay the price. Again. Austin has seen reason, son. Far as you're concerned, I'm the gods-damned emperor of this planet. And so help me, if that woman screws us again, then I will declare your sanctimonious ass an enemy of the state."

Pickus somehow managed to bottle up his response. It wouldn't help. This man hated Voria, and had since the moment Pickus had first seen the two in the same room. Nothing would change that.

"Do we have your permission to make the attempt, Admiral?" He took a deep breath and squared his shoulders as he waited for the response. This call wouldn't be even close to the hardest problem he had to deal with today, so he should be able to get through this without complaining or losing his cool.

"You got it, son. If you can save those people, then do it." Nimitz took on his most threatening scowl, which wasn't really all that different from his passive expression. "Just know that if you screw this up, Krox won't be your only enemy in this sector."

Pickus didn't bother replying. He terminated the connection, and then he left his quarters in search of breakfast. He couldn't do squat to help Voria, so he might as well stress out over a meal.

12

THE BAD GUYS

Skare smiled as he stepped onto the bridge of the single largest ship the Inuran Consortium had ever produced. The *Dragon Skull* was shaped exactly as its name suggested, and that shape was more than symbolic, as the sector would learn, to its peril.

The vessel was too small to be labeled a moon, but large enough that it did exert its own faint gravity.

Skare moved to stand next to the hologram dominating a quarter of the bridge, clasping his hands behind his back as he studied it. Several techs scurried from his path, their chrome gazes nailed to the decks.

The hologram displayed the ship's interior, which never failed to trigger a swell of pride. The engineering required had nearly broken even him, but he'd somehow managed to create the marvel Talifax had demanded. It both infuriated and terrified him that he had no idea what the ship's true purpose was. It wasn't merely a focus for the rebirth, but something much more; of that Skare was certain.

"Yes, much more," Talifax's emotionless voice sounded from behind him.

Skare rounded to face the taller alien, made imposing by the black armor. He'd give very nearly anything to know what lay underneath, though he doubted Talifax would ever allow it.

He noted that none of the technicians had reacted to Talifax's presence, which suggested they couldn't see him. None were staring and no one had whispered, but he'd bet more than one thought him insane. The question was, did he care? No. Let them wonder. Skare faced Talifax, and listened.

"You have done well." Talifax turned in a slow circle, his arms at his sides as he surveyed the bridge. "I can feel the strength of this vessel. It is all we need and more." The guardian turned back to Skare. "Where do we stand on production? This vessel is a marvel, but the rebirth depends on the entirety of the fleet."

Skare hesitated as he experienced an unwelcome, and rare, emotion. Embarrassment. "We're not proceeding as quickly as I'd like. Currently we've produced sixty-three percent of the required ships."

That got a stare. Several techs risked glances in his direction. They were responsible for many of the tasks related to producing the fleet, and rightly feared the consequences of failure.

"That isn't enough," Talifax growled, a rare hint of emotion. "Time grows short. If we do not possess the necessary number of ships, the ritual will fail. If it fails, Krox will devour you, your people, and this sector."

"I am aware of the stakes," Skare snapped, then remastered himself. He smoothed his jacket, and stared up at the senior partner in their little relationship. "I will ensure the ships are ready, somehow. But I've spent time studying

Voria's movements, and I'd say you have a much larger problem than my failure."

Talifax reached up and carefully removed his mask. He tucked it under one bulky arm, and took a step closer. "You wished to see my true form, did you not? You would not recognize my species, though a remnant still survives."

Skare studied Talifax's strange form, which was disturbingly familiar somehow. Long ivory tusks jutted from a wide mouth, and a prehensile trunk lay where a human's nose would be. Long, leathery ears covered the sides of his broad head. And then it hit him.

"I've been to the zoo on Ternus," he found himself saying. "You strongly resemble a creature from their home-world. An elephant, I believe. The implications are troubling."

"The same species are propagated all over the galaxy," Talifax explained. "Over many galaxies, in all likelihood. The same patterns are repeated over and over, with slight variations. Primates. Pachyderms. Reptiles. When you have seen as much of the galaxy as I have, you will understand this."

It drove home how much of a child Skare truly was, when viewed through the lens of godhood. That had been the lesson Talifax sought to impart. Skare could not afford the luxury of arrogance.

"I will see that a workable plan is sent by missive," he offered. "But I assure you...we will be ready. I will not be the reason the rebirth fails."

Every last member of the bridge crew worked overtime to avoid looking in his direction, or giving any indication that they could hear what he was saying. He ignored them.

"Excellent." Talifax slowly replaced his ebony mask, which snapped into place with an audible thunk. "And I will offer a similar assurance. I am aware of Voria's movements. She seeks to save the refugees of Ternus, and undo Krox's good work in that sector. This cannot be allowed to happen, and for more than the petty reasons you entertain. If I allow her miracle to stand, then she will capture the hearts of the sector. So she must fail. I will see to it."

Just like that, Talifax was gone, and Skare was alone with his people. He shot a glare around the deck, then stalked back to his quarters.

13

OUTMANEUVERED

Voria hovered in orbit over Ternus, close enough now to feel the residue Krox's presence had left. She could sense the lingering energies in the rock, the utterly incalculable amount of *earth* that must have been needed to alter the planet in such a way.

Likewise she could feel the millions of lives still trapped down there. Most of the wildlife had perished, though the canines Ternus seemed so fond of had survived in surprising numbers. She would save them too, of course, despite hating the way they smelled.

Voria extended both her hands, and concentrated. *Water* pooled in one, and *life* in the other. She clapped her hands together, and the energies exploded downward, rippling over the surface of the planet.

In the same instant Nara guided the *Spellship* down the gravity well, and made unerringly for the landing zone they'd designated.

Voria focused on the spell, and allowed the magic to play over every living creature on the world. Dogs and cats and people and even a few surviving livestock become one

one-hundredth of their former size. Her magic both stabilized and fortified them in a way that would allow them to
survive the sudden change, and their reduced size made it
possible for Nara to teleport them all at once.

Such a feat was beyond nearly any mage in the sector,
but Nara had been to more *void* Catalysts than anyone
living, save perhaps Aran. She could do it, if it could be
done.

The transformation completed, and Voria metaphorically held her breath as she awaited Nara's spell. It would
take long moments to build, as even the *Spellship* took time
to replicate a spell.

And, as Voria watched, she did feel a sudden surge of
void. The trouble was that surge didn't come from the
Spellship.

Voria focused her attention on the area where the pulse
had come from, and realized she was detecting a microscopic Fissure in Ternus's umbral shadow. It was no more
than a meter across, which was just enough space for an
armored fist to poke through.

Divine levels of *void* magic swirled around that fist, and
then *fire*, until a deep, angry purple obscured the Fissure.
Before Voria could so much as contemplate reacting, the
spell released and shot toward the planet. The arm
retreated, and the Fissure snapped shut in its wake.

The spell continued down to the world, and Voria iden-
tified it even as it hit. "My gods, he's disintegrating the planet." She instantly summoned a missive, and flung it down to
Nara. "Get out! Get out, now!"

The disintegrate spell slammed into a mountain range
on the southern part of the world, on the opposite hemi-
sphere from the *Spellship*, thankfully. A dark, purple cloud

oozed over the planet's surface, while hellish *void* energy filled the cracks forming across the planet.

The *Spellship* lifted off on the opposite side of the world, sluggishly clawing for orbit as the destruction spread. Unmitigated grief spread through Voria as the life signs were snuffed out, one after another. In less than a minute the entire surface had been covered by the cloud, and every last life sign ceased.

But that wasn't enough. The disintegrate continued its grisly work, and the planet began to quake. The core, both charged with magic, and no longer contained, detonated spectacularly, flinging billions of tons of rock and debris in all directions.

It took several moments for Voria to locate the *Spellship*, and a sliver of relief pushed into the grief. Nara and Pickus were fine, along with their people.

But Ternus? The twelve million survivors were dead, and from an external perspective, from the perspective captured by the drones watching the whole thing, Voria had just murdered a world. They'd seen her cast a spell, and at that spell's crescendo their capital had come apart, and their friends and family had died.

Someone had just doomed Voria's relationship with Ternus, and she strongly suspected she knew who it must be. Talifax had finally entered the game, it seemed, and she had no idea what she could possibly do to regain the ground he had just cost her.

Their chief ally would likely declare war on them.

14

DAMAGE CONTROL

Nara guided the *Spellship* into high orbit, and winced as the planet detonated. A translucent bubble appeared around them, insulating them from the magical explosion. Fragments of rock pinged off the ship's wards, discoloring them slightly with every impact.

The whole thing was over in moments, and just like that, all that remained of Ternus was a cloud of dust and debris. Nara waved a hand, and the scry-screen shifted to show that cloud, proving to Nara that what she'd felt was real.

She just couldn't wrap her brain around it. They'd been so close to saving those people, and at the very last instant a master strategist had cut them off at the knees. She didn't need to speak to Voria to know who'd done it. There was only one being it could have been. One being with the strength of a god, which is what such a spell must have taken to cast.

In that instant Neith's cursed gift sent her thoughts spinning in a dozen directions. How strong was Talifax? Could a guardian, which was theoretically a demigod, be stronger than some gods? Would a stronger god's guardian be correspondingly stronger than a weaker god's?

The questions were trivial right now, and she recognized her mind's attempt to reconcile the utter defeat she'd just witnessed.

"Nara?" Pickus called from the far side of the bridge where he sat at a hastily installed desk. "I've got Nimitz on the line. Sounds like he wants to talk to Voria, but even we haven't done that yet."

"Stall," Nara ordered. She turned to the scry-screen, and triggered a missive to Voria. It connected instantly, and her ghostly glow filled the screen. "You know who has to have done this."

Voria nodded wearily. "Talifax, yes. His motives make perfect sense. He's hamstrung our relationship with Ternus."

"He may have done more than that." Nara folded her arms, and wished she were elsewhere. "Nimitz is on the line, and I'm going to have to deal with him. There's a very real chance that they'll declare you an enemy of the state. This could mean war."

"I'm confident in your ability to handle it." Voria pursed her lips. "I'm going to retreat to the mirror and see if I can determine what to do next. Contact me when you're done speaking with Nimitz, and I'll translocate us someplace safe."

Nara bit back a hasty reply about Voria needing to take responsibility. "Of course. I'll handle it."

The scry-screen winked out, and Nara's shoulders slumped. She really hated this job. "Pickus, go ahead and put Nimitz on screen."

"Thank you, Voria," Pickus muttered. "He's all yours."

The scry-screen resolved into Nimitz's grizzled face. His eyes were alight with rage, and his hands were trembling. "I ain't even got words for what we're going to do to you. You tell her that. I don't know if this was a botched spell or some sort of con job, but it don't much matter. This means war. You gotta know that."

"Admiral," Nara offered as she struggled to rein in her temper. "That spell wasn't Voria. Ternus has other enemies, and one of them is trying to—"

"I don't even want to hear it," Nimitz broke in. He stabbed an accusing finger at the screen. "You *blew up our planet*. Twelve million people died, along with any hope we had of reclaiming our world."

Nara thought furiously. There was nothing to be said, and she knew it. But she tried anyway. "Admiral, there is now a second inhabitable system in the sector, and that was created by Voria. You can see that—"

"No one," Nimitz growled, "is alive to occupy that bloody planet. There are plenty of habitable planets out there. Depths, we've got Colony 3 lined up as a new capital. What we need are people. We've lost nearly six billion in the last year. That leaves less than four remaining across the entire sector. Humanity is in real danger of being wiped out. I know you like hanging out with Shayans, but you *are* human, right?"

Nara sighed under her breath. "I don't see it that way. This isn't about any one species."

"So you don't see yourself as human. Got it." Nimitz's expression went cold. The rage was still there, but lurking under the surface now. "You've got one hour to leave the system. If you're still here after that, then you will be treated the same way any other invading force would. If you are sighted at any Ternus world, you will be opposed. You ain't welcome here anymore."

Nara opened her mouth, and then closed it again. What could she say? Talifax had done his work damnably well.

15

GOING HOME

The massive doors swung shut behind Aran with imposing finality. He knew somehow that he would never be allowed to find this world again, and that he had all the answers he would ever get from Neith.

He drifted back toward the *Talon*, allowing his spellarmor to handle the navigation to free himself to think. Neith had given him a lot to unpack, so that was exactly what he needed to do. If Neith was the doctor, then he certainly didn't like the medicine.

This was going to be so much fun.

You fear home? Narlifex rumbled. *Why? We can destroy any Wyrm now.*

"Sometimes I wish I could see the universe like you do." Aran affectionately patted Narlifex's hilt. "I don't fear going home. I dread it. They're all going to try to use me like I'm the chosen one in some bad holodrama. I can't fight my way out of it. Quite the opposite. If anything, I need to find a way to bring them together when they don't even see Outriders as sentient beings. I hate politics."

Ah, Narlifex pulsed. *Then I hate politics too.*

Aran drifted up the ramp and through the blue membrane, back into the *Talon's* cargo hold. There was no sign of Bord or Kez, but both Rhea and Crewes were waiting. Crewes had removed his armor, which had shifted back to a cat and now lay curled up near his feet.

Rhea stood at attention, of course, and snapped a salute as he approached.

Aran removed his helmet, then returned the salute. "At ease, Outrider."

Crewes snorted out a laugh. "You look like you didn't hear nothing good. Get anything we can use, sir?"

"Yeah, but as usual, it sucks." Aran sketched a *void* sigil with his index finger, and slipped out the back of his spellarmor. At one time he'd felt naked without it, but now? He was formidable in his own right, just him and a spellblade. Formidable, right up until he had to go toe-to-toe with a god. "Neith wants us to go back to Virkon. She claims that Nefarius gets top billing right now, and that we need to stop her ASAP. She confirmed that Nebiat is controlling Krox, and thinks we can kick that can down the road a little ways, at least until Nefarius is beaten."

Rhea's face darkened into a scowl. "I have no wish to return to Virkon. They refused to cleanse me, and instead chose to make my corruption someone else's problem. The children of Virkon are cowards in this reality."

"They're many things, but I don't know that coward is one of them," Aran countered. He shook his head. "I get it. They're irresponsible, and their constant infighting is as exhausting as it is disgusting. But they represent the strongest remaining military in the sector, and they happen to have one of the few remaining gods. Neith told me that Virkonna might be the strongest surviving. Perhaps stronger than Krox, but if not, she's certainly the strongest god that might be considered an ally. Put simply, we need Virkon."

Rhea inhaled a long, slow breath through her nostrils, then gave a single nod. "I will put aside my personal feelings, and I will work with them if required."

"I'm not too fond of that rock either." Crewes spat on the deck. "They weren't too nice to the major, not until they realized she was more of a badass than they were. And they didn't do right by Kheross, neither. Scaly and I didn't get along, but he always had our backs in a fight. Wasn't right that they sent him away."

Rhea eyed Crewes as if seeing him for the first time, but said nothing. Crewes seemed oblivious, and his attention was still on Aran.

"I've got even more baggage on that planet than you guys." Aran started walking from the hangar, toward the bridge. Rhea fell into step next to him, and Crewes walked a few paces behind. "My sister is down there, and I used to work for Olyssa. For years. I did whatever she told me, and as far as she's concerned, I'm her favorite childhood pet. She doesn't see me as a person, and getting her to help us isn't going to be easy. The only mortal she ever respected was Voria, and Voria's got her own stuff to deal with."

"We got any allies there, sir?" Crewes called as they entered the bridge.

"Possibly." Aran frowned. "It could be tough to find them though. Apparently, Inura has gone to ground there. If we can find him, then he might be able to help us wake Virkonna. If we can do that, then we might be able to fight back. Gods, I hope so anyway."

Aran walked up the ramp into the *Talon*, and left Neith behind forever.

16

THE PITCH

F rit closed the cover of the tome and sat back with a contented sigh. The story of the Vagrant Fleet had been riveting, and she'd followed the adventures of Shaya across six books. Frit had never been overly fond of the planet Shaya, but the warrior Shaya was something else entirely. The books were hilarious, and she'd learned a lot about how the world she'd been raised on had come to be.

Frit glanced around her quarters, and tried to ignore the sudden emptiness she found there. They'd given her a bed, and a wonderful golden desk that was immune to her heat. She had as many books as she could wish, and even access to a holorecorder if she wanted to watch Ternus vids. Those she had to be careful with, as they did not react well to extreme heat.

Yet only when she was reading did she feel like she belonged. She could forget her situation here, which was both wonderful and terrible. It wasn't that she didn't feel gratitude, but she also wanted more. She wanted purpose. And friends who she saw every day. More people like Kaho, who'd been quite distracted over the last few days.

"Hello, child." The voice was friendly, but it crept down Frit's spine. "Have I come at a bad time?"

Frit looked up to see a spectral version of Nebiat hovering in her quarters, not far from the bed. She wasn't here physically, which meant that none of Frit's offensive spells would work. Frit relaxed a hair, but only a hair. Nebiat might not have the limitations that Frit assumed, especially given her newfound power.

"Hello, Nebiat." Frit rose from her bed, and eyed the woman who'd freed her and then used Frit's sisters to wage war against her enemies. She felt no anger or affection. She felt nothing. "This seems like an extraordinarily dangerous place for you to visit. Are you here to make peace with Voria? If so, I'm not the person you want introducing you. They aren't fond of me either."

"I came for you." Nebiat gave a half smile and a soft laugh. She gestured at Frit's quarters. "You can't tell me that you're happy here. That these people accept you for who you are."

"So you came to taunt me then?" Frit raised an eyebrow. This was beneath Nebiat.

"Hardly. I came to offer you power." Nebiat paused, then took a deep breath. "Let me rephrase that, because I know how you'll take it. I've come to offer you a voice in the future of your people."

Nebiat was right. Frit had been about to launch a retort about not being obsessed with power, but now she was curious. "Oh?"

"Your sisters have been granted a magnificent temple on my world, a world my children have chosen to call Nebiat."

Frit chuckled at that. "I'm sure they worship you. Why should I care?"

"Because your sisters lack leadership. Because they are

few, and right now they are in danger of fracturing." Nebiat's face softened into what appeared to be genuine concern. "If you return with me you can offer them the leadership they need. I will elevate you to guardian, giving you the strength to determine your destiny, and theirs. You can build a future for your people, and the cost is small, I assure you."

"Too small to believe, I bet." Frit folded her arms. "I'll admit I'm curious."

Nebiat sighed prettily. "You've misjudged me, Frit. Time and again. I want a future for both our people and I need your help to do it. For that future to have any prayer of success...you must help me extricate myself with the devil's bargain that Teodros created for me."

Frit's eyes widened as she suddenly understood. She gave a delighted laugh. "You're controlling Krox, but you're worried that you're going to lose that control. When you do, he'll destroy you. Is that it?"

"Something like that," Nebiat admitted, her smile evaporating. "I am no longer mortal, and cannot journey to the relevant libraries to do the research. I need help, Frit. And it is in your best interest to help me. Do you really want Krox free? Right now I am restraining him, but I assure you the fate he has planned for your sisters is much, much more cruel than you can imagine."

That gave Frit pause. Nebiat was evil to the core, in the sense that she would do anything to protect her own interests. But her interests seemed to be in building up her people. Krox would have a much more reductive set of interests, which would involve enslavement and wholesale slaughter.

"Let's say I agreed to his deal with you. What's involved?" She was skeptical of course, but also more interested than she probably should be. Going home might mean she wasn't so lonely, and there was a good chance she could persuade Kaho to go with her. She'd miss Nara, but that was pretty much the only thing she'd be leaving behind.

"If you agree," Nebiat explained. "I will invest you with a portion of my divine power. You will become truly immortal, and you will gain the ability to translocate anywhere in the sector. You can come and go as you choose, which would free you to stay here and research my...dilemma. I will not ask you to betray Voria or your friends. I merely seek a way to extricate myself from my father's trap, without loosing Krox on the sector."

It all sounded plausible. She wouldn't be asked to do anything untoward, and as she understood things, a guardian operated independently of its host god. Nebiat couldn't control her unless she used a binding. There was a chance this was merely a way to get Frit out of the *Spellship* so that she could be captured, but she tended to doubt it. That wasn't Nebiat's style, and she didn't gain enough from having Frit to make it worthwhile.

No matter how Frit looked at it she couldn't find a downside. She took a deep breath, and exhaled a puff of smoke. She might regret this, but it had to be better than wasting away here. "Will you give me some time to think about it?"

"Of course, child." Nebiat nodded. "I won't consider you an enemy either way, but I am very much hoping you will help me restore our people to greatness."

17

SIMULATION THETA

S kare watched the scry-screen from the command chair dominating the spartan bridge. The *Dragon Skull* drifted perilously close to the Ternus station, the ship so massive it could not squeeze into the largest berth.

The moment the ship connected to the station's umbilical port, the bridge chimed and Caelendra spoke. "Pardon me, Lord Skare, but we've received a request for admittance from Governor Austin. He's waiting to board."

"Escort him to the bridge with a drone." Skare waved absently, still lost in thought about Talifax, and what he'd managed to accomplish at Ternus. His destruction of the planet had been brilliantly orchestrated. So brilliant that Skare found it unsettling. Just how prepared was Talifax? He seemed to have an answer for everything.

It wasn't long before Skare heard booted feet approaching up the corridor. Several moments later Austin strode onto the bridge, and to Skare's surprise the governor was alone. Usually he had a retinue, and at least a few drones. Why had he come alone?

Skare raised a hand and waved at the quartet of techs working on the bridge. "Leave us."

The white-uniformed techs rose, almost as one, and scurried from the chamber.

"Thank you for coming on such short notice," the governor drawled. Austin gave a neutral nod as he moved to sit in one of the three chairs across from Skare. He loosened his tie, and withdrew a flask from inside his coat. "It ain't what you think. High grade stimulants. Keep me on my feet a few hours past when I should pass out."

Skare nodded, and rose. "I make no judgements, Governor. This war drives many of us to things we'd never have expected." He figured that was as good a segue as he could offer, and noted the shrewd way Austin reacted to the words. The context wasn't lost on him.

"Let's get right to it then." Austin's faced hardened, and Skare could feel the anger radiating off of him. "Voria destroyed our capital. Nimitz thinks it was intentional, but you and I both know she'd never do that. This was probably an accident. She's a new god, and so far as I know it don't come with a manual. But whatever the reason...we can't let this stand. My people will never forgive her."

Skare nodded sympathetically. He returned to the command chair and sat. "It must be answered, I agree."

"So...how do we do that? I need to give my people justice." Austin eyed Skare searchingly, and Skare eyed him back, his expression conveying as much sympathy as he could muster. Or his best imitation anyway.

"Well, Governor." Share mirrored the governor's posture, knowing it would make the man more amenable, if only slightly. "You're going to need magic. If you want to overcome Voria, it will require a counter to her immense Nature magic. You will need advanced magic of your own. You have ships infused with *spirit*. I would suggest obtaining a powerful source of *water*, and one of *earth*. Combined with *spirit*, these will grant access to Binding and Protection. Both will be key against Voria and her forces."

Austin looked even more uncomfortable, and licked his lips before speaking. "I don't understand magic, and we both know it. I've looked at your fancy circle, and I get what the words mean, but I don't understand their practical application. If I understand correctly, *earth* and *spirit* would allow my ships to bind things, just like the Krox. That what you mean by binding?"

Skare nodded.

"And *water* and *spirit*? What would that do?" The governor took a pull from his flask, grimaced, then replaced it in his jacket pocket.

"*Spirit* and *water* form the greater path of protection." Skare rose again, and approached the scry-screen. "Caelendra, please show simulation theta." He turned back to the governor. "This is how you fight a god."

The scry-screen resolved into an Inuran fleet, a hundred black ships in a spherical defensive formation. Magic flared around the center vessel, then rippled out to the others. Blue and white magic flowed from ship to ship, establishing a sort of latticework.

Krox appeared in the system, and raised a hand. He flung a tremendous ball of nuclear fire at the sphere of ships, but the sphere detonated on an invisible barrier a few kilometers out.

"Remarkable, yes?" Skare prompted as he eyed the governor. "*Water* and *spirit* would allow you to resist the assault of a god. *Earth* and *spirit* will allow you to control their dragons and their elementals."

Austin eyed the screen thoughtfully. The sphere broke

apart, and the ships converged on the god, their tendrils ripping magic from it in large quantities. A second and third fleet appeared, and the god was quickly overwhelmed.

"As you can see," Skare explained, "your ships will be all but unstoppable if you procure the right types of magic."

"And where do we acquire this magic?" Austin rubbed the legs of his pants, not a new habit if the wear on the pants were any indication.

"Right under our very noses." Skare offered a magnanimous smile. "I would begin on the planet Marid. Your colony shares that world with Drakkon, the guardian of Marid. The dragon is one of Voria's closest allies, and has no love for humanity. You could eliminate an enemy, and lay claim to the *water* magic you need all in one blow."

Austin was nodding now. "Yes, I could see that. It's our world, and the magic belongs to us. I'll speak to Nimitz and arrange the assault."

18

DRIFTER ROCK

After her horrendous failure at Ternus, Voria translocated on instinct. At first she wasn't sure why she chose Drifter Rock, a place she'd only frequented a half dozen times, but as she gazed down at the haphazard fleet around the porous asteroid she understood why.

They were the only people who still accepted her without reservation.

Going back to Shaya meant fencing with Ducius, and dealing with whatever accusations he hurled about her numerous failures. Yanthara was far too closely allied with the Inurans to be viable, and Skare would know the instant she arrived.

Virkon might tolerate her presence, but their welcome would be chilly at best, and violent at worst. Either way she'd be embroiling herself in a mess.

That left the most lawless station in the sector, one that had horrified her when she was a young officer, but gradually become a second home. Voria willed a missive to Pickus —just a message, not a request for communication. She didn't really want to deal with her crew or her followers. Not just yet. She needed to be around people who wanted nothing. Well, nothing except swindling her in a trade, maybe.

Voria teleported inside the asteroid's hollowed-out interior. Tunnels crisscrossed the entire thing, but they provided countless boltholes for drifters to scurry into if any military vessels or pirates showed up.

Hundreds of mismatched ships were parked in between brightly colored tents, and the haphazard marketplace extended across the interior. The low hum of conversations were welcome, and Voria lost herself in it as she threaded unerringly toward a specific stall.

Quite a few drifters, most clutching pints of beer, gawked at her as she passed. She'd muted the glow as much as she could, but there was no denying the luminescence. Shayans weren't unknown here, but they were rare enough to be worthy of comment. Most drifters knew that Shayans glowed if they drank lifewine, so she hoped that was what they assumed.

It didn't take long to reach the familiar green, blue, and red tents where Beadle ran his brewery. The very place she'd acquired the beer that had saved Bord's life. A steady flow of drifters, and a few humans, clustered outside the stall. Both Beadle and his wife were working the line and taking orders, and Voria stole a moment to watch them work.

She towered over the drifters, which made her presence impossible for someone as perceptive as Beadle to miss. The drifter froze when he saw her, and gently doffed his battered cap, which he pressed to his chest.

"As I livenbreathe, if it ain't the lady o' light herself." Beadle executed a perfect bow from the waist, which caused most of his patrons to turn and face her. "Gaze in wonder, lads. You're in the presence of a living goddess."

"Put yer jaw backin yer mouth, hoosband." Beadle's wife sidled up and planted both hands on her hips. "I don't like the way yerstarin, goddess or no. You've got a wife, and dontchu forget it."

Voria threw her head back and laughed. Something in her, a wound she'd been carrying, scabbed over in that moment. The pain lessened. There were still decent people in the sector. People who weren't trying to use her for their own ends, or to eradicate everything.

"Hello, Beadle." She approached the counter with a smile, and the crowd parted before her. "How has business been?"

"Can't complain, can't complain." He offered a gap-toothed smile. "Did you come for more beer? Didn't know gods could hold their liquor." Voria assumed it must have required supreme effort of will to make his speech under-standable, and appreciated the gesture.

"Quite the opposite." Voria folded her arms and looked to Magda. "I'm here to bless your beer. All of it."

Perhaps using the immense power she'd been given for something so trivial was negligent, but these people had stood by her. They'd stood by the sector. Even now, drifters were cleaning and repairing the parts of the *Spellship* that humans largely avoided. They worked tirelessly, and didn't complain. Yet they were disparaged across the entire sector as thieves and wastrels. She wanted to show them that a god believed in them.

"Whatcha gonna charge feraldis?" Beadle's eyes narrowed suspiciously, while Magda merely raised an eyebrow.

"Nothing." Voria folded her arms, and savored their expressions.

"Don't make no sense," Magda muttered. "Who goes around givin' stuff fer nothin'?"

"A goddess," Voria pointed out. "Your magic originated from Shaya, and I have come to reaffirm that magic. I've come because the drifters are the truest children of Shaya. Because you are still fighting and helping, and trying. And I want to reward that."

Voria raised her arms and wove *water* and *life* together. A potent wave exploded from her in all directions, the magic tailored to only target beer. It clung to casks, pints, and jugs, and the vats where it was brewed. The magic altered the beer, and gave it the ability to heal. Voria gave those potions all the potency a goddess could muster.

"And what do you except us to do now, lady?" Beadle blinked up at her in awe.

"Make a profit." She smiled, and for the first time enjoyed her godhood. "Go out into the sector and sell that beer. Sell it to people in need. Sell it to people fighting with us. Help them, and get rich doing it."

Beadle's eyes went watery, and then a ragged sob escaped. "Yer da most beautiful—". Magda elbowed him in the ribs. "*Second* most beautiful thing I've seen in all my years. We ain't never gonna fergetcha, lady. In fact, we're gonna start praying. You joost see if we don't."

Murmurs of agreement came from all around her, and Voria realized that she'd finally done something good. Something pure. The drifters were a balm on her soul, and more. Seeing them here, resolute and proud, gave her the strength to continue.

19

OPERATION RECLAMATION

Fleet Admiral Nimitz was now the highest ranking military officer Ternus could presently field. Not because he was the best. He knew he wasn't. No, because he was the best of what was left. All the better men were dead.

The last of those men had died in his sleep the previous evening. Fleet Admiral Kerr had leaned a little left for Nimitz's tastes, but he'd been a fine officer with a brilliant tactical mind. His death, especially when the man had been in such apparent good health, had shocked the senior officers.

Nimitz didn't like the circumstances surrounding Kerr's death, either. It happened less than twenty-four hours after he'd publicly chastised Skare over his callousness. Kerr had been a vocal opponent of the Inurans for a long time, and his death was certainly convenient.

He rose from the captain's chair, which wasn't entirely accurate since the ships didn't have a full bridge crew. It was just the chair. Nimitz approached the viewscreen, or whatever the magical equivalent was called, and spoke to the ship's computer, or fairy or whatever powered these blasted things.

"Caelendra, display the tactical disposition of the confederate forces on the edge of Malgoro Crater."

"Of course, Fleet Admiral Nimitz," a cultured voice replied. Was it supposed to sound like his wife?

The screen shifted to show a topographical map of the crater. A full brigade of Marines, veterans of New Texas every one, were assembled around three dozen hovertanks, the finest the Inurans had ever produced.

As impressive as the ground forces were, they were merely bait. The real offense came from the sixty black ships lurking above the ever present cloud cover. Once the head dragon engaged, they'd converge and destroy it. That would allow them to purify the Catalyst at their leisure, and thus satisfy the first phase of Operation Reclamation.

It was a simple plan, but through his four decades of command, Nimitz had learned that simple was almost always best. Simple left little margin for error, and your biggest risk was applying the wrong strategy. Complex plans had many points of failure, and could come apart for a variety of reasons.

In this instance, Nimitz wasn't really certain what he was dealing with. He hadn't been at the Skull of Xal, but he'd seen the footage. The demon that dwelled inside had torn those ships apart, and he didn't want to see a similar situation here.

They possessed some immediate tactical advantages, of course. There was no cover for the drakes, beyond the fog covering their blasted swamp. The lizards couldn't do anything about orbital bombardment, though Nimitz suspected the big dragon could probably put up one hell of a fight against their air.

"Colonel Brommel," Nimitz rumbled into the comm, "begin your advance into the swamp. If it slithers, flies, or hisses I want it dead."

"Yes, sir," the woman replied mechanically. She wasn't terribly imaginative, but she made things dead better than any other officer. Still, dealing with Brommel always troubled him. She was more machine than man, which wasn't any better than practicing that demonic witchcraft the Shayans were into.

Nimitz watched as the brigade fanned out into the swamp, each regiment forming a pincher as they approached the coordinates of the Catalyst. Thanks to Voria's incursion a year earlier, they had all the telemetry they needed, which would make the next part that much easier. At least something good had come from that botched op.

The brigade made good time, but it took several hours for them to reach the outskirts of the Catalyst. Nimitz spent that time gripping the arms of his chair and brooding. The same thoughts kept circling. He was out of his depth. He didn't understand the forces at play, but there was something intrinsically wrong with using these ships.

If magic was evil, and Nimitz knew to his core that it was, then how did they justify harnessing it? Because they knew that if they did not, their civilization was gone. No one knew the way back to Terra. Either they made it in this sector or they perished.

He leaned forward in his chair as a dense fog began rolling out of the center of the swamp. It was obviously a defensive measure. "Caelendra, why am I not seeing thermal signatures in that fog?"

"It is possible that there are no life forms," the pleasant

voice came back, "but I believe it more likely the fog is magical in nature, and is designed to cloak enemy units."

"All vessels," Nimitz rumbled as he pressed a button on the chair's arm console to switch to a fleet-wide channel, "prepare for orbital bombardment. Concentrate your fire on the area between our units and the fog." He tapped another button to turn off the fleet wide. "Caelendra, prepare nukes one through four please."

Her pleasant voice offered a caution. "As a warning, irradiating this area will have significant consequences to all life within this valley. I estimate with 84% accuracy that it will be uninhabitable to human life for many decades."

"Noted. Do it, Caelendra." Nimitz leaned back in his chair, and cursed the necessity for war. This valley was prosperous, and a tourist hotspot to boot. There weren't too many planets left, and irradiating one of the good ones didn't sit well. But when one was dealing with a god, they simply couldn't take chances.

Several glowing projectiles streaked from the base of the ship, and they were rapidly joined by nukes launched from the other vessels. All sixty loosed four each, and their spread pattern meant a dense overlap. Anything vulnerable to nuclear fire was about to get a face full of it.

The projectiles hit the swamp, and the viewscreen went white. It took several moments to return to normal, and when it did the fog was still there, though every tree, rock, and plant had been incinerated. "Order all Marines to take their radiation treatment and then enter the fog."

He wished they had some means of penetrating it. Maybe that required *fire* magic. He had no idea how their dark sorcery worked, but that seemed a likely way to counter magical *water*.

The Marines started into the fog, and Nimitz keyed in

the sequence to ride piggyback on Brommel's helmet cam. The colonel trotted through the fog in her silver power armor, the analog equivalent to the spellarmor that Ternus had once been so envious of. They'd definitely narrowed the gap since then.

Brommel set a ground-eating pace, and led her men deeper into the fog. She vaulted suddenly, twisting to allow the camera to catch the charred remains of a forty-meter snake. She passed another, and another. Very nearly everywhere she passed was covered in the creatures.

"Looks like we did for a significant chunk of their army, sir," Brommel's dispassionate voice came over the comm. "Proceeding to checkpoint alpha."

Nimitz didn't reply. He gripped the arms of his chair, and wished he were down there with them. This smelled like a trap. The snakes didn't even have wings. They must be young. There were no fully developed dragons in the mix.

The fog exploded outward in a titanic pulse that covered the whole of the swamp. Thick floes of dense blue ice bubbled up around every Marine, in every part of the swamp. Then it dragged them below the muck, armor and all, an entire brigade vanishing as if it had never existed, all within seconds

Brommel's head cam was quickly covered in dense black muck, and Nimitz switched the view back to orbital with a muttered curse. "Colonel, can you hear me?"

"Yes, sir." She sounded calm, at least. "I'm trying to extricate myself from the ice. I believe that—". The high pitched squeal of metal tearing drowned out her voice, and when it passed there was nothing but static.

"Caelendra, zoom in on the Colonel's position. Find me survivors." Nimitz rose from his chair and began to pace.

The camera obligingly adjusted to show the colonel's

position, which was nothing but muck-covered ice. Hell, if he didn't know ice had been involved, he'd have called it ordinary swamp.

Austin would chalk it up to standard losses. They'd assumed the ground forces would face heavy casualties, after all. But Nimitz couldn't help but feel like a butcher. How often had he cursed Voria for doing exactly what he'd just done? That kind of conduct wasn't befitting an officer, no matter the stakes. If he could have it back, he would. But he couldn't.

"Fleet Admiral Nimitz," Caelendra said, "I have detected movement from deeper in the swamp. Shall I adjust the screen accordingly?"

"Do it."

The screen shifted to show an orbital view of the center of the swamp. Sapphire light sprayed up from the ground in a roughly three-kilometer area, like the geysers back on New Texas.

"I'll add a magical overlay," Caelendra offered. The screen changed, and an enormous blue outline appeared under the valley floor.

"Is that...a dragon?" Nimitz whispered. "It's the size of a bloody continent."

"Indeed, Fleet Admiral."

Nimitz tapped the fleet-wide button again. "All ships begin full magical extraction. Focus on that sapphire light, and kill anything that tries to stop us."

20

OUTCLASSED

Drakkon hovered in the clouds, seeing through the dense mists as if it were clear. *Water* was, after all, his element, and that of his children. The disquieting ships the humans had brought reminded Drakkon of something, though he couldn't place his talon on the source.

The loss of the youngest drakes was tragic, and the land below had been made toxic and unlivable. He possessed the magic to cleanse it, though it would tax him greatly, and take several seasons. These humans and their incursion had succeeded in arousing something not even Nebiat's attempt to enslave him had wrought.

Drakkon was furious. These humans would pay for their temerity.

"My children," he rumbled, his voice as thunder among the clouds, his gnashing claws striking sparks that became bolts of lightning. "Let us show these humans the fury of the storm. Teach them that their technology is meaningless."

Drakkon dove, still wearing the clouds like armor. The vapor clung to him, and masked his approach until he slammed into the side of the largest human vessel. His claws bit into the armor, but weakly. They shredded the outer layer, but found more layers beneath.

He sucked in an immense breath, and expended a cloud of dense frost, which added to the weight of the vessel. Then Drakkon relied on physics. He kicked off the vessel with all his considerable bulk, and the ship plummeted from the sky, slamming into the mountains far below.

Drakkon gave a toothy grin of satisfaction...until the ship rose under its own power. Sparks played across one side of the hull, where the gashes caused by the impact had scored far deeper wounds than his own claws.

A tendril whipped up from the ship, snaking through the atmosphere in Drakkon's direction. He conjured his spellblade, Maladrieve, and knocked the thing away. He could feel the *void* pulsing from it, the eagerness and raw hunger of the beam. It wanted to drink his essence. It wanted to drink his mother's essence.

Only one being had ever been so consumed with power. These things were truly tainted by Nefarius, something Drakkon was now forced to admit he was trying to turn a blind eye to. He'd wanted to stay here, to build something. In doing so he'd ignored a growing threat until it had arrived on his doorstep.

Drakkon reached deep for his magic. He drew *air*, and *water*, and *earth* and *spirit* to bind it all together. He flung his magic at a section of the outer ring of the crater, a range of mountains containing many mighty peaks.

The largest mountain began to quake and rumble, and then millions of tons of rock abruptly tore loose from the world and flung itself at the terrible black ship. His makeshift missile slammed into the wound the fall had created, and sent a spray of metallic debris arcing out over the swamp.

Another mountain rose, and another. Drakkon hurled them into the same black ship, always digging into the existing wound. It took two more mountains before the ship stuttered and died. The vessel tumbled from the sky, its awful tendril dissipating into the wind. This time when it struck the ground, there was a tremendous detonation, and the vessel did not rise again.

Drakkon turned his attention to the rest of the combat, and knew despair. His children were young, and while strong, their ferocity was not yet tempered by experience. Most had already fallen. As he watched, Daradra, one of the fiercest youngsters, succumbed to a black tendril. Her essence was stripped away pulse by pulse, until the vessel finally discarded her pale corpse.

His rage grew, but in that moment wisdom prevailed. These ships were powerful. Fifty-nine remained, of sixty. Most of his children were dead. Their defenses had been stripped away, and so quickly. Drakkon could summon catastrophic magics, but the ships had proven resilient to direct magical attacks. What if he squandered his mother's power and the ships survived?

Uncertainty made him hesitate as another Wyrm fell from the sky. Drakkon needed aid, and needed it now. He began sketching a missive to the one being in the sector who might be able to save his mother.

21

TAKING A STAND

Voria stood before one of the oldest objects in creation, and dearly wished she could smash it. The blasted mirror felt as if it were taunting her, bobbing up and down endlessly while refusing to show her the things she wished to see.

Each time she tugged the possibility toward Krox or Nefarius, the mirror dragged it back to the planet Marid. However, the view refused to descend close enough to be of any use. The planet's blue-white surface glittered below her, with no indication as to why the mirror thought it important.

"We're in trouble, kid," Shaya said as she shimmered into view next to the mirror. "A god is manipulating possibilities. The mirror knows it, but it can't bypass whatever defenses the god has put in place. Something is happening on Marid, and someone doesn't want us knowing about it."

Voria tapped her chin as she studied the image. "This doesn't feel like Nebiat, though she's crafty enough to vary her tactics. So far as we know, Nefarius hasn't risen. I keep hearing about how powerful Talifax is, and after Ternus I'm inclined to believe the tales. Could he do this?"

Shaya nodded. She crossed her arms, and gave a shiver that couldn't have anything to do with the cold. "That and more. He's incredibly adept at crafting a cover possibility, one that appears a near certainty. Then he does something you can't possibly predict, which causes the near certainty to unravel. All of a sudden you have no idea what's going on, and while you're scrambling, he's winning the war."

Voria inhaled slowly, or mimed the motion anyway. Even calming breaths were denied a deity. She shook her head, and tried to find a way out of this trap. "If we go to Marid, then Ternus will see it as an act of war. They'll attack us, without a doubt. If we do nothing, then we risk Talifax somehow gaining control of the Catalyst, and maybe even killing Drakkon." Voria eyed Shaya. "I don't know what to do and am definitely open to advice."

Before Shaya could answer, the air around Voria vibrated and an incoming missive, audio only, began to play.

"Voria," Drakkon rumbled, "the humans have come, and they are winning. My children are dead, and I do not believe I can stop them from taking my mother. I have tried Inura as well, to no avail. You are my last hope, lady of light. Please, help me protect this place, or Nefarius will use her magic to slay us all."

Voria whirled toward Shaya. "I'll bet my best jacket it's those blasted ships. Ternus must be trying to secure *water* magic. I should have predicted this, visions or no."

"In your defense," Shaya pointed out with a shrug, "Talifax has worked hard to ensure that you cannot. The question is—what now?"

"We go to war," Voria answered without hesitation. She

raised a finger to sketch a *fire* sigil, then suppressed the instinct and willed the spell to complete. A moment later, Nara's face filled the Mirror of Shaya.

"What's up?" Nara had a mug raised, and had apparently been about to sip her coffee.

"Mobilize the crew. I'll be translocating us to Marid." She frowned to convey the urgency. "Ternus has declared war on Drakkon, and he is losing."

"What are you going to do?" Nara had already set the mug down, but the spell followed her as she departed her quarters.

"I don't know," Voria admitted. "If we can diffuse the situation, we will, but I tend to think matters have progressed too far for that."

Nara nodded and killed the missive. Voria closed her eyes and envisioned the entirety of the *Spellship* being elsewhere. She pictured a familiar world, the world where Aran and Nara had first distinguished themselves. The world where she'd murdered Thalas and made an enemy of Ducius forever.

The *Spellship* winked into existence in high orbit above the northern continent, where the crater lay. That put her closer to the Ternus orbital platform than she'd like, but she was gambling that it would take them time to respond.

Voria took several moments to extend her divine senses to the planet below, and immediately saw the extent of the crisis. Radiation blanketed Malgoro Crater, and while the steep mountains ringing it might have prevented that radiation from leaking across the planet, someone or something had wrenched several mountains from the earth, and apparently hurled them at one of the black ships, if the wreckage was any indication. That gap would allow the radiation to seep out to the rest of the region.

A few Wyrms desperately sought to defend the font of magical power at the heart of the swamp, with Drakkon's massive form leading the charge. A few of the black ships were down, but something like fifty still remained.

Voria felt a missive buzzing at her, and answered it. To her immense shock, Admiral Nimitz's grizzled face filled the screen. He eyed her with clear distaste. "I shouldn't be surprised that you showed up to help your demonic friends."

"Drakkon is hardly a demon," she snapped, struggling and failing to suppress her anger. "What you're doing here is murder, Nimitz. Murder of an ally, one who could have wiped out all human life on this planet long since."

"Could have, maybe, but not anymore." The admiral gave her a satisfied smile. "Now we've got the power to fight back. We don't need to rely on your 'generosity' any more. I'm going to give you one chance to leave this system, and then I'm going to turn my guns on you. We recognize you've done us some favors, but those credits are all spent. You murdered our capital."

"Are you threatening a goddess, Admiral?" Voria's voice had gone deadly calm. She saw no reason to correct him, as he wouldn't believe her about Talifax being the true culprit.

"That's *exactly* what I'm doing." He stabbed a finger at the screen. "You want to get between us and a resource on one of our few remaining colonies? Then I will order this fleet to destroy you. I saw what we did to Krox. We ain't helpless anymore, you arrogant slit."

"Very well, Admiral." Her eyes narrowed. "If you wish war, then you shall have war. Whatever happens today and the days that follow, remember that you had a choice."

She killed the missive, and extended a hand. The *Spellship* drifted into her palm, and she could feel the powers of the worshippers within. It was time to see what she could do against the awful tools the Inurans had forged.

22

THE POWER OF PRAYER

Nara sprinted onto the coliseum's stage, the same one where she'd help raise Voria to godhood. To her surprise and relief people were already filing into their seats. Thousands had already arrived, with more coming behind them.

Every one would likely be needed, if Nara grasped the situation. Voria was going to fight the black ships, and she would need all the strength her worshippers could deliver.

Getting the people to provide that energy meant uniting them in purpose. It meant bringing them together and making it clear what they were trying to accomplish here. Nara wasn't much of a speech writer, but she'd given a few recently and hoped she could pull this one off as well.

"Citizens of the *Spellship*," Nara roared as she strode out onto the stage. "Hear me!" Newly installed microphones picked up her words, and she could hear them echoing in the corridors throughout the ship.

The ones already seated turned in her direction, while those still trickling in found their seats. Nara licked her lips and continued. "Today, much as we hate the need, we are going to war again. Voria is about to engage a fleet of Ternus ships that are attempting to kill Drakkon, one of our greatest allies against the Krox. She will need every bit of our strength. Every bit of our devotion. We will need to give of ourselves to ensure victory today."

Nara bowed her head, and people all over the room did the same. She took a deep breath and intoned the prayer she'd recently written. It mimicked a prayer used by the dragonflight on Virkon, but it seemed fitting.

"Oh, great lady of light," she began, her voice ringing out over the audience. "Hear our prayers. Feel our strength. We bask in your light, and we reflect it back, gladly and strongly, and with the greatest of devotion. Take our strength, and use it to protect us."

All over the room people whispered the words, just a moment after she said them. A hum built somewhere beyond hearing, and then brilliant gold-white light exploded from the audience. It shot up into the walls and the ceiling, filling the ship with their collective magic.

Nara felt something rising from her, an energy that didn't reflect any of the eight aspects, but was no less powerful. She gave to it gladly, and fervently prayed that Voria would be able to use it to accomplish whatever she needed to do.

The energy built and built, huge pulses of it, and flowed directly into the ship. The analytic part of Nara's mind wished she could quantify and measure the amount. That should be theoretically possible, and would allow her to conduct studies.

How much faith could a single worshipper provide? Were all worshippers different? How different? Questions tumbled through her mind even as the final pulse of pure faith seeped into the ship.

She'd done what she could. The rest was up to Voria.

TRIAGE

Voria glided through Marid's atmosphere, dropping lower as quickly as she could manage without teleporting. Doing so would have gotten her there more quickly, but it would have made it impossible for the Ternus forces to predictably react to her presence.

As she'd hoped, a full two dozen black ships broke away from assaulting Drakkon, and moved skyward to engage her. The break in the assault allowed Drakkon to respond, and the colossal Wyrm seized a ship in his jaws, then flung it to the earth in a huge explosion.

Four other ships glided closer, and their dark tendrils seized parts of Drakkon's body. Pulses of blue magic flowed back to the ships, and Drakkon roared in pain and anger.

Voria waited until the two dozen black ships had nearly reached her, then teleported. She appeared right next to Drakkon, and extended the *Spellship*. Blazing blades of light extended from either end, and she twirled it like a staff.

The blades passed through the tendrils holding

Drakkon, and wherever light met dark Voria heard a high-pitched screech as if a living creature were being wounded.

"You've come!" Drakkon roared, regaining altitude with a mighty flap of his wings. "Where is the *Talon*? And Aran? We need every mage, or this world is lost."

"Aran is on a mission in the depths, so far as I know." Voria pivoted in midair, and used the *Spellship* to block a tendril that tried to seize her. She danced backwards and avoided two more. "I don't think we can win this, but I might be able to buy some time."

"What do you have in mind?" Drakkon breathed a cloud of dense frost, which caught two of the ships and sent them spiraling toward the ground. Both recovered before impact though, and quickly rose to re-engage.

"I will create a *life* ward around us and the Catalyst. Keep them off me for a moment." Voria dropped down to the Catalyst itself, and stood near the font of power jetting from the wound in Marid's chest.

She raised the *Spellship* and drew deeply from the power it offered. That power was stronger than it had been the last time she'd drawn on it, which suggested Nara's efforts were going well. The people had begun to believe, which made Voria believe.

A glowing golden latticework sprang up in a ring around the Catalyst, then began assembling itself into a dome. It took several moments, but Drakkon twisted and wove through the enemy ships, ensuring that they were unable to capitalize on Voria's momentary distraction.

Just before the ward closed, Drakkon's shape dove for it, and he shifted to human form, dropping through the last opening the moment before it snapped shut behind him.

Voria reduced her size to match Drakkon's human form,

and drifted over to hover next to him. His watery hair was more pale, and crow's feet radiated out from his eyes now. He'd aged, and if Shayans were any indication, that meant he'd lost a significant chunk of his magic.

"Are you all right?" she pressed, viewing him with her *life* sight. There was a wound in his side, and another on his right leg.

"I'll be fine, eventually." He stared up through the ward, where the Inuran ships had begun to cluster. They fired a volley of tendrils, which caught on the ward.

Voria could feel them draining its energy, and knew they didn't have long. A minute perhaps? She turned back to Drakkon. "We have very little time, and that means you need to make a choice. This world is lost. What do you want to do?"

She desperately hoped his answer wouldn't be to futilely throw his life away protecting his mother, but she also knew she wouldn't be able to influence his decision, whatever it was.

Drakkon darted an agonized glance at the font of magic power below them. "I do not have an answer, or not a good one at least. If we allow the humans to take this magic, they will use it to resurrect Nefarius."

"Is there any way we can prevent that?" Voria studied the magic, which sang to the *water* magic within her. Like calling to like.

"Partially." Agony flitted across his now-human features. "You and I are strong enough to take a significant portion of her magic. If we both drink deeply and then flee, we will lessen the amount they are able to recover."

Voria understood how much it must have pained the Wyrm to offer that course of action. What he was suggesting meant that his mother would never be resurrected, as he'd no doubt hoped for millennia. The magnitude of the sacrifice was humbling.

"Very well. Let's save what we can." Voria drifted lower, close enough that she was able to extend a hand to the magical font of power. She could feel Marid's essence and her memories. It was quite unlike the last time she'd been here, when she'd been a mortal at the whims of a dead god. Now she controlled the magical flow, and could pick and choose what she took.

That really came down to one of two things. She could claim power, or she could claim Marid's knowledge. Both were massive, and she didn't have the ability to take it all.

What should she save? Knowledge could help her win the war, but power would help her battle her foes. Plus, that power would be denied their enemies.

That decided her.

Voria reached for Marid's magic, and claimed as much *water* as she could drink into herself. Pulse after glorious pulse shot from the pool and into her outstretched hand. Not far from her she was aware of Drakkon sobbing, while he too drank of the magic.

High above, the black ships beat upon the ward, which was now discolored and beginning to crumble. Voria drew a few more pulses, and then with a titanic effort of will pushed the magic away. They needed to get out of here.

"Get inside the *Spellship*, and I'll take us away," she offered.

"Where will we go?" Drakkon asked, also breaking away from Marid's magic.

She considered that. Back to Drifter Rock? No, that would put the drifters in too much danger.

There was only one world that might take them in now, and having Drakkon with her made that more likely. One world that might fight back against these ships. Voria envisioned Virkon, and translocated just as the black ships broke through the ward.

24

SAND IN THEIR FACES

Aran fully expected an ambush the instant the *Talon* opened a Fissure into the Virkonan system, and kept his hand poised over a *void* sigil as he guided the ship through. There were no black ships, and no other visible threat, but he still didn't release the breath he was holding until the Fissure snapped shut in their wake.

Crewes cleared his throat nervously from the neighboring matrix. "What are the odds that giant dragon's gonna try to carry us down like it did the *Hunter*?"

Aran glanced at the scry-screen, which was dominated by the blue-white world above them. There was no sign of Cerberus on the screen, though Aran could feel the Wyrm's approach through the *Talon*.

"Good gods!" Crewes all but shrieked as a draconic eye filled the scry-screen.

It pulled back an instant later, and they were able to see Cerberus in all his glory. The sector's largest Wyrm, so far as Aran knew, weighing in at over twice Drakkon's size. The creature swam around them like an excited puppy, then darted up toward the planet, as if waiting for them to follow.

"Looks like we're invited." Aran struggled to keep the amusement from his voice, but failed.

"What is that thing?" Rhea whispered, her eyes rivaling saucers.

"That's Cerberus," Aran explained as he guided the *Talon* after their host. "He guards the Umbral Depths, and takes down any ship that he thinks is a threat. Last time we showed up he carried our entire battleship down in his mouth."

Aran followed the city-sized Wyrm down to the surface, and as Virkon grew, so too did the memories. Tall, jagged mountains ringed the blackened plains where the *Spellship* had crushed the Krox fleet. Nothing lived there now, the very soil irradiated by the nuclear weapons the Krox had employed.

The destruction was conspicuously absent in a patch of ground at the foot of one of the tallest mountains. Aran could just make out the gaping hole in the base of the mountain, which they'd entered through during his first audience with the Council of Wyrms. Or the first he could remember, anyway. Not everything had come back.

"You gonna land a ways off?" Crewes asked. He'd recovered his composure, though he still darted uncomfortable glances at the scry-screen whenever Cerberus glided by.

"Nope." Aran gave a mischievous smile. "Last time we landed a ways off because that's where Cerberus dropped us. Now we're playing on our terms. They don't have anything down there that can touch the *Talon*, not after the magic we took from Krox. I'm going to land right in their backyard, and we're going to walk right in. Let them chew on that for a bit."

"Are you certain that's wise?" Rhea ventured. She shifted

uncomfortably in the third matrix, then busied herself straightening her ponytail.

"Nope." Aran guided the *Talon* into the lower atmosphere, but they were completely insulated from the reentry, and didn't feel so much as a single bump. "Could be a mistake, but my instincts say this is the right play."

They passed through a thick canopy of clouds, which boiled around the ship for several seconds before dissipating. The *Talon* descended toward the Wyrm's mountain, and settled into a smooth landing a few dozen meters from the entrance. Aran parked the *Talon* off to the side, so he wasn't blocking the way in, at least.

"All right, people." Aran unbuckled himself from the matrix and ducked through the rings. "Let's go ruffle some feathers."

"Sir?" Rhea had risen from her matrix, and moved to stand before Aran. She was very nearly his height, and one of the few women he'd run into who could look him in the eye. "I don't understand. Why are you so intent on upsetting these Wyrms? I thought we were here in search of allies."

"I thought you didn't like these scaly—". Crewes cut himself off as he rose from his matrix, clearly realizing that he was talking to a Wyrm. "I mean, you don't like them either, right? So what's the harm in kicking a little sand in their faces? Shows 'em humans won't just lay down and do what they say."

"Because if we need allies," Rhea began, her irritated gaze flicking to the sergeant, "there is little sense in antagonizing them. It makes it less likely they will work with us, not more. There is a time and place for force, but I do not know if saber rattling is the wisest course."

"And you're encouraged to speak your mind about that. I'll explain once we're underway," Aran offered as he exited the bridge and threaded down the ramp toward the cargo bay. It was a longer walk now that the *Talon* had grown. He waited until they reached their makeshift armory before explaining further. "Get suited up. Full armor. Davidson?" Aran directed the question at the blond officer, who was wrenching something on the outside of his tank. Looked like he was bolting on something Pickus had made.

"Yo?" Davidson called back. He set down the drill he'd been using, and walked a bit closer.

"You've got command until I get back," Aran explained as he approached his armor. He paused before it, and glanced at Rhea. "Rhea, Crewes, you're with me. Everyone else will stay on the ship. This shouldn't take too long."

He slipped into his spellarmor, and fed it a bit of *void* to get it aloft. "All right, follow me, people." Aran glided through the blue membrane, and onto the world where he'd been born. He scanned the sky above, and was unsurprised to see dozens of Wyrms circling, all kilometers high.

"So that explanation, sir?" Crewes's voice crackled through his suit's speakers.

"Right." Aran cleared his throat. "This might be monumentally stupid, but if we're going to win this war we don't need to convince the council. We need to convince a goddess. And Virkonna was a warrior. If we can wake her up I don't want her seeing us as subservient. I want her seeing us as the people she wants to be dealing with. And kicking a little sand in the council's faces might also get Inura's attention. We don't know for sure where he is, but we do know he's got a workshop here, and that he was close with his sister."

"I'm relieved, sir." Rhea's voice carried no such emotion, and was as full of iron as ever. "I do not like the idea of confronting greater Wyrms, but I suppose if we do not do something extreme we will not attract Virkonna's attention. Even my people had legends of her."

"I don't really need the justification," Crewes growled. "These bastards tore at the major, and tore at her, and then when it came time to deliver on their promise of help they weren't nowhere to be found. We got it done, without them."

Aran agreed, though maybe a bit less vehemently. He took a deep breath as his spellarmor approached the council's mountain. They glided in an arrowhead formation, and passed through the cavernous entryway, into the chamber where he'd first met Astria.

Thick granite pillars stabbed up to the very top of the inside of the mountain, which had been completely hollowed to form their chamber. The entire peak was covered in caves and perches, many of which were occupied by very annoyed-looking Wyrms. Their bright scales glittered under the bits of sunlight filtering through the narrow hole leading out of the top of the mountain.

"Nineteen centuries," boomed a deep, feminine voice, "and in that time I have never seen such brazen temerity. Never witnessed a mortal so foolishly throw his life away. You must know that we cannot allow your impertinence to stand."

Aran slowly removed his helmet, then rose into the air, toward the alcove the voice had issued from. "If you feel like you have to attack me, I guess that's an option. I wouldn't recommend it. My people have been toe-to-toe with Krox, lady. You want a piece of us? Get in line."

Harsh, hissing laughter came from the opposite side of the cavern, and a wizened Wyrm appeared at the edge of a more natural-looking cave. "She'd have liked you, I think. I can sense the power brimming in you, so much, not just for one so young, but for anyone. You're Olyssa's pet, aren't you?

The Outrider who survived the March of Honor? My eyes aren't what they were, and your magical signature is quite different than when you departed."

"Matron, apologies, but I cannot allow this insult to stand," the first voice roared. The Wyrm leapt from her alcove, and spread large, leathery wings. She dropped into a swoop, and came up into a hover over Aran. She was larger than most of the Wyrms he'd fought, but a good deal smaller than Kheross, and likely a good deal younger, too. "Put your helmet back on. You should at least die in combat."

Aran raised an eyebrow. "You're certain this is how you want to play things?"

"I will—"

Aran raised a hand and clenched it into a fist. He reached for the immense reservoir of *void* magic that now lived inside him, and poured as much as he could manage into his fist. It began to glow and pulse as the violet energy crackled out around him.

The Wyrm sucked in a breath, and Aran knew if he allowed her, she'd spit a lightning bolt in his direction. No thanks.

He hurled the *void* energy at the Wyrm, and winced as Rhea shrieked from a few meters away. She'd probably assumed he was going to disintegrate the thing. Instead, the *void* slammed into the Wyrm's chest, and rippled out over the dragon's body.

The Wyrm was suddenly a hundred times heavier, and plummeted toward the base of the cavern. She flapped her wings frantically, and *air* magic billowed out around her as she tried to save herself. It wasn't enough, and she continued to drop. Aran let her fall to within a few meters of the floor, then unclenched his hand. The magic vanished, and she flapped back into the air.

"I am not just some Outrider," Aran thundered, adding a bit of *fire* to add volume. "I have come to wake your mother, and to bring her into the war against Nefarius. The Wyrm who slew Virkonna's mother is going to rise again, and if we don't stop her this entire world will be nothing but ashes. You want some time to adjust to that news? I get it. I'm here as a courtesy. Stay out of my way and let me do what I need to do, and we'll get along just fine."

The Wyrm landed, then kicked off the floor and launched herself into the air near Aran. Her eyes crackled with *air* magic. "You are powerful, true, but you are not a god, little human. You may have bested me, but I am merely a sentinel. Wait until Aurelius hears of your insolence."

"Aurelius is a pragmatist," Aran pointed out. "You go tell him what happened, and tell him that I don't want a fight. I just want to wake Virkonna."

25

SISTER

"Sir?" Bord's voice echoed over the *Talon*'s internal speakers, issuing from the walls of Aran's quarters. "Sorry for wakin' ya, but you wanted to be notified if anyone approached the ship. Kez and I are having a bit of a picnic on the upper hull. Looks like a single woman's approaching. I don't mean single like she's not dating. She's alone. She's wearing one of those mesh suits. Could be your sister, maybe?"

Aran sat up with a groan and rubbed at his temples. All that magic he'd pillaged did nothing to alleviate his need for sleep, and there'd been precious little of it lately. "Send her to my quarters if it's her."

He rose and buckled on his sword belt, then adjusted the scabbard so that Narlifex was within easy reach. Not that he expected to need it, but with Astria you never knew. She'd attacked him once, and even if she didn't, she'd expect him to be able to defend himself.

Vague memories of their childhood flitted through his mind, but they were disconnected. Distant somehow. He knew that these events had occurred, but there was no emotion associated with them.

"Brother?" came a soft, cultured voice from the doorway.

Aran turned to face her, and found Astria's tentative face. Her almond eyes were wide and hesitant. This must be just as difficult for her as it was for him.

"Hello, Astria." Aran crossed his quarters, and offered her a stiff hug. She awkwardly accepted it, but they disengaged as soon as they could. "I probably should have come and found you, but I wasn't even sure if you'd be living in the same place."

"Your ship is difficult to miss." She offered a tentative smile, and rested a hand on the hilt of her spellblade. "I'm told that you created quite a stir in the council chamber. The whole world is already abuzz. They claim you insulted Aurelius. Some even say you challenged him to a duel."

Aran couldn't help but laugh at that. He folded his arms, and leaned against the wall near the bed. "Not exactly. I did throw down a bit of a gauntlet, but with good cause, I promise." He offered a sheepish smile. "I'll admit I enjoyed it a little though. Payback for when he left us high and dry against the Krox."

Astria returned the smile, then moved to sit stiffly on the bed. "I'll admit it is nice seeing an Outrider treated as a serious threat for once, but I don't pretend to understand why. What do you gain, brother?"

"We're here to wake Virkonna," Aran explained. He sat next to her on the bed, and folded his hands in front of him. "I also believe Inura is here. I figured the best way to get the attention of a sleeping warrior goddess and her scholarly brother is to make a whole lot of noise right off the bat. If I did my work well, everyone on the planet knows I'm here."

She snorted a short laugh. "I believe you have succeeded in that regard. There is not a hall on this world where your arrival is not hotly debated. Some Outriders believe you will be the instrument of our salvation, that you will show the Wyrms that we are more than just servants and cannon fodder."

"You've got my sympathies, but I'm not here for that." Aran shook his head, then rose with a sigh. "Why don't we get something to eat? I have a feeling we might be talking for a while."

Astria nodded, then rose and followed him from his quarters. They headed to the mess, and Aran stopped in front of the food thingie. "Prime rib, rare. Mashed potatoes, with brown gravy."

A plate materialized and the heavenly aroma of New Texan beef filled the mess. Aran moved to the nearest table while Astria approached the food thingie.

"This thing truly is a marvel." She bent to inspect it, and when she was satisfied she glanced at Aran's plate. "Give me the same sustenance you have provided my brother."

An identical plate appeared, and Astria brought it over and sat next to him. Aran savored a mouthful of beef, and closed his eyes as he chewed. There were a lot of responsibilities, but this was one of his favorite perks. He so loved the *Talon*.

"I must admit," Astria began as she cut a tiny corner from the steak, "that I do not believe your arrival portends anything good for this world. Thus far, you have left strife and death in your wake, and I foresee more of the same."

Aran coughed, and his eyes began to water. He reached for a bottle of water, and drank about half of it before turning back to Astria. "The way you say that so matter-of-factly terrifies me."

"What will be, will be." Astria shrugged, then nibbled a

bite of steak. She seemed to approve, and began carefully chewing a larger bite.

"I can't say that you're wrong." Aran spent some time cutting up steak before looking up at her again. "Waking Virkonna is going to violently alter the balance of power on this world. Hopefully, some good comes of that and Outriders gain more autonomy. But there will be casualties, though I don't begin to know what they'll be yet."

"And why is waking her of such desperate concern now, when it was not just a few short months ago?" Astria cocked her head, her eyes full of genuine curiosity.

Aran dabbed at his mouth with a napkin, and then set down his fork. He eyed her soberly. "Krox changed everything. He kicked the crap out of us at Shaya, and got away with a weapon of incredible power. From what a goddess I trust told me...he's the lesser of two evils. Nefarius is far worse. If that's true, we're going to need Virkonna's help. We're basically screwed without it."

"Have we no other allies?" Astria tried a second small bite.

"We have Voria," Aran explained. "She's a goddess now, though not nearly as strong as Virkonna. And a few others. Drakkon."

Astria's eyelids fluttered in surprise. "You've met Drakkon? I suppose I should not be surprised. You know of the significance he holds for our style, yes?"

"Yeah, though I wasn't exactly in a position to question him about it when I met him." Aran's mind's eye shifted back to the world of Marid, deep in those seemingly endless swamps. "I didn't even know what an Outrider was then."

"Sir!" Bord's head poked into the mess, a lopsided grin plastered across his freckled face. "Voria just arrived in orbit. She's here, sir!"

26

NOT FOR YOU TO DECIDE

The *Spellship* appeared in orbit over Virkon, not terribly far from the umbral shadow. Voria manifested next to it, and waited while the largest Wyrm in the sector swam lazily toward her. She didn't know if the beast was intelligent, as Cerberus had never spoken, but she didn't want to intrude on the Wyrm's domain without allowing him to metaphorically sniff her hand.

The dragon's azure scales glittered in the light Voria cast, illuminating the beast as it swam closer. The Wyrm paused near her face, and she realized that her simulacrum, her visible manifestation, was several times larger. That made Cerberus roughly the size of a house cat, which perfectly captured the absurdity of finding oneself a goddess.

You are of Inura, the dragon's thoughts thrummed into her mind. *You have his power, a sliver of it. This cannot be coincidence. Inura recently returned to our world. Have you come to aid the master?*

Voria laughed and the sound somehow carried through space. She shook her head, and gave the Wyrm a real answer. "I didn't know your master was here, and actually came to speak to Olyssa. Inura being here changes things. Can you tell me where to find him?"

Cerberus's tail drooped, even as his scaled face sank into a frown. *He has hidden himself, even from me. I do not understand why he will not speak to us after so long away, but I will be patient. If you find him, will you tell him that we are waiting?*

Voria nodded gravely. "Of course, Cerberus. I will see that he doesn't shirk his responsibilities."

Shaya winked into existence with a raucous laugh. "Oh, this I've got to see. It's past time that Wyrm got his comeuppance."

Cerberus swam away without further comment, so Voria continued toward the planet. She needed to formulate a real plan. Olyssa was still the most logical starting point. If she could get the lay of the land, so to speak, she might be able to piece together Inura's location. His workshop seemed like a great starting point, though never having been there, she was going to have to rely on Nara to find it.

The atmosphere bubbled up around her as Voria descended toward Olyssa's spire, visible even from high orbit. She moved slowly and made no attempt to cloak her approach. Quite the opposite. She hoped a giant goddess of light would cause a stir. She wanted these Wyrms to take her seriously, and who knew? Perhaps one could carry word back to Inura that she'd arrived.

Though, she had to admit, odds were good that he knew already, but didn't care.

As Voria descended, Wyrms began to rise from the surface. Just a few, at first, but more and more the lower she came. By the time she reached lower atmosphere thousands of Wyrms, and even hatchlings, had taken to the skies. They swirled around her in a lazy cloud, all watching to see what she would do.

It reminded her of a Kem'Hedj board somehow, which shouldn't surprise her given that this was the last place she'd played.

She descended lower, until she recognized one of the Wyrms. Olyssa spread mighty wings, her white scales gleaming as she climbed toward Voria.

Voria paused, and waited there as her—well, if not a friend, at the very least an ally—approached. Olyssa was tiny beside her, and flapped to a halt a few kilometers before Voria's face.

"Welcome, Voria," Olyssa roared, her voice magically amplified so that it cracked over the land like thunder. "I can see that your circumstances have...changed since our last encounter."

"Indeed they have," Voria replied, amplifying her voice in a similar manner. "I've learned the true purpose of the *Spellship*. It is designed to elevate a god, and once created, to empower them in combat."

She extended her arm, and the *Spellship* landed in her palm. She ignited it, though with less magic than she'd use in combat. Voria twirled the staff a few times, then allowed the blades to wink out. She released the *Spellship*, and it moved to stationary orbit over Olyssa's spire.

"I've heard that you battled Krox." Olyssa flapped once and almost smiled. "You turned him away, and that is promising. It suggests that we should deal with you as an equal, as I've been trying to convince the council."

"I apologize for asking this." Voria tensed as she got to the business at hand. She hated being in someone else's debt. "The sector is in dire peril. The kind of peril that will mean calling for your mother to wake. Inura is already here, and it is him that I'm presently seeking."

"And just what is so urgent to warrant this heresy?"

boomed a new voice, a voice she recognized. Aurelius winged into the air, larger than Olyssa, but still comically small next to Voria.

Voria considered whether there was any value in concealing the knowledge, but couldn't think of a reason. So she told the truth. "Krox is more powerful than ever, but that isn't why I've come. Nefarius will be reborn soon, and as I understand it Virkonna will stop at nothing to prevent that."

"That isn't for you to decide," Aurelius roared.

Voria expected Olyssa to protest that, and could already see her opening her mouth to speak.

She fell silent when the air begun to hum and pop near Aurelius. A moment later Drakkon appeared, and his size made apparent just how young both Aurelius and Olyssa were. They were child-sized beside him, no larger than toddlers.

"Nor is it for you to decide," Drakkon roared. He spun in the air above them. "Any of you. Your mother, my aunt, is needed. We have come to ensure she is aware of the looming threat, before your world is stripped from you, as mine was. Even now the twisted creations of Nefarius devour my mother's essence. Our enemies grow stronger, while my wayward cousins spend time preening and scheming. The time for that has ended, Aurelius. Now, we are one dragon-flight, and unless you seek to challenge, I claim dominance."

Aurelius's tail swished, and he eyed Drakkon thoughtfully. "You being here changes much, cousin. You, I will follow. If you say my mother must be raised, then we will do all we can to aid you."

Aurelius nodded deferentially, and Drakkon's aggressive posture softened.

"We should allow Voria to rest and refresh herself,"

Olyssa boomed. "When she is ready we will hold a party to celebrate her arrival, and then we will see how we might aid her."

Voria wasn't ready for another one of their blasted parties, but she smiled anyway. "Wonderful. I will see you this evening."

27

QUESTIONS WITHOUT ANSWERS

Frit was blessedly insulated from the world at large, which was a relief after the events that had played out at Colony 3. She didn't have to worry about whatever Voria was doing on Virkon. She didn't even need to leave the ship, which meant that so far as she was concerned it didn't really matter what world they were orbiting.

The battle on Marid had been tense, of course. Frit had prayed alongside everyone else, and genuinely believed in Voria. It had been enough to survive, though not enough to overcome the enemy, apparently.

After that brief moment of excitement it was right back to her usual routine, which boiled down to about sixteen hours a day reading.

This time when Frit headed for the main library it wasn't to grab an armload of books and flee back to her quarters. She was here to get specific answers, and doing that was going to require the help of the most experienced true mage she knew.

Frit threaded through the tables and shelves, slowly

canvassing the room as she sought Kaho. The Krox was very difficult to miss, but he also tended to like hiding in corners, as he didn't like being noticed any more than Frit did.

She found him in a small alcove with a pair of over-stuffed chairs. Because of their magical construction they were able to accommodate Kaho's bulk, and he lounged comfortably with a knowledge scale in one palm. Data scrolled above it in a small illusion, and Kaho's eyes moved back and forth as he read.

He didn't notice Frit until she sat down in the chair next to him, and he gave a rather comedic start. "Oh! Frit. You startled me. I was engrossed in Eggenberger's account of the death of Shivan."

Frit smiled and propped a foot up on the table. "I like watching you read, sometimes. Your lips move. It's endearing."

"I'm glad you approve." He returned the smile, though he seemed skeptical. "It's good to see you. I haven't wanted to pry, as you've seemed like you wanted your space. Plus, I've had a lot to think about." The smile faded, and serious Kaho returned.

"I have too. I want to ask your help with something." Frit bit her lip and considered how best to approach this. "I want to better understand flame reading, so I can examine the future better. I've watched Voria with her godsight and she can literally see outcomes before she commits to an action. That seems like a depths of an advantage." One she could use to see how things turned out if she accepted Nebiat's offer.

Kaho rose with a grunt, and rubbed at his backside. "My tail fell asleep." He grinned at her sheepishly. "Not exactly the terrifying Wyrm. Anyway, I know where the flame reading section is. Many of the knowledge scales were recorded by the same unidentified scribe, and she seems to possess a singular command of both godsight and flame reading. I suspect we can begin there."

He led her between rows of shelves, and hummed to himself as he navigated toward a solitary shelf against the far wall. Kaho picked up a scarlet scale, and offered it to her. "This is her first treatise, and they go on from there. I don't even know how many volumes there are as I just got through that one before getting sidetracked. If I possessed *fire* magic I'd probably be more interested."

Frit accepted the scale and slid it into her satchel. She hesitated. Kaho was more likely than anyone else to have insight on Nebiat's problem with Krox. He could give her a starting point, at the very least. She still wasn't certain how she intended to answer Nebiat, but privately she admitted the offer was tempting. And she figured that having the knowledge wasn't the same thing as passing it on. Research wasn't wrong, so she hadn't done anything. Yet.

"I have another esoteric topic I was hoping to understand better," Frit asked, trying to manage a flirtatious smile, but having no idea if she succeeded. She'd never actually flirted before. "You know more about gods than anyone I know. I want to understand them better, particularly how they are formed...and how one might be...dissolved I guess."

Kaho's reaction puzzled her. He stiffened, and his irises narrowed to slits. Even his scent grew more acrid, and when he spoke his tone was brittle. "You've been speaking with Nebiat, haven't you?"

Frit froze like prey. How did he know? What had she said that had given it away? Well, there was nothing for it now. Her shoulders slumped.

"Yes," she admitted. "She came to me and offered to make me her guardian. She's agreed that if I accept I won't be asked to harm my friends. She's asked for help with a problem, and—wait, why are you laughing?"

Kaho's demeanor had changed yet again, and now he was chuckling. He raised a hand apologetically. "I'm sorry. It's just that she came to me two days ago with the same offer. She wanted to make me her guardian. I refused. I'll admit that the offer was tempting, but I don't trust her and you shouldn't either. It doesn't matter how good the offer is...there's a hook we're not seeing."

"But..." She struggled to suppress the tears, and only partially succeeded. Hot flame leaked down one cheek. "I was hoping you'd come with me. That we could start over on her world. Could help lead our peoples. It would mean having a purpose again. Having friends and family. Not being outsiders like we'll always be, as long as we stay here."

Kaho gave a sympathetic nod, then rested a scaled hand on her shoulder. "I understand your pain, and your desire for belonging. I share them. But I have made my choice, and do not take the vow I swore lightly. I must support Voria to the end, and I'm fairly certain she's the only god in the sector not looking to actively enslave mortals anyway. My mother? Frit, if you decide to accept her offer I will understand, but...I can't go with you."

Frit seized his hand in both of hers, and stared up at him, her stomach full of razorblades and acid. "I don't want to leave you behind."

"Maybe it doesn't have to be that bad," Kaho offered. He drew her into a hug and she relaxed against his waist. "If you accept you will be able to translocate. You can come and go as you please, and could probably still remain here. I won't reveal your secret, unless you place Nara or Voria in danger, of course."

"I'd never do that." Frit disengaged, and found her

resolve. "I'm going to speak with Nebiat one more time, then I'll make my decision. If I do decide to...take what she's offering, well, I'll still be around. I know you can't come with me, but I can still see you from time to time."

He beamed a kind smile down at her. "I'd like that, Frit. If we're both immortal, then we have plenty of time to find each other in the way I'm hoping for. I'll miss you. I do have one more piece of advice, though. Tell Nara, and soon. She's been hurt too many times, and she will understand even if she doesn't like it."

"I'll—". She was going to say 'I'll do it,' but she wasn't certain yet that she would. "I'll think about it."

28

REUNION

After hastily saying goodbye to Astria with assurances that he'd be in contact, Aran headed back to his quarters and triggered a missive to Voria. There was a momentary lump in his throat as he waited for her to accept, because Aran remembered the missive on Shaya, when he'd realized she'd been killed. Thankfully it connected instantly, and showed Voria's familiar face, elegant and dignified.

There was nothing to suggest she was a powerful goddess, beyond a soft golden glow.

"Ahh, Captain." Voria delivered a warm smile that his old commanding officer would never have indulged in. "It's damned good to see you, Aran. Are you in a position to pay a visit to the *Spellship*?"

"I don't see why not. Just give me a bit to grab—"

"No need," she broke in.

There was a swirl of violet energy around Aran, and he winked out of existence. When the teleport completed, Aran was standing in an unfamiliar room, though there were some familiar faces, at least.

Nara, Pickus, and Voria stood in a rough triangle near a large mirror. The mirror bobbed slowly up and down, while continuously rotating at the same time. It reminded him a little of a ship's matrix, except that he could feel an ocean of power contained within the mirror. *Fire* and *dream*, in equal measures.

Voria stood the closest, wearing her divinity like a second set of clothes, the *life* radiating faintly from her skin and hair in a way that hadn't been clear on the scry-screen. Pickus stood behind her in a dark uniform, looking every inch the commanding officer.

It was Nara who caught his attention though. She wore a simple set of dark-blue scholar's robes, but Aran could see her Zephyr armor peaking up over the neckline. She was ready for a fight, as always. Her hair had been left loose, and was a bit longer than last time Aran had seen her, now spilling a few inches past her neck.

"Hey." He smiled at Nara. "You look good." Then Aran realized with a start that they were all staring at him. "I mean you all look good, especially you, Voria. Divinity suits you."

Voria barked a short laugh then gave a self-deprecating eye roll. "I'm not certain I agree, especially not after what happened at Ternus."

Aran blinked a few times. "I take it you weren't successful."

Voria folded her arms, and her face folded down into the stern commander Aran had come to know. "Worse. Another god, or something just as powerful, opened a Fissure and destroyed the planet just as I was about to save her people. Someone wanted me to fail, and ensured that I did. This move effectively ended my relationship with Ternus."

Aran's hand tightened around Narlifex, and the sword

pulsed its smoldering anger. It was so frustrating dealing with unknown enemies. He turned to Nara. "There can't be that many beings capable of destroying a full planet. You're the only one of us who's met Talifax, and from what I understand he's a god in his own right. Do you think it was him?"

"He's the leading suspect." Nara shivered at the mention of his name, but her resolve seemed unshaken. "It's also possible it could have been an unknown, or even a player like Malila. We have no idea what her ultimate motivations are, after all."

"Good point." Aran nodded. "I wouldn't have even considered her as a candidate, but she might have the raw power, and she has no love for Ternus after our visit."

Voria's countenance hardened, though Aran could sense the turbulence underneath. Something was bothering her, even more than what had happened at Ternus. He considered asking, but waited to see if she'd volunteer the information.

After a few moments though, the major—he still thought of her that way—reached back and touched her bun, the radiant *life* energy surging just a bit as she did. "I haven't told you the worst of it. After Ternus...well, that was all the justification Governor Austin needed to declare full war on the sector's Catalysts. He began with Marid, citing that it is a Ternus colony, and therefore their property."

"Wait, but Drakkon is there. There's no way that..." Aran trailed off as he saw the sorrow in all three expressions. Even Pickus seemed to have been impacted. "Is Drakkon dead?"

"No, thank the goddess," Voria explained. She shook her head sadly. "The black ships drained most of the *water* Catalyst there, and as I understand it Marid was incredibly powerful. They drained a lot of magic. I was able to siphon some, and Drakkon did as well, but the bulk of it belongs to our enemies now. And I don't say enemies lightly. Ternus considers us as viable targets to drain; of that I have no doubt. They'd love to get their hands on my *life* magic, or Inura's."

Aran shuddered at the thought. The mirror spun again, and he glanced at its shining surface as it passed. He could feel its siren song calling to him, daring him to connect and probe its secrets. He stubbornly refused to give in. If Eros had struggled with this thing, who knew what damage he could do using it?

"I don't doubt it," Aran muttered. He shifted his attention to Voria. "And this makes waking Virkonna even more important. We need her, and we need Inura. Without them..."

Nara reached out a hand, and rested it briefly on Aran's shoulder. She squeezed it, and looked him in the eye. "We'll get them. I have to believe that."

"Well, we'd better," Pickus broke in with a nervous laugh. "'Cause after seeing Krox I don't even want to know how bad this Nefarius chick is."

Voria waved a hand in front of the mirror, and it resolved into a view of Virkon. "I can sense Inura on this world, somewhere. Unfortunately, I'm going to need to play nice with Olyssa. I've agreed to attend one of her blasted parties. I thought it best so I can take the measure of our possible allies."

Aran was mildly surprised that she was willing to explain this much of her plan. He'd expected her becoming a goddess to make her more uptight, but the opposite seemed to have happened.

Voria suddenly cocked her head as if hearing a voice none of them could. Then she shook her head with a sudden smile. "I am not telling him that. Aran, Shaya has great admiration for your accomplishments."

"Shaya?" Aran raised an eyebrow.

"The shade of Shaya was left behind to guide me, apparently. She's very, ah, colorful, but also wonderfully informative."

"Like the shade of Inura," Aran realized aloud. He turned to Nara. "Speaking of, that seems like the best starting place. Can you remember how to get back to the place where you found the *Spellship*?"

She nodded and brushed her hair from her face. "I was thinking the same thing. We can get there quickly, and if Inura is there we can ask him to meet with Voria. If not, at least we can speak to the shade and see if we can't glean his whereabouts."

"It's as good a plan as any." Voria heaved a put-upon sigh as she gazed at the mirror. "I have a feeling you'll have more fun traipsing through caverns than I will at this party."

29

BACK TO NORMAL

Aran met Nara in the predawn chill hanging over the outskirts of the town where Astria lived. The cobblestone streets would have been at home in some ancient society on a primitive planet, as would the squat adobe buildings. These people lived with almost nothing, all under the shadow of fear brought by their draconic masters.

"This way," Nara whispered as she started down a steep hillside toward a narrow crevice in the rock that Aran hadn't noticed.

He noted that she didn't use magic, so he followed her lead. He hopped nimbly down the slope, which his spellarmor made trivial even without gravity magic. Nara nearly faded out of sight as she entered the shadowed crevice, and he struggled to keep track of her as he followed.

"Does that suit have some sort of stealth magic?" he whispered once they were safely inside the cavern.

Nara raised a hand and clipped a halogen light to her collar. "I haven't fully puzzled out how it works, but it's a very subtle magic designed to make the eye slide off. I don't think it will attract any of the snakes down here."

"Snakes?" Aran asked, more in interest than fear.

"All sorts of primals are drawn to Virkonna," Nara explained as she picked an unerring darkness over the gravel-strewn path. Theirs weren't the first sets of foot-steps, but they were the first in a while. "The smallest are simple snakes, but the older ones are massive, and there are drakes besides." She gave a soft laugh, but didn't elaborate.

"What's funny?" Aran called softly as he crept after her. "And why aren't we using any magic?"

"What's funny," Nara explained with another soft laugh, "is how terrified I was the last time I came through here. So much has changed. We're so much stronger, and the prob-lems we had back then feel so trivial compared to what we're facing now. As for magic, the primals are drawn to it, so if we avoid using it we should encounter far fewer. They shouldn't be any sort of threat, but I figure why take chances?"

"Makes sense." Aran fell into step next to her as the passage widened, and he stared up at the sloped ceiling, which disappeared into the darkness high above. He slowed, and realized that he felt something. Something immense. "Below us. Do you feel that?"

Nara paused, and gave a sympathetic nod. "She's so powerful. I know we haven't talked much about relative strength, but Voria's is maybe ten percent of Virkonna's? I guess it's hard to know for sure."

"It's interesting being able to quantify a goddess." Aran stepped over a boulder, and noticed a tiny blue snake that slithered under it. He had no doubt there were others he couldn't see. "And I'd agree that Virkonna is the 'heavy'.

We're going to need her to go toe-to-toe with Krox or Nefarius, I imagine."

They walked a little further in silence, and the corridor widened into a true cavern even as it continued to slope down. Eventually Nara fell into step with him and they walked together in comfortable silence. It was the most normal things had been since the last time they'd been on Virkon.

"Aran?" Nara finally broke the silence, right after they'd paused to break out some rations. In this case, it was one of the protein bars they still had from the supplies that had been loaded onto the *Talon* when they'd taken possession of it. The chocolate chip cookie dough one wasn't half bad, though he didn't know what half those words were referring to.

"Hmm?" He set his helmet on the rock next to him, and ripped a mouthful off the end of the bar.

"What happened to you out there? I mean, if you can talk about it." Nara eyed him sidelong, those brown eyes just as mesmerizing as ever. If only things could be different.

"I don't know." Aran popped the rest of the bar in his mouth, then crumpled the wrapper and put it into his void pocket. He didn't speak again until he was done chewing, and he took his time at that. "We went inside Krox, and I used the ability that Xal gave me. I used it again when we were leaving Shaya and the Inurans ambushed us."

Nara nodded, and neatly folded her own wrapper, then tucked it into a plastic bag, which she tucked into her void pocket. She looked up at him. "We got your warning about the Inurans in the depths. It sounded like you won that engagement, though. Did something go wrong?"

"Maybe." He thought back to the feeling of exultation when he'd drawn the magic from the black ship. "I drank the magic from one of their ships in the same way they take it. And you should have seen the way the crew looked at me. I can't blame them. How am I different than those black ships? And how is Xal really different from Nefarius? Is working for him going to end up in bringing a different evil, dominating god to power? And how do we put the power back in the hands of mortals? I've got a lot of questions, and very few answers."

Nara gave a quick, musical laugh. "It feels like all we have are questions. I don't have answers, not about your ability or about our role in things. More and more I think Malila was telling the truth. Xal was the one who put us into play, and ultimately I think we're dancing to his tune. I just have no idea what that means."

"Guess we just focus on one task at a time." Aran rose with a stretch. "Shall we?"

She nodded, then shouldered her pack and started back up the trail, which threaded ever downward. "We'll reach a large cavern soon. That's where Wes and I had to use his pistols to distract them." She chuckled, but Aran didn't get the joke. "You had to be there I think." Nara offered Aran a more playful smile, one he hadn't seen in a long time. "I'm glad Voria sent us. It's nice catching up. I know things are... tainted between us. But I'd like to think we're still allies, and maybe friends." The last word had a question in it, and it forced Aran to finally ask it.

Could they be friends? Or even more someday? Maybe, if they lived that long. Which seemed incredibly unlikely. May as well enjoy the time they had left.

"We're definitely friends." Aran nudged her with his elbow. "Plus I've seen you naked."

Nara rolled her eyes. "I guess I walked into that one." She smiled at least, and that brightened the situation.

30

LEAVE ME BE

Aran stared down into the belly of the world, a seemingly endless cavern that stretched off in all directions, supported by immense pillars of varying sizes, stalagmites and stalactites that had grown together over the eons when this world was forming.

"We're beneath her, aren't we?" he asked, staring up at the ceiling, which vaulted into darkness high above them. He could feel the low, deep siren song of Virkonna's *air* magic.

Nara nodded, and her voice was small as she moved to stand at the edge of the cliff with Aran. "The facility we're after was built to capitalize on that. They built it under Virkonna so her signature would mask it. I think Inura built the place after she went into torpor."

She turned to face him, and her eyes widened slightly in a way Aran recognized. It usually meant she'd realized something that she considered obvious, though that was seldom the case.

"I think we can teleport from here," she explained, gesturing toward the far end of the cavern, where it disappeared in the distance. "I can manage that far fairly easily, and it will be much faster than navigating our way through this mess. Are you ready?"

She raised a hand and Aran nodded. Nara deftly sketched a trio of *void* sigils, which quickly fused into a teleportation spell. The world warped and folded around Aran, and when it stopped he was standing in a narrow stone corridor quite unlike the rest of the caverns they'd passed through. This place had clearly been constructed, and the walls were lined with endless glyphs. They glowed with a faint inner light, and Aran could feel the magic in them—weak, but persistent.

"Are they wards?" he asked, bending to inspect the closest set.

"I don't think so." Nara inspected the same set, the glow painting her in a ghostly light. "I think they tell a story."

"Indeed they do," came a dry Inuran voice, the accent unmistakable. "I see you have returned. Welcome, Nara of the Confederacy, though I imagine that title might be outdated."

Narlifex was out of his scabbard and in a guard position before Aran even realized what he was doing. The being before him looked human at first glance, but only at first glance. The leathery wings extending over his shoulders put the lie to that, as did the faint scales covering his skin. He looked much like Olyssa in her 'human' form, save that this being had what appeared to be real hair, long and white, with thin, fine strands.

"Shinura?" Nara straightened and faced the newcomer.

"Indeed." Shinura gave Nara a low bow. "And I must thank you again for that moniker. I find that I very much enjoy having a real name."

"Aran, this is the shade of Inura. I told you about him. We call him Shinura for short."

Aran sheathed Narlifex and approached Shinura, who stood before a pair of double doors, which had apparently opened silently when he'd appeared.

"Be welcome, Hound of Xal." Shinura executed a perfect bow, then gave a truly alarming smile, filled with the razored teeth he'd come to expect from Wyrms. "This is the crucible, and for the first time in millennia the forge fires are lit once more. The master has returned, and is crafting something marvelous."

"Inura is here?" Aran found himself tensing, despite the fact that Inura was supposed to be an ally. Ternus was supposed to be an ally too, but look where that had gotten them.

Shinura nodded, then stepped through the double doors. "Please, follow me into the facility. I will guide you to the master." The construct, if that's what Shinura was, strode purposefully up the hallway, and into a workshop the likes of which Aran could scarcely have imagined.

Golden devices lined the first chamber, most set on large tables and surrounded by a dizzying array of tools he didn't recognize. Nearly everything in the room glowed with some sort of enchantment, the most prevalent aspects being *air* and *life*, closely followed by the *earth* that had been used to construct the metallic parts.

"This way, please." Shinura plunged between a final pair of tables, then through a doorway and into a corridor lined with golden walls. Every few moments a pulse of blue-white light veined across the walls, then disappeared.

The shade led them down the corridor, past several more rooms filled with experiments, and finally stopped outside a room not unlike the others, save that it was occupied. Two men stood next to a large stall, which had been erected to hold a stylized suit of mecha. The metallic knight glowed gold, and Aran could feel the potency of the magic wafting over him, barely contained by the armor.

The closest of the two men bore wings similar to Shinura. In fact, those wings were identical. Nor were they the only parts. The being before him looked, on the surface at least, like an identical twin to Shinura.

"Inura," Aran called, plunging past Shinura, into the room with the mecha. He barely noticed the second man, until that man swept him up in a hug.

"Brother!" Kazon roared, his bushy beard scraping against the collar of Aran's spellarmor as he lifted Aran into the air. "You are the last person I expected to see."

"Kazon!" Aran returned the hug, then stepped back and took a look at the barrel-chested Inuran. Kazon's beard was longer than it had been, but the coarse black hair had been combed into a tight knot just below the chin.

He wore robes of shimmering silver cloth, that seemed to catch the light around them, drinking it in rather than reflecting it. Aran wasn't sure what magical properties the garment possessed, but he could feel the strength of it, though it was a tiny thing compared to the mecha, or to Inura himself.

Inura hadn't looked up from the mecha, and was deeply focused on a part near the knee, where he was using an unfamiliar golden tool to add *life* magic to the metal.

"Deal with them, Kazon," the god muttered, though his attention never left the mecha.

"Please, we shouldn't be in here," Shinura said, wringing his long, delicate fingers. "If you'd like I can provide refreshment. This way."

Shinura darted from the room, and Kazon began to

follow, so Aran did as well. Nara looked as if she wanted to stay and speak to Inura, but reluctantly followed them back up the corridor and into a room with four small tables. Aran recognized the golden triangle with the little box beneath it...the food thingie, or some version of it.

Nara entered the room, and moved to sit with Aran. Her eyes moved continuously, the hawkish intelligence clear as she categorized everything. Nara could probably accomplish a lot with a facility like this, if anyone gave her the time. She said nothing of course, which was fairly typical in Aran's estimation.

"Aran, it is so good to see you. How is my sister?" Kazon asked, as he slid into one of the seats. His grin hadn't slipped a millimeter.

"She's...well, she's a goddess." Aran could only shrug at that. "A goddess badly outclassed by the opposition, and in need of the kind of help only Inura can provide. We're here to wake Virkonna, and to ask Inura to actually help for a change instead of lurking in shadows. Planets are dying. Ternus is...gone."

"I know." Kazon's expression darkened, and guilt seemed to creep in. "It is true that Inura doesn't appear to be doing much, and that by extension I am not either. I assure you, however, that is not the case. Inura's work is of the utmost importance. This mech is his crowning achievement, and he believes we will need it if we are to triumph over our enemies. I don't know what he intends, exactly, but I believe his urgency is sincere. Inura never stops running from task to task, as if his time is nearly over."

Aran suppressed the hot flash of anger, and tried to be rational. It wasn't easy. He leaned across the table, and spoke quietly. "If we can't wake Virkonna, and if Virkonna won't fight, then we've lost, Kazon. You were the one who told me about Skare, and about the black ships. Since then I've seen them fight. And I've seen them drain the magic from a god. Even Krox wasn't immune. We don't have time for empty promises, and I don't see how a single suit of armor, no matter how large or powerful, is going to help us stave off annihilation."

"I realize that, but—"

"No buts." Aran rose from his chair and headed back toward the room Inura was working in. He made it to the doorway, but found Shinura there blocking his path.

"I'm sorry, but I cannot allow you to disturb the master. His work is of paramount importance." The shade had slid into a combat stance, which told Aran everything he needed to know. This guy wasn't going to budge, unless Aran moved him. Moving him would involve violence, and that did not seem like a good answer.

"Let me speak plainly," Aran offered, leaning in a bit closer. "I have a mission. I'm not leaving here until I speak with Inura. He can keep working, but he does need to at least address my questions. If you try to stop me from doing that, then things are going to get ugly and we're going to have to mess up this entire room. Do you really want to inflict that kind of damage on the facility? If you're a replica of a god, you know who I am and what I can do."

Shinura's wings drooped behind his back, and he wrung his hands. "You are putting me in a very uncomfortable position. But I agree with your logic. You may speak with him, but I'm going to wait here and pretend like you over-powered me."

Nara gave a soft chuckle at that, and even Aran managed a grim smile. He girded himself in his anger and headed back to Inura's workshop. The god hadn't moved, and was still adding more magic to the right knee joint.

"I can see that you're not going to leave me be." The god's tone carried his irritation, and he finally glanced up at Aran. The instant those slitted irises met his gaze he saw the very last thing he'd have expected. Fear. "Your kind have always been bullies, and I see that hasn't changed, dog. Ask your questions quickly, so that I can return to the work that will save us all."

"I know you're busy," Aran offered apologetically. He raised his hands, palms out. "We need to wake Virkonna. You know why, I'll wager. Just tell me how to do that, and I'll get out of your hair."

"Voria," Inura snapped. His attention had already gone back to his work. "She'll need to wake my sister. I don't have the time. She has both the power and the knowledge, if she applies herself. Instances like this are one of the primary reasons I elevated her, after all."

"That's it?" Aran asked. "You're just going to pass the responsibility, and assume Voria will figure it out?"

There was no answer.

Aran turned to Nara, who was leaning against the doorway, watching. He raised an eyebrow, but she shook her head. Aran considered whether there were any more important questions, and decided it would be pointless anyway.

They had the only answer they were likely to get.

31

PARTY CRASHER

Voria was damnably tired of parties, and she hadn't even attended her first one since becoming a goddess. But she had little choice save to play their blasted political games. This planet was the fulcrum on which the entire sector's fate turned. The idea of discussing that fate in snippets of conversation around bits of finger food was so damned inefficient.

In the end it was Drakkon who convinced her to see reason. If she truly wanted to build a religion she needed to earn their respect at the very least. Their allegiance was too much to hope for, but if they were willing to oppose Nefarius, Krox, or both, then they'd make strong allies.

"Are you ready?" Drakkon called from the doorway to Voria's quarters.

She rose from the desk she'd been sitting in when Nara had killed her. Voria had made her body solid, but it didn't feel like a body. She wasn't the woman who'd lived in these quarters. She didn't even need sleep, much less have a heartbeat.

"As ready as I'll ever be." Voria mustered a smile. "I'm

focusing on the positive. At least we'll get to awe them a little bit."

Drakkon smiled, though the wisps of white in his liquid hair and the lines around his eyes prevented it from warming her too much. He raised a hand, and Voria didn't resist as he translocated them. The ability had a cool-down period before it could be used again, which she'd timed at about three hours, for her anyway. Was that different for every god? She made a mental note to find out as it could be important.

They appeared near the center spire, where Olyssa was already holding court. Perhaps two dozen Wyrms stood in clusters, all within easy earshot. Many were oriented toward Aurelius, perhaps even more than Olyssa, despite it being her party. The power balance had certainly shifted since the last time Voria had been here.

"Ah, welcome." Olyssa swept forward, a too-wide smile looking even more out of place with her bald head. The utterly hairless Wyrms were disquieting at least in part because they were so similar, yet entirely different from humanity. "This is the first time in many, many centuries that I have had a goddess grace one of my parties." She inclined her head to Drakkon next. "Cousin. It has been even longer since we've last spoken."

Drakkon gave a friendly grin. "Little 'yssa. I still remember when you were just a hatchling and you couldn't pronounce your full name."

She gave a throaty, inhuman laugh. "And you were the stalwart warrior, always off to war with mother against some grave threat." Something flitted across her features. Sadness maybe. "There were tragedies in the past, but there were also victories and celebrations. I hope those will come again now that you have returned."

"Why *have* you returned, cousin?" Aurelius boomed as he strode over. The taller Wyrm moved to stand near Drakkon, but there was nothing aggressive in his stance and he kept his hand far from the hilt of his spellblade.

Drakkon's expression hardened. A goblet floated over to his hand and he crunched it into uselessness, then flung it at the ground. "The humans are rising up. They came for me on Marid. They killed my offspring, and nearly killed me. They would have if not for Voria. In the end we salvaged but a scrap of Marid's power. The rest belongs to puppets of Nefarius."

"Nefarius?" Olyssa clutched her hands to her breast, and for a moment Voria feared she might flee. "Surely you must be mistaken. Nefarius is dead, and has been for countless centuries."

"Nefarius may be dead," Voria said grimly, "but Talifax is not. I've seen first hand how powerful Talifax is. He's expertly guided Ternus into a war against us, all to power up magical artifacts they'll no doubt use in the ritual to raise their goddess. They gained *spirit* when fighting against Krox. They've claimed *water* from Marid. If they decide that *air* would be a useful addition, then you may find yourself in a war you are unable to win."

Aurelius began to laugh, and many other Wyrms took it up.

An unquiet rage roiled in her gut, or where her gut would have been if she'd still had a body. "Is there something particularly comical about the news I've just delivered?"

"You believe humans can overcome the last dragon-flight?" Olyssa sounded as if the idea were the most preposterous she'd ever heard. "Respectfully, if they come for us we will crush their vessels, devour their leadership, and then savage their worlds."

"Will you, cousin?" Drakkon roared. He stalked over to her, and his eyes promised swift death. So much so that Voria nearly intervened. Drakkon stopped her with a hand. "Look at me, Olyssa. Really look. I know you all see it. You can feel it. My power has diminished. I am weaker than I was, even after taking a portion of my mother's magic. Had you met me an hour ago that would not have been the case. My power was ripped away by the humans I was forced to run from. Do you think yourself my equal, Olyssa? Do any of you?" He turned in a circle, glaring at anyone willing to meet his gaze.

It didn't appear any of them were, not even Aurelius.

"The humans will come," Drakkon continued. "When they do, if we do not have the full strength of your mother, and the full aid of Inura, then we are doomed. We are likely doomed even with that aid. It is past time we—"

The air popped and spun next to Voria, and she readied a counterspell as a being materialized.

A short, slender Wyrm who only came up to Aurelius's shoulder appeared, but unlike every Wyrm there, long, white hair cascaded down his shoulders, and the divinity pulsed off him in waves.

Inura flexed his wings, and looked around until he spotted Voria. "Ah, there you are. Your vassal has badgered me into offering you remedial instruction on waking my sister. I will offer you a few minutes, but it must occur while I am working. Come with me."

Wyrms genuflected all around her. Some prostrated themselves, pressing their faces against the stone. Even Drakkon sank to one knee, though Voria noted the bitterness in his eyes. Inura had lost whatever friendship might have once been there.

"I'm not going anywhere with you." Voria folded her arms. "You teleported into my chambers, told me to become a goddess, and then vanished to leave me to deal with Krox. Millions of my citizens died in the aftermath, but you were nowhere to be found. I am not your servant. I am your ally. If you wish cooperation, then you must at least explain your plans."

Some of Inura's franticness left him, and he turned his full attention on Voria. He towered over her, though of course she could change that in an instant if she chose to. She did not. She merely waited for Inura's answer.

"You are every bit as stubborn as she was." He shook his head sadly. "I suspect it's merely a defect in your species, one I have neither the time nor inclination to repair. We do not have time for your petulance. My sister must be woken, and you need to do the waking. Now come with me to the crucible, and I will teach you what you need to do."

"Recently," Voria continued as if the Wyrm-god hadn't spoken, "I attempted to save our allies, the very humans who assaulted Marid. While there, Talifax acted openly, and doomed an entire world. I could do nothing to stop him. I am out of my depth and you offer no guidance. No aid. All you ever do is demand. I'm here to tell you, Inura, that we are not your playthings. I am a goddess, and you will treat me as an equal. You will explain your plans, or I will no longer participate in them."

Inura gave an exasperated sigh. "Very well. If you accompany me, I promise I will answer any questions you may have. Is that acceptable?"

"Barely." Voria folded her arms and wished for a universe with no gods.

32

THE CRUCIBLE

O nce Voria had agreed to go with Inura she assumed the matter was settled. She could not have been more mistaken.

Much to her shock, Olyssa stalked over, looming menacingly over Voria. "How dare you speak to the Wyrm Father as if you were in some way equal? You were made from a shred of his power that he chose to give up. There are gods, and there are *gods*. And you are an up-jumped mortal, clinging to the lowest rung of divinity. You are only a short step removed from a *human*."

The way she delivered the term made Voria grateful Aran hadn't been there. He would not have reacted well, and at this point he might have been able to kill Olyssa before anyone stopped him. Voria didn't want the Wyrm dead, but she couldn't condone the casual racism. It was the same sort Thalas had delivered to the drifters, and just as damaging.

Inura gave Olyssa an irritated wave of his hand. "Be quiet, child. It is not your place to speak for me."

The shock and horror on Olyssa's face was the last thing

Voria saw before Inura teleported her elsewhere.

She'd seen enough translocation and teleportation to know the difference. The former had no side effects, but the latter had made her stomach queasy for hours...when she'd had a stomach.

"That wasn't terribly polite," Voria pointed out. "She's going to hold that against me. And Drakkon may be annoyed that you left him behind."

"I don't care." Inura didn't even look at her, and instead hurried through a nearby doorway. "Follow me."

Only in that moment did Voria comprehend their surroundings. The walls were a golden metal, but magic played across them like slivers of azure lightning. She couldn't begin to fathom the magic, or its purpose. This must be the crucible Nara had told her about.

She followed Inura from the chamber, and he led her through a row of darkened workshops before stopping outside the only one with a light inside. He turned to face her, and clasped his hands before him. "I promised you answers. I want to ensure that you get them, so that I can get back to my work uninterrupted. You've no idea how important this final piece is."

"Sister?" Kazon's voice boomed from inside the workshop. A moment later his bearded face appeared, split by an equally massive grin. "He found you! Aran will be so pleased. Come in, come in."

"Still your enthusiasm, disciple." Inura waved absently at Kazon, and she noticed that Inura treated him with a good deal more respect than he'd offered Olyssa. "Your questions, Voria. And I'm aware that Shaya is probably standing there suggesting all manner of juvenile options."

"I totally am," Shaya said, as she shimmered into view, into Voria's view at least. "Well, I would be if I thought you'd say them out loud. I'm just as curious as the lizard to see what you're going to ask."

She stilled her mind and prioritized her questions. There were many, but she considered which one she'd ask if it were the only question the Wyrm would answer. Her choice surprised her. "Ikadra was severely damaged during the ritual of elevation. How can I repair him?"

"An astute question." Inura cocked his head. "Ikadra still has a large role to play. Repairing him will require greater enchanting. You need someone with tremendous *air* and tremendous *life*. After you've performed the task I have in mind for you, you can ask my sister to imbue you with such magic. If you are respectful, the literal opposite of your treatment of me, then she may grant it."

"Don't you possess both *air* and *life*?" Voria demanded.

"Of course I do, and since I know you'll ask...no, I won't fix him. My strength is allocated to another task, one I assure you is far more vital than you believe." Inura's snowy eyebrows knit together, and his ever-present scowl deepened. "You will be quite equal to the task if you can swallow your pride and accept my sister's leadership. You want Nefarius to stay dead, do you not?"

Voria nodded, and waited to see where he was going with this.

"Then work with her. Do as she asks. Kneel before the throne. After Nefarius is dead you might even persuade her to assault Krox. Or, you can go your own way." Inura heaved a put-upon sigh. "I will not be able to change her mind. Virkonna always does as she will. But I can control my own actions. Two more tasks remain. First, I must imbue a guardian. Then, I must complete this eldimagus."

Voria glanced over his shoulder into the workshop where Kazon had been working. A suit of golden mecha, perhaps thirty meters tall, stood in a stall designed for its construction. All manner of tools hovered around different parts of the armor, some feeding the suit magic while others performed some sort of divination.

Why Inura thought such a weapon worthy of his time didn't concern her in the slightest. She wrote it off, as she wrote him off. But the bit about a guardian? That very much interested her. "I've done some reading on guardians."

Inura snorted a laugh. "I'll bet you have. I wonder what claptrap passes as 'lore' these days." He shook his head. "You could make a guardian, theoretically. But in practice I wouldn't recommend it. I mean no disrespect, but you are effectively *my* guardian. The amount of magic I passed you is significant, but if you were to make a guardian they would gain little beyond simple immortality. Save your strength for the battle to come."

Voria gritted her teeth. Not because his words made her angry, but rather the opposite. Because they rang true. She wanted to imbue Nara with the kind of power that would make her a near equal, but it sounded like she lacked the strength to do that.

"All right." Voria considered her next question. "How do I wake Virkonna?"

"At last." Inura finally perked up, and his tail swished happily behind him. "The ritual is not terribly difficult, and requires a small quantity of *spirit*, a moderate amount of *life*, and an equal amount of *water*." Inura ducked past her into the corridor they'd taken to reach the workshop. "Shinura! Come here."

An identical copy of Inura came sprinting up the corridor, and slid to a halt near the real Inura. "Yes, master?"

"Take Voria to the library. Get her the *Ninth Treatise of Divine Restoration*. She's going to wake my sister."

33

LEGACY

Aran spent the next few days indulging in something he'd not had the time to do in months. Train. Some might argue that the best training was experience, but Aran disagreed, particularly after gaining a new type of magic.

Experience was wonderful, but training, especially sparring against other mages, forced you to think creatively about how you used your powers. It forced you to adapt as other mages did the same, and all of you improved in the process.

When the *Talon* had expanded it had created several new rooms, and he'd commandeered the one next to the hangar as a makeshift gym. A squat rack stood against one wall, and a ring of mats lay in the center of the room.

Right now Aran danced across those mats, Narlifex humming through the air as he executed the very first kata he'd ever learned, one of the memories restored to him by Neith not so long ago. He executed it perfectly, and found comfort in excellence.

After the first kata Aran added *air*, and leapt off the

ground, soaring through the air in precise movements. This too was part of his routine, and he found comfort in the simple magic use. He repeated the next three steps of the kata, each requiring him to twist gracefully in precise measures.

Then Aran got bored. Instead of the usual last twist he shifted his entire body to *air*, and zipped to the far side of the room. He repeated the seventh kata, and this time he used *void* to blink to the far side of the room, ending the movement with a wicked slash that would have decapitated an opponent.

I enjoy this, Narlifex pulsed. *We prepare to kill, but safely, when combat is not dangerous.*

Aran smiled as he twisted into the ninth kata, but added a hop backward where he flung the shattered shards at the end of Narlifex toward an imaginary opponent, a fan of death that would be very lethal in a real situation. Aran snapped up his wrist, and a shield of ice formed. It afforded a different balance, and he shifted from Drakkon stance into a lighter form he'd seen Erica use back on Shaya.

A deep male voice spoke behind him. "You use improvisation. That is a necessary skill for any master, but one that most students cannot approximate."

Aran spun in surprise, and slowly drifted to the ground when he realized who the speaker was. He was taller than Aran, with liquid blue hair that flowed as water would, all down his shoulders. They framed a face most would call perfect, the scales so tiny they might have been pores. Drakkon's slitted eyes stared impassively at Aran, though he inclined his head in an almost imperceptible nod.

"I'm sorry about Marid," Aran offered lamely. No words of his were going to make anything better. "I'm glad you got out alive."

"As am I." Drakkon stepped into the room and extended his left hand. A wide-bladed great sword appeared, the spellblade radiating intense power.

Narlifex gave a wordless growl at the sight of it.

"At first," Drakkon continued as he glided into the first kata, "I wished to end my life. To give my power to Voria, and be done with this endless war of gods. Almost, I took my own life."

Aran said nothing, but shifted into the eleventh kata. He added no flourishes, instead listening to the Wyrm who'd founded the style Aran sought to master. Every motion Drakkon made was perfect, and made more graceful through the use of his wings and tail.

"In that moment I think I finally understood Virkonna, my aunt." Drakkon landed, and sheathed his blade. "I had been mistaken about why she chose torpor. I'd thought she did it because she was weary. Because her mother's death was one loss too many. I'd lost my mother, after all, or so I'd thought. But I hadn't lost Marid, not truly. My mother still existed. She could still be restored, if I could find potent enough magic to do such a thing. But now? Now she is gone. Her essence ripped apart by scores of those cursed ships. Now, I can never bring her back. This is what Virkonna understood. The futility of it all. The idea that no matter what we do, that we cannot overcome our enemies. They are always one step ahead. Always a little bit better."

Aran continued the eleventh kata to completion, then ritualistically sheathed Narlifex, the fragments rapidly reassembling themselves into the end of the blade just before vanishing inside the scabbard. He turned to Drakkon and bowed, and then he squatted down against the wall where he'd left his water bottle.

"So you think it's hopeless then? That's what you're

saying, right?" Aran was surprised at the ice in his own tone. He sounded so cold. So emotionless. That wasn't him. Was it?

"Virkonna certainly did." Drakkon sank down against the wall opposite Aran, and lay his blade against the mat next to him. A rime of frost immediately formed on the blue fabric. "When Nefarius slew her mother, Virkonna realized the full scope of Nefarius's plans. Not just their scope, but their range and depth. Nefarius had planned for everything. She'd seen moments eons from this day, and used her knowledge of the most likely timelines to engineer things in her favor." Drakkon shook his head sadly, his eyes unfocused as only memory can do. "The cost of killing Nefarius was incalculable, and she orchestrated all of it, even her own death. She knew she would need to die, but that when she came back there would be no one strong enough to oppose her. We were too busy worrying about Krox, or encroaching humans, or countless other distractions. Meanwhile Nefarius quietly won the war."

It saddened Aran that Drakkon had given up, and he wished he had the words to make things better. He knew that trying would be a mistake. The Wyrm needed to process his grief, so Aran let him talk, and just listened.

"When I realized that, I nearly went to Voria. That was my lowest moment." Drakkon rose from the wall, and bent to retrieve his blade. "But then I asked myself a question. How do I want to die? It's something you mortals ask yourselves every day. I imagine all of you have an answer. But if you are a true immortal, as Marid has made me, then prudence means we never need ask that question. Gods, and demigods, do not question their legacy, for we are our own legacy. We are eternal. But I realized that my own death is probably near, and I asked myself how I might want to face that death. How might I want to be remembered by the gods and mortals that survive the coming conflict, for there will certainly be those, unless Nefarius's victory is total."

Aran rose as well, and slowly drew Narlifex. He watched as Drakkon moved to the center of the training mat. The Wyrm faced him, and beckoned. Aran stepped onto the mat, and slipped into a guard position.

"My decision, ultimately, is the only one I can make and remain true to who I am." Drakkon smiled then, the sea of teeth showing just how inhuman he really was, much more so than the tail or wings. "Come, Outrider, and dance with me. Give me a month, and I will turn you into the finest swordsman the sector has ever seen. You are the instrument of my vengeance, and while I may not see the end of this current iteration of the godswar, I will ensure that my enemies never forget my name."

Aran gave a yell, and charged.

34

I ACCEPT

The next two days were a special kind of hell for Frit. Even though she hadn't actually done anything wrong she felt like she had. It was too similar to when she'd spied on Eros for Nebiat, and it dredged up all the same feelings. Even remorse over Ree's death, she was shocked to realize.

Frit spent most of her time in her quarters, with occasional trips to gather more knowledge scales. She'd also had several more conversations with Kaho, and he'd been wonderful about providing insight into Nebiat's situation. Unfortunately, he'd pressured her relentlessly to tell Nara what she was considering.

It was so tempting to do exactly that. Nara would probably understand. Probably. But whether she did or didn't, it would put her friend in a difficult position. She'd have to choose between her loyalty to Frit and to Voria, and it wasn't fair to put Nara in that position.

"Child?" A soft voice wafted over her from behind, and she twisted to see Nebiat's spectral form in her quarters. The dreadlord-turned-goddess wore a hopeful expression, her flowing gown as elegant as it was flattering. "Is this a good time? I can come at another, if you wish."

In that moment Frit experienced a revelation, one very similar to something Nebiat had shown her back on Shaya. She'd taken Frit to a sweetshop for her first sticky bun. A dreadlord had casually dined in the capital of her enemies, and now here she was doing it again. Virkon contained at least three gods that Frit knew of, none of whom would react well to Nebiat's presence. Yet the dreadlord seemed utterly unconcerned that she stood in the stronghold of her enemies.

"Now's as good a time as any." Frit rose and approached the specter. She stopped before Nebiat, and eyed the deity searchingly. "I'm assuming you still want to make me your guardian. Have you considered what might happen if I disagree with you? I've done my homework. I can take whatever magic you give me to Voria. That would empower your enemies, and gain you nothing."

"Only if you betray me." Nebiat gave a musical laugh. "Oh, Frit, I so love your candor. I still remember the cafe on Shaya where we shared your first sticky bun. You aren't that girl anymore. You're ready for this. I want you not in spite of your willfulness, but because of it."

Frit paused at that. Leaders like Eros were careful not to keep strong dissenting opinions close to them, but in many ways Nebiat was more crafty. Perhaps she saw the value in a strong subordinate, or perhaps she was just telling Frit what she wanted to hear. "Kaho told me that you approached him first. I'm your second choice."

"And I stand by my first choice, though you shouldn't see that as an insult," Nebiat replied smoothly. "Of course my own son is first, for obvious maternal reasons. You know how intelligent Kaho is, and what he might accomplish in the role. He would bring my children to greatness, whereas you are far more likely to look after your sisters, though you can't be blamed for that."

Frit gave a grudging nod. She couldn't fault any of Nebiat's logic. Kaho would be the best choice, if he was loyal to Nebiat at least. And he would likely favor Wyrms more than she would.

"I don't understand your motivations, and it really bothers me," Frit found herself saying. "You're evil. You wipe out worlds. You tried to destroy Shaya, and killed countless people in the process. Why should I ally with you? It doesn't matter how pretty the dream you're offering if it's all a lie. I know you're capable of being friendly until you get what you want from me, but I also know you'll discard me, and anyone else, without a second thought."

Nebiat listened gravely with her hands clasped before her. "It's important you realize that evil is merely a word used to justify the destruction of one's enemies. The condemnation of our actions is how they dehumanize us. Yet they use exactly the same actions. Let me tell you a story of an evil Ifrit." Nebiat gave a dramatic pause, and a smile as she continued. "There was a girl on Shaya, a slave who served the noble Tender, Eros, hero of Shaya. One day she betrayed Eros to his enemies, foul dragons who seek to slaughter all children, and shave all livestock."

Frit snorted a laugh, despite the gravity of the situation.

Nebiat continued, giving her a wink. "This Ifrit was given the key to her collar, and could have fled on her own. Instead, she created a resistance among her sisters. She convinced nearly forty treacherous Ifrit to betray their noble Shayan masters. They burned several war mages alive during their escape, and later killed more when those brave Shayan pilots were sent to bring the traitors to justice."

"I've heard enough," Frit growled. It hit too close to home. Even Nara blamed her a little for Ree's death. "I see your point. Everything said about you to me is from one of your enemies. But you seem to forget that I'm capable of observing you myself. I watched you during the war. I saw the way you treated Nara and the people you bound. You can't seriously believe that I'll accept you as some magnanimous deity."

Nebiat tilted her head back and laughed. It was a long, loud, freeing sort of laugh. The laugh lines bunched around her eyes as the goddess focused on Frit again. "I think we're going to get along wonderfully, Frit. You know better than any that I am utterly ruthless. You understand my goals and motivations, and know that I will listen to you, even if I do not always do as you ask. You are exactly the same sort of moderating influence my father lacked. Teodros died, not just because he over-reached, but also because he didn't have any allies. He kept his children at arm's length, and used us as fodder. In the end he died for his hubris. I do not wish to make the same fate."

Frit took a deep breath, and exhaled a puff of smoke. She wasn't certain this was the right decision. Part of her screamed that she should talk to Kaho, or Nara, or even Voria. But she'd been over this ground too many times. This decision was hers, and hers alone. It was simple really. Did she stay here as an outsider, miserable, and marginalized, or did she take up the mantle of demigoddess and help shape a culture that would be a home for her people?

It was no choice really, despite needing to ally with the personification of evil she'd grown up fearing. Reconciling propaganda with observation had been difficult, but Frit believed she might know Nebiat better than anyone living. She understood the dreadlord, her sacrifices and her triumphs. If she was wrong, the price was likely to be high, but at least Frit was going in knowing that.

"Very well," Frit intoned, solemnly. "I'm willing to accept your investiture of power. And in exchange I will do everything in my power to help you escape from Krox. However, I will not take any action I disagree with. I will not be your slave, and if you attempt to make me such, you will find me very quickly defecting to your enemies."

"I wouldn't dream of putting you in that position." Nebiat nodded and raised a hand to sketch a sigil. After a moment she lowered the hand, as if suddenly realizing it wasn't needed. "You are making the right decision, Frit. I will give you the power I've offered, and when I am finished I will leave you here to solve my dilemma. You'll have both the power and space to do whatever you wish. First, though, I have one request."

"Oh?" Frit asked suspiciously.

"Come home, Frit." Nebiat took a step closer, and looked as if she wanted to hug Frit. "See the world you will be defending and shaping. Meet your sisters, Frit."

Frit hesitated. She knew that the next words she spoke would dominate her fate forever, but when she spoke them, she spoke them gladly. "Okay. Take me home."

35

FRAMED

Aran rolled his shoulder as he reluctantly crawled from bed. Drakkon had beaten the everliving crap out of him on the mat. Again. But for the first time Aran had actually landed a blow. That showed he was improving, right? In another century or three he might win, if Drakkon was asleep, maybe.

He rose with a grunt and tugged on his uniform. He buckled Narlifex on over it, and the blade thrummed a greeting. It talked more when spoken to, but the blade still rarely initiated a conversation.

Aran exited his quarters and headed to the mess, where there was coffee, a more vital fuel than magic at this point. Davidson was the only one there, and to Aran's immense surprise the stoic blond officer was crying. He glanced up as Aran came in.

"You're gonna want to see this." Davidson wiped at an eye. He shook his head, and nodded at the image playing on his portable viewscreen. "Ternus just did a real hack job on us from a PR angle. So far as they're concerned we're the enemy. That means my folks are gonna get persecuted. Gave birth to a traitor and all that."

Aran ordered his coffee from the food thingie, and moved to sit next to Davidson. "All right. Hit me with it."

Davidson hit the reset button and the newscast started from the top. A pretty blonde reporter announced the story, with the headline *Victory at Marid*. She started with a smile. "We've just received news from Governor Austin himself that Ternus has enjoyed its first victory of the war."

Footage of the battle for Starn played in the background, and Aran winced. He didn't want to remember that battle. It had ended badly, for everyone involved. Draconic Krox gutted starships and slaughtered Marines.

"We discovered a nest of dragons lurking near a resort community on the planet Marid." The smile became a concerned frown, and the reporter's eyes shone with unshed tears. "Our sons and daughters rose to the occasion, but the magic they were up against was...well, I'll let you judge for yourself."

Footage from a Marine's helmet cam played, and showed the ground erupting around them. Then they were sucked down into the swamp, and the camera went dark. The screen cut to a trio of hatchlings tearing apart a tank, and then the people inside.

Something clicked in Aran's head. The newscast hadn't said that these dragons were in any way affiliated with the Krox, but they'd shown some very suggestive footage first. Most viewers would assume the two were one and the same.

The camera changed again, this time to a view from orbit. The reporter shed a single emotionless tear as she spoke again, her expression all empathy. "Casualties were heavy, as they always are when dealing with supernatural monsters. This time, though, Ternus was ready. This time we had an answer to their dark sorcery."

The camera cut to the terrifyingly familiar ships, and majestic music played as the camera slow-panned around the midnight vessels. Smiling young officers, attractive men and women every one, gazed up at the ships, their faces rich with hope.

The ships suddenly zoomed into combat over Marid, and Aran watched as they descended toward Drakkon en masse. Dragon after dragon died, and when the dust had settled, and Drakkon stood alone, only nine ships had been destroyed.

The rest converged on the doomed dragon, and Aran winced. Drakkon fought hard, but there could only be one end.

A flash of white light drowned out the screen, and when it cleared, Voria was there. A literal lady of light, standing protectively over Drakkon. She whirled the *Spellship* and the shining blades sliced through the tendrils the black ships had attached. Drakkon was free!

Voria raised her free hand, and a *life* ward sprang up around her, Drakkon, and the Catalyst itself. The black ships began assaulting the ward, and it immediately began to discolor.

"As you can see," the reporter said, her tone forlorn now, "a woman we thought our ally has chosen to consort with alien powers, rather than help our brave men and women. She protected the dragon lurking in our swamp, one that has no doubt slain countless humans over the centuries it has terrorized that world."

Aran snorted. "Terrorized. Drakkon has been in torpor since before this colony was founded."

"Facts don't much matter to our media." Davidson shook

his head. "Public opinion is far more persuasive. Keep watching."

The dome began to melt, and as it did Voria and Drakkon teleported away. The black ships swooped in, and their tendrils began eagerly drinking the magic.

"The dragon and the traitor Voria fled the scene, leaving our boys to safely dispose of the magic left behind." She shook her head sadly. "I'm told it will be a generation or more before the swamp can be made habitable again, effectively ending tourism to a once vibrant community. In the wake of all the recent tragedies it's almost too much to bear. Our heart goes out to—"

"I don't want to listen to this." Aran spoke over the woman, though the footage was still playing. "This is complete—"

"Many are asking," the reporter continued as the screen filled with an outdated picture of the *Talon*, "where Captain Aran and his Outriders are during all this. They won't be coming to our rescue this time. They've made their choices, and as much as it broke the governor's heart, they have also been declared enemies of the state. All Outriders are to be killed on sight, and are considered extremely dangerous."

As she said the word 'dangerous,' the screen resolved into a darkened view that could have taken place in any planet's umbral shadow. A fleet of Ternus ships engaged a single vessel. His vessel. The *Talon* tore through them, though much of the actual combat had been cut from the footage.

It went straight to the *Talon* seizing one of the ships with its own tendril, and draining the magic from it. The process was horrifying to watch, and it was unmistakable that the *Talon* was the aggressor.

"It appears a man we once revered has been corrupted

by dark powers. It is a sad day indeed." The reporter was suddenly all smiles again, and there was no sign of the tear now. "Our boys will do what they have to do. They're going to eradicate every magical threat in the sector, until our worlds are safe once more. In the meantime, Governor Austin has temporarily moved the capital to Colony 3 in the wake of Voria's treacherous attack on our capital."

Aran sat heavily, and stared down at his coffee. "Man, there are some days when I really, really hate this job."

36

WAR COUNCIL

Aran headed straight back to his quarters, and the instant he reached the scry-screen he triggered a missive to Nara. It connected, and Nara's sleepy face filled the screen. She brushed dark hair from her eyes and covered a yawn. "Another emergency?"

"Not precisely," Aran explained as he began to pace. "If Pickus hasn't shown you yet I'm sure he'll be along presently. Ternus just released a news report showing Voria as the villain, and they included me. They've declared us enemies of the state. Not a surprise, but I figured she'd want to know."

Nara blinked away sleep, and instantly arrived at the same conclusion he had. "Talifax is clearing the board so Voria doesn't have any pieces to work with."

"That's my thought." He scrubbed his fingers through his hair. "I was hoping we could meet and discuss what comes next. I don't need a lot of Voria's time, but I figured you, me, her, and maybe Drakkon. We need to figure out what Talifax's ultimate plan is, and we need to do it soon."

Nara nodded and crossed her chambers, the missive

following over her shoulder. "Hold on a moment, and I'll bring you here."

Aran closed his eyes just in time for *void* magic to settle around him. He very nearly fought it off, memories of Nara as she'd been before tugging at him. He ignored his instincts and relaxed into the teleport. A moment later he appeared in Nara's chambers aboard the *Spellship*.

Once that prospect would have delighted him, but after everything that had happened he wasn't sure he even thought about her like that anymore. Or anyone. He'd effectively cut romance out of his life, because there was never time when running from crisis to crisis.

Nara's quarters resolved around him, and Aran quickly regained his balance.

Nara is the same as we are, Narlifex pulsed. *She is linked to us. I feel her.*

Yeah, she is, he agreed.

"It's good to see you," he said aloud, then smiled. "World's coming apart, as usual."

"It feels like it never lets up." She gave him a smile that was reminiscent of her old self. "Speaking of, can you share more about this crisis or does it make sense to wait until we're with Voria?"

"The short version? We can see what Talifax is doing, and we need to stop it. It's time for a plan. We can't sit back and wait. We need to find the threat and stop it before it comes for us. We can't fight a reactive war." Hearing himself, it didn't sound nearly as compelling as he'd hoped. "The long version is better, I promise."

Nara gave a musical laugh, something Aran realized he missed hearing. It really was good to see her. They continued in silence, but it was a comfortable silence, both of them lost in intense thought. In Aran's case it was about how to approach this council. They needed to all be on the same page for once.

The golden doors to the Chamber of the Mirror stood open as they approached. Voria and Drakkon stood chatting near the Mirror of Shaya, but that stopped as Aran and Nara approached. There was no sign of Pickus, but Aran figured that if he needed to know, Nara or Voria could relay what they discussed.

"It's good to see you, Captain." Voria smiled warmly. "Circumstances are dire as always, of course. What can we do for you?"

Aran rested a hand on Narlifex and tapped the pommel thoughtfully. How best to approach this? Straightforward, as always. "Talifax is manipulating public opinion in Ternus space. He's painted you as the destroyer of their capital, and me as your willing lapdog."

"Yes, I am aware." Voria's glowing eyes tightened, the only sign of anger he was used to seeing from her.

"I've been thinking about the reasoning," Aran continued. "Talifax isn't merely denying you worshippers. I think he's actively positioning Ternus to be Nefarius's power base when she returns."

Drakkon barked a bitter laugh. "That would certainly fit her style, though I don't understand how they'd pull that off. Humans hate magic. They hate gods. I cannot imagine them following one."

"I can." Nara's voice was a near whisper. She eyed each of them before speaking. "Talifax is smart. Ternus trusts technology, not magic. To them these ships are technology, even if they're powered by magic. Those black ships are giving Ternus an edge, and he's teaching the people to put their faith in them. We know the ships are tainted. Does that mean that, in a way, the people are worshipping her by worshipping the ships?"

Voria cocked her head as if listening to someone they couldn't see. "Shaya doesn't believe so. I think worship needs to be consciously directed at an entity for a god to make use of it. The worshipper needs to intend to give you that power."

Nara nodded as she processed the information. "Then I don't see how Talifax is going to pull this off. But that doesn't matter. We know he's turning our former allies, and that we're now fighting a two-front war."

"Ternus is recovering quickly, too," Aran pointed out. "The factories at New Texas are coming back online, and Colony 3 never stopped producing. And while I noticed their PR machine didn't mention it, they've also got New Ternus as a resource. You give them a year or three and they'll be right back to the same strength they were before."

"Greater," Voria said. "Much greater. Before, they were not backed by a goddess."

"Speaking of, where do we stand on waking Virkonna?" Aran asked. "Having another god might be more trouble than it's worth, but at this point I'll take all the help we can get."

Voria squared her shoulders, and the golden halo around her brightened noticeably. "Inura has given me enough information to wake her, but was maddeningly light on the specifics, of course. I have no idea what to expect, and I feel like I've been asked to throw the magical equivalent of a rock at a sleeping god. But, whatever the consequences, I will begin that ritual shortly."

Aran nodded and scrubbed his hands through his beard. He wished he'd had time for a real shower. "I guess I'll get back to the *Talon* then, just in case. Any plans we make before she wakes will be pointless, but I'm hoping she'll respect either you or Drakkon enough to listen. I feel like we're almost out of time to react to Talifax and Skare."

"That time probably came and went before we met," Nara said with a sad shake of her head. "They're orchestrating this whole thing. Maybe since before we were born. There's so much we can't see, and I feel like we're playing right into their hands."

"Perhaps," Drakkon allowed. "But have we a choice? We must struggle, and hope. Either it is enough, or it is not."

"I knew there was a reason I liked you." Aran nodded respectfully to Drakkon. "We'll keep swinging until we can't any more. Good luck, Voria."

The deity gave him an absent smile, but he could see that she'd already returned to her work.

37

WAKING A GODDESS

Voria retreated to lunar orbit before beginning the ritual that would awaken an elder goddess. She hovered in the sky, large enough that the people on the night side of the world would see her rivaling the moon.

"You're quite fond of theatrics, aren't you?" Shaya appeared, a tiny speck near Voria's cosmic cheek. "This ritual could have been performed on the ground."

"Of course it could," Voria agreed. She raised a hand, and began to slowly draw upon *life* and *water*. "But I have no idea how Virkonna will react. I can see her magical signature. She's the size of a continent. In addition to pragmatism I understand the value of the theatric. How many humans are gazing up at me right now, seeing someone who looks like them perform a divine feat?"

"You are so much better at this than I was." Shaya gave a self-deprecating laugh. "I would never have considered that a goddess being suddenly woken up might throw a tantrum. And she might."

"Well," Voria muttered as the magic filled her. "We're about to find out."

She extended a tendril of pure creation, the greater path of Nature, and touched the mountain peak that sat directly over Virkonna's head. The magic seeped into the rock, into the planet, and into Virkonna.

A shining beacon appeared where Virkonna's mind was, and though Voria didn't understand what she was doing, or how, she stepped into that beacon. The planet vanished, and she appeared inside a memory.

Voria had seen this enough times to understand how it worked. Virkonna was lost in her own mind, reliving snippets of a vast life. Voria would need to find her and convince her to wake to reality, just as Crewes had managed when he'd retrieved Rhea.

She was on a rocky hillside on some long forgotten world, and a battle played out all around her. In the sky a great darkness had devoured nearly everything, and when she examined it with her godsight she realized she was seeing a supermassive black hole. That put this world at the core of some galaxy. Probably their own, though she had no way to verify that.

An azure-scaled hatchling bounded over a rock, and breathed a lightning bolt that caught a tech demon in the knee. The creature's knee exploded, and it tumbled down the rocky slope in a tangle of limbs.

Voria had seen the demons at the Skull of Xal, and these were identical. Its black armor and wicked rifle were very nearly the same style, and it had the same prehensile tail and leathery wings.

That made Virkonna's assault all the more impressive.

The hatchling drew a pair of spellblades as she landed, then cut through a trio of demons as if they were beneath her notice. Behind her, other hatchlings charged, with less success, but the demons were forced back, down the slope toward the valley floor.

A roar shook the world, causing the land to quake and buck. Voria glanced up, and her jaw fell open as she saw the combat playing out on the edge of the black hole. A star-sized eight-headed dragon surged into view in the southern sky, and she moved unerringly toward the darkness. As she did so Voria realized that darkness wasn't empty.

Scarlet eyes larger than most moons flared in that light-less expanse. This creature dwarfed Krox. The leather wings flaring out behind it were similar to the dragons, but the rest could not have been more different. This creature had thick, bony hide. Demonic hide. A tail curled behind it, long enough for the barbed end to be flung at worlds on the far side of a system.

The creature was terrifying. Utterly terrifying.

"It makes our epoch of the godswar look quaint, doesn't it?" Shaya shimmered into view, now the same size as Voria. "I don't even know what that thing is, but Xal looks pretty similar. Might be a relative. Dad maybe? Guess it doesn't matter."

"When are we?" Voria studied the monstrosity, which continued to fill her with an almost supernatural dread.

"A million years ago? More?" Shaya gave a shrug, and brushed dark hair from her face. "Long before our race came to prominence, that's for certain. Our ancestors, if they've discovered language, are beating each other with clubs and spears on some forested world."

"And that would mean Virkonna, given her current size, is less than a century old, yes?" Voria watched the future deity, and already spotted the hints that had likely led to her elevation. She cut down her opponents with the same fluidity Aran used. She was efficient, lethal, and utterly merciless to her demonic foes.

"That's my take." Shaya planted a hand on the spellblade belted around her waist. "Drakkon gets a lot of credit for inventing a truly new style, but he'd be the first to tell you that Virkonna is a better swordsman. She used more traditional styles, but to devastating effectiveness, as you can see."

The hatchling blurred past a quartet of demons, who stood rigidly as electricity crackled through their bodies. Virkonna swept an archaic spellrifle from a void pocket, and finished all four with a single fireball.

"At some point she must have attracted the attention of that thing." Shaya nodded at the eight-headed dragon.

"That must be the Wyrm Mother, the one who elevated Virkonna."

"And Nefarius," Shaya pointed out. "Virkonna is hiding here because her sister murdered her mom, and now sis is back to murder everyone else."

Voria tried to see the situation in those terms. Gods didn't seem all that different than mortals. They had emotions and failings. Their senses were greater. Their lifespans immeasurable. But ultimately they were just old, powerful mortals. Could she really fault Virkonna for retreating from reality? How many millennia of war had Virkonna seen by that point?

Virkonna leapt into the air and flared her wings. She glided upwards to join several dozen of her siblings, and they descended toward the greater battle on the plain below. Gods, demigods, ancient Wyrms, and strange magical war machines tore apart the very land around them as they clawed at each other.

"The scope of it," Voria whispered in awe. "The amount

of magical power here is so far beyond what we currently have in the sector. I count hundreds of demigods, and half that number of gods, most of them elder. What are we witnessing?"

"I know that whenever someone referred to the battle with Nefarius as the godswar she looked at them as if they were insane." Shaya also wore a look of awe. "I'm guessing this is why. There are so many of them. I wonder what they're fighting over."

"I suppose it's time we find out." Voria concentrated, and exerted the magical force she'd imparted into the spell.

The memory froze.

Only Virkonna still moved, completing the sword stroke that decapitated another demon, then landing gracefully a few dozen meters away. The hatchling whirled, and looked around in confusion. All over the sky the battle had frozen, even the eight-headed dragon, and the demonic elder god she fought.

"What...what is this?" Virkonna's blades lowered a hair.

Voria stepped into her field of view, and waved a hand. "Can you see me?"

Virkonna sucked in a breath, and a bolt of lighting shot through the space Voria occupied. She felt nothing as the phantom spell passed through her, thank the goddess.

"What are you? How have you frozen everything like this? Are you—". Her reptilian eyes widened. "Are you...Om?"

"Who?" Voria asked, then realized that she was going about this the wrong way. She raised both her hands. "I'm not whoever this Om is, but I *am* a goddess. A lesser one. I've been sent to wake you from torpor. This isn't reality, Virkonna. This is a memory you've retreated into, because you were stricken by grief over the death of your mother."

Virkonna's head snapped up to view the eight-headed dragon. "So many of the things you've said are impossible. Nothing can kill the Wyrm Mother, not even Xakava."

Voria gave a sympathetic sigh. She was forcing someone to process their grief, but it had to be done. "Virkonna, you are a goddess. The strongest goddess left in the sector. Krox has already risen. Nefarius is about to rise. Talifax has been orchestrating her rebirth, and we can't stop it. Not without your help. Inura sent me to wake you. Even now he's preparing for battle with Talifax and Nefarius."

"Who?" Virkonna cocked her head. "That name is familiar, but I can't place it. I feel as if I should know this...Nefarius."

"You do know her." Voria frowned. "She murdered your mother. She's your sister, Virkonna."

Virkonna's slitted eyes widened again, and her fanged mouth worked as she struggled for words. Nothing came out. Finally, Virkonna sat on a nearby bolder, granite crunching under her weight. Voria said nothing. She let the Wyrm think.

Several minutes later Virkonna rose to her feet. She faced Voria, and her entire demeanor was different now. All compassion and all curiosity had been replaced with harsh pragmatism. "I remember now. You speak the truth, but I don't love you for it. Why would you want to pull me from this place? This time? This is when I was happiest, and I've earned a few cycles to tarry here."

"You've been absent from the galactic stage for a dozen millennia or more," Voria pointed out as calmly as she could manage. "In that time most of your siblings have died. Only Inura and your, ah, elder sibling in the depths remain."

"Neith." Virkonna blinked. "I remember. It's good that she lives. And Inura too you say?"

Voria nodded, but said nothing else. She let Virkonna piece it together.

"I remember Nefarius now. She...how is it possible for her to live again? After we slew her I scattered her body myself. I dropped bits in distant galaxies. There should be no way for her to have returned, not even with that scheming sorcerer's endless meddling. I do not understand how he could possibly bring her back." Virkonna shook her head, and flared her wings behind her. "How he did so doesn't matter. Nefarius must be stopped. It is time for me to wake. You have done well, servant. I will speak to my children, and then I will summon you."

"Servant?" Shaya snorted out another laugh. "I forgot how, ah, forward thinking Virkonna is about non-draconic servants."

Voria suppressed a sigh. This did not seem like it was going to be a very enjoyable experience. Virkonna had all of Ducius's arrogance, but with cosmic power to back it up.

38

HOLY ONE

Voria returned to her own mind, and stared down at the planet Virkon to see the results of her actions. At first there was nothing. Then the clues began. They began at a seismic level, one that very few on the world below were capable of measuring.

The trio of tectonic plates under the area where Virkonna slumbered began to shake and rumble. The shaking intensified, and the resulting quakes tore apart vast swathes of the land. It looked like a Fissure forming, the land falling away beneath certain areas and being thrown up into others.

That was only the beginning.

A tremendous white wing tore loose from the world, and as it rose entire mountain ranges slid off, crushing human settlements that had been built across the valleys at the base of those mountains.

Voria winced knowing that thousands must have died. The tragedy rivaled Krox's assault on the tree, yet it wasn't a foreign enemy inflicting the damage. Virkonna's rise was killing her own people.

Another wing emerged, then an arched, scaly back. Snowy scales glittered as the sector's largest dragon, Cerberus's much older mother, clawed herself free of the world where she'd been slumbering. Even amidst the carnage it was breathtaking, a singular experience the survivors would relate to grandchildren. Were any alive to tell such stories.

Virkonna's departure shifted tides, awoke volcanoes, and sent earthquakes racing around the planet. She flapped away from the carnage, and rose into the sky near Voria. It put their relative sizes in perspective, and Voria realized she was roughly the size, if not the shape, of Virkonna's foot.

Countless dragons ascended from the planet, swirling like a cloud of bats. They swirled around their mother screeching cries of joy as they congregated around her. Not a one seemed concerned with the carnage left in her wake.

"Even I have to admit how beautiful that is." Shaya shimmered into view near Voria's face. "There aren't nearly as many as the first time I saw it. Back then Inura still had his own Wyrms, too."

"What comes now?" Voria asked. Virkonna seemed preoccupied with her children, which was fine for now.

"Virkonna is the last of the warriors," Shaya explained. "Neith, Inura…they were scholars. Marid was a warrior, but she died millennia before my time. Virkonna thinks like a warrior. Strength matters. She'll start by consolidating her power, which will mean asking all the other gods and demigods to publicly abase themselves. As soon as she realizes Nefarius is coming back she'll mobilize for war. The very instant she determines the site of the resurrection she'll lead her flight into battle."

That eased something in Voria. "I can deal with a bit of

humility, I suppose. So long as she's willing to oppose Nefarius."

Virkonna's wings stretched to their full width, and she gave a cry that defied physics and echoed through space. Then her gaze fell on Voria, and she swam through the void in her direction. Voria stood her ground, and made no move to alter her size. She was tiny compared to the elder goddess, but that didn't mean she had to abandon dignity.

"You have accomplished the task for which my younger brother imbued you." Virkonna's head swung around, and one baleful eye stopped before Voria. "I understand that you are merely a messenger, and will not fault you for the slights you offered, so long as you offer obeisance now."

Obeisance. Did she mean worship? Or merely respect? Voria had no way of knowing, so she made her choice. Humility was one thing. Abject servitude quite another.

"I am pleased to have played a role in returning you to the galactic stage." Voria executed a perfect curtsy, the kind she had absolutely detested as a teen, and hadn't used since.

Virkonna eyed her through one of those slitted irises, but Voria could make nothing of the gesture. The Wyrm-goddess's face was utterly alien. Unknowable to a mortal.

One thing Voria found interesting was that Virkonna seemed to have a physical body. She was no pool of light, but a full dragon, with scales and claws, and fury. That evoked a whole host of questions, none of which were appropriate in that instant.

"You have not been instructed in the art of service." Virkonna gave the faintest of sighs. "I should have expected little else. That is my brother's fault, not yours." Her massive head swung toward the planet, and stared down at the crater her passage had left. A golden city lay near the center, and Voria could feel the power radiating from it. That must be the crucible. "I will return to my domain and set my house in order. You will be my guest until then. I will allow you to keep the *Spellship*, for the time being. Take care that no harm comes to it. You've no idea its power or importance. Every elder god will realize this, and they will covet that ship for the advantage it conveys. There is no other worship amplifier in this sector. Guard it well. It would be a pity for you to experience my wrath so soon after having woken me."

It had never occurred to Voria that she might have to give the *Spellship* back. She considered it hers, but then she hadn't made it. Inura and Virkonna had. She needed to honor that, whatever her personal feelings.

"Thank you, Virkonna." She probably shouldn't be using the deity's name, but given her own godhood she thought it an acceptable lapse. She was mistaken.

Virkonna's eyes narrowed. "The proper title is either holy one, or master."

Rage thundered through Voria, and it took everything she had not to lash out at the arrogant Wyrm. There was no way she was calling anyone master. Ever. "Thank you, holy one."

Virkonna gave a mollified nod, then swung to face the planet. She began to descend, and her body shrank as it fell. She made for the side of the planet that had not been ruined, and the Wyrms followed.

Voria could only watch. She wondered if she'd done the right thing. Virkonna would likely oppose Nefarius, but her winning might not be better for the sector in the long run. It would be nice if, for once, she didn't have to choose the lesser of two evils.

39

KHEROSS OF THE LAST DRAGONFLIGHT

K heross flared his wings behind him and walked with pride as he navigated the terrace. Conversations ceased in his wake, and each group of Wyrms studied him as he passed. Any new Wyrm, in any society, was immediate cause for curiosity, and sometimes hostility.

A mixture of both met him in their expressions, some wonder at the long white hair fluttering in the wind behind him, and some anger that an outsider might so boldly approach their newly risen mother.

Virkonna became aware of him long before her retinue. Several quiet conversations were taking place around her, but Virkonna's slitted eyes had locked on him. Kheross stared right back, and strode calmly through her people until he stood near the base of her throne.

He waited patiently for her to acknowledge him. There were some social niceties even he wouldn't shirk. After several moments Virkonna leaned forward on her throne, her ivory hair fluttering as a sudden gust caught it.

"Who are you?" she demanded quietly.

All speech around her ceased, and the sudden silence rippled out until every last Wyrm was staring at them. Kheross waited a few more moments to let the tension build, and then rested his hand on the hilt of his spellblade.

"My name is Kheross," he explained simply. "I am a traveler from another reality. A reality crafted by your brother, my uncle Inura."

Virkonna leaned back on her throne and studied him, her expression unreadable. She drummed her fingers on the arm of her throne, then ceased and spoke. "You come from the reality where we hid the *Spellship*?"

Kheross blinked his surprise. She was far more astute than he'd have expected for a goddess known more for her abilities in war. "I do. In that reality, Nefarius arose and tore apart the sector. She won."

Virkonna rose from her throne, and gracefully approached. She wore a pair of slender spellblades, and her scaled hands rested on the hilts. Not in a threatening manner, but in the manner of a master swordsman prepared to defend herself.

"If she won," Virkonna wondered aloud, her slitted eyes narrowing, "then why didn't she claim the *Spellship*?"

Kheross gave a bitter laugh. "What use was it to her? There is no point in amplifying worship if you devour all your worshippers."

Virkonna shuddered visibly, but her posture didn't slacken. She eyed Kheross imperiously. "She devoured worshippers, and yet you survived somehow."

"Only because I was her creature." Kheross's fingers squeezed his hilt as if choking the life from Talifax. "I was corrupted by the blood of Nefarius. Slowly, over several centuries. In several more I would have ceased to exist. I would have become her blood, which covered every sentient world in this sector, and all the galaxy for all I know."

"Talifax removed the blood?" Her eyes narrowed. "And why might he do that? Why relinquish his hold over a vassal as ancient as you? It makes little sense."

Kheross hesitated. She was right, and he knew it. "I don't know. I've given it endless thought, and have no doubt I will continue to. It makes little sense, unless the power he stripped from me was more valuable than the prospect of another servant. Perhaps he needs the magic, every scrap of it."

Virkonna's expression softened a hair. "You have my sympathy for the horrors you have witnessed, my child. But Talifax is no fool. There is likely a scrap within you, though I confess I can't see it."

Kheross resisted the urge to correct her. She wasn't his mother. His mother was dead.

"What is it you seek from me?" Virkonna asked. She returned to her throne, and sat.

"Vengeance," Kheross offered. "Or redemption, I suppose. I was a creature of Nefarius. A tool of Talifax. I know that very soon you will ride to war. When you do, I wish to be allowed to go with you. I wish to be your hound, to slay the sorcerer Talifax, or to die trying."

Virkonna gave an approving nod. "Then you shall. Make your vows, Wyrm."

Kheross sank to his knees, and rested his chin against his chest. He'd exposed himself, his crimes, and his weaknesses. Not the whole of them, maybe, but the fact that they existed, and their dark nature.

Virkonna was willing to accept him anyway. She would let him ride to war. He offered his allegiance gladly. "Holy one," Kheross began, "accept my fealty. Command my claws to rend, my teeth to tear, and my magics to slay. I bask in your light, and reflect it back, gladly and strongly, and with the greatest of devotion. Take my strength, and use it to protect us."

A pulse of pure golden brilliance rose from Kheross, the visible manifestation of his faith. It shot into Virkonna's breast, and the deity glowed with golden light. Then an answering pulse shot from Virkonna's breast, back into Kheross.

Golden power washed through him, and he felt a binding settle over his soul, connecting him to his goddess.

"The dedication is complete," Virkonna said. She rose once more. "Be welcome, Kheross of the Last Dragonflight. Rise."

Kheross rose to his feet, and gazed around in wonder and disbelief. He had a home once more.

"In a few hours I will begin the contest," Virkonna rumbled, "to fill the role of my guardian. Your strength would make you an excellent candidate, and I welcome you to compete if you wish."

Kheross considered that. He'd certainly enjoy competing with his cousins, and hopefully besting them all. He knew he could take Aurelius, who seemed to be the strongest of these Wyrms.

An uneasiness washed through him, though. A nagging thought that would not be silent. What if Talifax still controlled him? What if he was using Kheross to take some of Virkonna's magic?

"I dare not risk it, mother," Kheross explained. "It may be my paranoia, but I fear Talifax's influence. I fear that you investing any amount of power in me could be a ploy. And, to be truthful, I would rather kill Talifax with my own strength."

Virkonna nodded. "An honorable choice. Very well. In the battle that comes you have my permission to hunt the deceiver as you will."

40

VOICE OF THE OUTRIDERS

A ran and the rest of the company kept largely to themselves in the wake of Virkonna's awakening. No one wanted to talk about the destruction on the planet below. They'd seen it on Marid. They'd seen it on New Texas. Ternus. The list just kept getting longer. So many people dead, and for what? So a goddess could wake up?

Over the past week he'd thrown himself into tactical study and sparring with Drakkon. They'd met twice a day for the past seven days, and while Aran was beginning to grow as a swordsman he was also cognizant that no one was stopping Talifax or Krox from whatever screwed up plots they were hatching.

Yet here they sat, doing nothing. Voria hadn't yet been summoned, and so far as Aran could tell, Virkonna was busy solidifying her position just like any other Wyrm would have done. She was more like Nebiat and less like Neith, and his level of bitterness at that fact surprised him. He'd have thought he was over petty gods.

Gods. Mortals. We are all the same, Narlifex thrummed.

The blade was becoming quite the philosopher. *Life is magic. Magic is life. Gods are old mortals, but they have mortal failings.*

"You're not wrong about that," Aran agreed.

The scry-screen in the corner of his quarters chimed, and Aran rose with a yawn. He walked to the screen and accepted the incoming missive. His sister was one of the last people he expected to see.

Her almond-shaped eyes and dark hair were familiar, but there was still more awkwardness than affection in her pretty face. His probably looked exactly the same from her perspective.

"Brother, I apologize, but I come to you with a request for aid. One you are uniquely suited to fill." She paused, and seemed to be waiting for permission before continuing.

"Go on," he prompted. Aran folded his arms, and gave her his full attention.

"Virkonna is raising a guardian," Astria explained. "There will be a contest, and she will choose a champion from among the survivors."

"And?" Aran's heart beat a little more swiftly as fight or flight overtook him. He wasn't going to like this ask.

"And this contest is generally for Wyrms." Astria's eyes grew wet, though no tears escaped. "There is no official prohibition for an Outrider entering. After...what she did to our world, we need a voice, brother. We need to show the Wyrms that we are not fodder. We are not merely weak servants, to be discarded and spent where convenient. To be trampled underfoot."

Aran exhaled a long, slow breath. He didn't want to react too quickly to this, but his initial instinct was to simply say no. "I don't have any interest in being a lapdog for Virkonna, and it sounds like that's the job I'd be signing up for. That's effectively what a guardian is, right? Her right-hand man?"

Astria nodded. "Yes, but also no. A guardian can serve as a check on their master's power. Some guardians have even rebelled against the god they serve. Elevating you may provide social expectations, but it will not bind you. It will not force you to obey."

"I don't see that as any better." He shook his head. "She'll expect me to jump when she says jump."

Astria barked a bitter laugh, and the lines around her eyes tightened. "She already expects that. Every Wyrm expects that. Aran, you represent our one chance to be free. There will always be wars. Do you think that it will somehow end after you kill Nefarius, or Krox? The godswar is eternal, and Virkonna will attempt to aggressively expand the last dragonflight. She will see it as her duty."

Aran had to fight to keep his posture from going slack. The slight slumping of the shoulders, the bowing of his back. His body wanted to give up. It wanted to give up because it had seen the cost of waking Virkonna, but only now did the real cost become apparent. They'd unleashed another elder god on the sector, and no elder god seemed to have the sector's best interests in mind.

"You think that if I embarrass the Wyrms competing in this contest, it's going to somehow make Virkonna treat Outriders better?" Aran didn't bother hiding his skepticism.

"It has to begin somewhere," his sister pointed out. "And there is another reason. You wish to slay Talifax, and Nefarius if she truly rises, and Krox. Can you accomplish any of those things without Virkonna?"

She had him, and he knew it.

"Maybe, but I don't see how," he admitted. He sighed, and scratched at his beard. "I can't really see a way out of doing this. What's involved?"

"It's quite simple," Astria explained. "All combatants are

placed in a pre-defined arena. Your goal is to disable or kill all other combatants. When the combat is over, Virkonna chooses a winner."

"Which is theoretically the last person standing." Aran raised an eyebrow. "Couldn't Virkonna choose a Wyrm anyway, even if I win?"

"She could," Astria allowed. Some of the enthusiasm bled away. "I do not think she would, though, and even if she did all would know that a human had bested every Wyrm on our world."

"Okay." Aran rolled his shoulder, which still ached from yesterday's workout. "Give me a bit to get suited up."

"You will not be able to use your armor."

Aran sighed. "Of course not. Can I use Narlifex?"

"Of course. Many Wyrms will fight in their bipedal form to increase the level of challenge. Aurelius will be one. Olyssa another. If they fought as full Wyrms they would crush their opponents, and there is little honor in that."

"That makes me feel better, at least." It didn't, though. There would be a great deal of resistance to an Outrider entering the contest, and every Wyrm involved would have a common cause.

They would remove him before focusing on each other.

41

THERE CAN BE ONLY ONE

A ran walked down the *Talon*'s ramp, his teeth chattering in the frigid wind. He'd set down near the spire Virkonna had claimed, the remains of a mountain peak at the edge of the crater she'd created when clawing her way free of the earth.

Hundreds of supplicants were clustered around the base of the spire, where they were met by white-robed acolytes who sorted them into different groups. From what Aran could see the line was only getting larger, and he seriously doubted that any of those people were ever going to make it up to see Virkonna.

High above, dozens of hatchlings drifted in lazy flights, all orbiting the top of the spire where their elders would be mingling and likely playing Kem'Hedj.

Aran channeled a bit of *fire* to warm himself, and his teeth stopped chattering. He walked down the ramp to Astria, who stood by herself. The rest of the company had volunteered to accompany him, but Aran saw no reason for them to leave the warmth of the ship. The contest wasn't to the death, so there wasn't anything to get worked up about. Theoretically, at least.

"I thought you were going to bring your Outriders," he called, his voice nearly ripped away by the wind.

"I did," she called back gravely. Her expression was as dour as ever, visible only because her cowl had been pulled back. "Not a one is willing to risk themselves publicly. For good reason. Aurelius put it about that any Outrider who stood for you would be exiled, alongside their families."

Aran wrapped a hand around Narlifex's hilt, and forced a long, slow breath. He'd dearly love to hit something, though he knew it wouldn't help. It took two more breaths to push the frustration away, and he only spoke once he had.

"Then why are we doing this?" he asked quietly. "If your own people don't believe in this, why antagonize a goddess?"

"Because if you succeed," she gave back without hesitation, "then children born tomorrow will know that a human can become a god."

Aran released Narlifex's hilt, and the anger evaporated. She was right. The people were afraid, because they should be. Humans were less than dragons, and when your god made you literal second-class citizens, what kind of message did that send to your children?

The best you could hope for was to be a loyal hunting dog, not so very different from how Xal intended to use him. It wasn't right. People deserved better. They deserved freedom, and to stand as equals if they were to fight as equals.

"So how do we do this?" Aran asked, staring up the three-kilometer length of the spire.

"We follow them to the killing field," Astria explained. She raised a slender hand and pointed to a field to the west. "Virkonna will arrange it to her liking, and then she will allow the melee to begin. After she creates the field, but before she allows the fight to begin, you must get her attention and request that she allow you entry."

Aran was about to ask a follow-up question when deafening thunder cracked across the plains and mountains, drowning out any possibility of speech. Lightning veined across the sky in all directions, every bolt coming from the peak above.

A single tiny figure jetted into the air, no larger than a human. Behind her came dozens of Wyrms, the largest in the front. Aurelius's wingspan was easily a hundred meters, and behind him came Olyssa's nearly equal bulk. In their wake came smaller Wyrms—a dozen, followed by more.

Aran counted twenty-two in all, and assumed that since they were flying after Virkonna, they must be the ones who'd be involved in the fight to be named guardian.

"Shall we?" He used a bit of *void* to lighten himself, then *air* to guide himself into the sky. It was more costly, magically speaking, than using his spellarmor, but still a trivial act.

His recent brush with Xal and Krox had dramatically increased his reserves, and Aran still hadn't found a daily limit to the number of spells he could cast. Today would be the first real physical contest since he'd gotten the abilities, though.

Plus, he was fighting some of the largest adult Wyrms on the planet. They could bring their own magic to bear, and it might be greater than his. As arrogant as it sounded, even in his own head, Aran doubted it. He was stronger than any mere Wyrm.

That is not arrogance, Narlifex protested. *We are strong. We do not age as they do. We are a breed apart.*

That piqued Aran's curiosity. Had he passed some sort of

divine threshold that meant he no longer aged? The blade seemed to think so.

"Brother?" Astria called over the wind as she pulled even with him. She'd pulled her cowl up, and the white fabric fluttered around her as they picked up speed. "You do not seem at all concerned by this fight. Why is that? Does the prospect of doing battle with Aurelius not frighten you?"

"No," he realized aloud, yelling to make himself heard over the wind, "it doesn't. Not because I think I'll win, but because my pride isn't on the line. So what if he beats me?"

"I see you do not yet understand. Look." Astria pointed, and Aran followed her finger with his gaze.

Virkonna had stopped over a relatively intact portion of the plain near her spire. She raised both hands, and bolts of lightning stabbed down in rapid succession. They slammed into the plain, their strikes so numerous that they carpeted the earth. The ground heated, and within moments topsoil melted, then the granite underneath. The entire plain became a field of lava.

"Virkonna loves her games. She will set the terms of this one, and tell all combatants."

"Couldn't you have mentioned this part?" Aran watched in a mixture of horror and amazement as hunks of lava drifted up into the air.

They assembled themselves into a mirror of the solar system, with the largest hunk of lava representing the sun. It was easily six or seven kilometers across, while the hunk representing Virkon was smaller than Aurelius.

"Ages ago this system housed a colossal battle," Virkonna's clear voice echoed over the plains, as clear as if whispered into his ear. "My brother Inura and I fought to claim this world from one of the last demon lords. His forces flooded the system, innumerable and implacable. They were many, and we few, yet every one of us was a god in our own right."

Countless globs of earth rose into the sky, and the wind shaped them into monstrous shapes of all sizes. Some were tiny, no bigger than Aran's fist. Others were twice Aurelius's size.

"Today we will re-enact that great battle. All supplicants for guardian will defend Virkon." She gestured at the representation of her world, and that hunk of rock began to glow a bright azure. "The demons come. Defeat them and each other. Claim Virkon, and let none bar you from it."

Astria floated a little higher than Aran, and lowered her cowl. Her hair whipped around her like a sea of dark snakes. "Now is the time, brother. You must intervene!"

"Here goes, then." He nodded at her, which seemed more fitting than a hug, and then Aran willed *void* to carry him aloft. He streaked skyward like a meteor reversing course, and rose toward the edge of the three-dimensional map Virkonna had created.

By the time he reached the goddess every eye was on him, both the Wyrms and the humans clustered around the base of the spire so many kilometers below.

Now that Aran was close to Virkonna he was able to see what she looked like, and she wasn't what he expected. Like Olyssa, she was bipedal, with wings and a tail. Tiny scales covered her body, but where her eyes should be there were only pools of intense blue radiance. Pure *air*.

Like Nebiat and Kheross, she possessed a full head of hair, though. Hers was a mixture of snowy white and azure blue, a color which rippled and changed against the sky behind her. Her hair sat still against her, completely untouched by the gale winds only a few meters away.

Only in that moment did Aran realize why his mind had

supplied Kheross as a comparison. The Wyrm had lived on the *Talon* for months, and Aran recognized him instantly, standing in midair behind Virkonna. His arms were crossed, and there was no sign of his spellaxes. Apparently he wasn't fighting today.

Aran gave Kheross a nod, and Kheross returned it. Nothing more needed to be said.

"You've clearly sought to disrupt these proceedings," Virkonna called imperiously. She drifted closer to Aran and her eyes narrowed. "And I am aware of who you are, Outrider. What is your intent, and could it not wait for a more opportune moment?" Curiosity softened the anger, though Aran sensed the balance could shift at any moment. Virkonna was as changeable as the wind.

"I've come to enter the contest for your favor," Aran called, using the ritual greeting he'd been taught. "You will choose a guardian, the strongest on this planet. That's me, and I want a chance to prove it."

"An Outrider?" Aurelius scoffed, his laughter booming like thunder.

"Even one as accomplished as you would fare poorly," Olyssa offered, a flap of her enormous wings bringing her closer to Aran. "You have earned much honor, but this is not the way, Outrider. Stand down, before you lose face, and possibly your life."

"I don't care about losing face," Aran pointed out. He met Aurelius's slitted gaze, and then Olyssa's. Virkonna hadn't said anything further, which suggested she wanted him to fend for himself. He could do that. "My life is mine to do with as I will, and I choose to risk it here. I will win your contest, and by the end you'll realize that a human is more powerful than any of your children."

Many Wyrms began to laugh, but that laughter was silenced when Virkonna raised a clawed hand. "The Outrider may fight." She lowered her hand with a dramatic flourish. "Let the battle begin."

42

SKY BRAWL

Aran shot skyward the instant Virkonna's claw came down. He twisted around one of the outer 'planets', which still glowed an angry molten orange as it rotated past him. Swarms of demons shot up all around him, though most of the living rock constructs plunged deeper into the system, toward the representation of Virkon.

The Wyrms reacted almost as one, each winging up to defend that planet. It was a stable, predictable strategy. Get between your opponent and their target. Unfortunately, defending a single point in three-dimensional space was difficult when your opponents were attacking from many directions at once.

Wards sprang up around miniature Virkon, and Wyrms breathed bolts of lightning to surgically remove larger targets, while swiping at smaller ones with their claws or tail. Aurelius and Olyssa both fared well in the initial rush, but not all the Wyrms were so lucky.

Magma demons swarmed around those fighting alone, and quickly engulfed them. The first Wyrm's body tumbled end over end toward the lava below, and Aran glanced around frantically but no one was making a move to save the unconscious creature.

Aran shot toward the Wyrm and wrapped a tendril of *air* around the creature's tail. He used gravity to lighten its body, and flung it gently behind the bounds of the lava. The dragon might not enjoy the landing, but at least it would be alive to complain about it.

He glanced back at the combat, and could no longer see any dragons. Virkonna's demons swirled around the planet she'd erected, where Aran assumed the dragons must be. That was confirmed when another body tumbled out of the swarm, and another.

Virkonna did nothing, merely hovered in the sky watching. She made no move to save the fallen Wyrms, and seemed utterly oblivious to their potential deaths.

Rage rolled through Aran.

Why are you so angry? Narlifex asked, his confusion evident. *We should join the killing. The fallen have no one but themselves to blame. They chose this.*

Aran extended both hands, and used gravity to seize each Wyrm as it fell from the cloud around Virkon. One by one he got them to safety, though it meant avoiding combat completely. Perhaps for that reason the demons ignored him, and instead focused on the surviving defenders.

Neither Olyssa nor Aurelius had tumbled free, so they were probably forming the center points of the resistance.

Aran quickly realized that playing a reactive game wasn't going to win this battle. There were thousand of demons, most smaller than him, all attacking at once. He needed to neutralize them, and do it in a way that wouldn't kill the dragons.

He flew up a few dozen meters, and surveyed the system.

The 'sun' still glowed an angry red, and dwarfed everything in the system. If this were a real battle that would be the largest source of gravity in the system.

Aran darted down toward the sun, and extended a hand toward the cloud of demons obscuring the vision of tiny Virkon and whatever defenders might still be alive.

We fight now? Narlifex pulsed hopefully. The blade so badly wanted to kill.

"Sorry, bud." Aran gritted his teeth and reached deep into the well of *void* in his chest. "This is going to take something a lot more broad than swordplay."

Aran extended the gravity magic toward the makeshift sun, and pulled a tendril of molten rock away from the core. He added *fire* to keep it heated, something he wouldn't have had to do with matter from a real sun, and wove that rock toward the cloud of demons.

The molten rock slammed into them, pulling most of the demons away in a shower of magma. Aran yanked them back toward the sun, and flung all the demons he'd collected into the blazing ball.

The reduction in attackers allowed Aurelius to make a push, which Olyssa quickly supported. The two flew back to back, picking off demons as they cleared a space around the planet. Only a handful of other Wyrms still flew, and most were visibly wounded. One had a shattered wing, and was only aloft through the use of *air* magic.

"Okay, now you get to show off." Aran unsheathed Narlifex and flew toward the combat. He surged *fire* to increase his strength, and *air* to become more agile.

Then Aran became one with the combat, as Drakkon had taught him. He flowed through the battle, Narlifex darting out in quick strikes, the shards at the end of the blade exploding into furious death that shredded every demon it touched.

Aran forced a path through the remaining demons, twisting around answering blows as he made for the blue rock Virkonna had created to represent her world. He became one with the blade, and time itself seemed to blur.

How long he killed he didn't know, but suddenly it was over. The last demon was down.

Aurelius's form swept toward him, and human-sized claws slashed toward his face. Aran used a bit of *void* to blink down about twenty meters, under Aurelius's blow... and into a lightning bolt fired by a large white Wyrm he didn't recognize.

The bolt caught him in the back, and the magic played through him, causing his muscles to seize. Had he not been naturally resistant to *air* from the gifts Virkonna had given him, Aran doubted he'd have survived the breath weapon.

As it was his shirt burned away, and second-degree burns made his back a sea of fire. Adrenaline made the pain bearable, but only just. He blinked again, this time behind the Wyrm who'd attacked him.

Aran flung Narlifex toward the creature's back, directly over the heart. He channeled his rage into pure *void*, and increased the sword's weight a thousandfold. The weapon punched through the creature's heart, and its body fluttered weakly toward the lava below, blood spurting from the wound.

Narlifex ripped free from the creature's body and shot back into Aran's hand even as he touched down on the blue rock Virkonna had demanded the victor hold.

Looking around only Aurelius and Olyssa remained. A few demons survived, but whenever one approached either Wyrm it was ruthlessly crushed.

"Come, cousin," Aurelius roared as he swung his massive head in Olyssa's direction. "Let us tear apart the mortal, and then give this farce the only end it could have ever had."

"There is no honor in that," she snapped. Olyssa's form rippled and changed, until she stood in her human form a few dozen meters from Aran. "You pride yourself on your skill as a blade master. Do you really think yourself unable to best an Outrider in such a contest? He has proven himself this day, as I expect Mother will agree. You owe him your respect."

Aurelius's slitted eyes narrowed, but he didn't answer. Finally he looked directly at Aran. "I am accounted the finest swordsman this world has ever—"

Aran was kind of done.

Today had shown him something. He wasn't mortal any more. He wasn't playing by the same rules. The level of magic Aran had been gifted, and the magic he'd stolen, had elevated him far beyond some stupid, petty Wyrms. No matter how old those stupid, petty Wyrms might be.

Aurelius's tail, arms, and legs were suddenly crushed against his body. Aran lifted a hand, and tightened it into a fist. The Wyrm's long neck scrunched inward as his massive body was forced into a fetal position. The magic was frighteningly easy to maintain.

"Drakkon is the finest swordsman this world has ever known," Aran pointed out. "Though I hear Virkonna makes him look like...well, like you, maybe."

He walked calmly over to the Wyrm, and stood before his massive jaws. Aurelius huffed an enraged breath, but that was the extent of the resistance he was capable of offering. "You might be able to take me in a duel, but I think it's a lot more likely I'd kill you instantly, and the last dragonflight would be deprived of one of its strongest warriors. And that would be a real shame."

Aran lifted his hand, and the Wyrm rose into the air. Aran made a flinging gesture, and Aurelius was flung several kilometers away, still unable to control his body. He crashed down, quite painfully Aran hoped, just outside the lava field. Only then did Aran release him. He didn't know if that disqualified Aurelius, but he had to imagine that it did.

Aurelius struggled to his feet, and leapt back into the air with an angry flap of his wings. He did not approach the battlefield.

That meant it came down to him and Olyssa. He turned to find her standing in a guard position, a slender spellblade clutched in one hand. Her stance said she was a master, but then, so was he.

When he beat her, and Aran was almost positive he could take her in a straight fight, he would be named guardian. Virkonna would ram a piece of her magic down his gullet, and own another piece of his soul in the process.

Aran sheathed Narlifex. He gave Olyssa a respectful bow, and then kicked off the blue rock. He let her stand there, and hovered in the air by himself.

"You win." He rested a hand on Narlifex, and hoped the blade understood. That was twice he'd denied it a good fight, in one day. "Congratulations."

Olyssa's sword tip never wavered, but she watched him curiously through those slitted eyes. "Why? I do not understand. After seeing what you did to Aurelius you cannot possibly fear me."

Aran laughed at that, then shook his head sadly. "You're right. I don't fear you. Or any Wyrm on this rock. There *is* a dragon I'm afraid of though, one that we should be out fighting instead of here playing games. Virkonna needs a guardian, then fine, let that be you. But here's my ask, Olyssa. You know I could have taken you today. You know that an Outrider had your fate in his hands, and chose to allow you to live, and to claim a position of immense power."

"Say no more." Olyssa gave a tight, inhuman nod. She sheathed her blade, and gave Aran a bow. "If Virkonna picks me I will ensure that your kind are given more of a voice. Of that I can assure you."

"I do *not* choose you," Virkonna thundered, literally. Her voice drowned out all other sound, and Aran's ears rang as the echoes faded away. The goddess glided to a landing next to Aran, but her angry glare had settled on Olyssa. "You are weak. And passive. You seek nothing further than to prevent the erosion of your power. The idea that you could claim more power or territory would never occur to you. You are no predator. You are prey. Begone from my sight."

Virkonna waved a hand, and Olyssa's body was carried away by a tremendous wind. She went spinning away from the arena Virkonna had constructed, out of Aran's sight. He tensed, and waited for Virkonna to turn toward him.

Her eyes were barely contained storms, the power of it crackling all around them. But being this close to her he sensed something completely unexpected. The greater part of her power was contained elsewhere somehow. This human representation of her was...vulnerable. She was weak right now, not much more than a mortal. Not much more than him.

Aran stowed that thought, and hoped she couldn't read his mind. Idly imagining killing a god was a great way to die or start a war.

"You declined my guardianship," Virkonna said, her voice painful, but bearable. "Why enter a contest, one you are clearly quite capable of winning, if you never intended to claim the prize?"

"I intended to win it initially," Aran explained. May as well give her the truth. "I changed my mind when your top Wyrms started plummeting to their deaths. Our sector is engulfed in war. This is the last dragonflight for a reason, and the very last thing you need to do is further weaken it. Yet you were more than willing to allow your strongest Wyrms to kill each other. If that's the kind of leader you're going to be, then I don't want to work for you."

He gave her a level stare, and waited for her response.

43

WARRIOR GODS

Aran had no idea how Virkonna would respond to a blunt subordinate, but realized he didn't really care. One of the biggest advantages in being a cat's paw of the gods was that the gods needed you. Thus, they were reluctant to suddenly obliterate you for being rude. So he hoped anyway.

Virkonna's expression tightened in what he guessed was probably anger, though he couldn't say for sure. Aran forced himself to meet that tumultuous gaze, knowing that looking away would be taken as a sign of weakness. He'd already seen what Virkonna thought of weakness.

"Your perspective is limited by your mortal nature, as mine was when I made a very similar utterance to my mother," Virkonna finally said, her voice thundering down to the waiting crowds, dragon and human both. "Striving for mastery, for greatness, is necessary in a guardian. I must select one who is powerful and bold, but also compassionate enough to counsel me to caution when my followers are in danger. I do not have the luxury of caring for each tiny human or hatchling. I must chart a course through history amidst the titanic forces of the gods."

"If you're expecting me to give you a pass," Aran boomed, using a bit of *air* to amplify his own voice, "then you are sadly mistaken. The simple act of waking you wiped out cities across this continent. My people suffered, in great numbers. You expect loyalty from humans, and admit you need them and their worship to win the war against Talifax, Nefarius, and Krox, and anyone else who tries to trample this sector under foot. But what happens when you're the one doing the trampling? I won't be a party to that. I don't care what kind of power you're offering. I've got plenty of power."

"Not like this." Her eyes narrowed. "I do not enjoy your tone. It's been countless millennia since even my brother spoke to me that way."

"Seems like you could use more of that, not less."

Virkonna closed her eyes for a moment, and sighed. She opened them. "Do not erode the ground you've already conquered. I admit I need a strong voice that will teach me to see as a mortal sees. I must understand them if I am to win their hearts, and win them I must if we are to prevent my sister from rising once more. You've no idea how terrifying Nefarius can be. If she rises there will be no stopping her. Not enough warrior gods remain. We're down to sniveling cowards like Neith, and artificers like Inura. I cannot best Nefarius alone, but you? You would be a potent addition to my arsenal. Particularly given the gifts Xal has already imparted."

Aran opened his mouth to remind Virkonna that he hadn't agreed to anything, but it didn't matter. Lightning shot from her eyes and into his, her power exploding through his body, invading it. Remaking it.

Something—her consciousness, he realized—entered his mind and began sifting through his experiences like the pages of a book. It wasn't painful, but the intrusion enraged Aran in a way he couldn't articulate. There was just something unclean about another being entering your most private thoughts without so much as a 'by your leave.'

Aran gritted his teeth, and drew upon the enormous power Xal had given him. What he did next was instinctual, and he wasn't certain he could duplicate the feat. Aran poured the magic into his own mind, somehow strengthening his defenses. A dense magical shell formed around his mind, and Virkonna's consciousness was flung violently away.

Whatever changes she was enacting on his body continued, some sort of infusion of *air*, a far greater quantity than she'd imparted before. This much was akin to the void Xal had given, a significant, divine quantity.

"I may come to regret this," Virkonna thundered. *Air* continued to play through Aran, but somehow he forced his gaze up and met hers. "You are powerful. More so than expected. But that is a good thing. Take the power I offer, and use it to help me strike down Talifax before my sister is resurrected."

One final pulse of *air* magic surged into Aran, bringing with it tremendous euphoria that was in no way congruent to his current circumstances. He felt like giggling, when a moment ago he'd wanted to draw his weapon.

The result of drinking such power, Narlifex growled. *It will pass, but we will need to find a place to rest, to absorb the power fully.*

"I won't be your puppet," Aran managed through gritted teeth as the magics finally abated. "I'll help you fight, but I am not a pet. Not a dog you can order to attack."

Virkonna cocked her head, and stared hard at him. "There you are mistaken. If I order you to kill, you will kill. But neither will I expect blind obedience." Her wings drooped. "I have given much of myself, and I must rest. Return to your vessel, and await my summons. When I awake, I will call the flight and we will make war on our enemies."

Virkonna vanished, and left Aran the center of a whole lot of unwanted attention. He ignored everyone, and flew toward the *Talon*. He badly needed sleep. When he woke up he could figure out what Virkonna had done to him, and what the hidden cost would be.

She'd given him power, without a doubt. But if she thought she was going to control him she'd soon find out giving him this strength was a mistake.

44

COMMITTED NOW

Frit had experienced translocation when Voria had brought the *Spellship* to Marid, but she'd been in the library when it happened. Beyond a sinking in the pit of her stomach, which quickly faded, she felt nothing.

This time, though, her entire surroundings changed. Her quarters vanished, and abruptly she hovered in the sky over the world Nebiat had shown her in the vision. It was somehow more beautiful in person, the rocky world glittering below her.

"If you were a human, like Nara," Nebiat's shade said as she winked into existence near her, "then you'd already be dead. The vacuum would have shredded your fragile body."

The move lacked Nebiat's characteristic subtlety, but in this instance Frit supposed it wasn't needed. The reminder that she wasn't any more human, or Shayan, than Nebiat hit home. She looked like them, because they had literally shaped her that way. But she wasn't like them.

"If I were Krox, like you," Frit replied, evenly, with no animosity, "then I'd have lured you into a trap, and killed you. The research seemed pretty clear. If you manifest as a shade you are incredibly vulnerable. Certainly vulnerable enough that Nara, myself, and Voria together could have overcome you."

"Then it is fortunate for me that you are not Krox." The shade smiled, and gestured at the sky above and behind Frit. "It is precisely that difference that I hope will allow you to free me from *that*."

Frit pivoted and stared up at the sky. A human observer would have said there were two suns, and in a way they were right. Both celestial bodies contained the properties of a star, but one of them was a god. She could perceive many spectrums humans could not, and the god's brilliance was pleasant, not blinding.

Krox looked much as he had on the footage she'd seen of him invading Shaya, four arms extending from a cosmic torso, full of stars and other celestial bodies. Two of those arms cradled the spear he'd wrested from the great tree. Worldender, its black length utterly alien, and hostile in some way.

The god hovered there, unmoving. Uncaring. Its existence terrified her, and she knew with absolutely certainty that it hated her. It wanted to consume her. The being inspired the very last emotion she'd expected. Sympathy.

"We will find a way to free you," Frit promised, staring up at the god. "That thing is terrible, and I can't imagine being trapped inside. Back on the *Spellship* you asked me what things would have been like if Krox rose without you to control him." She faced Nebiat's shade, and wished she could comfort her, as she'd comforted Frit back on Shaya all those months ago. "I don't need flame reading to answer that. The world below would not exist. And soon, no world would exist."

Nebiat nodded earnestly. "You understand then. I am this generation's terrible tyrant. Everyone thinks me evil. They do not know what I have sacrificed, or why. I have salvaged what I can from a bad situation, but I am also painfully aware that I am moving inexorably toward oblivion. That thing will consume me, in a decade, or a century. You know what happens then."

Frit shivered at that, though not from the chill of the void. "Then let's make sure it doesn't happen. Give me this investiture, and I'll return to the *Spellship* to find a cure. There must be an answer." She paused then, but decided that the secret was worth revealing. "One of the things I've never told you about is a place Nara knows of. She's spoken of it often, though obscurely. She returned from the Umbral Depths changed. She'd been touched by a goddess, and in a deliberate way. That makes me wonder if this goddess isn't some mouldering Catalyst, but rather very much alive."

Nebiat's expression tightened, and her eyes took on a very interested cast. "Go on."

"I think there's a world in the darkness," Frit explained. "I think this god or goddess runs a library or repository of knowledge of some sort. I've tried to puzzle out who or what they might be, but haven't come up with anything concrete. It's the place where they found the *Talon*, and learned about the *Spellship*."

"And you believe that this god might know of a way to free me." Nebiat gave a slow smile. "I knew you were the right choice. Come, taste of divinity."

The shade vanished. Frit spun around slowly, but there was no sign of Nebiat. She was just beginning to wonder what was going on when light pulsed from the star. That light didn't behave as other quanta might. It shone only on her, the favor of a divine being so old it remembered the birth of the stars in this galaxy.

The magic that was washed over her was hot and soothing. Pure flame, an ocean of pure flame, swam around her. It found her nose, and her mouth, eyes, and ears. The magic flooded into her body, pouring in through any avenue it could find. Power exploded through every part of her body, more than any mortal could hope to contain.

That power brought more than raw magical strength. Understanding filled her mind, ripping away veils she hadn't even known existed. All the theoretical texts she'd read about flame reading and godsight, like Voria used, were suddenly practical.

Possibilities rippled out in all directions, some more probable than others. The further they stretched the more fragile they became, until they disappeared into a mass of indistinct possibilities at the edge of her vision. There was so much, but somehow she was able to comprehend it all.

"I have increased your cognitive ability," Nebiat explained, the shade giving Frit a triumphant smile. "I have also unlocked godsight, which will enable you to counter our enemies. If you wish, you may translocate back to the *Spellship*, or you may linger here and visit the temple your sisters have erected."

Frit peered longingly down at the world. She very nearly translocated down to the surface. It would be wonderful to catch up with her sisters, to hear them laugh and to hug them. But it would be short-lived. They'd soon realize she'd been elevated above them, and the jealousy would begin. The politics. She just didn't have the strength for it yet.

Soon, she'd return home and try to lead these people. For now, though, she owed Nebiat. She'd find a way to free her, if that way could be found.

45

UNDERESTIMATED

What *have you done?* Krox's voice thundered through Nebiat's mind, and while she no longer felt pain in the same way, it was still uncomfortable.

She smiled down at Frit, watching as her creation began to experiment with the enormous amount of *fire* magic Nebiat had invested in her. Oceans of the stuff. Likely far more than had ever been given to a guardian before.

Fully a third of our fire *now resides in that creature. If her species were not uniquely suited to interface with that magic, she would have been obliterated by that much power.*

Nebiat's shade gave a delighted laugh. She stared up at Krox, or rather at what she had made from him. The god would prefer to be an amorphous star, which seemed such an unimaginative waste.

Every primitive society, in every sentient species, worships the sun, Krox rumbled, his irritation undiminished. *Your thoughts are so...chaotic. Why would you do this? I cannot see your rationale. You are hiding much from me, it seems.*

Hope swelled in Nebiat. She'd been learning to hold her

own in this eternal game of tug of war, something she very much sensed Krox would prefer she not know.

Your perspective is the literal opposite of a mortal, Nebiat explained. *All mortal species, at least those I have encountered, are tribal in nature. We work together. This is as true for my species as it is for weak species like humanity. Mortals understand intrinsically that we are greater than the sum of our parts.*

Krox's irritation deepened into true anger, the first time Nebiat had truly witnessed it. The god swelled, immense strength surging. But surging impotently. Krox could do nothing, thanks to Teodros's binding. *You do not possess even a wisp of understanding of what you have done. You have not created a servant, which even I understand the need for. Servants can greatly extend our influence. You have created a rival. This godling is far weaker than us, but make no mistake, she is a god in her own right. She possesses so much strength that she could make her own guardian. Why? What benefit does imbuing her with so much strength provide you?*

The outburst stoked Nebiat's hope into certainty. Krox was afraid. Not of her, but of what she might do. *I will keep my thoughts to myself on this matter, but since I know that you will not leave me in peace otherwise, I suppose you are owed an explanation. Frit is now powerful enough that Voria will be forced to treat her as an equal. Voria believes that I think the same way you do. The idea that I could give so much power to a being who isn't explicitly loyal to me will be inconceivable. This will create the possibility I need to exist. Surely even gods understand the concept of misdirection.*

She left it at that, and watched as Krox pulsed thoughtfully. It did not take the god very long to puzzle out her true motivations. *You suggest that the reason for this folly is to make your enemy fear you, which is plausible, but a lie. I have watched your mind. You are too cunning not to have considered what might happen if your new servant decides she is your enemy. What will you do if Frit betrays you?*

She will not. Nebiat's confidence was total, and she reveled in Krox's consternation. The god could feel her certainty. *You want to know why, but you are literally incapable of understanding how mortals make their choices. Frit has the power of a goddess, as I do, but the truth is both of us are still mortals. We think like mortals. Frit will not turn on me, I assure you. Because I will give her no reason to turn on me. The key to an alliance, which is what I have forged, is mutual interest. Frit wants the same things I do.*

Krox's anger broke like a tidal wave hitting a granite shore. Amusement leaked in, then overtook the rage. *Ah, little goddess, your hubris is incredible. Frit wants the same things you do, FOR NOW. We shall see if you come to regret this little decision.*

Nebiat's amusement also grew. The god thought it knew her ultimate plan, but it had no idea. None of them did. When her plans came to fruition the entire sector would be shocked. Until that day let them continue to underestimate her, as Krox did.

46

GOODBYE

Frit found translocation to be the most intuitive of all magic. Think about a place, and then simply be there. She arrived in her quarters on the *Spellship*, which were cold and empty. A single flower sat in a vase on the nightstand, which hadn't been there when she'd left. One of Kaho's little gifts.

He left them regularly, and never once accepted credit when she'd thanked him. Instead he liked to pretend they must be from some other secret admirer. She smiled, then exited her quarters and made her usual walk to the library.

No one accosted her. No one looked up at her. She was invisible, as usual, which was terrifying from a tactical perspective. Frit had been bred for combat, and had read countless treatises on erecting defenses. Allowing an enemy guardian to enter your ship at will was a massive security flaw. What if Talifax translocated in and executed Nara, then left?

She entered the library's vaulted room, her smile growing when she spotted Kaho at a table near the door. He had several tomes spread before him, and his snout was deeply buried in one on the table before him.

A group of scholars clustered around a table on the opposite side of the room, and Frit heard Nara's voice, though she couldn't make out what she was saying. She paused, and decided she wanted to speak to Kaho before saying goodbye to Nara. That she wanted to put off as long as possible.

"Kaho?" she called as she neared the table.

He looked up, his slitted eyes focusing on her. They widened and he rose hastily to his feet. "Frit, I—I had no idea. You're glowing like, well, I don't really have a basis of comparison. The only word I have to describe you is goddess, and I am not speaking of how attractive you are. Though you are certainly a goddess in that respect as well."

She gave a delighted laugh, and flung her arms around Kaho's waist. "Thank you."

"For what?" He wrapped his wings protectively around them.

"For believing in me." She pushed gently against him, and disengaged. Kaho released her, and understanding lay in his gaze.

"You're not staying," he muttered, the words stripped of all emotion. His tail drooped though, revealing his disappointment.

"I can't." She bit her lip. "I've had a lot of time to think. I need to find a way to free Nebiat. I've agreed to do that, and after having spent time with her I think it's in our people's best interests."

"Our people?" Kaho eyed her curiously. "Are you speaking of her world?"

"It is that, true, but it is also our world." She smiled as she thought of it, entire continents full of their respective peoples. That's what it would grow into, given time. "I know you don't understand my rationale. In time, I think you will. I have to solve this, and it can't be done here. If I want to help Nebiat I need to speak to an elder god. The same one that Nara went to in the Umbral Depths."

Kaho shook his head sadly, his tail drooping. "I believe she's under some sort of magical compulsion that will not allow her to speak of it. They all are. It seems a prudent precaution, one I don't see an easy way to circumvent."

Frit's eyes narrowed and she gave a wicked smile. "One of the few advantages to being a fly on the wall is that people say all sorts of things in front of you. Voria had a map into the Umbral Depths, and if I can get a look at it, then I can translocate to that world."

Kaho eyed her sidelong, and settled back into his chair. "I suspect it may not be...quite that simple."

Frit couldn't help but laugh at that. "Probably not. I'm going to miss you."

Kaho faced her fully, and his emotions played across his scaly face, all the things she knew he wanted to say made clear in those soulful eyes. "I'll miss you too. I wish I could go with you, but I have made my choice, and do not shift allegiances lightly. I hope we never have to meet in battle."

Only in that moment did the magnitude of what she'd done come crashing down on Frit. Going to war with Kaho and with Nara, was now a definite possibility. She needed to accept that.

"I'll do everything I can to prevent that." She licked her lips, a puff of smoke rising with a hiss. "Give me time to work with Nebiat, and I will push for peace. We all know Nefarius is the real enemy at this point, and that Krox has to be contained or he'll be just as bad. Nebiat can do that, if she's allowed the space. People don't have to like her. They just need to stay out of the rift."

He shook his head sadly. "I do not know what will happen. Come and see me if you can."

"I'd like that." She rested a smoldering hand on his arm. "And I'll come back, I promise."

She turned from him and hurried off, before her emotions got the better of her. This was going to be hard enough as it was. Leaving Kaho behind had been difficult, but facing Nara could lead to armed conflict, though she suspected her godsight suggested that possibility was remote.

Frit strode across the marble floor, carefully navigating a path even as she considered the extravagance that had gone into this vessel's creation. It showed her, in one more small way, the field she was playing on. She'd just agreed to serve the type of being who created this ship.

Nara sat at a table surrounded by perhaps a dozen scholars, each of whom jealously guarded their position. Frit moved to the back of the line, and tried to edge her way closer. She earned a few annoyed glares, but didn't make it any nearer to her friend.

Old Frit would have meekly turned away and come back another time. Unfortunately, that Frit was now a luxury. One she could no longer afford. Frit stepped forward and gently stoked the *fire* magic within her.

Heat radiated from her, intense enough to be painful. The closest scholars backed away with cries, and Frit flared her aura again. Now *fire* rose from every portion of her body, white and pure, and hot. Hot enough that every last one of the scholars began backing away.

Only then did Nara look up and notice her, and her eyes went comically wide. "Frit, uh, you're melting the edge of the table." Nara reached out and moved an ancient tome that had been sitting near the part of the table turning red from heat.

Frit dampened her aura, but only slightly. She folded her arms, and met Nara's gaze. "We need to talk. In private would be best."

"Could we maybe do this—"

"Send them away, Nara." Frit closed her eyes, and kept a tight rein on her anger.

Shuffling feet sounded all around them, and Frit finally opened her eyes to find Nara sitting alone. The scholars hadn't retreated very far, but Frit no longer cared if they watched. She'd say what needed to be said, and then be on her way.

"I've made a choice you aren't going to like," Frit began, licking her lips. "Nebiat came to Kaho with an offer."

Nara froze, and her face drained of blood. So Frit kept on.

"Kaho refused that offer," she paused, but only for an instant. She needed to do this. "Next Nebiat came to me. She needed a guardian, and I agreed."

Nara's face fell, and tears began to flow from her eyes. "Why, Frit? After what she did to Shaya you have to know what that means."

The scholars backed further away, and more than a few had erected *life* wards in apparent anticipation of the combat they believed was about to play out.

"Krox wants to enslave the galaxy," she explained. "The only thing keeping him from doing that is Nebiat. She's repopulated her world, somehow. There are tens of thousands of Wyrms, and thousands of Ifrit. They're prospering. The world is amazing. In a generation it will exceed Virkon. Maybe even sooner. Nebiat agreed to give me the power to help protect that world, and to shape its people. She's offered a home, one where I won't be a freak."

"You have to know she's just telling you what you want to hear," Nara snapped. Her eyes flashed as she shot to her feet and planted both palms on the table. "I cannot believe how disappointed—"

"Oh, get over yourself," Frit roared. She stabbed an accusing finger at her friend. "You're the same type of traitor I'm accused of being, but of course they welcomed *you* back with open arms. Gave you a position of power, and their trust, of course. Don't act like you're better than me, Nara. You don't have all the facts, and if our friendship ever meant anything to you, then you'll consider those facts before making any decisions."

Nara took a deep breath and sat back down. Her expression softened, and tears fell unheeded. "You're right. I'm sorry. Tell me, please. I'm sorry I wasn't there for you."

"It's not your fault." Frit dimmed her aura and moved to sit across from her best friend, grateful that Nara had proven reasonable. She regretted her outburst. That hadn't been fair. "I still remember how scared and lost you were when you first came to the Temple of Enlightenment. That girl became my friend, and she still is."

Another tear slid down Nara's freckled cheek. "I don't understand. Help me understand, Frit. Please."

"Nebiat is keeping Krox in check, for now." She sighed and leaned back in her chair. "Eventually Krox will devour her, and when he does he'll be free. When that day comes he'll be as dangerous as Nefarius, or maybe even more so. Nebiat is the only thing keeping him in check. She asked me for one thing. She wants me to find a way to free her before Krox wins."

"So that's it." Nara straightened and gave Frit a calculating look. "Nebiat needs you to save her, and you need me to do that. That's why you're here."

Frit nodded. "I want to find the world you went to in the Umbral Depths. I want to find the same answers you did."

"But you have to know I'm not allowed to talk about that." Nara sighed. "I'm not sure I would even if I could."

"You don't have to say a word," Frit said. "Just tell me where you found the map."

"I can't help you." Nara shook her head sadly. "The map was in the *Big Texas*'s computer, and the ship didn't survive the trip."

"That's all I needed. Thank you." Frit leaned across the table, and tried to ignore the tears in her own eyes. "I'll find a way to help you win this war, Nara. We don't have to be enemies."

"I hope you're right." Nara rose, and they hugged, perhaps for the last time.

47

THE FIST

There was no fanfare when Skare arrived in the system known by its Catalyst—the Fist of Trakalon. The system was far enough out of the way that few had reason to come here. There were no natural resources and no habitable worlds.

The only features of note were three gas giants, each a different boring shade of orange, all orbiting an equally boring star.

Even the Catalyst wasn't much to look at. The untrained observer would have called it a planet, and it did fit many of the criteria. Most of the structure was mineral. Granite and iron and osmium and many other metals and rocks veined through what were clearly the fingers of the galaxy's most titanic fist.

Those fingers were attached to a hand that had been severed at the wrist, but it was easy to extrapolate the size of the god from that one severed appendage. Trakalon wouldn't even notice the *Dragon's Skull*, or the sizable fleet Skare had brought. They were smaller than insects. More on the scale of bacteria, perhaps.

Skare rather enjoyed the reminder of his relative size, because it underscored the sheer immensity of the beings he was dealing with. Soon Nefarius would rise, and when she did he would learn the true meaning of service.

He had little doubt that his own ambitions would be secondary, but he'd seen how Talifax operated. The guardian was free to accumulate power. Free to do as he willed for millennia at a time, so long as he was always tending to the needs of his master.

Skare was more than prepared to sacrifice whatever Nefarius wished. He doubted she would ask much, as any intelligent deity would see the value in a willing servant. Not a servant with their own interests, but rather a servant willing to skim power off the top while accomplishing the goals of their master.

"Caelendra, plot a course inside the fist, please." Skare rose nervously from his chair, and watched as the scry-screen showed their approach.

The bridge crew, nameless techs as far as he was concerned, busied themselves at various consoles. It would have been a simple matter to automate their work, but Skare valued skilled subordinates. They often spotted things their masters were blind to.

The vessel swung ponderously around the fist, to the part where the thumb curled over the index finger. The *Dragon Skull* slipped into the shadowed recesses, disappearing into the area where the fingers met the palm. The area where Talifax had been quietly orchestrating the return of his mistress for who knew how many millennia.

The ship entered the cavernous center chamber, where a pool of immense *void* magic undulated and pulsed, confined by the magical wards etched into every visible inch of the surrounding rock. Those wards did more than just contain the magic...they hid it from scrying.

"That was the reason," Talifax's voice rumbled from barely a meter away, "that I chose this place."

Skare darted an irritated glance at the guardian in his bulky black armor. In his surprise Skare had very nearly activated his new armor, which was, so far as he knew, still a secret from Talifax. Keeping it that way was vital. It was possible the armor was strong enough to overcome Talifax, but if they ever clashed, Skare knew overwhelming and unexpected force was his only hope for victory. It must be a surprise.

He considered chastising Talifax for sneaking up on him, but any reaction was a victory for the mysterious semideity. So Skare gave him nothing beyond the glance.

"Yes, yes, I understand." Skare waved dismissively at the near-deity. "The fist's *earth* magic cloaks the blood of Nefarius. Not even the watcher in the depths can pierce your wards. We are all very proud, I assure you."

Talifax barked a very human laugh, and shook his helmeted head, the unreadable visor focusing on Skare. "I suspect there may be a note of sarcasm there. I admit I will miss our little chats after we accomplish what we set out to do."

Skare ignored the obvious bait. Talifax was implying Skare wouldn't survive the rebirth, but Skare refused to ask why. He wouldn't get a straight answer, and suspected Talifax was just trying to distract him. In a way that was good. If Talifax thought him worthy of misdirection then he must see Skare as a threat.

Talifax gestured at the wards. "You aren't wrong, but you did not capture the whole truth. Many mortal mages do not understand the true nature of magic. In time, one god can digest another. *Earth* can be converted into *void*."

Skare's eyes widened as that single bit of knowledge reordered his entire world view. It was so simple. How had he missed it? "So in addition to hiding our endeavors, you are using the fist as a sort of incubator."

"Precisely." Talifax approached the scry-screen. "I have been draining the magic for centuries, gradually strengthening my mistress while drawing from the fallen titan." He turned back to Skare, that mask as inscrutable as ever. "That process is nearly complete. When that happens the wards will fail, and all our enemies will realize what we have done. If you have not accumulated the requisite number of ships we will not be able to conduct the ritual. Either way...they will come for us."

"The fact that you don't know if I have enough ships is promising." Skare folded his arms, and delivered a confident smile. If Talifax hadn't seen the ships it was that much more likely he had no idea about the armor. "I've kept those vessels cloaked from all possibilities, but I assure you...we have enough. More than enough."

"Excellent." Talifax took several booming steps closer. "Then only one piece remains. Our enemies will bring it to us, we will claim it, and our mistress will be reborn. I must admit, Inuran, that I am quite pleasantly surprised by your dedication and ingenuity. You have accomplished more than any other servant I have ever employed."

"Thank you, mighty one." Skare gave a respectful bow, not too deep. Talifax might believe him a servant, but once Nefarius rose he would find out how very mistaken he was.

Skare would only serve one master.

48

NO

Voria had retreated to the *Spellship* in the wake of Virkonna's grand stunt. She was painfully aware that she needed Virkonna, and Inura, to help fight Krox. If Talifax succeeded, they'd be needed to stop Nefarius too.

She simply could not do this alone.

The problem, of course, was the same Aran faced. Virkonna's motives clearly did not take into account her followers, and despite elevating a guardian—a guardian she'd agreed to listen to—Voria remained skeptical.

It seemed far more likely that Virkonna would trample a path toward her enemies, and anyone in the way would get crushed. The best she could hope for was minimizing the people in the way.

Voria had spent every free moment in the Chamber of the Mirror trying to determine the best course to that end. The mirror had been helpful, and she was finally learning how to master its abilities.

She was about to summon another weave of possibilities when the air near her began to vibrate, then resolved into a simple one-way missive. Virkonna's thunderous voice was unmistakable.

"Greetings, vassal. My brother has informed me of the role he intends you to play, and I have acquiesced and will allow you to ride to war with us. Before that can happen you must come to my spire and take your vows. My patience is not infinite. Be swift."

Voria's heart ached as she considered how Ikadra would have reacted. She still had no idea how or when Inura would restore the staff, and without a significant increase in her *air* magic she couldn't do it herself.

As it stood Voria had to decide how to react. She could try sending a response, but doing so would force Virkonna to come in person, and Voria sensed that the deity considered such things beneath her.

She could go, of course, but doing so signaled that she was willing to follow Virkonna as a master. She wasn't. Voria would be part of an alliance, and would cede control of any pantheon they created, but she wasn't going to be anyone's lap dog. Certainly not a god who murdered swathes of her own population with that kind of casual abandon.

In the end there was only one choice. Voria concentrated, and translocated down to Virkonna's spire. The more she used the ability the faster she recovered and could use it again.

She appeared in the midst of a decadent party, with Virkonna seated near the center of a half dozen Kem'Hedj boards, all of which she was playing at the same time. And winning. Voria understood how, of course. Godsight made the game pointless, and Voria wondered why Virkonna still indulged. It couldn't have been simple ego. There were easier ways of proving her superiority to her followers.

"I have come, as you have requested." Voria offered a low

and proper Shayan bow, the kind she'd only ever offered to Aurelia when she'd been Tender.

"It wasn't a request." Virkonna rose from the air cushion she'd fashioned, but continued to play all six games while speaking to Voria. Scales drifted from her body, landing on each board with the same precision. "I ordered you here so that we could clarify the nature of our relationship."

Power wafted off Virkonna in waves, and the display wasn't lost on Voria. She was flexing her divine muscles to underscore their relative differences in strength.

Voria folded her arms, and kept her tone as neutral as she could manage. "And what do you see that nature as?"

"Master and servant," Virkonna answered without hesitation. "Your power comes from a sliver of Inura, my younger, weaker brother. Because you've done well with that sliver I am willing to grant you a sliver of *air* as well, enough to make you a proficient enchanter. You will serve as a battlefield medic, and when not in battle you will aid my brother in creating his engines of war."

"My power," Voria replied, as mildly as if relating the weather, "comes from Shaya, and from Marid, and from my own followers. It's true that some of the magic originated from your bother, but Inura was nowhere to be found during my ascension. That was left to one of my very mortal followers."

"You quibble over the gap between scales," the deity snapped. Lightning crackled in her eyes, clearly designed to intimidate. Voria decided she was having none of it and stood her ground as the elder goddess continued her tirade. "The bulk of your power comes from my brother, and the rest comes from my elder sister. Marid is dead, and I speak for her. I speak for Inura as well."

"Only because he's otherwise occupied," Voria countered. "And I don't accept that you speak for Marid. Drakkon does."

"My nephew," Virkonna growled, "is not capable of speaking for a god. He is a potent ally, but barely a demigod. He's only seen a few dozen millennia. He is hardly qualified to make the kind of decisions an elder god must make. Now we are done with this discussion. You will do as you are told, and I will hear no more of it."

"No," Voria said mildly, the word carrying across the top of the spire, enough so every Wyrm heard. "I won't. I do not work for you. If you seek allies, then I would be happy to count myself among them. But I am not a pawn to be expended as you see fit. I will not die as Shaya did. I will find a way to help the mortals of this sector, to shield them from you, and all the other callous gods."

She realized she'd raised a hand at some point, and had stabbed an accusing finger at Virkonna. Only then did she grasp the magnitude of her words. Even knowing that, Voria wouldn't have taken them back. Someone had to stand up to these gods, to teach them that mortals were worthy of consideration.

"Out of affection for your forebear I will not slay you out of hand." Virkonna's wings flared behind her, and she took a threatening step closer to Voria. "My nephew thinks highly of you, as does my new guardian. I will allow you to live, but only if you vacate my sight. You will not be present at the battle against Talifax. You have lost that right, child god. After we have dealt with that threat we will speak again, and you will learn your place. Now go. Before I change my mind."

Voria considered several choice responses, but delivered none of them. Instead she teleported back to the *Spellship.* Virkonna was sending her away like a child, and she doubted there was any way to stop that, short of capitulation or outright war.

Virkonna was still taking Aran, though, and the *Talon*. Voria needed to make certain Nara was on that ship. That was the next best thing to her being there personally, and whatever Virkonna believed, they were going to need every god and every mage.

She had no illusions about the newly awakened goddess, either. Virkonna could and would attack Voria; of that she had no doubt. Retreat had been her only option, even if it felt like cowardice.

49

REASSIGNED

Nara sat alone in one of the *Spellship*'s dining halls, which reminded her of the *Talon*'s mess, only far larger. She pushed the plate away, and decided not to pick at the last few crumbs of the chocolate cake she'd just devoured.

She knew she was an emotional wreck, but she took great pride that no one else knew it. Throwing herself into her work gave her the occasional moment where she was blessedly free of thinking about Frit, and all the reasons her best friend had left.

Only one fact mattered, in the end. A fact she hadn't even confided to Voria, which, given the circumstances, couldn't really be laid at Nara's feet. Voria was busy dealing with Virkonna, and before that had been dealing with waking her, and before that had been dealing with the attempt to save Ternus.

Frit had become the guardian of their oldest enemy. There would be no amnesty. No reconciliation. If Voria learned of it there was a real possibility her and Frit would fight, and one of them would end up dead.

For that reason Nara had kept Frit's secret to herself, for now anyway. She prayed that Frit was smart enough to depart swiftly, and after she was gone Nara would speak to Voria.

The hairs on the back of her neck rose, and a moment later a fiery missive flitted up to her. Nara withdrew her scrypad, and let the message play. It was Voria. Did she know?

"Is everything all right?" Nara couldn't see much behind Voria, just the sky, which was consistent with Virkonna's spire.

Voria's face fell. "Pretty much what we'd expect. The worst case scenario. I've been banished from Virkon, and forbidden to attend the battle with Talifax, once we've discovered the location."

Nara blinked a few times, and tried to decide how to react to that. "I don't...why? What benefit could leaving a full god behind do? Presumably Talifax has an entire fleet of those ships, and Inura must have told her about them."

Voria shook her head, the frustration clear on her glowing features. "She will not see reason. But we still have an opportunity to influence the outcome. Virkonna will keep Aran close to her now. I'd like you to move to the *Talon*, and be my eyes and ears for whatever comes next. If there is a battle I cannot afford to be blind."

"Of course," Nara said without thinking. "Pickus should be able to manage the bureaucracy we've created, at least until I come back."

Voria appeared relieved. "I'm glad you see the need. I'm going to the chamber. Since we won't see each other again until this is over—good luck, Nara."

"Thank you, Voria. We'll do you proud."

The missive dissolved, leaving Nara alone in the dining hall. She needed to fetch her things and get over to the

Talon. Seeing Aran would be good, at least. She still wasn't sure where she stood with the others, but she hoped that some of them might be happy to see her.

She could use a silver lining at this point.

"I apologize," Kaho's deep voice rumbled from behind a neighboring shelf, one full of knowledge scales. He stepped out from behind it with a knowledge scale in either hand. "I did not mean to overhear. You are leaving?"

Nara started at the hatchling's sudden appearance, but relaxed once she realized who it was.

"Before you go I wanted an opportunity to tell you something." Kaho looked eminently uncomfortable, and his tail swished in agitation behind him. "I am not...practiced with emotions. I wished to tell you that, while I do not expect you to reciprocate the sentiment, I consider you to be my closest friend. Perhaps even closer than Frit, who has my heart, in spite of her rash decisions. From one outcast to another... take care of yourself, Nara. For whatever it's worth, I am sorry for our former conflict on this world. I regret my actions."

Nara found herself tearing up unexpectedly. She hadn't realized it, but she'd grown quite attached to the big lizard. "You've become a close friend, Kaho. You taught me that dragons, the Krox specifically, are not inherently evil. Nebiat is evil, but your people are not. Thank you for teaching me that lesson. I'm going to miss you."

"I hope we see each other again soon, and that Frit somehow escapes the choice she has made." Kaho offered a tentative smile.

Nara sighed at that. "I don't see it happening. She's made her choice. If we see her again I expect it will come to blows."

She hoped for all their sakes that she was wrong, but in her heart she knew that she wasn't.

50

BROKEN

Frit appeared inside a room that, until this morning, she'd never have assumed she'd find herself inside of. The walls were deeply shadowed, and the only light source came from a large mirror bobbing up and down in the center of the room as it rotated in an endless circle.

The Mirror of Shaya, perhaps the most powerful scrying device in the sector. It was a device Nebiat no doubt coveted, and she'd probably have encouraged Frit to steal it had she known of its proximity. Thankfully, Nebiat had no idea. Frit wasn't here to steal it. She was here to use it.

As she understood it, flame reading, or fire dreaming—they seemed to be the same thing—required both *fire* and *dream*. At a simple level it seemed that *dream* provided the glimpse into the endless possibilities, and *fire* allowed the user to burn away the unlikely possibilities until they'd found the most likely. She knew it wasn't that simple, but that was the best overview she'd yet found.

"Let's hope they don't have any wards," Frit muttered. She didn't detect any, and suspected that if there were any, they were around the outside of the room. It explained how

Talifax always moved around without anyone knowing. Translocation was cheating, basically.

She moved to stand in front of the mirror, which showed her reflection on its silvered surface. The mirror stopped as she approached, then turned to face her, like a pet paying attention to its master. She sensed a disturbing amount of intelligence from the device.

"Can you understand me?" she asked, extending a hand to touch the mirror. A shock went up her finger, and she yanked her hand back. "Okay, I guess that was pretty stupid."

The mirror didn't answer, but the surface swirled with mist, then resolved into the bridge of an unfamiliar ship. Rusted metal walks lined narrow corridors and low ceilings, the hallmark of dirt-cheap Ternus vessels.

"That certainly matches the description of the *Texas*," she muttered to herself. "You can sense what I need, can't you?"

Frit gasped. The mirror was gone. The room was gone. Suddenly she was on the bridge of the tiny frigate. The crew was gathered around the console, watching the scry-screen, which showed nothing but darkness.

And then she saw it. Right there on the screen in blocky green letters. Frit fixed her attention on the first set of coordinates, and committed them to memory. The vision continued, and the ship passed through some sort of illusion. It now showed the silhouette of a planet. This must be the place. If she could only glimpse those final coordinates.

She poured more strength into the vision, channeling as much *fire* as she could hurl into the device. A river of star stuff flowed into the mirror, more than any mortal had ever dreamed of touching. It was working! The image stabilized, and she saw the final coordinates.

Agony, immeasurable as it was irresistible, seized her in its icy jaws. She fell to her knees and in the distance heard shattering, as if a large pane of glass had been smashed into the marble floor. Frit desperately sought to master the pain, but the best she could manage was cradling her skull.

She had no idea how much time passed, but when she regained full consciousness she was staring up into Voria's stern face. The glowing woman was even more frightening now that she was a goddess, and Frit snapped into a sitting position.

"You've managed to achieve something I thought impossible," Voria murmured, eyeing Frit with the kind of curiosity reserved for a magical phenomenon one wished to study. "You've destroyed the Mirror of Shaya. Shattered it into a lump of magical materials that I may as well melt down and forge into a club, so I can beat myself to death. It would be both quicker and kinder than the fate you've left me. So far as we knew, that mirror was older than any object in the known universe, save Worldender."

Frit rose shakily to her feet, and wished she'd brought her staff, or anything else to lean on. Her head ached abominably. Did Voria know why she was here? Did she know about Nebiat? "I'm sorry. I know I shouldn't have been using it, but in my defense I thought it was indestructible."

"As did I," Voria admitted. "What's even more troubling, to my mind, is the vast amount of magical strength you now possess. You didn't merely visit some Catalyst. You've been touched by a goddess." Voria folded her arms, and gave Frit what Nara had termed the confession stare. "Which one?"

For one terrible moment Frit couldn't locate words. Should she lie? Flee? No, she owed Voria better than that. She owed her the truth.

"Nebiat," Frit admitted, then rose to her full height, and

found she was taller than Voria. She met Voria's stare pound for pound. "I'd hoped to avoid this meeting, but it doesn't look like I can."

Voria tapped her lip and said nothing, though the hard stare didn't slip. It was subtle, but Frit could also feel magic building within the goddess. *Life* and *water*, probably forming some sort of defensive magic. She hoped so at least.

"I'm sorry about the mirror." Frit offered her palms apologetically. She took a careful step back, and winced when glass crunched underfoot. "Listen I know we're technically enemies now. Again. I mean, I can't keep it straight."

"Why?" Voria asked. "You had a home here."

"This ship and your kindness to me isn't the reason, but we both know this wasn't a real home for me. It was a large prison cell. Why did I take Nebiat's offer? Because she needs a handler," Frit said, a better explanation than she'd given Kaho or Nara. She'd had time to think about the question. "She needs someone to curtail her mad schemes, and she needs someone to suggest reason once in a while. To exert at least some influence, and to curb her ambitions."

Voria gave a sad sigh. "You realize you've left me only one option?"

Frit struck an instant before Voria could. She called *fire* from the deep, endless well in her chest. But Frit colored that magic with *void*, tapping into the greater path of Destruction. She fired a bolt of disintegration, even as she hated herself for doing it.

Self-preservation took over.

Frit rolled backwards even as Voria dodged the disintegrate. She came to her feet and flung a pair of fireballs, one from each hand. "Try dodging this."

The overlapping explosions washed over Voria, and temporarily obscured her from view. When the fire faded,

Voria stood behind a *life* ward, glaring. "You will not slay me so easily."

"I'm not trying to slay," Frit cried, all the desperation alive in her voice. "I just want to leave. I'm sorry Voria. I never meant to betray you, or to destroy the mirror. Can't we just...walk away? The mirror won't be the only thing broken if we let this escalate."

Voria hesitated, then gave a nod of resignation. She bent to pick up a shattered shard of the Mirror of Shaya. The *life* ward winked out, and she offered the shard to Frit. "Take it. Bring it back to Nebiat. Tell her that her little scheme worked. She's deprived me of a powerful tool, and left me all but blind before the rebirth of Nefarius." Voria's face went ugly, and her next words were snarled. "You've cost me more than you can ever know, Frit. If we fall to Nefarius, know that it was you who caused our destruction. Now get out. If I ever see you again, then we'll find out if Nebiat gave you enough strength to withstand my wrath."

Frit gazed sadly down at the shard she held in her hand, and nodded. She couldn't blame Voria, but she wouldn't alter her actions, even if she could. She knew where to go now. Frit translocated, and left her old life behind.

51

BITTER ANSWERS

F rit would have preferred to collect her thoughts before venturing into the Umbral Depths, but Voria had put her on the spot, and she'd instinctively translocated to the coordinates she'd seen in the vision the mirror had shown her.

That probably wasn't the smartest approach, as she had no idea what using the ability in the Umbral Depths would do.

She appeared in the sky over a darkened world, one that may never have known the touch of a sun. Her senses had already been honed to see in the void, but Nebiat's tremendous gift further enhanced her sight. She could see the magma under the surface, sustaining the world in the frigid depths.

Yet there were also places she could not see. Somewhere in the northern continent lay a mountain surrounded by incredibly intricate wards. There were thousands of layers of them, each interlocking with the one above and below. The hand that had crafted them must be the most deft to ever weave a spell, or perhaps it had been erected by many pairs of hands.

Frit drifted toward the planet, willing herself to accelerate with a bit of *void*. The planet's atmosphere buffeted her, but her body had been designed for the rigors of space. Re-entry was...pleasant.

She arrived at the strange mountain, so much larger than any of the others around it, and immediately spotted the very man-made entryway. It was quite unlike the caves on surrounding mountains, and further proved that someone or something dwelled here. She landed gently outside, and walked into the wide tunnel.

"Ah, you have arrived," came a strange voice from the shadows. It articulated words in strange places, and the sounds were mushed together in an inhuman way.

Frit flared her aura, exposing the creature. Eight black eyes studied her, matched by an equal number of scaly limbs. She had no idea what manner of creature she was looking at, but it had spoken, which meant it could be conversed with.

"You were expecting me?" she demanded. She tried to sound imperious, like she imagined Nebiat would when imposing her will on the world.

"Of course." The creature sounded scandalized, as if it were unthinkable it not know of her arrival. "Please, I will escort you directly to Neith. The goddess is quite enraged. I have never seen such a fit from her. She is not prone to temper, and if you are the cause then...I would do what you can to set your affairs in order."

Frit blinked a few times, but followed the creature up the corridor. It led her to a pair of golden double doors, which stood open. She noted that every temple she'd been to had incorporated gold. It seemed too prevalent to be coincidence, and she wondered idly if the metal had properties she were unaware of.

"What is this place?" Frit hurried to keep up with the creature, which shuffled forward quite rapidly despite its odd gait.

"The first library," the creature calmly explained. It passed through the doors and into the mountain's hollowed-out interior.

Frit gazed around her in wonder, and realized what this place must be. Shelf after shelf after endless shelf lined every available wall, and all of them contained hundreds of knowledge scales. This place had to be the largest repository of knowledge in the sector. Far, far, larger than Shaya or the *Spellship*.

"This way, please." The creature sounded cross, and Frit realized she'd been standing there staring.

She fell into step behind the creature, which shuffled through rows of shelves seemingly at random. Within moments, Frit was hopelessly lost, and even being able to see the top of the mountain didn't do much to orient her. She had a sense that they were working their way toward the center, but beyond that had no idea where they were going.

The strange spider-creature stopped in front of an enormous pair of double doors, predictably made of gold. It turned to face her, and perhaps pity entered its gaze. "If you survive, and are permitted, we will be happy to find any data you wish to acquire."

"Thanks." She blinked up at the doors wondering what to do. She didn't have to wonder long. They swung silently open, as if beckoning her.

As soon as she stepped through them Frit detected immense strength. She could feel a god, a powerful one. It wasn't so strong as Krox, but it was much, much more powerful than Voria. And it was almost entirely comprised of pure *fire*, her primary aspect.

"Hello?" Frit called as she flew into the air and drifted toward the magical signature. "I'm told that you were expecting me, whoever you are."

"Indeed," a voice thundered, too alien to assign any sort of gender to. The words were painful, but Frit ignored the discomfort.

Frit scanned the darkness, and saw a roughly Wyrm-shaped creature scuttle forward. It looked like the creature that had guided her here, but a thousand times larger, and with thick, scaly wings behind its back.

"You have aroused an emotion I have not experienced in sixty-seven centuries." The creature scuttled forward further, and a thick white ball of flame appeared near the top of the cavern, illuminating its terrible visage. It contained the worst parts of spiders and Wyrms, and bits of nightmare stuffed in between. "Anger. Rage, perhaps. When a god reaches my age all emotions are rare, special occasions. So, for this reason, I will not devour you before learning more of your transgressions. I do not know how you have done what you have done, but I will have the tale."

"Uh." Frit knew she didn't sound very demigod like, but she'd just been caught redhanded doing something very, very bad. And she didn't even know what it was. "It's pretty short. I was trying to find this place. I knew you didn't want it found, but I figured out that you'd left clues so that Nara could come here. I used my godsight to scan their memories. That required the mirror. Everything seemed to go fine, right up until I saw this world."

"At which point," Neith thundered, all eight eyes blazing with inner flame, "the wards around this world and this reality snapped into effect. They did what they were designed to do and protected this place. In the process they destroyed one of the most ancient eldimaguses the galaxy, and perhaps the universe, has ever seen. The Mirror of Shaya was properly called the Mirror of Zelek, and predated any of the politics in this sector. It comes from the Great Cycle. Such objects are of incalculable worth."

"Respectfully, it was *your* magic that broke the mirror," Frit pointed out. She was so sick of being blamed for things, and in this instance there was no way she could have anticipated this. "You have all the knowledge in the galaxy here from what I can see. People are dying out there. We have so many questions, and no answers. Can you blame us for doing whatever we can to find help?"

The gods jaws quivered as it seemed to consider the problem. Finally, its body began to ripple and change. Frit watched in awe as a towering mountain became a woman roughly her size. Her skin was covered in a sea of scarlet scales so dark they could pass for black, and a pair of wings jutted majestically behind her.

She resembled the Wyrms on Virkon, until one reached her midsection. Instead of legs she had a thorax, with four legs attached to it. Four arms extended from her upper body, all covered in the same scales. There was not a bit of hair anywhere on her body.

"I have not worn this form in...well, longer than your species has existed." Neith scuttled forward, and Frit suppressed a shiver. She hated spiders. Neith fixed her with eight beady eyes, set into an all-too-human face. "I wear it now, because I have finally met a student capable of understanding divination as I understand it. Your transgression should not have been possible. That it was means you have a singular gift. If you can acquire a divine quantity of *dream*, there will be nothing you cannot see."

"Thanks?" Frit cleared her throat. "Listen, I don't want to sound hostile. I realize I'm bad at this diplomacy stuff, but, I came here for a reason. I was hoping for help."

"I know. You seek to free Nebiat from her binding." Neith's mouth broke into an amused smile, made terrifying by so many eyes and an utterly inhuman mouth. "She would be free of Krox, which is a sentiment many gods before her have voiced. From Shivan to Marid...so many great gods and goddesses died because of that monster. Krox is terrible beyond imagining."

Frit considered the awful star Nebiat had shown her, and agreed. She'd seen Krox firsthand, and that was enough to take the threat very seriously. "So you understand the problem. Will you help her? Nebiat is hardly a good person —or deity now, I guess—but she's far from the worst. I believe Nebiat can be persuaded to fight Nefarius, and we all know she's coming. I don't know where you stand in all this, but I can't believe you want her to come back."

"Ahh, child." The creature rumbled with laughter, which threatened the cavern and caused dust to rain down. "I would give almost anything to return to a time when I only needed to consider the simple circumstances surrounding this moment. When I only had to make one choice, made easy by visible cause and effect."

Frit sort of expected the patronizing tone, and didn't take offense. Eros had done it all the time, and he wasn't nearly as old as this...thing.

"I'm only just beginning to understand how to perceive other possibilities," Frit admitted. She didn't like ignorance, but the first step to eradicating your own weaknesses was identifying them. "You, from what I can see, might have invented divination. That's why I've come. You can show me the answers I cannot hope to find on my own, and you can warn me of implications I do not understand."

"And the first step to that is critical thinking." Neith raised a pair of scaled arms and rubbed them together. "Tell me, Frit, if we released Nebiat today, if she were suddenly her own being, what would the immediate implications be?"

Frit considered that. She knew that there was probably something obvious she was missing, but she stuck with what seemed to be the biggest problem. "Well, Krox would be free, unless we simultaneously find a way to keep him bound."

Neith nodded sagely. "Indeed, and I'm pleased to see you've considered that at least. Let's say we modify the ritual so that it will keep Krox in stasis. Let's assume doing so requires you to sacrifice another consciousness, one that will eventually be consumed, as Nebiat would be."

"That's horrible," Frit realized aloud. "There must be some other way."

"There is not." Neith seemed to take no joy in the words. "Krox will escape any trap we set for him. He is ancient and cunning. It takes a powerful will to shackle such a being, even for a short time. Nebiat has managed this. Finding a replacement would be nearly impossible."

Frit fell silent, and thought about that. They couldn't free Nebiat without also freeing Krox, unless they were willing to sacrifice someone else. That someone would need to be powerful, and powerfully motivated, or they'd be right back to Krox being free.

"We have to leave her where she is." The realization was a bucket of icy water over her shoulders. "Krox has to be contained."

"Why?" Neith leaned a bit closer, and studied Frit curiously. So close to human, but not. It was damned disturbing.

"Krox can resist Nefarius." Frit drifted a bit higher, and a bit of excitement leaked into her tone. "Krox is *necessary* to beat Nefarius."

"Very good." Neith gave an encouraging smile that landed nearer predatory. "No victory against Nefarius is assured, but in the few possibilities I have gleaned, Krox played a role. We must take that into account when making our calculations. Could I free Nebiat? Certainly. Will I? Quite the opposite. I will actively oppose anyone who seeks to liberate her."

Frit knew in that instant that she'd failed her new mistress, because she patently agreed with Neith's logic. There was no saving Nebiat. Not if they wanted survival for the rest of the sector.

52

ARE YOU MAD?

Nebiat spent countless hours crafting spectral forms. It was one of her few entertainments, and she indulged it often. Currently she'd focused on crafting the perfect spectral Wyrm.

The trick was making herself larger than any of her children, but not so large that they could not relate to her. After much thought Nebiat decided that being Drakkon's size was perfect. It was large enough to instill awe, as she'd learned to her horror back on Marid, but not so large that one would crater a continent simply by landing. That would prompt too much fear, and she didn't want to rule her people the same way her father had done. Besides, when her children grew she could simply adjust her avatar to match.

You spend too much time on these trivialities, Krox rumbled, his first words in more than a day. *You have convinced me that form matters, to an extent, but it cannot come at the expense of your greater strategy. Nefarius will come soon. You see the possibilities as clearly as I, those few not obscured by Talifax's meddling. Yet you do not seem to fear this, and take no steps to plan for it.*

Is that what you believe? That pleases me, old god, because it shows that I am better at hiding my thoughts than you would admit. Nebiat reveled in that. There were many problems she couldn't find solutions for, the greatest being Krox eventually devouring her mind. The idea that she was building defenses he couldn't penetrate gave her a shred of hope. *I will reveal a bit of my plan, but know that I do not care what your opinion is. Like it or don't. I will not change my plans.*

Very well, Krox rumbled back. *I will not attempt to sway you, though if I see flaws in your limited plans I will not be silent.*

Nor would I ask you to. Nebiat actually valued Krox's experience. She just understood the cost of relying on it. *I know that you place little value on underlings, but much as I hate it, I must rely on my guardian. Frit is intelligent, capable, and most importantly well liked by the right people. Gods and mortals alike are more likely to deal with her than with me. Particularly because she is operating under her own auspices, and they will know that. They will see she has not been coerced in any way.*

Krox pulsed thoughtfully. *I see value in this plan. You continue to surprise me. Your enemies revile you, as those who remember me do. They will not trust us or ally with us, because they know we will betray them when it suits us.*

But Frit, Nebiat pointed out, *is honorable. She is just. She is concerned with equality and fairness. As difficult as it may be, I must allow her to operate on my behalf. At best I might create another servant or two, but acting directly is foolish. You've made it very clear that Talifax can predict our movements. Well, if I choose not to move, to remain here, then I ensure I am no threat. Nefarius, if she rises, will focus on Voria and her allies. We are free to grow in strength, and to breed an army on the world below. By the time Nefarius can turn her attention to us we will be strong enough to resist her.*

There my faith in your plan ends. Now Krox pulsed amusement. *I have watched many cultures erroneously assume that they could resist Nefarius when she came. You have no idea what she is like, or how difficult to resist she will be. If she comes for this world your schemes will not save you. Any allies you make will not save you. Capitulation will not save you. Your only course is total, overwhelming victory against the greatest warrior of the greatest portion of the godswar still recorded in Neith's annals.*

Nebiat knew Krox wasn't deceiving her. She could see his thoughts, the memories of Nefarius's many victories. She had been terrible, and only bested through a coalition of powerful elder gods. Most of those elder gods no longer existed.

She was saved from having to answer when a being suddenly translocated into existence a mere few hundred kilometers from Krox's bulk. Frit had returned.

Nebiat joyously assumed her new spectral Wyrm form, and appeared in the sky near Frit. The Ifrit turned to face her, and Nebiat could tell from her guardian's facial expression that things had not gone well. She opened her jaws, and spoke in a deep, sonorous voice. "Tell me, guardian. What have you learned?"

"I've seen a great deal," Frit began, drifting closer, near Nebiat's slitted eye. "Some thing you will like, and I suppose I'll lead with that. In trying to uncover the location of the hidden world in the Umbral Depths, I was forced to use the Mirror of Shaya."

"And?" Nebiat demanded. She dearly wanted to get her claws on that device, but Frit wasn't carrying it now.

"The defenses of the deity I scryed kicked in." Frit's face fell, and she looked tremendously embarrassed. "The mirror shattered, and cannot be repaired. I was knocked unconscious in the blast, and woke up to find Voria standing over me."

"You are fortunate to be alive." Nebiat desperately sought to contain her curiosity. She'd been cooped up for entirely too long. At least Krox had stilled his commentary.

Frit shook her head, long strands of flaming hair drifting in space around her like a sea of writhing snakes. "No, I am not some tool, as it turns out. You may have given me a bit more magic than you meant to. I fought Voria to a standstill, and I might have been able to win that fight. She knew it, so we stopped, rather than destroy the *Spellship*. She asked me to tell you that your plan had succeeded, and to tell you that she hopes you are happy. She's lost the tool she needed to find Nefarius."

"Was the *Spellship* damaged?" Nebiat fought to contain her emotions. That ship was of paramount importance, but she could not afford to reveal that fact, not to anyone.

"No, thankfully." Frit's embarrassment deepened. "Just the room where the mirror was held."

"I'm sorry you were placed in that situation." Nebiat experienced a tiny bit of satisfaction. "Voria will be pleased to know that I *am* happy. We have deprived an opponent of a potent tool, and it cost us nothing. It was always my plan for Voria to fall fighting Nefarius. This changes nothing, and ensures she will be blind to my schemes. You have done well."

"The next part you'll like less." Frit gave a heavy sigh. "I made it to...my destination, and I'm now under a geas that will prevent me from speaking of the place, or the being who dwells there. I can relate our conversation, though."

"Does this mysterious goddess know of a way to free me?"

"I believe so," Frit explained, "but she was unwilling to

share it. The being explained to me what would happen if you were removed. Krox would be free, and the sector would pay the price. She would not provide the knowledge we needed. What's more, I was promised that if I continued to search that I would be actively opposed by a very powerful, and very much living, deity."

Nebiat closed her spectral eyes, but it did not stop her from seeing. Her options were narrowing. She hadn't really believed Frit would find a solution, but confirmation that she hadn't still stung. She reined in her anger, and tried to be magnanimous.

"Thank you, Frit. You've done what you can." She gestured at the world below with a titanic leg. "If you wish, you may retire to your temple. Your sisters have prepared quarters for you, and are eagerly awaiting your arrival. If I learn anything I will call for you."

"Nebiat?" Frit asked, rather more tentatively than Nebiat had come to expect.

"Yes, child?"

"This being believes Krox will be instrumental in stopping Nefarious." Frit eyed her searchingly. "Surely we should work together with Voria. If we combined forces we could better prepare, and maybe win this fight. I saw what Nefarius was like before and...we don't stand a chance. Not on our own. Nefarious is far stronger than anything you've seen, even Krox."

"Are you mad?" Nebiat demanded, her eyes flying open. "We attacked Shaya a handful of weeks ago. We killed tens of thousands of their citizens, and tore apart their blasted tree. Voria will never forgive me, and she will do anything to best me. If we put ourselves in a vulnerable position they will pounce, I assure you. No, they live or die without our intervention. Now go. Please. Before I grow angry."

"Of course." Frit executed a standing bow, and then translocated to the planet below.

I told you, Krox taunted. *There is no escaping me.*

Nebiat fought to suppress the growing panic. There appeared to be no way out, and she couldn't ever recall having been this terrified.

Do you know the goddess my guardian spoke of?

Of course, Krox rumbled. *The description is unmistakable. She is the watcher in the depths. Neith, the first Wyrm elevated by the Wyrm Mother. She has been an ally, at times, but more often an enemy. That is especially true now that we know where she is located. I suspect that even now she is moving her world.*

That gave Nebiat much to think on. Neith sounded like the one most likely to pierce the possibility that she was oh so carefully crafting. But that didn't matter, so long as Neith was on the run and unable to warn her allies.

She only needed to keep it secret a little longer.

53

YES, PHARAOH

F rit felt awful as she translocated down to the planet. She was terrified of the temple beneath her, its fluted spires curling up into the sky like wisps of flame. There was no way the structure could exist without magic, which Frit could feel even three hundred meters away.

As she watched, a hatchling glided in for a landing on a balcony, and an ash-scaled elder Wyrm leapt off another. Quite a bit of traffic flowed to and from the temple, though she didn't spy any of her sisters.

She hated the idea of simply knocking, but if she was Nebiat's guardian she was going to have to learn to conduct herself with authority and grace, like Voria, or Nebiat herself. Frit drifted lower, toward the base of the structure. The most traffic flowed here, with dozens of hatchlings seeking admittance through a wide doorway seemingly cut into the middle of the dancing flames.

Before she could step inside, something flared above her and she glanced up to see a cloud of native Ifrit, living flame, descend toward the temple. The flames disappeared into the tip of the central spire. Curious. What had brought them here and why?

Frit joined the hatchlings at the back of the line, which moved very slowly through the doorway. She couldn't see much of what awaited them inside, and instead listened to the hatchlings chat as she waited her turn.

"Is this your first time?" the smaller hatchling asked, his voice a deeper rumble than Kaho's. He sounded nervous.

"Third," the other hatchling replied with more confidence. "The sisters can do as they claim. Hedjet read my futures, and foresees my rise in a Great War. I will lead, she says. I've come to speak to Deshret, though he is much harder to obtain an audience with."

Frit cocked her head at that. The titles were in ancient draconic, and roughly translated as 'white crown' and 'red crown'. Two leaders perhaps? Maybe a chieftain and a spiritual leader? Frit was hardly conversant in cultural anthropology, so she hoped she was understanding correctly.

The line inched forward and she finally stepped inside the temple. The walls were the same living flame, dancing and undulating with a will of its own. A trio of Ifrit stood in white robes, which were untouched by their considerable heat. Two were recognizable as her sisters, but the third gave Frit pause. It was a man.

"Hedjet!" One of the Ifrit suddenly called. She was pointing frantically at something, trying to get the attention of the woman in the middle. "Hedjet, look!"

Frit glanced around to see what she was pointing at, but everyone around her was just as mystified as she was. She turned back, and found all three Ifrit, including the male, staring at her with their mouths hanging open.

"Uh, hi there." Frit took a cautious step forward. She was

not off to a great start as a supreme god-like leader. "Is one of you Hedjet, and if so, are you in charge?"

The Ifrit in the center had short hair, just barely touching her smoldering shoulders. She was perhaps six inches shorter too, which was more variance than the Ifrit back on Shaya had ever displayed. Of course neither of those was as odd as the male Ifrit off to the right. He was handsome, in a classic Shayan sort of way.

"I am Hedjet, Pharaoh." The sister dropped to her knees and prostrated herself. The other Ifrit copied the gesture, and all over the room hatchlings mimicked it. Within a few moments she was the only one standing.

"You can all stand up." She reached down and helped Hedjet back to her feet. "Don't ever get on your knees, not for anyone. Certainly not for me. Is this what Nebiat is making you do?"

"Making us?" Hedjet gave Frit a scandalized glance, then dropped it to the obsidian floor. "Pharaoh, mighty Nebiat does not speak to us. We are left to discover our own forms of worship. But the wisest among us realized she would appoint a prophet, one to lead us. And you have come. We recognize your strength, the touch of our goddess."

Frit couldn't really argue with any of that. It sounded pompous, but she supposed she was the divine instrument of a goddess. And these people did need leadership, if this was the best society they could come up with.

"It looks like I have my work cut out for me." She shook her head, and looked around. "We are equals. All of us. Wyrm, Ifrit, human...we are all sentient beings worthy of respect."

Hedjet blinked a few times but eventually nodded. "Of course, Pharaoh. If I seem hesitant it is only that this is new and will take time to adjust. Many Wyrms do not feel that—"

"That Ifrit are the equal of a true Wyrm," interrupted a deep, cultured voice. A hatchling strode down the wide stairs, his feet hissing each time they touched a flaming step. He walked boldly down to them, and as he approached, Hedjet started to drop to her knees.

Frit's hand shot out and caught her sister's wrist. She guided Hedjet back to her feet, and moved to intercept the smug hatchling. "I take it you must be Deshret?"

"I see word of my wisdom precedes me." The hatchling puffed up, and many other hatchlings in the room aped the gesture.

Ah, so that was how it was.

"Tell me, Deshret, do you believe that a mere Ifrit can be the equal of a...mighty Wyrm such as yourself?" She sauntered forward in the way that often drew Kaho's attention.

"I do not care what title you have been given," the hatchling growled. "I will—"

Frit extended a hand and summoned the *fire* Nebiat had given her. A river of blinding white flame burst from her palm, and slid across the floor toward Deshret. The flames pooled around his feet, binding him to the stone. He seemed concerned, but not frightened. That would change in a few moments.

"I have a difficult choice to make." Frit walked calmly to stand beside Deshret, who towered over her. "My natural inclination now that I am in a leadership position is tolerance. My best friend would tell me to be patient, and my former mentor would urge me to discuss our differences until we reach an accord."

The flames had risen past Deshret's thighs now. He began to thrash, but was unable to lift either foot from the stone. That bit came from *void*, but the rest was pure *fire*, and it was the flame that would be the end of him. They continued to creep up his body, now covering his waist.

"Then I realized," Frit continued, "that I was bred for war. I was baptized by Shaya, in battle. I don't have the stomach for politics, and I certainly don't have the patience for anyone who asserts that their species is better than mine." Frit extended a hand, and the flames shot up the rest of Deshret's body.

He opened his mouth to scream, but the fire flowed inside, burning away the oxygen he'd have needed to cry out. The hatchling collapsed to the stone as the nuclear flame ate through his skin, flesh, and bone. Frit made it quick, and several seconds later nothing but a smudge of grey soot lay on the obsidian.

She turned to Hedjet, whose face had gone carefully neutral. "I do not know how you select the next Deshret, but however you do it, I'd ensure it is someone who sees our kind as equals."

"Yes, Pharaoh." Hedjet bowed, and backed slowly away. In fact, they'd all backed away.

Well, it looked like Frit had chosen to rule through fear. She wondered what Nebiat would make of it, and if it had been the right decision. If she'd been asked yesterday what she'd have done, incinerating the opposition would not have been on the list of answers.

But today Frit became a war leader. She didn't know if they could survive Nefarius, but she was going to do everything in her power to ensure they won.

54

WE RIDE TO WAR

Aran returned to the *Talon* after Virkonna's latest 'war council', which was a party where no actual strategy had been discussed. It seemed more like an excuse for Wyrms to tell war stories and boast of past battle prowess.

He was unsurprised to find Drakkon waiting in the sparring room, but was shocked to see who he was sparring with.

Nara, a good half meter shorter than the burly Wyrm, circled low and fast near the outside of the ring. Drakkon darted forward, and Nara parried the blow with her staff, then tried to land a jab. Drakkon blocked it easily.

"Good, good." He gave her a smile as he circled, though he did spare a moment to nod to Aran. "You are getting better at reading my moves and then reacting, rather than the blind offense you've been using."

"Better you than me," Kezia said. Aran hadn't realized she'd been crouched against the far wall, but the diminutive blonde was coated in sweat. "I could use a few pints after that. Come join me when you're done, Nara."

"I—" Nara began to reply, but Drakkon instantly pounced, and threw her to the mat. "Oof. I will."

Rhea ducked into the training room, and Aran offered her a welcoming smile. She inclined her head in a neutral nod, but then froze. Aran traced her gaze, and noted that she was staring at Nara. Rhea's eyes narrowed, then she turned without a word and departed.

That wasn't good. He'd expected some resistance toward Nara, but hadn't realized Rhea might share in it since she hadn't been present for Nara's betrayal. Rhea had been on edge since she learned of her father's presence here, though so far as Aran knew she hadn't talked to anyone about it.

Theoretically that was his responsibility, but Rhea was tough, and time was of the utmost importance. Virkonna had said she was going to move soon, and he wanted to be ready when she did.

HEAR ME, MY CHILDREN, Virkonna's voice thrummed through his mind. For a moment Aran thought only he could hear it, but everyone else suddenly clutched their heads, groaning in pain as the voice continued. *THE TIME FOR WAR HAS COME. OUR ANCIENT ENEMY HAS MADE A GRAVE ERROR, AND WE HAVE LEARNED THE LOCATION OF THEIR SECRET CABAL. THE TIME HAS COME TO VISIT OUR WRATH UPON THEM.*

Aran could feel her stirring, several dozen kilometers away. Somehow Virkonna could store the bulk of her power while in human form, then recall it as she wished. She'd just recalled it, and her strength surged like an ocean.

"All right, people," Aran said, drawing everyone's attention. "You heard the lady. Looks like we're riding to war. Drakkon, will you be joining us this time?"

Drakkon nodded gravely as he offered a hand to Nara and helped her to her feet. "My mother is dead and gone.

There is no reason for me to live any longer. My life is mine to do with as I will, and I choose to spend it thwarting the humans who devoured my mother's corpse."

"Glad to hear it. The rest of you enjoy what R&R you can, because this will be the last of it. I'll take us into orbit, and we'll see precisely what Virkonna has in mind."

Aran tapped into the *Talon*'s senses, and willed the ship to lift off. It drew a tiny tendril of *void* from him, almost imperceptible, then they were airborne. He walked to the bridge as the *Talon* flew, and kept one eye on the growing dragonflight.

It was quite impressive, thousands of Wyrms all rising up from the planet together, all clustered around Virkonna's gravity-effecting bulk. Even Cerberus swam up to her, though his form was dwarfed by hers.

My children, the hour is at hand. Talifax seeks to resurrect my dark sister, and I have seen the precise moment of her ascension. We must stop it, no matter the cost. Every Wyrm, every Outrider, must work together to overcome the forces arrayed against us.

A brilliant light shot from the planet and streaked up into the sky near Virkonna. At first Aran hoped it was Voria, but quickly realized the figure was too large for that. A snow-white Wyrm about half the size of Virkonna swam up into the stars near her. Inura, in his dragon form at last.

Welcome, Brother. Virkonna spread her wings, and settled them protectively around the dragonflight, which included the *Talon*. *Gather your strength. In moments the battle begins. Let us terrify our foes.*

55

CONTINGENCIES

Skare's finger hovered over the scry-pad built into the desk he'd ordered installed on the *Dragon Skull's* bridge. It lent the same feel he'd grown used to in his office, and gave him the illusion of control. He knew it to be an illusion, but that made it no less necessary, and no less potent.

All around the bridge techs sat at their terminals, none daring to look up, much less speak. They were terrified of the pair of cyborgs Skare had posted at either end of the bridge. The cyborgs had been born human, but none of that humanity remained in their cold, black exteriors. They were smooth, with no visible mouth, eyes, or anything else a human might recognize.

"I can feel their strength," Talifax's calm voice rumbled from the corner of the bridge. Skare glanced up, but didn't rise.

"You're referring to my guards, yes?" Skare turned from the cyborgs, once again wondering if Talifax knew about his armor. He fingered the bracelet under his uniform, then stopped when he realized what he was doing.

"Indeed. Why so many?" Talifax glanced over his shoulder, up the corridor leading deeper into the ship. "You have enough firepower on this ship to give a god pause. Did you not feel that the tanks and mechs were enough? These new tools feel like you are...compensating for something."

"If a god takes issue with the ritual I am about to initiate," Skare explained, tapping the first sigil on his screen, "then I want the best magical defenses in the sector. My creations only grow stronger when attacked with magic. I suspect even you might find them a challenge."

Talifax casually walked to the cyborgs and inspected them. "Perhaps. And their presence reassures you?"

"Indeed," Skare said, aping the obsolete demigod. He tapped the second sigil, and waited for it to turn purple before tapping the third and final. His desk flared, and the screen flashed an icon indicating that the ritual was complete.

Outside the ship the spellcannon filled with immense *void* magic, which pulsed out in a fat tendril, the very same used to drain magic. This one did the opposite, though. It emptied its reserves, delivering pulse after pulse of black power into the pool that would drive the ritual, just as countless ships had delivered their own payloads over the last few months.

"There is enough." Talifax sounded pleased as he strode to the desk, and stared down at the images playing across the surface. "Your metrics are accurate. In a few moments the wards will devour the last of the *earth* magic, and we can begin in earnest."

Even as the near-god spoke, the screen showed the process. The latticework of runes across the interior of the fist flared once, and then fused. Droplets of brown rained from the rock, drifting lazily toward the pool of *void* still undulating in the center of the cavern.

The *void* magic quivered as the *earth* reached it, then surged forward like a living thing. It clung to the rock and began to siphon the magic from it. The rock cracked and splintered, and the *void* oozed into those cracks. The rock itself dissolved, and the *void* grew stronger.

"There is no stopping it now," Talifax said, and sounded pleased. It was the first time he'd ever expressed such an emotion. "They will come for us now, in strength."

"What about Krox?" Skare asked. His own godsight was a weak, pitiful thing. He hated that he needed to rely on Talifax for information.

"Krox will not intervene. Not directly, though in the aftermath there are some intriguing possibilities," Talifax explained. "No, Virkonna will lead the charge, with Inura yapping at her heels, as always. They will bring their ragged progeny. If your vessels live up to your promises, the ending is a forgone conclusion."

Skare glanced at his guards. Talifax had paid them no mind. He had no idea if that meant Talifax had a huge blind spot where technology was concerned, or if the guards were simply not a threat. That terrified him, as they were his only real contingency plan. No one understood how powerful they were, but they'd find out soon enough.

"The vessels will live up to expectations, I assure you." He tapped a sigil on the screen, and it shifted to show the two hundred vessels arrayed outside the Fist. Beyond them lay an additional five hundred conventional vessels, which were every bit as powerful in their own way. "I've not seen a goddess in battle, but you've asked for seventeen minutes. Be assured I can give you that."

"Excellent." Just like that, Talifax was gone.

Skare turned back to his screen, and watched the *void* devour the fist. It had begun.

"Lord Skare?" Caelendra's pleasant voice sounded from the air around him.

"Yes?" He suppressed the irritation.

"Fleet Admiral Nimitz has requested a secure channel."

"Open it," Nimitz ordered. That was even faster than he'd expected. He waited until the admiral's leathery face filled the screen on his desk. "Ah, Admiral. I've been expecting your call. I imagine there is some alarm about the magical phenomena enveloping the Catalyst?"

"I've got every captain on the line asking for orders," Nimitz groused, his bushy eyebrows knitting together. "You assured me that construction on this super weapon was nearly done. You got any word, son?"

Skare found the title amusing as he was three times the Admiral's age. "I do, Admiral. What you're feeling is the NEF-1 unit's activation. And we are going to need it."

"What the depths does that mean?" Nimitz leaned back in his chair. "We don't have any active engagements or known enemies. Unless Voria's managed to get some rabble together. What is this, Skare?"

"The goddess Virkonna has awakened, Fleet Admiral." Skare leaned back and perfectly mimicked the Admiral's posture. Mirroring was powerful when seeking cooperation. "An elder god is coming for us, with a fleet of dragons. All your experience with the Krox is about to become very relevant. A different flight of dragons is coming, and they are seeking vengeance for your actions at Marid."

"So you're saying this is our fault." Nimitz sounded skeptical.

"I'm saying that cleaning up the sector won't be easy," Skare countered smoothly. "What we're doing is necessary, and was bound to make some enemies. You do have the option of fleeing, of course. My own fleet will stay. If you leave, though, I will not be able to protect NEF-1. Our best counter will be lost, and possibly used by our enemies against us."

That got his attention. Nimitz sat up straight. "They won't get past us, son. You got my word on that."

56

PREMONITION

F rit had settled into her quarters, which were wonderfully crafted with an Ifrit in mind. Her bed was magical *air*, wrapped in a layer of swirling smoke to give it definition. The floor, walls, and most of the furniture had been shaped from obsidian, each piece crafted magically into the shape that best fit its purpose.

Rockshapers had sprung up all over the planet, and many had been employed in the creation of the temple. Frit didn't know where their *earth* magic had come from, and made a mental note to ask Nebiat. Whatever the source, it gave their people options, and she found that reassuring.

Frit's people were naturally gifted with *fire*, with provided them with battle mages. Their *earth* mages could supplement that, and if Nebiat could be convinced to part with some *spirit* they could create the binders that had made the Krox so feared throughout the sector.

Right now, though, Frit needed intel if she was going to formulate any sort of defensive plan. She needed to understand how and when Nefarius would return, and what role she might play in it. If they really could help Voria turn the tide, then Nebiat was going to have a very difficult time stopping Frit from marshaling every last dragon and every last Ifrit.

She walked to a small nightstand she'd dragged to the center of the room, and sank into a cross-legged position before it. The shard Voria had given her sat on the center of the night stand, glittering and refracting the light.

"I can still feel magic from this thing," she whispered aloud, while internally praying wordlessly to any deity that would listen. "Let's hope it's still got some of the same enchantment."

Frit drew slowly on her *fire* magic, and fed it to the shard. The jagged piece of enchanted glass drank greedily at the magic, so Frit added more. And more. The effort began to pull at her, but Frit gave it still more. "I hope this isn't going to explode."

A wave of energy washed out from the shard, and Frit was suddenly elsewhere. She floated in an unfamiliar system, and immediately spun around as she sought to orient herself. An angry star sat in the center of a system littered with asteroids and a trio of gas giants.

A debris field had accumulated around the system's only planet, a large rocky world with no apparent atmosphere. Some of that debris was clearly the remains of spacecraft. Hundreds of them. Perhaps more.

But one feature leapt out over all the others, its magical signature rivaling the sun in brilliance. For the planet wasn't a planet at all. A tremendous fist, made remarkable by its sheer size, orbited the star. The fist was bigger than most planets, and pulsed with *earth* magic.

Frit glided closer and attempted to see what kind of creatures might live on the fist, as she could feel many life signatures there. She hadn't made it very far when a blinding pain shot through her temples. The closer she flew, the greater the pain. Frit stopped, and the pain lessened.

She withdrew a few kilometers, and it diminished further. Then, just to be certain, she flew closer again. The pain was blinding, and it took long moments for her to blink the spots away.

Frit released the vision, and reappeared in her quarters. Something was happening at the fist, which she guessed must be the Fist of Trakalon she'd seen on the Shayan sector map back in Eros's office.

She wished she could talk to Neith and get her opinion, but knew that returning to her world, especially via translocation, would be a terrible mistake. She was on her own with this one, and she'd need to decide how to proceed.

Something bad was going to happen at the fist. Soon. And she had a feeling Nara was going to be at the heart of it.

57

NEF-1

The *Talon* materialized in a system that should have been unfamiliar to Aran, but somehow he recognized it. He'd been here, though how or when wasn't clear. His memories had been restored, but evidently this was one of the pieces that hadn't come back.

The orange star and matching gas giants were unremarkable. Only the fist itself was worthy of note—well, unless you counted the largest fleet in recorded sector history.

Hundreds of conventional Inuran vessels ringed the planet-sized fist. Behind them lurked three fleets of black ships, each containing a hundred vessels. Having the seen the footage on Marid, a hundred was more than sufficient to kill your average demigod. How well would a full god do against them?

Dragons swam through the void all around the *Talon*, with clusters of spellfighters flying parallel as Outriders supported their Wyrms. It was an impressive sight, especially when considering that they outnumbered their opponents by a margin of two to one. Twelve hundred Wyrms were riding to war.

They fanned out with expert precision, with Wyrms like Olyssa and Aurelius leading the flanks. The center was dominated by the single most impressive sight Aran had ever seen. In that moment he felt a small surge of pride at being so closely connected to Virkonna, though he certainly wasn't blind to her flaws.

The sky-blue Wyrm-goddess swam through the void at the head of their fleet, so large that their enemies would not be able to ignore her. Behind her came Inura, his white scales painted orange by the ambient light in the system.

The way he flew made it clear he wouldn't be participating on the front lines of the combat, more like a squire following a knight than even a lesser partner.

Bord's voice broke the silence, reminding Aran that his physical body was standing on the bridge. "See now that's a god I can understand. Inura's smart enough to let his lady lead the way, while he stands back and casts wards and heals and whatnot."

Aran focused on his own physical senses, and looked around the bridge. The company had assembled, and were awaiting his orders. Rhea and Crewes had both moved to their respective matrices, and Aran moved to stand before the central one.

Bord, Kez, and Nara sat in the chairs against the far wall, within easy view of the scry-screen. Bord's quip had gone unanswered, and all three sat in somber silence. They all knew how dangerous what they were about to face could prove to be.

"Listen up," he said, quietly, but loud enough to gather their attention. Aran nodded at the scry-screen, which showed the fleet awaiting them. "We've got a job to do. Until now, we've been able to cheat. Back on Marid when this all began, Voria brought Bord back from the dead. We've deferred costs, and sought magical workarounds."

Even Bord had gone serious at the mention of his resurrection.

"Today we no longer have that option." Aran ducked into the matrix, and tapped the first *void* sigil. "We're riding to war against the worst god this sector has ever known. Worse than Krox, because at least Krox wants to enslave us instead of devour us. Rhea can tell us all about the horrors Nefarius will bring."

The Outrider went pale, and gave an almost imperceptible nod. "Victory will be costly. Perhaps impossible. But I will accept annihilation before I will ever go back to the theft of my very will."

He let his gaze roam between them, and took pride in how straight they stood. How confident they appeared. His people were ready.

"Thats why," Aran continued, his words tinged with the same confidence, a certainty that what they were doing was the right course, "we're going to cut the head off the snake. Skare is out there somewhere, on one of those ships. Skare will be orchestrating the ritual. We're going to find his ship, break in, and kill him before he finishes. Odds are very high that he'll have the highest concentration of magical and physical security available to the Inurans. This isn't going to be like New Texas. There's no eleventh-hour savior. Either we get the job done, or Nefarius rises and the sector is doomed. Skare knows that. Talifax knows that. They're shrewd, powerful, and impossibly well connected. They know our capabilities, and their answers are going to be designed with our abilities in mind."

"What are you saying, sir?" Kezia asked as she brushed

blonde curls from her forehead. Her hair had gotten much longer since she'd started dating Bord.

"He's saying," Crewes broke in, spinning the matrix's command couch to face her, "that some of us ain't coming back. We're gonna take casualties."

"Oh, bloody depths," Bord cursed, shifting uncomfortably in his chair. "This is going to be a Starn situation all over again, isn't it?"

"I wasn't at Starn," Aran pointed out, "and we're a whole lot more powerful than my first op back at Marid." Aran flared his eyes with the same lightning Virkonna used, showing the depths of the magic he'd been given. "But the sergeant isn't wrong about possible casualties. We'll be lucky if any of us make it out. So I don't want you to focus on that. I want you to focus on the mission. If we succeed, the sector gets to live. That's worth any cost up to and including our lives. Agreed?"

"Agreed," Crewes said without hesitation.

Rhea simply nodded.

"Joost do what you can to keep us breathing, sir," Kezia said. She eyed Bord with a clear tinge of fear. "I've got something to lose now."

"I'll do everything I can."

"I know not everyone here trusts me," Nara began. She paused to make sure she had everyone's attention. "I know we're not really...friends anymore. I'm sorry for that. It's my fault. But I want you to know that you are all something greater than that. You are the only family I can remember, and I will fight to keep you all alive. I promise."

"Nara's got some strong spells, and Rhea is almost as lethal as her sour-faced primping lizard of a dad," Crewes pointed out. He nodded toward Aran. "The captain ain't even mortal anymore. I heard that Olyssa chick call him a demigod, if you can believe that. He don't even age. If the captain could keep our asses breathing when he was just some wipe, then I bet he can get us through this now. I believe in you, sir, and I'm going down swinging."

Aran hated the finality of it all, as if they were pre-accepting their own deaths. He understood, though, that separating themselves from this would give them the head-space they needed to win.

"Sir, we've got an incoming missive," Rhea said. She extended a hand, but didn't quite tap the *fire* sigil that would put it on the scry-screen. "Shall I?"

Aran nodded. He'd already felt it through the *Talon*, and knew who it was.

Admiral Nimitz's grizzled face filled the screen, his beard longer and bushier than the last time Aran had seen him. Nimitz's gaze swept the bridge, but stopped when they reached Aran. He gave a slight nod, still infused with respect.

"Hello, son." Nimitz rested his elbows on the arms of the chair, and leaned toward the screen. "I don't see that up-jumped war criminal you like to ride around with. Was even she a bit squeamish about betraying her own race so she could suck up to gods and monsters?"

Aran looked up from the command matrix, and felt nothing but pity. Nimitz's rage had consumed him. The admiral had presided over the deaths of most of his nation, and had watched as the Krox destroyed their way of life. The only road left to him was attacking anything that threatened what survived.

"I'm sorry it came to this, Admiral." Aran returned the respectful nod. "Unfortunately, you don't have all the facts. I warned Admiral Kerr about those ships, and I was sorry to hear about his loss."

That scored a point. Nimitz winced. "Kerr was a good man and a fine officer. You don't get to say his name, son. Not if you're here to attack a Ternus fleet, the same way you attacked them in orbit over Marid."

"I wasn't even at Marid." Aran's eyes narrowed, and he forced down the anger. Railing at this man would only confirm his beliefs that Aran was somehow a monster. "You've been duped. The footage of us battling those ships came from Shaya. I was ambushed by Skare when I entered the Umbral Depths. You know me, Admiral. You know my principles. You know what I stand for and why I fight."

Nimitz's expression thawed a few degrees. "I admit it don't sit well with me, and it ain't at all like the man I've always believed you to be. You got a chance to prove it right now, son. If you tell me you're here to kill the dragons advancing on our position then I'll order every one of my ships to include you as a friendly. But if you're here to attack us, then all that nonsense you said doesn't much matter, does it?"

"I guess it doesn't." Aran shrugged. He met Nimitz's gaze. "I want you to know, man to man, that I didn't do it. I'm still going to kill you and your fleet. I'm going to kill all those black ships. I'm going to kill Skare. Because if I don't, another god rises. And this one won't be nearly as gentle as Krox was."

"That's rich." Nimitz barked a short, bitter laugh. "Son, unless I'm blind it would appear you've brought two gods of your own to attack us. But you're worried about us doing the same? We ain't raising a god, son. We've created a magitech device designed to *kill* gods. NEF-1 is gonna wipe the floor with your pet lizards, and I'm going to enjoy watching the atmosphere leak out of that fancy ship before it detonates. I hope that slit you work for shows up too, but if she doesn't you can rest assured that when we're done here I will find Voria, and I will make her pay for each and every Ternus life she's responsible for."

Void roiled deep within Aran. Nimitz had finally given something away, though Aran wasn't certain yet how he could use it. NEF-1 was a pretty obvious moniker for the goddess they were about to resurrect.

Aran killed the missive and poured *void* and *fire* into the *Talon*. They accelerated, and began to catch up to Virkonna. She'd be at the center of the battle, and Aran wanted to be able to react quickly.

They had to find and stop that ritual, and they needed to do it now.

58

SOMETHING SENSITIVE

The conventional fleet, all five hundred ships, moved as one to block the Virkonan lines. They interposed themselves between the approaching dragons and the fist, further reinforcing Aran's belief that the ritual was somewhere inside.

About two thirds of the black ships hung back, mostly clustered around the ridges of the fist, which provided cover and an easy means of escape if they were pursued. Aran knew the ships were valuable, but was puzzled as to why the Inurans wanted such large reserves.

Two smaller groups of black ships moved to support the conventional Inuran vessels, each group containing fifty vessels. Those would be their god-countering squads, Aran imagined.

Dragons began fanning out, supported by their Outriders. Then the lines met. Dragons began tearing apart starships, the atmosphere venting out like spurts of white blood. Spellfighters engaged capital ships, some blown up from Inuran cannons, while others began whittling down their opponents.

Virkonna raised a single scaled hand, and lightning crackled from each clawed finger. The *air* magic flowed like a living thing, arcing between ships as it clawed its way deep into the Inuran ranks. Everywhere the lighting touched metal melted, and ship after ship came apart, their keels breaking as the magic savaged their vessels.

Inura spun out magics as well, so quickly Aran had trouble tracking it all. The spells were designed to increase everything from a target's speed to toughness, to creating fear in the mind of anyone who beheld the target. It was an incredible partnership, and dramatically increased Virkonna's already considerable combat abilities.

Much of that magic also spilled over to Drakkon, who'd taken up a position behind Virkonna as well. Unlike Inura, however, Aran could tell from Drakkon's posture that he was ready to support her flank.

Virkonna's assault opened a gap in the Inuran ranks, and she began flying through, toward the fist. Aran considered sending her a missive and explaining that bypassing an enemy and leaving them at your back was a terrible plan.

Instead he guided the *Talon* into Virkonna's wake, and spun to face the Inuran ranks. "We need to make this shot count. I need everything you're capable of giving me, Crewes."

"Can do, sir," Crewes gave a wide, predatory smile as the *fire* rolled out of his skin, and into the matrix.

Aran poured an equal amount of *void* in, and if he'd left it there, the spell would have simply been a wide-beam disintegrate like he'd fired at the Battle of Shaya. Instead, Aran decided with a grin, he was going to take it to the next level.

He added roughly twice as much *air* as he had *void*, shaping the spell to give it one of lightning's most common attributes. The cannon discharged a black bolt of lightning that arced between Inuran ships, hopping from ship to ship to ship in rapid succession.

Each ship the bolt touched simply ceased to exist. They exploded into particles, and then...nothing. There wasn't even visible debris where the ships had been.

"By my count," Rhea said matter-of-factly, "you wiped out fifty-nine capital ships with a single spell. I believe that is a record, sir, for any Outrider."

"What was the previous record?" Crewes asked with a grin. "'Cause I was a part of that spell too."

"Seven, sir."

"Let's not get too cocky." Aran tried to make sure he took his own advice, though it was difficult. The feeling of the divine levels of *void* and *air* were...heady. It separated him from other mortals, and he already saw the trap there. "These are their conventional vessels. The black ships are the real threat."

Aran increased the *Talon*'s velocity, and they shot through the now much wider gap in the Ternus ranks. The Wyrms on that side of the battle were already capitalizing on their opponents' weakness, and that Ternus flank threatened to crumble under the weight of the last dragonflight.

The black ships entered the fight, the first group of fifty moving unerringly toward Inura. Each fired one of their terrible tendrils, which snaked their way across the void toward the sector's oldest *life* Wyrm.

Virkonna twisted her bulk with impossible speed, and interposed a wing between the projectiles and her younger brother. She batted most of the tendrils away, but two clung to her wing, and pulses of white were siphoned back to the ships.

The dragon goddess roared in rage, and loosed a bolt of

pure, primal *air*. It engulfed both offending ships, and several of their neighbors.

At first the ships merely shifted in color, their hulls becoming a shade of blue that matched the lightning.

Virkonna did not relent. Her breath continued, and one by one the ships popped in comparatively tiny explosions. Only when the last had detonated did she cease and turn back to the battle.

Their opponents hadn't been idle. For the first time Aran realized one of the black ships was much, much larger than the rest. It wasn't the command vessel that Nimitz had no doubt been given. It was larger, for one thing, and shaped differently. As Aran studied it he realized the ship was modeled to look like a dragon skull, complete with eye and nose sockets. It was the strangest configuration he'd encountered, but he doubted it made the ship any less lethal.

That was answered an instant later when dozens of bolts of disintegration shot from the skull—from each eye, from the nose, and from the mouth. Those spells converged on Drakkon's exposed back in a hail of magical death.

The Wyrm, Aran's mentor, was busy dismembering one of the black ships, and his claws were finally penetrating the thick armor. Impossibly, he twisted out of the way of many of the bolts. Somehow he dodged them, even though they were everywhere. For a while. Then one struck his wing, which began to unravel. The next two hit his back, causing Drakkon to release the black ship as his body wildly spasmed.

"No!" Aran roared, knowing it was futile.

The last flurry of bolts caught Drakkon just above the tail. The tail and one of the legs simply dissolved into parti-cles. Drakkon's blood sprayed out into the void in a glittering constellation of droplets, each infused with some of the most potent *water* magic in the sector.

Drakkon might have died then, but Inura scooped up the wounded Wyrm, and began carrying him toward Virkonna. Pure white *life* magic pulsed from Inura into Drakkon, stabilizing his wounds, though not regrowing his lost limbs. Perhaps that would take time. In either case it removed Drakkon as a factor on the battlefield, and put them in a much worse position.

"Guardian!" Virkonna roared, her voice magically amplified through the void. "That ship is the primary threat. Destroy it. Rip it apart. Kill its occupants."

Aran was already planning on attacking the ship, since that was almost certainly where Skare, and perhaps Talifax, would be hiding. He guided the *Talon* in an evasive path that carried them toward the enemy command ship.

The black ships responded immediately, many rising from the fist to protect the *Dragon Skull*. "Guess we found something sensitive."

59

SACRIFICE

"Rhea," Aran ordered as he guided the *Talon* deeper into the Inuran ranks, "we're going to need some wards. Bord, relieve Crewes and get her some help."

"Sir?" Crewes asked as he spun his command couch in Aran's direction. "That will leave us light offensively if you're flying the ship. Rhea can handle defensive."

Aran shook his head. "Negative. Bord, get in there. This is going to be more about speed than damage. We need to slip past those ships and engage that skull directly. And I have a feeling they're not at all interested in letting us do that."

"Whatever you say, sir," Crewes leapt to his feet and rolled out of the matrix. Neeko trotted after him as he moved to take the seat Bord had vacated. "I hate sitting it out is all."

"You aren't. Get the others down to the hold and get suited up and ready for boarding. If you don't see Davidson, go to his quarters and get him. Tell him we're going to need his tank for my plan to work."

"Your plan involves a tank?" Crewes asked as he walked to the bridge's doorway. "This I gotta hear."

"We're going to blast a hole in the rear of that ship, just above the engines. Then we're going to park and follow Davidson's tank as he blasts a path toward the bridge." It didn't sound nearly as impressive out loud as it had in his head.

"Well, shit, I could have come up with that." Crewes gave a grin, then exited.

Bord was already sitting in the command chair, and turned toward Aran. "You want me to get some wards up, sir, or should I wait for them to engage?"

"Now would be good. Rhea, use your discretion." Aran guided the *Talon* closer to the enemy.

Black ships began closing ranks around the *Dragon Skull*, which had begun retreating back toward the fist. As soon as he closed to range they began firing their tendrils, which in a way was better than having to face more conventional spellcannons. Spells could be fast, and could have a variety of effects. These tendrils were slow, and while it was risky to let one catch hold, it was very possible to simply evade them all.

Which made Aran wonder why there was a need for so many of them. The ships provided certain advantages, but they were hardly the weapon Aran would have created if given the same resources.

He twisted around the first volley of tendrils, then blazed past several more. Only one caught them, but it slid off Bord's wards as they rocketed out of range.

"Sir," Rhea said, "there are far too many vessels surrounding the fist for simple evasion. Do you have a plan for facing that many?"

Aran studied the enemy position, while still flying the

Talon through their ranks. "You're not wrong. There's enough of them to immobilize us, if we're not careful. Thing is, I don't really have a backup plan."

Rhea turned her matrix in his direction. "We could get the sergeant back up here and try the offensive approach."

He shook his head. "No, the battle in the depths near Shaya showed how resilient these things are. They're not going to go down like the conventional ships. We stick to defense. Keep those wards primed. I just need to fly perfectly."

Aran focused on threading the eye of the needle, and flew as he'd never flown before. Dozens of tendrils converged on their position as Aran glided ever closer to the crack that led inside the fist. The *Dragon Skull* had nearly disappeared inside, but they were gaining on it.

The *Talon* rolled around a group of tendrils, then Aran teleported them five hundred meters. He repeated the spell, hopping ever closer in an unpredictable pattern that the Tendrils couldn't react quickly enough to.

The cost in *void* magic was high, but he let it pour out of him as he narrowed the gap to the skull. Then it happened. Three tendrils predicted a hop, and caught on the wards. That slowed the *Talon's* reaction times, and two more tendrils predicted their next hop.

Each hop came more slowly, and cost him more. And the ships were converging on their position. Aran thought furiously, but short of going full offensive couldn't think of a good solution. There were just so many blasted ships, and in the distance he could see the *Dragon Skull* getting away.

"I can't sustain this forever," Rhea called, the strain evident in her voice.

"She ain't wrong," Bord gave through gritted teeth. "I'm

still trying to impress a girl and all, but...I could use a break."

Indecision stole Aran's attention for a single instant. What was the right answer? He couldn't see it. Nara was downstairs getting her spellarmor on, and she was the only other one who might have had a creative solution.

Shit.

Something punched through the closest black ship, a shining blue-white projectile that shattered the hull and left exploding fragments in its wake. The projectile shot into another ship, which also exploded. After the third ship it paused long enough for Aran to recognize it.

"My gods," he murmured. "Is that Kheross?"

The mighty Wyrm tore into the Inuran ranks, twisting around tendrils, and clawing apart vessels with ruthless efficiency. In many ways, he was faring better than Drakkon, despite being a quarter of the size.

"Tell me, Captain," Kheross bellowed as he assaulted another vessel, "are you a lover of good tales?" Kheross breathed a bolt of lightning, which nicked a ship's engines, slowing it enough for him to catch up. Two tendrils snaked toward him, but Kheross rolled over the ship's hull, using it as cover.

The tendrils latched onto their own companion, and began draining the black ship. Kheross took the opportunity to shred the hull of the vessel he was sheltering behind, and it detonated. The Wyrm rode the explosion, using the momentum to hurl away from those ships desperately seeking to entrap him.

Three of the ships arrayed themselves into a perfect line, and Aran just couldn't ignore it. He poured *fire* and *void* into the *Talon*, and a wide-beam disintegrate lanced out. All three ships came apart, their particles dispersing as Kheross zipped away to safety. "I like a holodrama as much as the next guy, but this eleventh-hour stuff is pretty stressful, you know?"

"In every great tale there is a sacrifice, Captain." Kheross curled into a ball and tumbled past a tendril, then banked and reversed course, attacking the ship that had fired it. "There are too many ships. They will attempt to follow you inside that behemoth, and they will slow your progress. You'll never catch the lead ship, and you will never stop them before they complete their ritual."

"Those stories are stupid," Rhea cried. She raised a hand toward the scry-screen, where her father's draconic face was now displayed. "You do not have to do this. Not to redeem yourself, nor to prove anything to me, if that's what this is about."

"You're right, daughter," Kheross replied as something exploded behind him. "I do not have to do this. I choose to do this. We must stop Nefarius, or this reality is as doomed as our own. We have one chance to ensure that our mistakes are not repeated. I choose *life*, not *void*. I choose *your* life. Live, and slay Talifax. Somehow. Find a way. If it can be done, then I believe you will help do it. And who knows? I might survive this."

Tears streaked Rhea's face, but she seemed unable to muster words. Finally, she choked one out. "Live."

Kheross kicked off another ship, and gave a roar of pain as a tendril seized his wing. "Stop that ship!"

The scry-screen went dark, and Aran focused on flying. He guided them inside the fist, disappearing into the gap between the thumb and forefinger. He could still sense the *Dragon Skull*, and with Kheross slowing the black ships, they were rapidly narrowing the gap.

Aran pulled his teeth back in a grimace and poured *void*

into the ship. He accelerated and increased their mass. "That bastard is not getting away."

The *Talon's* mass continued to increase, even as Aran increased their momentum. The *Skull* loomed larger and larger, and then he braced himself as the *Talon* slammed into the rear of the ship, which was far, far larger than it appeared at a distance.

They punched through the dark metal directly behind the ear hole. If not for the wards both Rhea and Bord had erected, he had no doubt the *Talon* would have been torn apart. Instead, they broke through the outermost layer of the enemy hull, and lodged inside like a bullet.

Aran rolled from the matrix, and paused to check on Bord and Rhea. "Everyone okay?"

The pair gave nearly identical nods, both weary and devoid of emotion. They were running close to the redline, which was not how he wanted to begin a hostile incursion into a heavily defended enemy vessel.

"Let's get suited up. It's time to end this." Aran strode from the bridge, and the others followed.

60

TOO EASY

Nara sketched a *void* sigil before the spellarmor, then quickly slipped inside. It was the first time she'd used a set in several months, and the first time she'd ever been inside of a Mark XI. She still remembered how jealous she'd been when Aran got his, and the rest of them were still cruising around in their old Mark V's.

All five potion loaders had been filled with counterspell potions, which was perfect. She could handle whatever offensive spells they needed using her spellrifle. Speaking of....

Nara opened her void pocket and retrieved the rifle she'd recovered from the Ternus facility where she'd been trained. Now that her memories had returned she understood it like an extension of her own body.

That had been true back when she'd been a Zephyr, but now she understood magic well enough to know why. The rifle was alive, even if it only had a primitive consciousness. It understood why it existed. What its purpose was. Each time Nara used it to kill, it felt complete.

The rifle was going to feel very complete today, because

she wasn't going to stop killing until Talifax was dead or on the run. The latter was far more likely if he was actually losing, and she was under no illusion that they'd be able to stop that sneaky bastard from getting away if he thought victory impossible.

If they thwarted him, that would be enough for her. She'd surprised him at Shaya, and was hoping to do so again here. Of course, she'd also expected to have Voria in this battle and wondered if Talifax was somehow responsible for Virkonna leaving her behind.

Nara paused as she felt tremendous magic rolling into the ship somewhere above her. Most of that was *life*, with *water* and *spirit* in lesser quantities. Wards. Powerful ones. And they were being continuously renewed. That kind of magical expenditure couldn't be sustained for very long.

The ship suddenly lurched, which was a little surprising only because the *Talon's* inertial dampeners had always blocked the impacts they'd felt, even when they'd punched through the skin of a god. What had they just hit that had been tougher than Krox?

The flow of magic ceased, and Aran appeared a few moments later, quickly followed by an exhausted Bord and Rhea.

Aran made a beeline for the membrane, then turned to face the company, who were clustered around Davidson's hovertank. "Davidson, are you in there?"

Nara turned to face the lieutenant's tank, which had grown considerably since she'd seen it on Marid. The sleek, blue behemoth pulsed with its own inner magic, now a powerful eldimagus in its own right. And probably alive, for that matter.

She tried not to think about Ikadra.

"I'm good to go, Captain." Davidson's voice came back

over the speakers. "You sure about driving a tank inside their flagship? Aren't we going to reach some pretty tight quarters?"

"Most likely," Aran admitted with a nod. "We'll leave it behind if and when we have to. The thing is, Ternus is known for their love of mechs. Skare will have some nasty surprises for us, and I want a nasty answer."

"Makes sense, sir."

Aran turned to the rest of the squad, and included Nara in his gaze. "All right, I'm going to get suited up and will follow you out. Rhea, Crewes, you're on point. The rest of you deploy behind them. Nara, can you cover our rear?"

Nara rested her rifle on her shoulder. "Can do. Do you want an invisibility sphere?"

"Yeah." Aran sketched a sigil before his Mark XI, then disappeared inside. When he spoke again his voice came over Nara's internal speakers. "Keep us cloaked. That may or may not fool some of Skare's troops, but it's a small investment."

"Sir, I don't have many spells left," Rhea admitted. "I'm down to mostly *fire*, and I expect their tools to be resilient to such magics. Permission to focus primarily on melee?"

"Do it. Get up close and personal. Crewes will support your advance."

Nara felt a pulse of strong *fire* and *earth* magic from Rhea, and immediately recognized it as a spell that would increase her natural attributes. Not just strength, but toughness as well. On top of her spellarmor it would make the Outrider formidable in close quarters. Perfect for the interior of a ship.

"Let's do this," Aran said. He stepped through the membrane into the enemy ship. The section of the ship had been depressurized, and there was no sign of resistance.

Nara waited for the rest of the company to follow Aran, then trailed after, just ahead of Davidson's tank. As soon as she was through the membrane she cast an invisibility sphere, and drifted a bit forward to make sure it caught Rhea and Crewes at the front of their column. The squad rippled, then disappeared from sight.

Kezia's heavier armor clanked up beside her, and her faceplate hissed open, though Nara couldn't see her with the invisibility. "Back there you said you know we don't trust you."

"Yeah, and that's okay," Nara whispered back. "I wasn't trying to guilt you. I'm sorry."

"I didn't take it like that." There was laughter in Kez's voice, the kind Nara hadn't heard directed at her in a long time. "I joost wanted to say that I do trust you. I understand why you did what you did. We *are* family, and you're a part of that family. You always will be, even if we squabble sometimes."

"Thank you," Nara whispered back.

Kez's faceplate hissed shut, and the pair continued forward in silence. It meant more to Nara than her friend would ever know.

Nara focused on the combat, and scanned the metrics filling her HUD. It was reassuring to be surrounded by tech again, especially since her rifle was perfectly capable of casting any spell she needed to deliver offensively. Hard-casting was a great skill for all mages, but she valued it a lot less than Voria had.

"Sir," Rhea's voice panted over the comm, "the area beyond this door is pressurized."

"I'll maintain the seal," Aran replied smoothly.

Nara felt a flow of *air* snake over her shoulder, then form a thin membrane in the corridor right behind them.

Rhea shoulder-checked the bulkhead with her armor, then Crewes did the same. They kept it up for several seconds before one of the sergeant's blows caused the door to buckle, and he charged into the next room, with Rhea in tow.

An explosion of flame washed up the corridor, and obscured Nara's vision for several moments. When it cleared most of the rest of the company was already into the next room, and Nara rushed to follow, her invisibility sphere still in place.

She sized up the combat as soon as she arrived, which was easy to do with Crewes and Rhea charging beyond the confines of her spell, and thus taking all the fire since they were the only two visible targets.

They'd emerged into a large hangar, with some sort of magical reactor near the center, its blue flickering light dancing on the walls. Two dozen mecha, each ten meters tall, were arrayed at the far side of the room. A line of Inuran hovertanks, like Davidson's, but a bit smaller, were parked in front of them.

Every last one fired at Rhea and Crewes, but Rhea vaulted over them and a brilliant latticework of blue and grey burst out from her hands. The ward surrounded her and Crewes, and while the withering volley discolored the surface the ward was still intact when the storm of death finished.

Nara snapped her rifle to her shoulder, and sighted down the barrel at the tanks, which were probably the bigger threat even though there were fewer of them. If even a single tank got a direct hit the mage was unlikely to survive.

She flipped the selector to four, the maximum the rifle was capable of channeling, and filled the weapon with *void* magic. Since her second trip to the Skull of Xal, her reservoirs felt nearly limitless, so she knew she may as well hit as hard as she could.

Nara fired her spell, which appeared to go wide of the target. It arced into the air over the central tank, and then began to crackle and pulse. The micro-singularity quickly grew in strength, and all three tanks were ripped up into the miniature black hole. A moment later the spell winked out of existence, and the tanks were just...gone.

"Man, I love having you back, Nara," Crewes panted over the comm. "Come on, people, let's do for the rest of them."

Crewes leapt forward and breathed a river of flame toward a pair of mechs that were advancing on him. Their legs heated to an angry orange, then began to run like wax. Both mechs collapsed, and their ammunition began exploding, which only spread the destruction to several more mechs.

"Fall back to defensive positions," Aran's voice came over the comm.

"Sir?" Crewes gave back incredulously. "We've got 'em on the run."

"This is way too easy," Aran said. "They're luring us in. Davidson, Nara, keep picking off targets. Make them come to us. I want to see if we can spring this trap early."

Davidson's tank kicked back a full five meters, and a spear of blue streaked into one of the surviving hovertanks. Sparks exploded out of the impact point, and a moment later the powerless tank clattered to the deck, inert.

"Can't disagree," Davidson's drawl came over the comm. "They haven't even really fired back yet."

As if on cue, the enemy hovertanks bucked, and fired a volley of depleted uranium rounds. Aran stepped in front of the company and raised a hand. The rounds, all of them, just...stopped. Then they began to reverse course, and streaked back into the guns that had fired them, blasting the cannons to slag.

Nara went numb, for a moment anyway. The casual display of power was utterly terrifying. Aran wasn't playing on the same level as the rest of them, not any more.

"I think it's about to get a whole lot harder." She pointed to the far side of the hangar.

A suit of spellarmor flashed into view, then crashed to the deck in a perfect landing. It looked very much like the suit Kazon had given Aran, though this was larger and much bulkier.

Her HUD put it at 2.2 meters tall, though that was the only information it displayed. The passive divination that would normally give her basic information came back with nothing. "That armor drinks magic. It isn't like the others. This is going to be a lot tougher."

Another suit of armor crashed down next to the first, and two more sprinted into view after it. She could hear more of them up the corridor where the first had emerged.

61

BOSS FIGHT

Aran's stomach roiled as their armored opponents lumbered into view. They were tall enough that they might be more mech than spellarmor, which made them larger and stronger than anyone in the squad.

Worse, Aran felt nothing from them. No signals, and no magic. They had the same oily black exterior as the black ships, and he realized that would make them terrifying opponents.

"Focus on physical attacks and counterspells," he ordered over the comm. "We have no idea what these guys can do yet. Crewes, Rhea, why don't you give the first one a poke and see how they react?"

"On it," Crewes roared. He surged forward, bounding across the hangar with ten meter steps. "I dumped a whole bunch of *fire* into pumping my strength, and I really want to see what happens if I hit something."

Crewes dropped his spellcannon, and flicked both wrists as he charged the first enemy mech. A pair of gleaming silver spurs extended from each wrist, and the blades were coated in thick, undulating flames.

The sergeant leapt into the air over his opponent, and the mech shifted its cannon to track his flight. The cannon bucked and a roar drowned out all sound as fifty-caliber rounds streaked into the sergeant's spellarmor.

They knocked him about like a ship in a hurricane, but somehow Crewes stayed on target. He landed on the mech's shoulder and dug the spurs into the thing's neck. The mech raised an arm to swat Crewes off, but the sergeant seized the arm, and bent it back away from him. "Nnnnnghh...this thing is strong. Somebody give me a hand."

Rhea and Kezia sprinted together as one, each aiming at the mech's legs. Rhea fired a stream of hip-shots from her spellrifle, each acid bolt melting the deck under the mech's right foot, then she tossed her rifle into a void pocket and drew her spellblade.

Kezia slammed her hammer into the left leg, and the mech toppled onto its back with a tremendous crash, its cannons spraying rounds all over the hangar. They clanged off friend and enemy alike, though neither side was significantly damaged by the conventional rounds.

The remaining trio of mechs charged into the fray, and the first one shoulder-checked Kezia away. Her armor tumbled, but she rolled back to her feet, and grunted into the comm, "That one hurt. Joost popped my first two healing potions, and I still feel a little woozy."

"Careful, luv," Bord pleaded. "I ain't got much left if you run out."

Aran knew he needed to end this, and quick. Any direct magic wasn't going to hurt these mechs, but while strong, they didn't seem superhumanly so.

He looked up at the bulkhead, then down at the floor. The exterior of the ship was some sort of magitech alloy, but the interior had been damaged by Rhea's simple acid bolts.

Aran extended both hands, and reached deep into his reserves of *void*, so deep that he barely heard his own yell. He used gravity, more than he'd ever tapped into. Aran began to tug at the bulkhead above, and the ceiling gave a groan of protest as the metal began to buckle.

All four mechs glanced up, as did the rest of the company. That took their eyes off the floor, and Aran extended his rifle in that direction. He fired a level five void bolt, and disintegrated the center of the floor under the mechs.

That whole area of the hangar buckled and collapsed down to the next level of the ship. In the chaos, Aran shifted his full focus to the ceiling, and yanked down with all his magical might. The level above tore free and toppled onto the mechs.

The devastation was larger than expected, but the company quickly scrambled away from the destruction, then winked out of sight as Nara cast another invisibility sphere.

"Rhea, Bord, do you have enough left for a ward?" Aran asked as he zoomed around the mess he'd created, and focused on the pulsing blue reactor at the far side of the hangar.

"I can manage," Bord panted, "but I ain't gonna have anything left to heal."

The shoulders of Rhea's armor slumped. "I have nothing left, sir. I am sorry."

"Bord get the best ward you can get, pronto." Aran turned back to the light. "That thing looks really important. Sure would be a shame if someone hit it with a level four void bolt, wouldn't it, Nara?"

She laughed into the comm. "A real shame."

Aran couldn't see her under the invisibility, but he could

see her aura with the ability Xal had given him. Her rifle snapped to her shoulder, and a void bolt streaked into the reactor.

An instant later a wave of magical, nuclear flame rolled out, melting everything it came into contact with.

The squad all dove down to Bord's position, where he already had his hands in the air, erecting a ward. The white latticework of sigils snapped into place just before the explosion impacted, and Bord sagged to his knees with a grunt.

"Crewes." Aran spun to face the sergeant. "Can you direct the flow of fire?"

Crewes's arms came up. "Can do, sir."

The wards began to discolor, and then break apart. By that time the sergeant had seized the explosion, and he hurled the river of flame down into the gaps in the wreckage over the mechs.

The fire melted the metal, and it fused into one giant piece that covered their enemies like the lid to a massive sarcophagus.

"Everyone okay?" Aran called, spinning to conduct a visual check. Everyone seemed okay, and a moment later a chorus of yes's came back over the comm.

Streamers of smoke pooled in corners of the room, and obscured most of the passageways leading to other parts of the ship. Sparks shot from exposed wiring, which had been ripped loose when Aran had torn apart the bulkhead above. All in all the destruction was rather impressive.

"I should have known," Skare's smug voice echoed through the hangar, "that I would have to tend to this personally. I must admit that I am rather surprised at how quickly you disposed of my arcanomechs."

A larger black mech jumped from the level above, and

crashed down into the floor not far from the company. It was a good three meters tall, the better armored version of the mechs they'd just faced.

"Be careful, Aran," Nara whispered over the comm. "That thing is a lot scarier than it looks."

"A good deal scarier," Skare's voice echoed over the deck. "Yes, Captain, I have been monitoring your communications since your arrival in the system. Virkonna's assault...Ternus's capitulation. Each was merely a piece in my plan. And now, I will execute the final phase of that plan. Before Nefarius arises you will be dead, and I will present the corpse of her rival's guardian as proof of fealty. I can feel your strength. She will enjoy feasting on you."

"What makes you think you can pull all that crap off?" Crewes demanded. He stalked forward. "You know what I think? I think we're about to paste bits of your smug face all over the inside of this ship."

"Do you?" Skare asked mildly. His hand came up, and a spear of *void* streaked out from each finger. All five twisted through the air like living things, and Aran realized in horror that they were identical to the tendrils the ships used.

As the tendrils approached Crewes, each broke into a dozen, which broke into a dozen more. Hundreds of tendrils streaked from his fingers, entire clouds of them moving to envelop Crewes. The sergeant inhaled deeply, then loosed a cloud of flame. The tendrils cried out beyond hearing, but not in pain...more in pleasure. They greedily drank the flame, and continued on toward their target.

Black, ropy tendrils wrapped around the sergeant, and yanked him toward Skare. Crewes gave a hoarse roar of agony, and pulses of *fire* flowed up Skare's tendrils into the armor, as Skare began to drain Crewes's magic.

62

THE COST

Kezia stood frozen in the middle of the battle, and squandered several precious seconds. Sarge had charged this guy and was getting his ass kicked. Behind her Bord stood half hunched over in his armor, clearly running on fumes.

Her superior officer was about to die, and her only choice was to go in without her support. Bord had kept her alive through things that had killed planets, and her heart thundered as she charged into combat without him.

She wasn't alone, thank the gods.

The captain glided forward, his spellblade everywhere at once as Aran slashed through any tendrils that Skare whipped in his direction. There were so many, but somehow the captain twisted around those he was unable to sever. She'd never seen anyone, not even the captain, move like that before. He left afterimages as he flowed around them, literally too fast for the eye to follow.

She might not be a god like him, but that didn't mean she couldn't help Sarge. Kezia focused on the combat. She trotted to an area outside Skare's vision, and then charged the bastard from behind. Kez had plenty of time to pick up speed, and she coaxed her heavy spellarmor into a full run.

Kezia's breathing quickened, and *fire* magic boiled out of her into the armor. It increased the suit's already considerable strength, making the massive hammer she hefted all the more dangerous.

Skare had some sort of spell immunity, but she wondered how he'd handle a massive hammer to the back. Physical force, in sufficient amounts, was pretty hard to ignore.

Kezia charged, and at the last moment flung all of her strength into the swing. The hammer hummed through the air, far faster than a weapon of its size should have been capable of.

All that stored kinetic energy slammed into Skare's back with a tremendous crack, and flung the smug bastard fifty meters into the wall at the opposite side of the hangar. The sergeant clattered to the deck, and quickly began scrambling to his feet.

"Ugh," the sergeant muttered. "I don't feel so good."

Skare began doing the same on the opposite side of the hangar, but Davidson's tank bucked and a spear of ice knocked him to the ground again.

Crewes lobbed a ball of napalm onto Skare's arcanomech, but while the flames clung to the metal they didn't seem to damage it in the slightest. Kezia froze, and tried to decide what the next move should be. How did they hurt this bastard?

"Nice work, Kez. Looks like this is going to be about physical force, people. Bring this bastard down." Aran's confident voice filled Kezia with resolve. The captain had gotten them through every scrape, but this one was more important than all the rest put together. It wasn't just one planet on the line, but theoretically the whole sector.

Kezia set her feet and readied for another charge. She sprinted forward even as Skare flipped back to his feet. She'd nearly reached him when he twisted suddenly, like a matador dodging a bull in that stupid cartoon. She tried to adjust her course, but all that enhanced strength worked against her. She simply had too much momentum, and went stumbling past.

Kezia twisted in time to see a forest of tendrils stabbing down in her direction. Their tips had gone flat and rigid, like blades, but thinner than any sword. Kez rolled away, but there were so many tendrils. The first punched through the shoulder of the armor, but missed her arm.

The next came through the cockpit, and sank into the headrest, pinning her blonde curls, but missing her neck.

Third punched through her chest, and awful, acidic pain rippled out as something hot bit into her. The fourth tendril punched through her leg. By the time the fifth fell she could no longer focus through the pain. It came from too many places.

The rain of blows continued, and Kezia's mouth filled with blood. She thrashed wildly to escape the pain, until the last blow fell and darkness came.

63

VENGEANCE

Aran's heart broke as the blows continued to rain on Kezia. Time seemed to slow, and he became aware of Bord's scout armor charging toward the fallen drifter, oblivious to Skare still standing there.

Aran did the only thing he could. Kezia was past protecting—part of him knew that, but if he didn't stop Skare right now, the bastard would kill Bord too, and then maybe the rest of them.

Aran channeled his magic inward, as he'd seen Kezia do. He used *fire* to increase his strength and *air* to increase his speed. He used levels that the purely mortal version of himself would never have been able to manage.

So much so that when he glided toward Skare, wisps of magical energy rolled off his armor. Aran poured *void* in to increase his mass, and then slammed into Skare with the force of a meteor.

"Oof." Skare's black, emotionless armor tumbled end over end across the ground, the tendrils going limp as he rolled.

Aran spared a glance at Kezia, but only a glance. The

corporal's armor clattered limply to the ground, and Bord skidded up wordlessly to tend to her.

Aran returned his attention to Skare, who was already rising to his feet. He was about to charge again, when Rhea's armor quite literally exploded. The magic was blinding, and when it faded, Aran found himself staring at an adult *air* Wyrm in the prime of its strength. Her mottled scales were similar to Kheross's, though she was only a third of his size.

Wyrm-Rhea scuttled forward, and fell upon Skare in a storm of claws and teeth. His tendrils struck out, stinging the Wyrm's face, but doing little to dissuade her rage. Rhea's enormous mouth clamped down over Skare, and bit down with a crunch.

She shook his body like a rag doll, then hurled the arcanomech into the wall. The wall buckled with a tortured scream of metal, and sparks flew from the elbow joint of Skare's armor. The Inuran rolled to his feet, his tendrils already rising as well.

Aran flashed forward, and drew Narlifex in the same motion. The forest of tendrils came for him, but Aran glided through them, twisting to avoid one that reached for his face, then another that came perilously close to his leg.

Narlifex flashed out toward the Inuran, and Aran blended every type of magic he possessed. He brought the blade down with his enhanced strength, and the blow connected just below the mech's waist, where the leg met the body.

Magic fought magic, but Aran's *void* overpowered Skare's spellarmor. Xal devoured Nefarius, allowing the blade to slice Skare's leg completely off. The Inuran patriarch gave a high-pitched shriek, and teleported to the far side of the hangar, where he tapped a potion loader. Gold flashed as the healing potion began its work, though there was no replacing the limb.

"Nah, you ain't gettin' no respite, you son of a bitch." Crewes didn't let up, and rocketed up into the air. He came down on top of Skare, and began slamming his fists into the mech's helmet. The first few blows merely knocked Skare to the deck, but then the cracks began to spread across the oily black faceplate. "This is your invincible armor, huh? Your masterful weapon? Don't look so impressive anymore. Looks like you're missing a leg. Might be you're about to be missing a couple arms, too."

Tendrils exploded out from Skare, and began to encircle Crewes, but Aran flashed down, and sliced through them as quickly as they appeared.

"He's mine!" Bord shrieked.

Aran glanced over his shoulder to see Bord standing there, Kezia's hammer cradled in both hands. Towering flames rose from Bord, his *fire* magic flaring as the rage over-took him.

The specialist's scout armor was covered in blood, but not his own. There was only one reason Bord wouldn't be at Kezia's side, and Aran felt the tears begin when he realized what it was. Only death would take him away from her.

"I finally found happiness," Bord's voice cracked. "And you took it away. You burned my home, and killed my friends. But this? This is too much. She was the best of us. The very best." One of Bord's hands shot up, and he wrenched off his helmet and hurled it to the deck. Tears streamed from his eyes as he tightened his grip on Kez's hammer. Magical flame burned away the tears, and his mouth twisted into an ugly snarl. "I want you to look me in the eye when I kill you."

Bord charged forward, *fire* exploding out all around him.

He leapt twenty meters into the air, and brought Kezia's hammer down in a high arc. Skare reached for his potion loader, but Crewes lunged forward, his gauntlet immobilizing Skare's hand. "Oh, no, you don't."

Bord's yell grew into a wordless shriek of grief and rage. The thick head of Kezia's gleaming hammer slammed into Skare's cracked faceplate, and crushed it with a sickening crunch. Blood spurted in all directions, and the helmet fell away to expose Skare's ruined face, teeth missing and one eye crushed.

The hammer clattered to the ground, and Bord staggered back over to Kezia with a sob.

Skare struggled to rise, somehow still able to function despite the hideous damage his body had suffered.

Rhea's clawed foot settled over the mech, and pinned it to the deck.

Aran walked wearily over, and kicked the remains of Skare's helmet away.

"I don't understand," Skare whispered through mangled lips, one eye clogged with blood. "How is this...possible?"

"You do understand," a calm voice answered, and Aran realized a new figure had appeared. It wore dark, bulky armor which revealed little about the figure wearing it. It seemed utterly unobtrusive compared to the mechs they'd just fought. "You know the answer, but you do not wish to face it."

Skare coughed, then spat a mouthful of blood onto his chest. Then he gave a ghastly grin. "I—I was never really that important. The ritual didn't require me."

"Oh, it did," Talifax corrected. It could be no one else, Aran realized. "Your sacrifice is appreciated. And as you expire, know that I found your ambitions...amusing."

Skare's remaining eye closed, and after one last ragged

breath his chest went still, and the life signs monitor inside his mech gave a single tone to indicate pilot death.

Aran twisted suddenly, but as fast as he was, there would have been no way to avoid the spell. Thankfully he wasn't the target. A disintegrate passed through Talifax's face with a ripple, then dissolved the wall on the opposite side of him.

"Illusion," Aran cursed as Nara stepped into view with her spellrifle in hand.

"Of course," Talifax said. The armor turned toward Aran. "Skare ensured that my presence here was unnecessary. That the rebirth would be complete. Now you will see that all of your plans, and all of your effort has amounted to *nothing*. Every bit of it happened because I allowed it to happen. You dance to my tune, puppets."

Then he was gone. Aran whirled, but the last of the Inuran resistance in this part of the ship was dead. It really had been too easy, despite the enormous cost the company had just paid. Bord's horrified sobs ripped into Aran from behind, but he knew he had to keep moving.

"Bord," he said solemnly. "Take her back to the ship. Davidson, Crewes, Rhea...fall back to the *Talon* and get prepped for flight."

Aran glided over to Nara while the company headed back to the ship.

"You know it's not likely we did enough damage to stop this thing," Nara pointed out.

"And I don't know if killing Skare did anything at all. I thought the ritual would be happening here, but it looks like we were wrong. There's no magic circle to disrupt this time. Whatever their ritual is...I'm sure it's bad for us. I don't think we're going to find it here. This was a diversion. The thing is...I have no idea where to look next."

Nara glided toward the *Talon*, and Aran followed. She

raised her helmet, and tucked it under her arm as she flew. "I don't have any great ideas. We got played again. Maybe we fall back and see how Virkonna is doing."

Aran wanted to punch a wall. It felt like there was no right answer.

They darted into the ship, and Aran willed the *Talon* to prep for take off. Just before he reached the ship he turned back to Skare's distant body.

"Nara, you have enough juice for another disintegrate?" Aran asked.

Nara nodded.

"Clean that up, please. I don't want to take any chances."

64

SHOULD HAVE KNOWN

Nimitz had presided over many battles, usually in charge of a single vessel. Later in his career he'd been entrusted with an entire carrier group. He'd distinguished himself commanding the 9th, though they'd ceased to be a functional unit at Starn.

All those battles shared a common theme, one that scoured a man down to the raw materials the all mighty, if he existed, had originally imbued them with. A commander couldn't really control a battle. The best they could hope for was that their subordinates obeyed orders, and that whatever plan they cooked up actually worked.

Yet in spite of his experience, Nimitz had trouble stifling the rage, frustration, and sheer helplessness overwhelming him. He sat alone in his blasted ship, the screen before him judgmentally displaying the carnage.

Aran had made good on his threat, and a single spell had eradicated a large swathe of the fleet. It had shown the incomprehensible forces they were dealing with. Nimitz's fervent hope was that this NEF-1 unit, whatever it was, might even the odds. Otherwise these dragons were going to overwhelm them.

"Caelendra," Nimitz rumbled as he rose from the command chair. "Status report."

"Only nineteen Ternus ships remaining," she gave back cheerfully. "At our current rate of casualties our remaining reserves will be wiped out unless we receive aid."

Nimitz glanced at the scry-screen, which showed the unholy ritual at work. The planet-sized fist was coming apart, and quickly joined a pool of floating black liquid. That liquid filled Nimitz with unease, though he couldn't precisely say why.

"Order our vessels to get away from that stuff. Disengage, and regroup—"

"I cannot comply, Fleet Admiral," Caelendra interrupted.

"Why the bloody depths not?" Nimitz snarled, wishing there were something close at hand to smash.

"Protocol 9 has been initiated," the voice explained cheerfully. "All control has been relinquished to the *Dragon Skull*."

And there it was. Nimitz had suspected that pasty-faced clown might try to double cross them somehow. He knew that if he sent a communication Skare would ignore it, or feign ignorance, or explain why the transfer of control was necessary.

Nimitz sat heavily in his command chair. "Ha! Command. I was never in command, not from the moment we accepted these things. That kid was right. We made a devil's bargain. Caelendra, will you send a message back to Ternus?"

"Of course," she confirmed, "but only if that message is

personal in nature. Any attempt to divulge the events of this battle, or to discuss NEF-1, will be deleted."

Nimitz began to laugh. Skare had thought of everything apparently, and he imagined that bastard sitting in an office somewhere, laughing maniacally.

He watched as his ship and the other surviving vessels flew into a precise pattern. Their enemies had tricked them so completely that even though Nimitz had expected treachery, he was still caught off guard by the magnitude of it.

NEF-1 was clearly rising. But she didn't belong to the people of Ternus. She wasn't their savior. She belonged to the Inurans, or whatever dark powers they worked for.

Ternus had been duped, and the few surviving humans were about to be enslaved. There wasn't a damned thing he could do about it either.

He reached down and unhooked the flap securing his sidearm. Nimitz had put in the time. He'd done his duty. He had operated to the best of his ability until the very end. He could take pride in that, at least.

Nimitz raised his pistol and pressed the cold metal to his temple. It was finally over. He stroked the trigger, and slipped into blessed, well-earned oblivion.

65

REBIRTH

Virkonna belched another lightning bolt, this one charged with a primitive intelligence and sent to devil these blasted ships. It twisted between them, feeding them so much magic their reactors went critical. The spells were expensive, but unfortunately had proven the most expedient way to kill her opponents.

Even she had to admit that those vessels were works of art. Their ability to channel magic inward at a slow enough rate to drink it was something she'd never encountered before, not in thousands of battles across hundreds of millennia. Nefarius had never used such objects before.

But then Nefarius had never corrupted her brother's power base so completely that he'd utterly lost control of it. She didn't pretend to understand how or why he'd allowed that to happen, or Inura's accusation that choosing to mourn as she had removed her ability to have an opinion on the matter.

Resentment still simmered between them, but thankfully they were experienced enough to put that aside during such a monumental battle.

Virkonna's tail lashed out and encircled one of the smaller black ships. She whipped it around, adding a touch of *air* magic as she flung it into a larger ship. Both were damaged, but the larger ship crept back into combat.

"What does it take to kill these abominations?" she bellowed.

"They are impressive, and based on my own research," Inura admitted. He still cradled Drakkon to his chest; the *water* Wyrm lived, but was unable to fight. The pair were surrounded under intense layers of wards, which would keep them safe from anything short of an elder god's magic.

The few black ships that had tried to force their way through those wards were quick to receive lightning bolts from Inura, so they'd moved on to other targets. Most had selected smaller, younger Wyrms and many of Virkonna's children had already fallen.

Their claws had found blood before then, however. Much of the Inuran fleet, both the conventional vessels and the sleek black ones, littered the space around the Fist of Trakalon.

Virkonna still remembered that titan, and wished that he were here now. He would never have stood for Talifax's meddling, and would have been strong enough to find and kill the crafty sorcerer.

Magic surged within the fist, and Virkonna twisted to observe the phenomenon. At first with mere curiosity, but increasingly with apprehension, then horror.

Void magic, familiar *void* magic, rippled outward and consumed the rock around it. The great titan's fist, which had weathered countless solar storms, meteors, and endless wars, began to implode. It melted inward and quickly joined the *void* energy, which grew considerably stronger for having absorbed all that primal *earth*.

"Inura, what are we witnessing?" Virkonna demanded. She kicked another of the blasted vessels away from her, and realized that it was one of the last few attacking her.

Most of the black ships had retreated, and were now clustered around the cloud of undulating *void* magic that had consumed the fist. Didn't they fear the *void* magic? Perhaps they could withstand it, and that was why they took shelter there.

"That magic is a part of her rebirth," Inura shouted back. He shook his head. "I do not understand what role the ships play, but destroying as many as we can would be advisable."

"What do you think I've been doing?" She swept her wings together, and knocked a trio of ships into each other, then breathed a bolt of lightning that shattered all three.

The surviving ships began to arrange themselves in a strange configuration, and Virkonna frantically struggled to destroy as many as possible. There were simply too many. Each one took so much effort to slay.

A chill swept through Virkonna when she recognized the form the ships were taking. Many had joined together somehow, end to end, and were now simulating parts of a skeletal structure. Wings and ribs, and an elongated neck.

She sucked in a deep breath, despite there being no air in space, and exhaled the most powerful lightning bolt she'd ever flung, enough *air* to slay a god. The magic slammed into the largest ship, the one that looked like a skull. Her magic played over it, but the metal drank it eagerly, and the lighting flowed down all the ships, fueling the ritual.

"Can you counter this?" She whirled and shot a desperate look at her younger brother. Doing so forced her to glance at her children once more, at how few had survived the battle thus far. Their ragged ranks were close to breaking, and had only survived because the black ships had fallen back.

Fallen back to become the skeleton for a reborn goddess.

The ships had completed their work, and a dragon not much smaller than Virkonna herself hovered in space—or its skeleton anyway. The flagship, the *Dragon Skull*, had maneuvered into position, and clicked into place with the ship that formed the last vertebra.

"I have been so blind," Inura cursed. He raised a clawed hand, and flung a multi-aspected spell at the undulating pool of *void* magic before it could reach the skeleton.

The skeleton didn't truly live, not yet, and her brother had sensed something in that magic. The last piece, perhaps. An iridescent sphere appeared around the blood, confining it and forcing it together as the sphere constricted.

Inura yanked his arm closer to his body, and the pool of *void* shot away from the skeletal dragon. For a moment elation surged as Virkonna realized what he was doing. If he could deprive the ritual of blood, then Nefarius would never truly rise. The skeleton was a powerful eldimagus, but hardly a god.

Virkonna flew closer to her brother, and scanned the space around them for threats. Their enemies would have no choice but to act now. And she was right.

The sun itself sputtered and died, plunging the entire system into darkness. She could feel the strength of the spell that had snuffed the star. This was no illusion. No trick. An elder god, or something just as strong, had eradicated it.

Fissures cracked into existence above Inura, then below, behind, and in front. Dozens formed, some opening, while others closed. Virkonna knew it was designed to distract, and tracked every portal as she swam around the Fissures looking for the sorcerer who'd cast them.

"Come forth, Talifax! Face me." She roared her displeasure, but there was no answer of course.

No answer except a storm of disintegrates, hundreds upon hundreds. They rained through every Fissure at once, an endless stream of negative energy. Hundreds of spells quickly overwhelmed Inura's wards, which discolored and then broke.

Inura raised a claw to sketch a teleport, but a tiny hand emerged from one of the Fissures, and flung an incredibly complex counterspell. It slammed into Inura's growing spell and shattered it.

The disintegrates continued to rain on Virkonna's doomed brother, a brother she'd sworn to protect, from every direction, each spell ripping a new wound in his body. Inura clutched Drakkon close to him, and sheltered the younger Wyrm with his own body. It wasn't enough.

The spells continued to fall, and her brother's struggles grew weaker. Weak enough that the shell containing the *void* magic cracked, and the contents oozed a path back toward the ritual.

Virkonna raised a claw, and attempted to mimic Inura's spell. She wasn't nearly as powerful a caster, but she was an ancient goddess, and quite familiar with true magic.

A counterspell slammed into her spell, just as it had Inura's. Virkonna could only watch as the final flurry of bolts slammed into her brother, and her nephew. They may or may not be dead, but without greater *life* magic than she possessed, there was no way to heal them or return them to consciousness.

Blast it. Her own pride had made her send the Shayan goddess away. She'd spited herself, and perhaps denied her brother the very thing he needed to survive.

As she watched, the blood of Nefarius began to flow over

the skeleton. It formed sinew and tendons, and muscles. They flowed over the skeleton with incredible speed, the body growing back far faster than either science or magic should have allowed.

The flow of unholy flesh had nearly reached the head when a vessel jetted away from the rear of the skull. Virkonna sensed her guardian within, the strength of him truly magnificent. She also sensed his turbulent emotions, and that things had not gone well inside.

"Talifax," she growled to herself, wishing for the trillionth time that she'd killed him when they'd first met, all those millennia ago.

The guardian had somehow outplayed her, and all she could do was react.

The rebirth continued, and a layer of midnight scales began to cover Nefarius's newly created body. They flowed ever upward, beginning with the tail, and working their way up the midsection.

Eventually they covered the skull, and when the process completed, Virkonna's greatest nightmare opened her eyes.

Nefarius lived again.

AFTERMATH

Aran zipped away from the *Dragon Skull*, and hadn't taken the *Talon* very far when he realized what was going on. A god was being reborn.

"My gods," he muttered, "what is that thing?"

"That is Nefarius," Rhea said sadly, "the Wyrm that devoured my entire reality." The Outrider limped to her matrix, and dropped down into it. Crewes settled into the other one.

Everyone else was below decks, too tired and too emotionally drained to react. "How's Bord holding up?"

Aran knew it might not be the most important thing right now, but it was impossible not to care. Kez had been such a huge part of their lives, but nothing like she'd meant to Bord.

"Kid's strong," Crewes said, with a note of pride. "He'll get through this. I'll help him. I owe him that. Depths, I owe her that." Crewes closed his eyes, but it didn't stop the flow of tears down his dark cheeks.

Aran focused on flying, and took them up and away from Nefarius as the god continued to rise. The midnight

Wyrm was very nearly the size of Virkonna, and there seemed to be no gaps in her body despite the number of ships that they'd destroyed.

Somehow Skare had made enough to spare.

He poured *void* into the *Talon*, and zipped toward Virkonna. As they twisted around the wreckage of ships and dragons both, he spotted Inura and his heart sank. The *life* Wyrm floated, apparently lifeless, in the void. Cradled in his arms was a smaller Wyrm. Drakkon. The *water* Wyrm appeared just as lifeless. The amount of magical power the pair represented would make an incredibly tempting target for any god.

"Sissssstteeeerrrrrrrrrrr," the newly risen dragon goddess rumbled. Deep purple light, bordered by scarlet, flared in her eyes. Nefarius gave an experimental flap of her wings, which carried her closer to Virkonna. Her neck craned around, and she fixed Virkonna with that awful gaze. "I warned you this day would come. Your schemes have failed. I live. And today, I will finally rid myself of you, as my children have already done with our mewling brother. Then, only Neith will remain."

Aran could feel Virkonna through the magic she'd infused him with. Her emotions were normally muted, distant things. But right now an ocean of brittle rage surged through her. She glided closer to Nefarius and flexed her claws.

"You've killed our mother and most of our siblings," she roared. "You are a treacherous, evil creature that should have been crushed as an egg. Perhaps I will die today, but if so, it will be clawing out your throat, you traitorous witch. I will make your rebirth the shortest in history."

Virkonna hurled herself into Nefarius, and the dragons began snapping and clawing at each other, exactly as their much smaller children might have done. It was ferocious, brutal combat that consumed both gods.

It left Virkonna totally unprepared for the tiny Fissure that opened beneath her. A small pulsing ball of *void* energy shot through, and arced upward into her back. The energy crackled across her scales, and seeped in everywhere it touched.

The effect was instant, if short lived. Virkonna's spine arched, and her entire body went rigid...for a few seconds.

Nefarius used that few seconds to clamp down on Virkonna's throat with her wicked jaws. She tore out a tremendous hunk of flesh, and sent divine blood spraying across the cosmos. Virkonna tumbled away, flailing desperately as she sought to escape her more violent sister.

"Sir, you got a plan?" Crewes asked, his voice half an octave higher than normal.

His eyes narrowed as he focused on Nefarius. "We're going to kill a goddess, but first I'm calling for backup. Sit tight for a sec."

Aran did the smartest thing he could think of. He sent a missive to Voria, a one-way message, "Virkonna is about to die. Nefarius has risen. We need you now, or the war is over."

By the time the spell completed, Crewes had already dumped a huge amount of *fire* into the *Talon*. Aran dug deep and added the last of his reserves to the spell. Those reserves had seemed so endless, but after everything he was finally running dry.

Nara had slipped into the third matrix, and Aran felt a surge of grateful relief when *void* rolled out of her, further strengthening the spell.

He focused on Nefarius, on the head which contained the ship where Kezia had died. "Let's make this count."

A bolt of negative energy, twin to the one that had destroyed such a large swathe of the Inuran fleet, zipped into Nefarius's face. The targeting could not have been more perfect, and the bolt caught the dragon in the eye.

Wave after wave of *void* and *fire* tore into the dragon's face, and scales boiled away on that side, leaving a patch of oily, black metal. When the spell ceased, that was the only visible damage. Both eyes still glowed just as brightly, and the dragon's titanic head swung around to face Aran, enraged.

A precise four seconds later, Voria's unmistakably brilliant golden light flooded the system. It exposed hundreds of Fissures, each disgorging countless monstrosities from the Umbral Depths. The only type Aran recognized were the arachnidrakes, and many of the others were both larger and more disturbing.

Voria's brilliance spilled over the portals, and they began to dissolve. Her light served as a beacon, and the few surviving Wyrms and their Outriders swam in her direction.

Aran tapped all three *void* sigils, then all three *fire*. "Dig deep, Crewes. We need to keep this up a little longer."

"Can do, sir," Crewes managed through gritted teeth.

They raced through the system casting low-level spells as quickly as Aran could manage, each designed to clear a path for the survivors. There weren't many, and it didn't take nearly as long as he'd have liked, simply because there was almost no one left.

Voria extended the *Spellship* and blazing blades erupted from either end. She charged, but she was tiny compared to the warring elder gods. Voria streaked forward and landed on Virkonna's shoulder.

Wonderful golden light, the hallmark of *life* magic, poured through Virkonna, healing the dragon goddess's wounds, the scales on her throat regrowing until the wound was gone, though Aran sensed that the loss of magic remained. Virkonna flapped away from Nefarius, who banked away toward another target.

Inura's floating body.

Options tumbled through his mind. He could try draining Inura so he could save some of the magic. He had a feeling they were going to need that. Unfortunately, his encounter with the ships in the depths had taught him that draining took time. It had taken many seconds to destroy even a single large ship. How long would something as large as Inura take? Hours, maybe. Minutes, certainly.

That the left the unthinkable. If they couldn't save Inura, then they had to deny his magic to their enemies.

Aran broke off from attacking the remaining monstrosities, and winged toward Inura. "Rhea, relieve Crewes. Nara, I'll take whatever *void* you've got left. Rhea, give me whatever *fire* you can scrape from the bottom of the barrel. We make this shot count, or Nefarius is about to get a whole lot stronger."

Crewes stumbled from his matrix and sat heavily against the wall. Neeko crawled into his lap and began to purr.

Neither Nara nor Rhea spoke, but both wearily poured what magic they still possessed into the *Talon*. Aran poured in his own dwindling resources as well, everything he could still muster. That wasn't much, and he silently prayed to the ship to give him everything it could.

Magic gathered for several seconds, an immense amount, more than Aran could possibly have hoped for.

Aran loosed the bolt, and Nefarius dodged, up and away. A tiny shred of relief rippled through him when he realized she'd had no idea what his true target was. That meant she wasn't all powerful.

A single bolt of disintegration, perhaps the largest and most powerful ever fired in the sector, streaked into Inura's corpse. Wave after wave of negative energy disappeared into the dead god's chest, until a critical mass was achieved.

Then Inura exploded into nothingness—the entire god, just like any other target would have. Billions of particles drifted away, leaving nothing in their wake.

"Nooooooo!!!" Nefarius roared, her hateful gaze settling on the *Talon*. "Do you have any idea what you've done? That *life* magic was irreplaceable. I will devour you and your entire race for denying me what is mine." Nefarius casually grabbed Drakkon's corpse and ripped a leg off. She wolfed it down, then flung his body aside for later consumption.

"Sir, uh, I do not like the way that thing is looking our way." Crewes was suddenly very small against the far wall. "She seems a mite pissed about the face thing."

High above them Voria extended her arms. Aran's stomach flopped as the translocate overtook him, and a moment later they reappeared in high orbit over Virkon.

He quickly assessed the survivors. There were less than two hundred dragons, and only a handful of Outriders. Drakkon was dead. Inura was gone. Virkonna had arrived as well, but her wounded form was already descending through the atmosphere, shrinking as she approached her spire. If that wasn't a capitulation he didn't know what was.

An elder goddess had run away so hard she couldn't even talk to her surviving allies after a battle, and she'd been their strongest asset.

Where did that leave them?

67

UNEXPECTED ALLIES

Frit appeared in the sky near Nebiat's spectral form. She curtsied at the waist, and waited for her mistress to acknowledge her. Frit no longer wore subservience very well, but when one came asking a favor it was wise to be as polite as possible.

"What is it, child?" Nebiat's very human form appeared in the void a few meters away. She was roughly Frit-sized. "You seem quite distressed."

"You know why, don't you?" Frit bit her lip. She was almost positive that Nebiat had felt the battle playing out at the fist, but didn't want to assume.

"I know that our enemies are weaker now than they were this morning." Nebiat held up spectral fingernails for her own inspection. "And I know that Voria is in an absolute panic. I also know that our own position is slightly stronger than it was this morning, as it is every day."

"I know you hate Voria, but if you're being honest with yourself, you have to admit that Nefarius is the greater threat." Frit folded her arms, and tried to muster as logical an argument as she could. "Virkonna is wounded. Inura is dead. Drakkon is dead. Marid has been consumed. Nefarius even possesses some *spirit* magic from the ships that assaulted you at Shaya."

"All true," Nebiat allowed. She stopped inspecting her hand and gave Frit her full attention. "How would you suggest we capitalize on the situation?"

"We ally with the weaker side," Frit gave back instantly. Nebiat would like that reasoning. "Voria and her allies aren't strong enough to fight back, and Nefarius knows that. She'll be on them soon. They're desperate."

"And you want to capitalize on that desperation? Go on." Nebiat drifted closer, her gaze firmly locked on Frit.

"We should ally with them, temporarily. Offer them help," Frit explained, hoping that Nebiat would at least hear her out. "They'll need assistance. We give it to them. We help them recover, and help them defend themselves against Nefarius. We have Worldender, and you are the strongest remaining elder god now that Virkonna is weakened."

"I agree that they need us." Nebiat gave a musical laugh, and her eyes narrowed. "What I don't agree with is us profiting from aiding them. If we do nothing Nefarius will spend strength overcoming them."

"Will she?" Frit countered. "If she devours her enemies she gains their magic. She becomes stronger, and eventually she comes for us with that strength."

Nebiat's frown deepened. "That is an excellent point. In the short term this will weaken her, but if we do not strike during the aftermath of Nefarius's attack then we will lose. It makes far more sense to hang back and await that confrontation, then attack the victor, most likely Nefarius."

Frit shook her head. "That's too risky. There is too much chance that Nefarius will pick off gods one by one, and slowly get stronger while you stay roughly the same. If we ally with Voria, then we can ensure her and most of her allies die during the final confrontation. And we can force the offensive in a time and place of our choosing."

Frit didn't want Voria to die, and certainly didn't want Nara to, but she realized that if she didn't speak Nebiat's language there was precisely zero chance of the goddess going along with this.

"Very well," Nebiat allowed. "You may approach Voria as my emissary. Tell her I am willing to come to her world to discuss our common enemy. Tell her this must be done quickly, before Nefarius recovers from devouring Drakkon."

68

THE SCORPION AND THE FROG

Voria knelt next to Virkonna's human-sized form and pressed her hands against the hideous wound in the goddess's back, which had apparently been inflicted before her arrival at the fist. *Life* magic pulsed out of her in quantity, and the wound gradually grew smaller, then finally scabbed over. Virkonna gave a groan through gritted teeth.

"You have my gratitude," Virkonna growled. "If not for your intervention, I would have died alongside my brother. As it stands, the only reason for our survival is that Nefarius will need time to recover after devouring my nephew and whatever remains of my children."

High above, the *Talon* screamed into view, and the ship dropped into a perfect landing on the far side of the pillar. The ramp began to descend, and Nara rushed out, running over to stand near Voria.

"How is she?" she whispered, staring at Virkonna in horror.

"I will live," Virkonna rasped. She pulled herself into an elaborate throne that had been installed in their absence. "Until my sister comes to relieve me of that life. When that day comes I do not see how we can resist her."

Aran came striding down the *Talon*'s ramp like the vengeance of the gods incarnate, but curiously there was no sign of the rest of the crew. The captain approached and moved to stand near Voria. He eyed Nara and something unspoken passed between them.

"I haven't told her yet," Nara whispered.

"Told me what?" Voria asked, rising to her feet now that Virkonna was safely on her throne.

"Kez—" Tears filled Aran's eyes, and he struggled for several moments before he could continue. "She didn't make it."

Voria closed her eyes, and wished for simpler days. "Somehow that is worse than everything else that has come this day. She was a kind soul."

When Voria opened her eyes she realized that everyone was staring at something behind her. She turned, and a mixture of shock and rage washed through her when she saw that Frit was standing there.

The flaming demigod clutched her hands before her, and somehow managed to look the frightened slave she'd been when they first met.

"I'm sorry," Frit said, in a small voice. "I know I'm not welcome here, and I promise I will leave after I deliver my message."

"Which god do you represent, daughter of Ifurita?" Virkonna demanded. Her hand settled on her spellblade, though Voria wasn't positive the goddess was strong enough to use it.

"Nebiat." Frit curtsied to Virkonna. "I guess you might know her as Krox."

"She is a treacherous serpent," Voria snapped, then immediately regretted her choice of words.

"Mind your tongue, little god." Virkonna's eyes narrowed, but she shifted her attention back to Frit. "And what is it your master wishes?"

"An alliance," Frit said, looking up to meet Virkonna's gaze, but only for an instant, then she dropped her gaze. "You can't defeat Nefarius by yourselves, and we don't want her around any more than you do."

"Not three weeks ago your mistress assaulted my world." Voria stalked forward, and resisted the urge to attack. "She killed tens of thousands of my citizens. She has bedeviled my people for decades. Why would we possibly trust her?"

"Because you have no choice?" Frit shrugged. She held up her hands in a placating gesture. "If you're not interested, say the word and I'll be on my way."

"No," Virkonna growled. She rose shakily from her throne. "I might be willing to work with your mistress, but to do so I require a gesture of good faith."

Frit curtsied again. "I'd be happy to relay your requests."

"Bring me the spear Worldender, and then we will talk. With that weapon I can truly slay Nefarius." She rose to her full height. "This provision is not negotiable. Can you relay that to your mistress, daughter of Ifurita?"

"Of course." Frit bobbed a final curtsey.

Voria took the opportunity to use her godsight. She examined the timelines, and instead of focusing on Nefarius she looked for Krox. The deity was out there, and the possibility existed that he might come here, to this world. If so, there didn't seem to be any combat immediately after, but Voria couldn't see any more than that.

It was possible that meant a turbulent future, but it was also possible that Nebiat was somehow hiding her true intentions. Voria was not inclined to trust her, whatever Virkonna decided.

Gasps sounded all around her, and Voria glanced up at the sky to see a second star appear. Krox had arrived.

Voria tensed, but did not immediately pursue combat. That would ruin any chance they had of an alliance, and doing that might drive a rift between her and Virkonna. Voria felt trapped.

"I—" Frit looked skyward, and turned a troubled glance back to Virkonna. "I don't understand why Krox is here. I wasn't told that he'd be—"

Krox's hand opened, and hundreds of Wyrms flew out like a flock of bats. Another opened, and a cloud of Ifrit flowed out, as the Wyrms had. At first Voria feared they were attacking Virkon, but noted that they were fanning out in orbit. An honor guard? Her gut said otherwise.

"Virkonna, this is an attack. Do not be lured in," Voria counseled.

The Wyrm-goddess turned a baleful eye in her direction. "I sense no attack. I—"

The Wyrms fanned out and assaulted the ragged remains of the Virkonan spellfighters, all those still in orbit. They savagely destroyed vessel after vessel, while a good three dozen Wyrms began to assault the *Spellship* itself, which now stood alone.

"We have to stop this," Voria demanded, pointing at her vessel. She rounded on Frit, whose horrified expression told her everything she needed to know. The Ifrit was just as shocked as everyone else.

Voria tried to translocate, but realized she'd just used the ability. Blast it. Nebiat had almost certainly chosen this moment for that exact reason.

BITCH, I INVENTED BETRAYAL

Nebiat stretched out a hand and seized the *Spellship*. She wrapped it in layers of *spirit*, *water*, and *earth*, sheathing it in protective wards and bindings, like a spider spinning webs around trapped prey.

Once the ship was completely obscured under potent magics, she turned from Virkon and began flying away as fast as she could, toward the outer edge of the system.

That wasn't very fast when one considered the speed of translocation. She was barely moving as fast as ordinary light, which was glacially slow in cosmic terms.

I do not yet grasp the full extent of your plan, Krox mused. *I had assumed this an invasion, yet you clearly do not seek combat. Was this ship your goal?*

Nebiat was all too happy to explain. She examined the possibilities back on Virkon, and was reasonably confident pursuit would be too slow to catch her. They'd already wasted precious seconds dithering. Voria couldn't translocate, and Virkonna had no reason to.

As expected, Voria was the only one to act. Her blasted nemesis teleported into orbit where Nebiat had been mere moments ago, and stared after her as if considering pursuit. In some possibilities Voria did, and in others she realized the futility and did not.

Ahhh, I understand. Krox gave an amused rumble. *You knew that your rival would be unable to use translocation so soon after escaping Nefarius.*

I did, Nebiat agreed. *But it's more than that. I also knew she'd fear Nefarius. She has no idea how long it will take him to devour Drakkon. What if he comes for Virkonna while she is chasing me? She cannot afford the risk, and she will soon realize it.*

And you feel stealing the Spellship *was that large of a victory? It is an interesting toy, but hardly worthy of the same effort you utilized to retrieve Worldender. The* Spellship *is only a few dozen millennia old, and a pale shadow of the weapons created at the height of the godswar.*

Nebiat laughed. It pleased her that Krox was ignorant both of her plans, and of the true uses a ship like this could be put to. She held the vessel before her cosmic face, and inspected it through her wards and bindings. Somewhere inside, her wayward son had given way to despair, now that he realized what she had done. They were going to have a long talk, Kaho and her.

This ship allows us to amplify worship. I have just created a planet full of worshippers. More importantly, I have deprived Voria of her greatest tool. She cannot oppose Nefarius in direct combat, and neither can Virkonna. They are doomed when the god moves on their planet.

And what will you do when Nefarius comes for you? Krox demanded

I will kill her and devour her, Nebiat gave back. *I have Worldender, and I have the* Spellship. *I also have the largest army in the sector. The only army in the sector. What do my*

rivals have? *Nefarius is no doubt powerful, but she sacrificed her fleets for her rebirth. Her strength cannot be infinite.*

Krox pulsed thoughtfully in silence for long moments. *I believe you may have done something brilliant. I do not understand how this has come to pass, but I now see the possibility of our dominion over this entire sector, something I have failed to achieve for longer than your species' existence.*

Nebiat smiled. Everyone had underestimated her once again. Now it was time to finish this. She would wait for either Nefarius or Voria to act, and the moment either displayed weakness she would crush them.

If either moved directly against her she'd ruthlessly slaughter whatever force they brought. In a few short weeks she would be the only god of any significant strength still living.

EPILOGUE

Kazon set the spanner down, then crossed the workshop and sat at the table he'd converted into a makeshift mess. He'd even taken to sleeping there. Every free moment had been spent tinkering with Inura's golden creation.

What he did came through instinct, and there was no conscious decision. He worked on what felt right, as he had every day since Inura had left.

Kazon wasn't a war mage like Aran, or a true mage like Voria. He was just a tech mage with a basic understanding of engineering principles. And that meant that there was a force at play here he didn't understand. That didn't mean he was ignorant to its existence, though.

Inura had modified him somehow; of that Kazon was certain, even if it wasn't clear how or what the god had done, precisely.

He pushed a stack of plates aside, and fished out a hunk of this morning's pancakes. It was soggy with syrup, but at this point he'd take the sugar high. Afterwards he might even be able to sleep.

"You are still toiling, I see," came a cultured voice from the workshop's doorway.

Kazon looked up guiltily, about to pop another bite of pancake into his mouth. Inura stood in the doorway. Kazon dropped the pancake, but before it hit the plate he realized the truth. "Shinura. For a moment I thought..."

He hadn't seen the shade in several days, and had wondered what had become of the magical servant. Thanks to whatever compulsion Inura had laid on him, he hadn't wondered very much, though. That would have interfered with the work.

"You thought correctly, in a way." The simulacrum entered the workshop, and moved to stand before the golden knight, which was now complete.

"What do you mean?" Kazon retrieved the pancake and popped it into his mouth. He was hungrier than he'd thought, and might actually need to go prepare something. Or ask the facility to anyway.

"I mean," Shinura began as he turned to face Kazon, his scales gleaming in the golden light, "that I am more than I was. Inura...updated me, to put it in terms you'll understand. Our consciousness diverged many millennia ago, when Inura left and Virkonna entered torpor." Shinura's tail flicked in agitation. "Inura layered all his experiences during those millennia right over my memories. He showed me all the things he'd seen, and brought our consciousnesses much closer together. I am him, in a way, but I retain my...perspective?"

"That is wonderful." Kazon's face split into a wide grin. "You can tell me what this mecha is for. And maybe even help me deploy it in time for whatever Inura had planned. You've no idea how timely this is. Our side desperately needs some sort of hope."

"They cannot know," Shinura snarled as his eyes flared with immense *life* magic. Far more than the servant had possessed when last Kazon had seen him. The gesture was more in keeping with Inura, which was deeply troubling. "I sacrificed half my magic so that Nefarius and Virkonna would believe me dead. If Talifax learns of my survival, then Nefarius will arrive within hours. We cannot risk alerting anyone."

Suddenly Kazon understood. Inura had bequeathed a massive chunk of his power to Shinura, and he'd entrusted his memories to the simulacrum as well. He'd effectively cloned himself, all in an effort to escape the notice of his enemies. It was very much like a lizard cutting off its own tail so that it could escape a predator.

Kazon sat back and tried to comprehend the kind of desperation required to do something like this. "You sacrificed half your power and your very life, from my perspective at least. All so you could hide? Why? Aran needs you. Voria needs you. They cannot count on Virkonna, and you know it." He rose and stabbed a finger at the mecha. "And what is that even for? If it is so important, why aren't we using it? Why not bring it to our allies? We could use it and your survival as a rallying cry."

Shinura gave a bitter laugh and shook his head. "Our future is balanced on the edge of a blade, an inferno on one side and oblivion on the other. Only one chance for our survival remains, and it requires absolute secrecy. You will take my creation, and you will do what must be done. You will ensure that *no one* learns of my survival."

Kazon had nearly endless questions, but Shinura, who'd always been patient, now bore Inura's characteristic impatience. It was probably safest to treat him like the fallen god.

He stared up at the golden knight, and prayed that Inura's contingency offered some chance of survival.

He didn't know what came next, but for good or ill everything would be settled soon. Of that he was absolutely certain.

NOTE TO THE READER

Hey guys, thanks for sticking with me this far in the series! We're six books in and primed for Godswar, the epic conclusion. That should launch on or around June 30th, 2019, with many spinoff series after that.

If you're interested enough to want to know when the next book comes out, pop over to magitechchronicles.com and sign up to the mailing list on the right-hand side of the page.

I'll give you a chance to beta read the next book, work on the roleplaying game, and you'll hear about a small Magitech Chronicles Facebook Group with like-minded readers where we talk about everything from the roleplaying game to what's coming in the next book.

We'd love to have you!

-Chris

Made in the USA
Coppell, TX
05 January 2021

47591268R10207